Acclaim for Kean Soo's
MARCH GRAND PRIX

"March Grand Prix delivers on charm
and excitement! March is fun, fun, fun!"

—Gene Luen Yang,
American Born Chinese

"March Grand Prix is a candy-colored racing comic that fires
on all cylinders. It's fast-paced frenetic fun that captures the
speed and excitement of racing in comics form — you can
practically hear the tires squealing and the engines roaring!"

—Ben Hatke,
Zita the Spacegirl

"Finally! A story that combines the compelling cuteness
of *Richard Scarry's Busytown* with the high octane thrills
of *The Fast and the Furious*."

—Dave Roman,
Astronaut Academy

"March Grand Prix will march its way . . .
right into your HEART!"

—Ryan North,
Adventure Time comics

BY KEAN SOO

CAPSTONE YOUNG READERS
a capstone imprint

March Grand Prix
published by Capstone Young Readers,
a Capstone Imprint
1710 Roe Crest Drive
North Mankato, Minnesota 56003
www.capstoneyoungreaders.com

Cataloging-in-Publication Data is available on
the Library of Congress website.

ISBN: 978-1-62370-171-0 (paperback)
ISBN: 978-1-62370-532-9 (eBook)

Summary: A new, turbo-charged graphic novel
by Kean Soo, author of the acclaimed, award-
winning series Jellaby. March Hare wants to be
the fastest and furriest race car driver around.
But first, this rabbit racer will have to prove his
skill at the speedway, on the streets, and in the
desert. With pedal-to-the-metal illustrations and
full-throttle action, March is sure to be a winner!

Printed in China,
03302015   008868RRDF15

KEAN SOO

MARCH GRAND PRIX

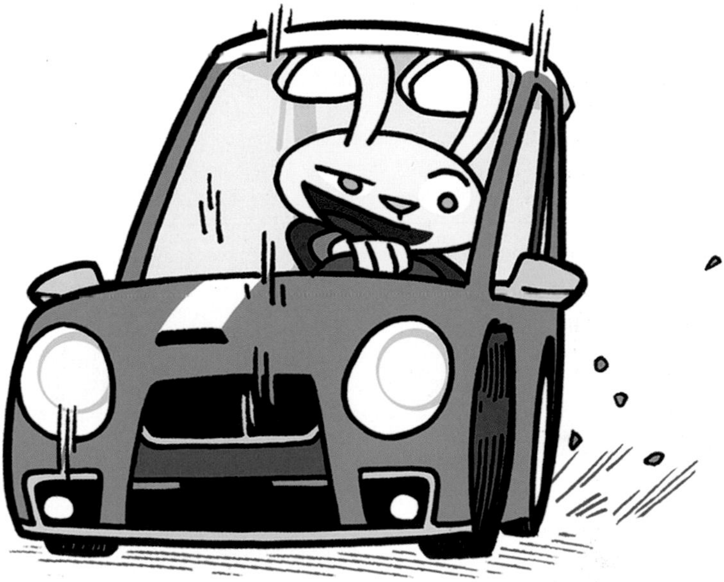

THE FAST AND THE FURRIEST

To Mom and Dad,

For all the times you drove me around in the backseat of the car, trying to get me to fall asleep. And for all the times I woke up as soon as we got home.

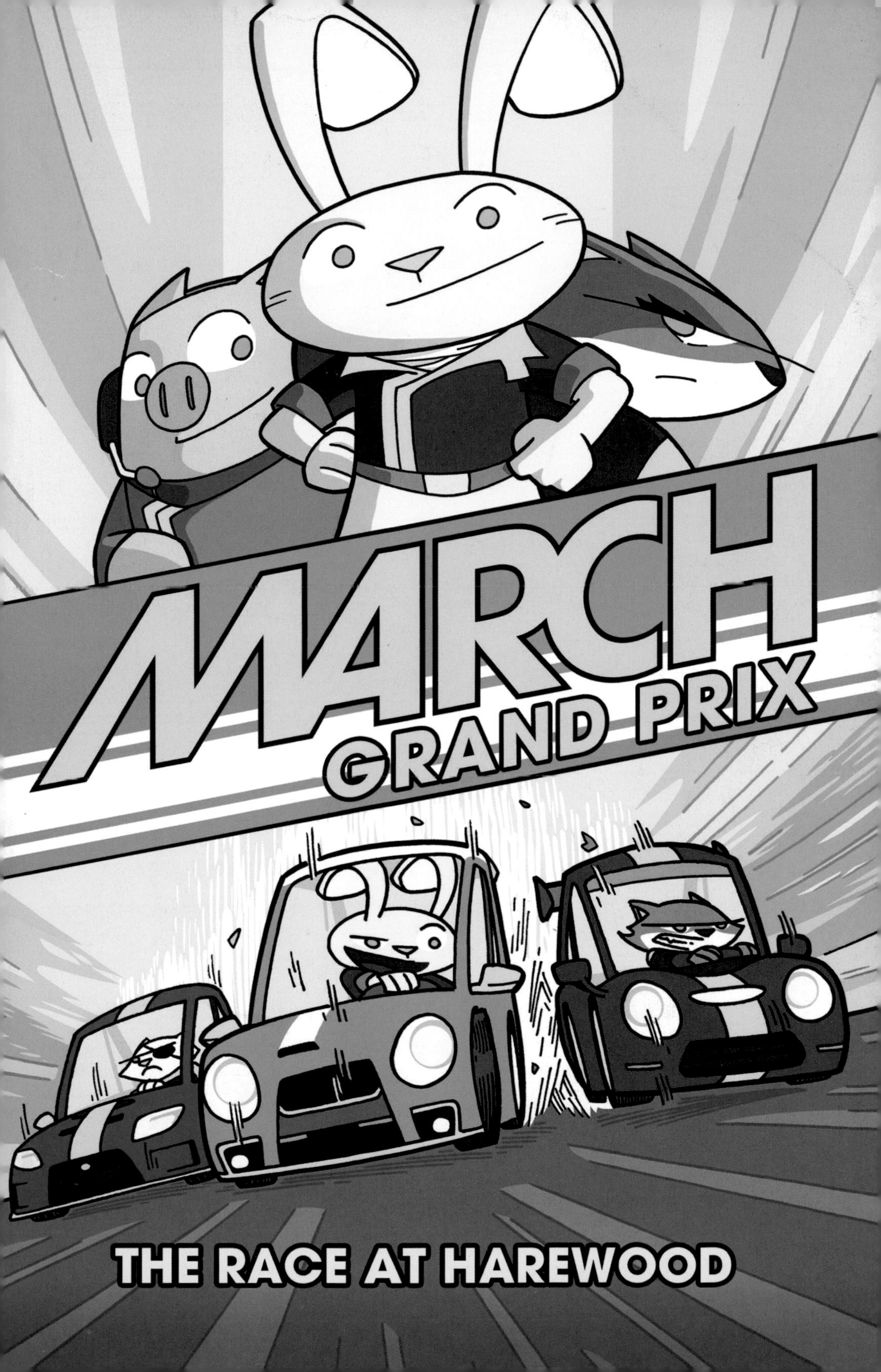
MARCH
GRAND PRIX
THE RACE AT HAREWOOD

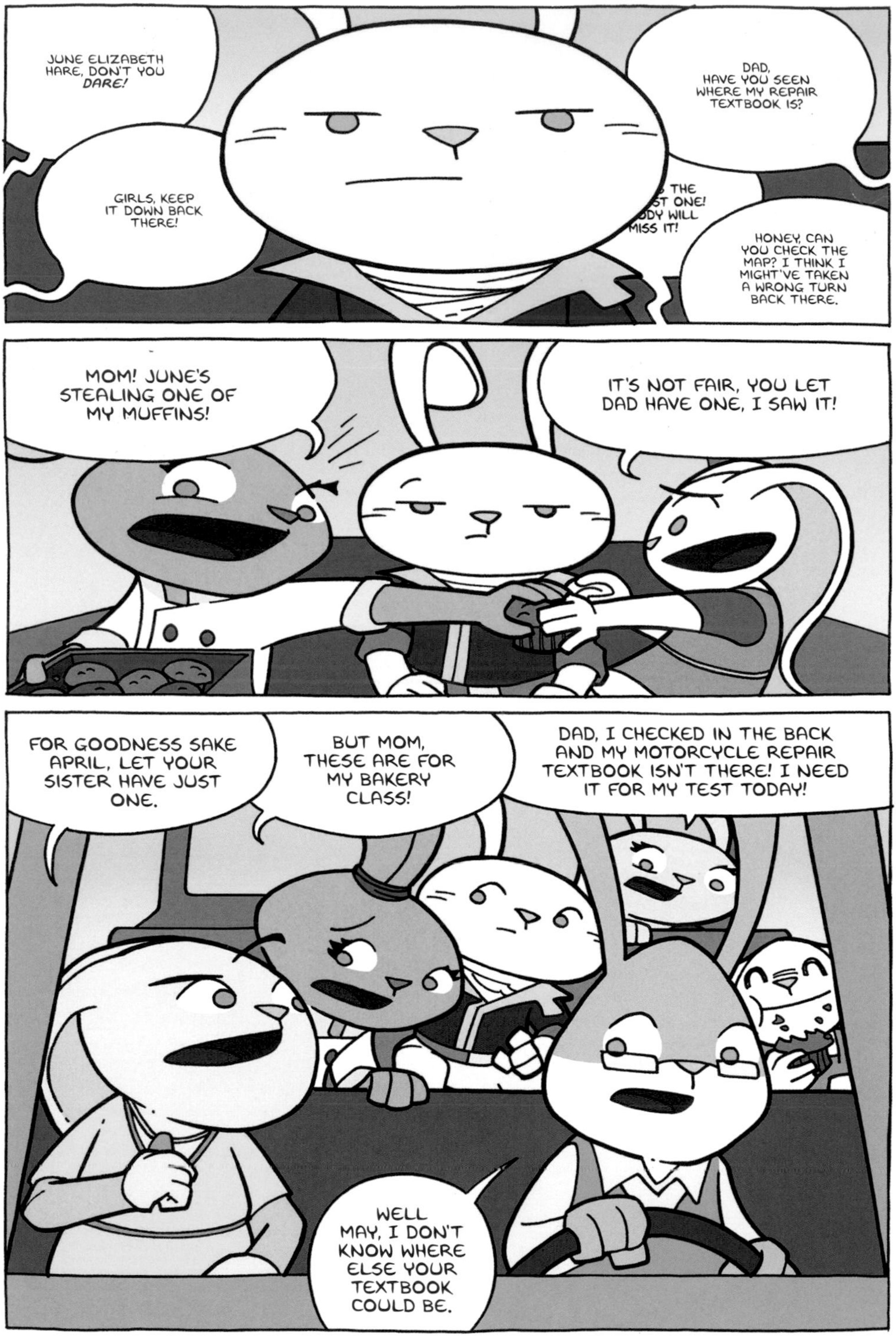

JUNE ELIZABETH HARE, DON'T YOU DARE!
GIRLS, KEEP IT DOWN BACK THERE!
DAD, HAVE YOU SEEN WHERE MY REPAIR TEXTBOOK IS?
HONEY, CAN YOU CHECK THE MAP? I THINK I MIGHT'VE TAKEN A WRONG TURN BACK THERE.
MOM! JUNE'S STEALING ONE OF MY MUFFINS!
IT'S NOT FAIR, YOU LET DAD HAVE ONE, I SAW IT!
FOR GOODNESS SAKE APRIL, LET YOUR SISTER HAVE JUST ONE.
BUT MOM, THESE ARE FOR MY BAKERY CLASS!
DAD, I CHECKED IN THE BACK AND MY MOTORCYCLE REPAIR TEXTBOOK ISN'T THERE! I NEED IT FOR MY TEST TODAY!
WELL MAY, I DON'T KNOW WHERE ELSE YOUR TEXTBOOK COULD BE.

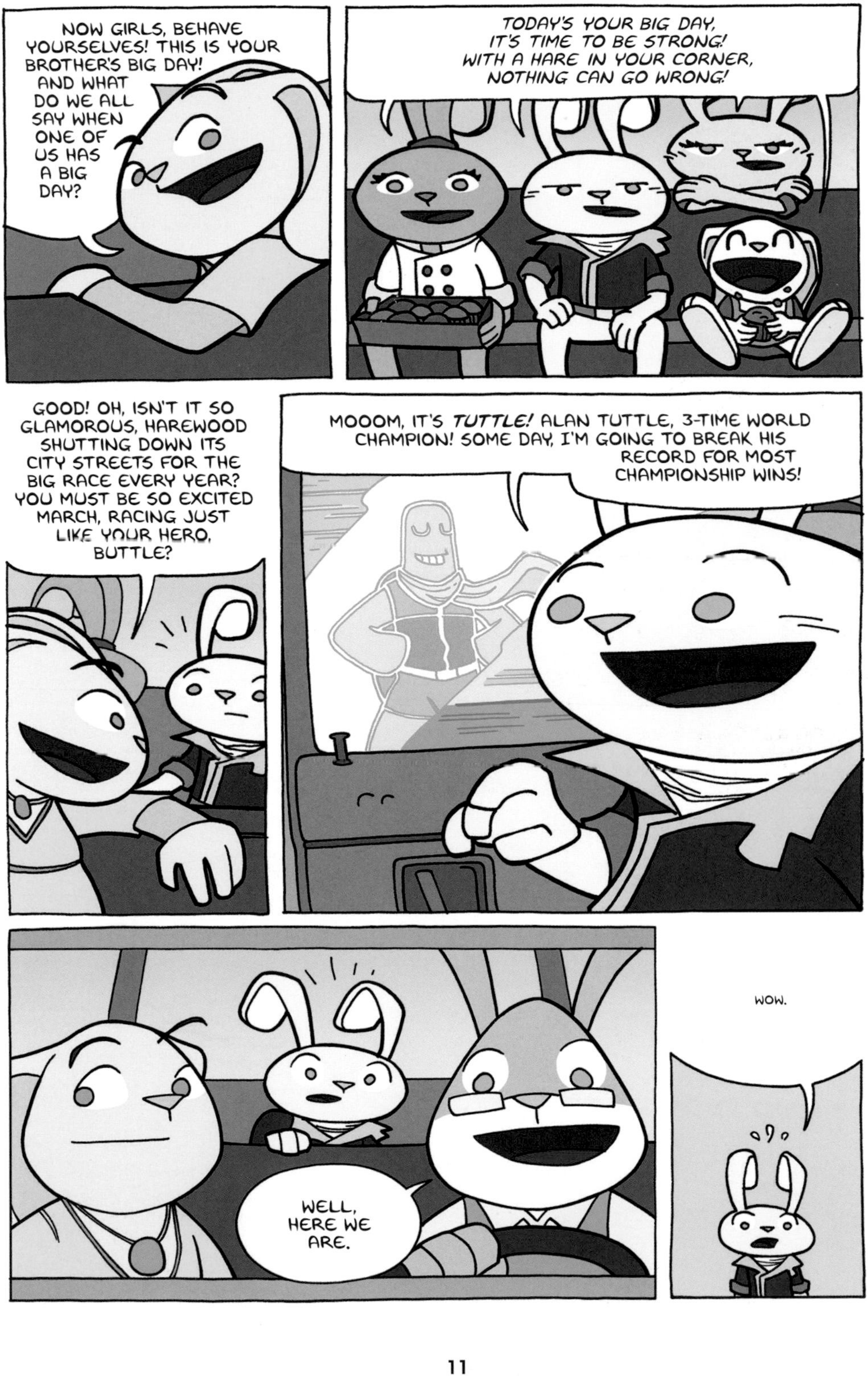
NOW GIRLS, BEHAVE YOURSELVES! THIS IS YOUR BROTHER'S BIG DAY! AND WHAT DO WE ALL SAY WHEN ONE OF US HAS A BIG DAY?
TODAY'S YOUR BIG DAY, IT'S TIME TO BE STRONG! WITH A HARE IN YOUR CORNER, NOTHING CAN GO WRONG!
GOOD! OH, ISN'T IT SO GLAMOROUS, HAREWOOD SHUTTING DOWN ITS CITY STREETS FOR THE BIG RACE EVERY YEAR? YOU MUST BE SO EXCITED MARCH, RACING JUST LIKE YOUR HERO, BUTTLE?
MOOOM, IT'S *TUTTLE!* ALAN TUTTLE, 3-TIME WORLD CHAMPION! SOME DAY, I'M GOING TO BREAK HIS RECORD FOR MOST CHAMPIONSHIP WINS!
WELL, HERE WE ARE.
WOW.

GOOD LUCK SWEETIE! HAVE A GREAT DAY!

MA, NOT IN FRONT OF THE OTHER DRIVERS! IT'S SO UNCOOL!

KISSY KISS ♥

OH.

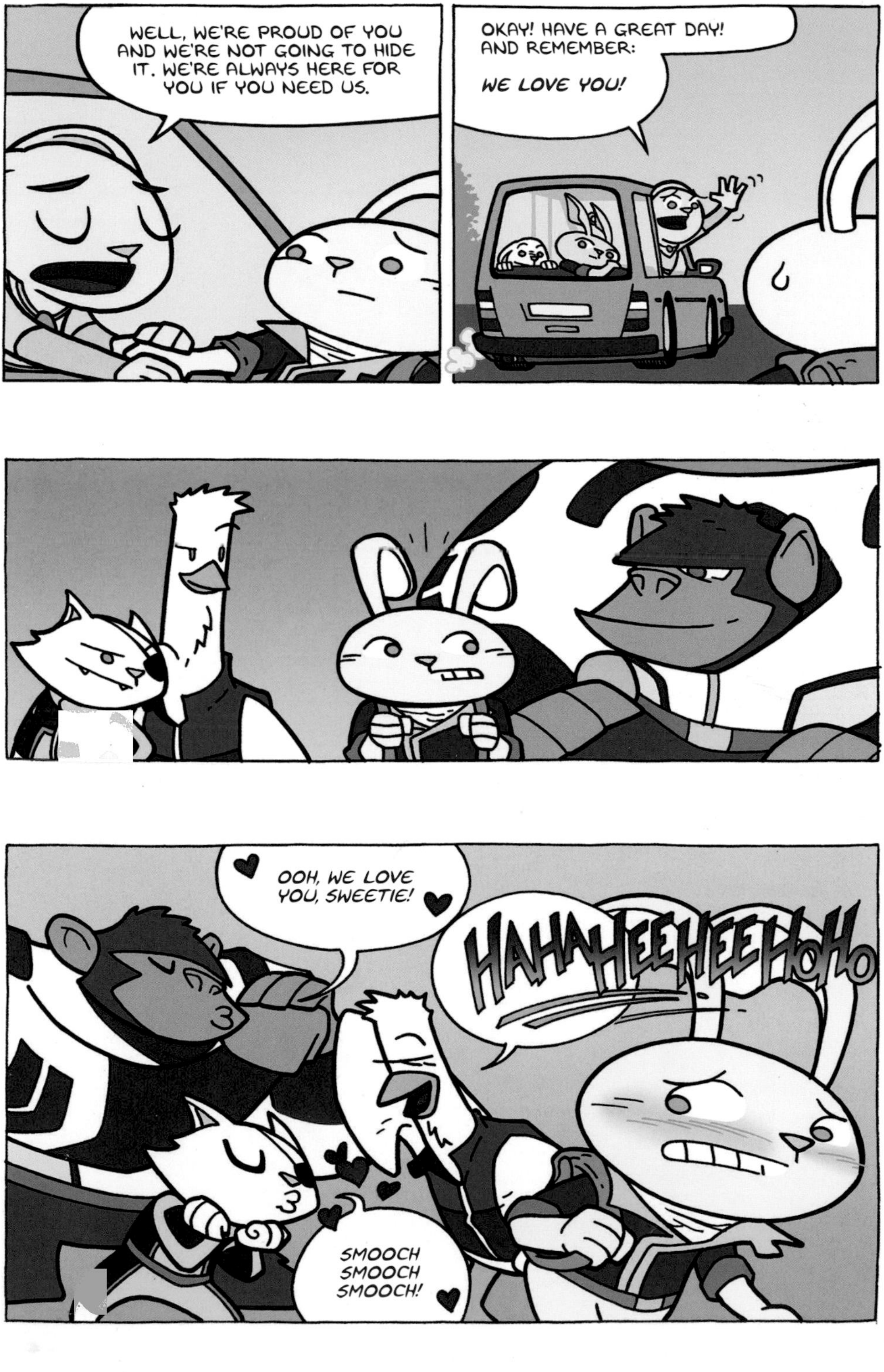
WELL, WE'RE PROUD OF YOU AND WE'RE NOT GOING TO HIDE IT. WE'RE ALWAYS HERE FOR YOU IF YOU NEED US.
OKAY! HAVE A GREAT DAY! AND REMEMBER:
WE LOVE YOU!
OOH, WE LOVE YOU, SWEETIE!
HAHAHEEHEEHOHO
SMOOCH SMOOCH SMOOCH!

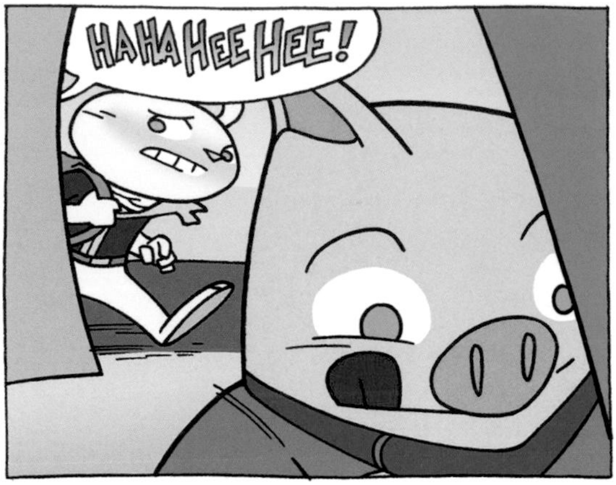
HAHAHEEHEE!

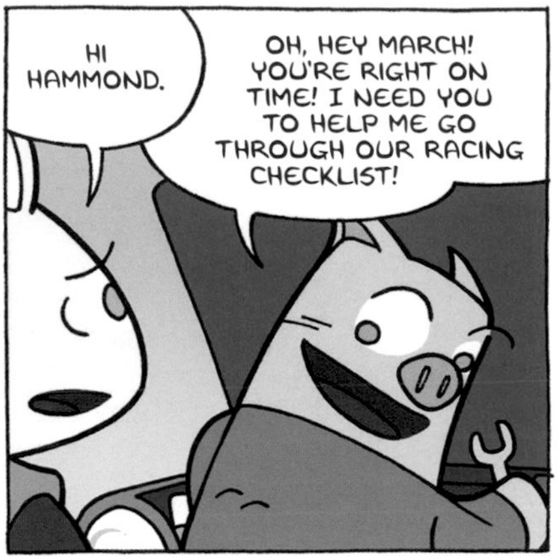
HI HAMMOND.
OH, HEY MARCH! YOU'RE RIGHT ON TIME! I NEED YOU TO HELP ME GO THROUGH OUR RACING CHECKLIST!

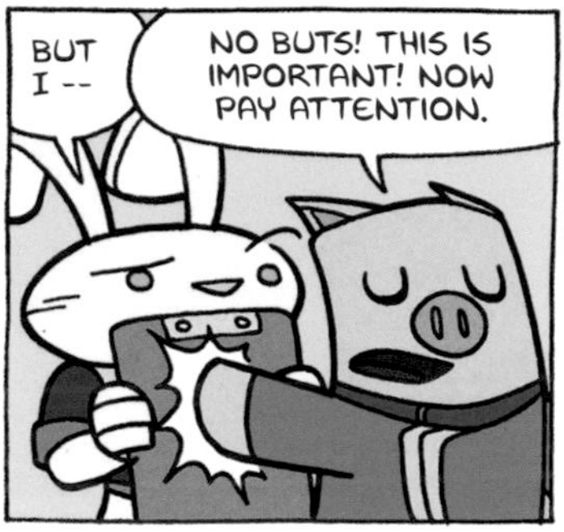
BUT I --
NO BUTS! THIS IS IMPORTANT! NOW PAY ATTENTION.

GT-R Superturbo

Speed
Acceleration
Handling

Class: Subcompact 3-door racing hatchback
Layout: FF layout (Front-engine, Front-wheel-drive)
Engine: 1.4-Liter, 16-valve twin charged inline four-cylinder
Power: 200 hp
Torque: 220 lb/ft @3000 rpm
Transmission: 5-speed manual
Curb weight: 1,488 lb
Top speed: 125 mph
0-60 mph: 6.5 seconds

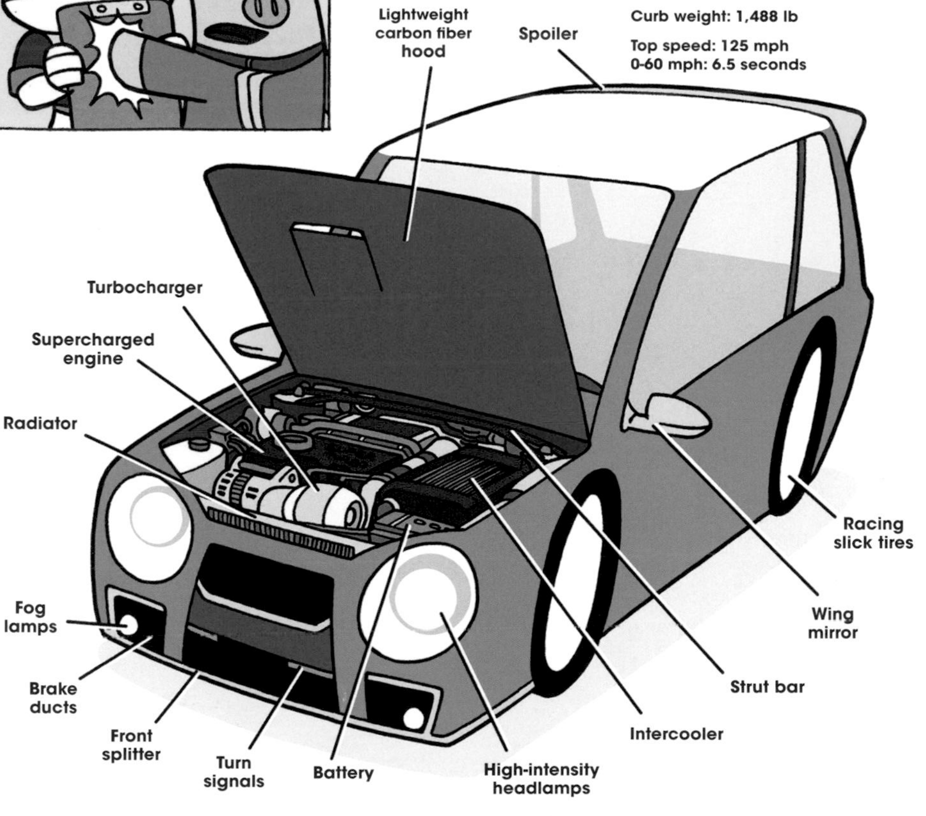
Lightweight carbon fiber hood
Spoiler
Turbocharger
Supercharged engine
Radiator
Racing slick tires
Wing mirror
Strut bar
Intercooler
High-intensity headlamps
Battery
Turn signals
Front splitter
Brake ducts
Fog lamps

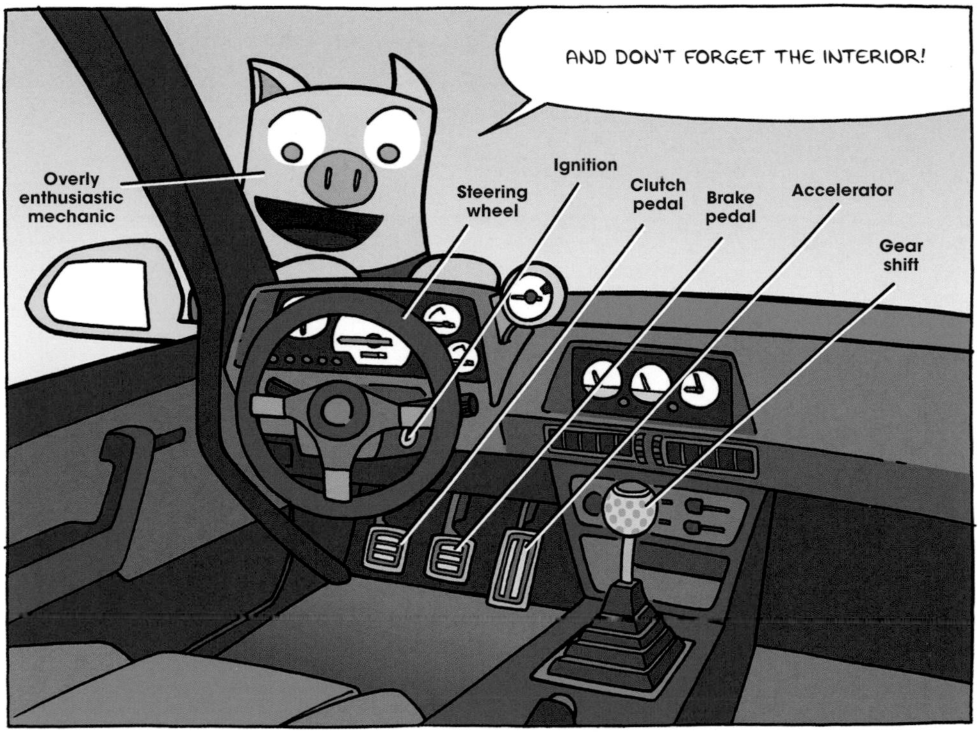
AND DON'T FORGET THE INTERIOR!
Overly enthusiastic mechanic
Steering wheel
Ignition
Clutch pedal
Brake pedal
Accelerator
Gear shift

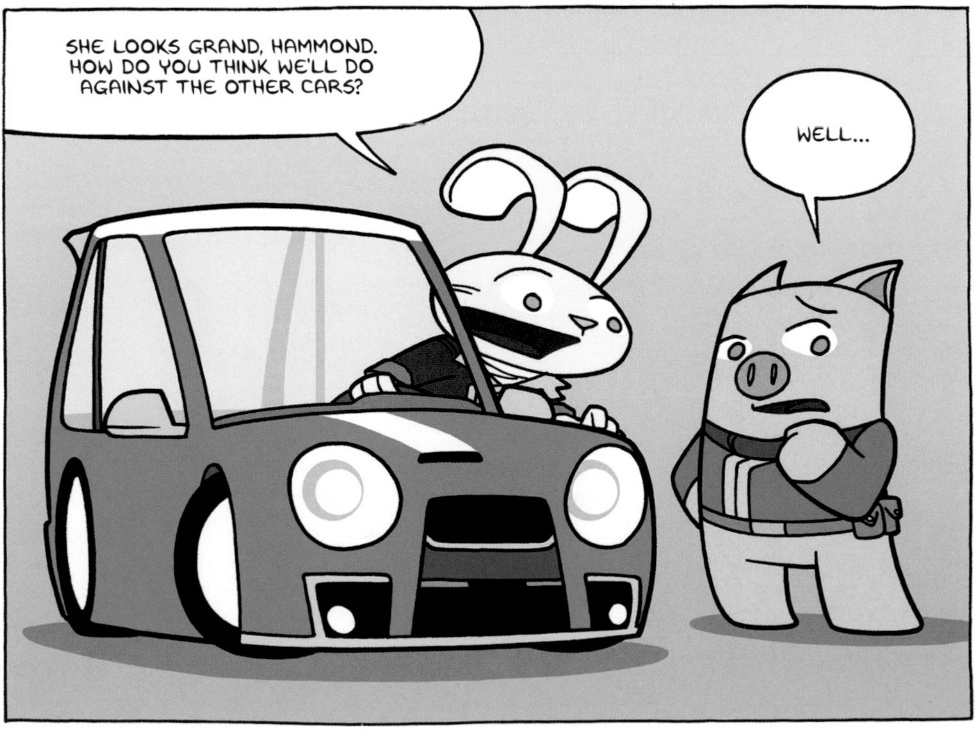
SHE LOOKS GRAND, HAMMOND. HOW DO YOU THINK WE'LL DO AGAINST THE OTHER CARS?
WELL...

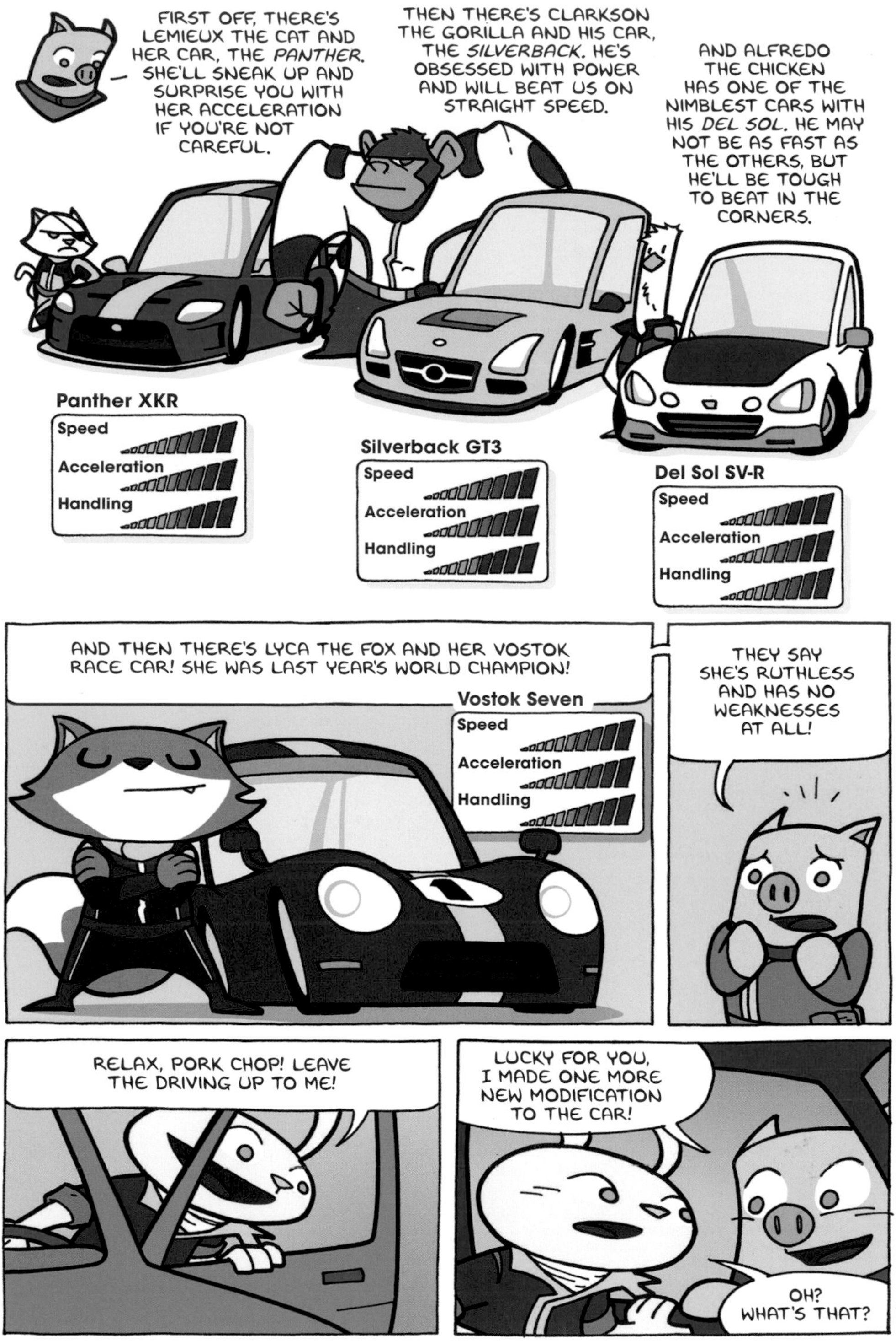
FIRST OFF, THERE'S LEMIEUX THE CAT AND HER CAR, THE *PANTHER*. SHE'LL SNEAK UP AND SURPRISE YOU WITH HER ACCELERATION IF YOU'RE NOT CAREFUL.
THEN THERE'S CLARKSON THE GORILLA AND HIS CAR, THE *SILVERBACK*. HE'S OBSESSED WITH POWER AND WILL BEAT US ON STRAIGHT SPEED.
AND ALFREDO THE CHICKEN HAS ONE OF THE NIMBLEST CARS WITH HIS *DEL SOL*. HE MAY NOT BE AS FAST AS THE OTHERS, BUT HE'LL BE TOUGH TO BEAT IN THE CORNERS.
Panther XKR
Speed
Acceleration
Handling
Silverback GT3
Speed
Acceleration
Handling
Del Sol SV-R
Speed
Acceleration
Handling
AND THEN THERE'S LYCA THE FOX AND HER VOSTOK RACE CAR! SHE WAS LAST YEAR'S WORLD CHAMPION!
Vostok Seven
Speed
Acceleration
Handling
THEY SAY SHE'S RUTHLESS AND HAS NO WEAKNESSES AT ALL!
RELAX, PORK CHOP! LEAVE THE DRIVING UP TO ME!
LUCKY FOR YOU, I MADE ONE MORE NEW MODIFICATION TO THE CAR!
OH? WHAT'S THAT?

I PAINTED ON A BRAND-NEW RACING STRIPE!
RACING STRIPE? HOW WILL THAT HELP?
EVERYONE KNOWS RACING STRIPES MAKE YOU GO FASTER.
RIIIGHT.
CHK-VRMMMMMMMMM
VVVVVVRRRMMMMMM

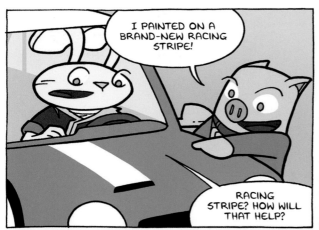

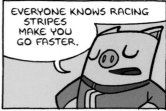

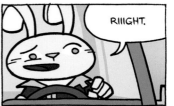

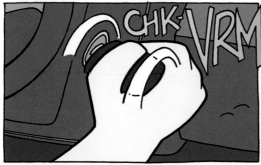

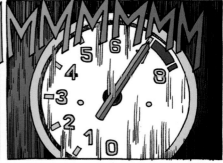

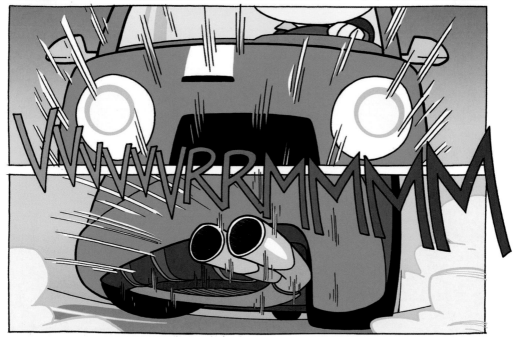

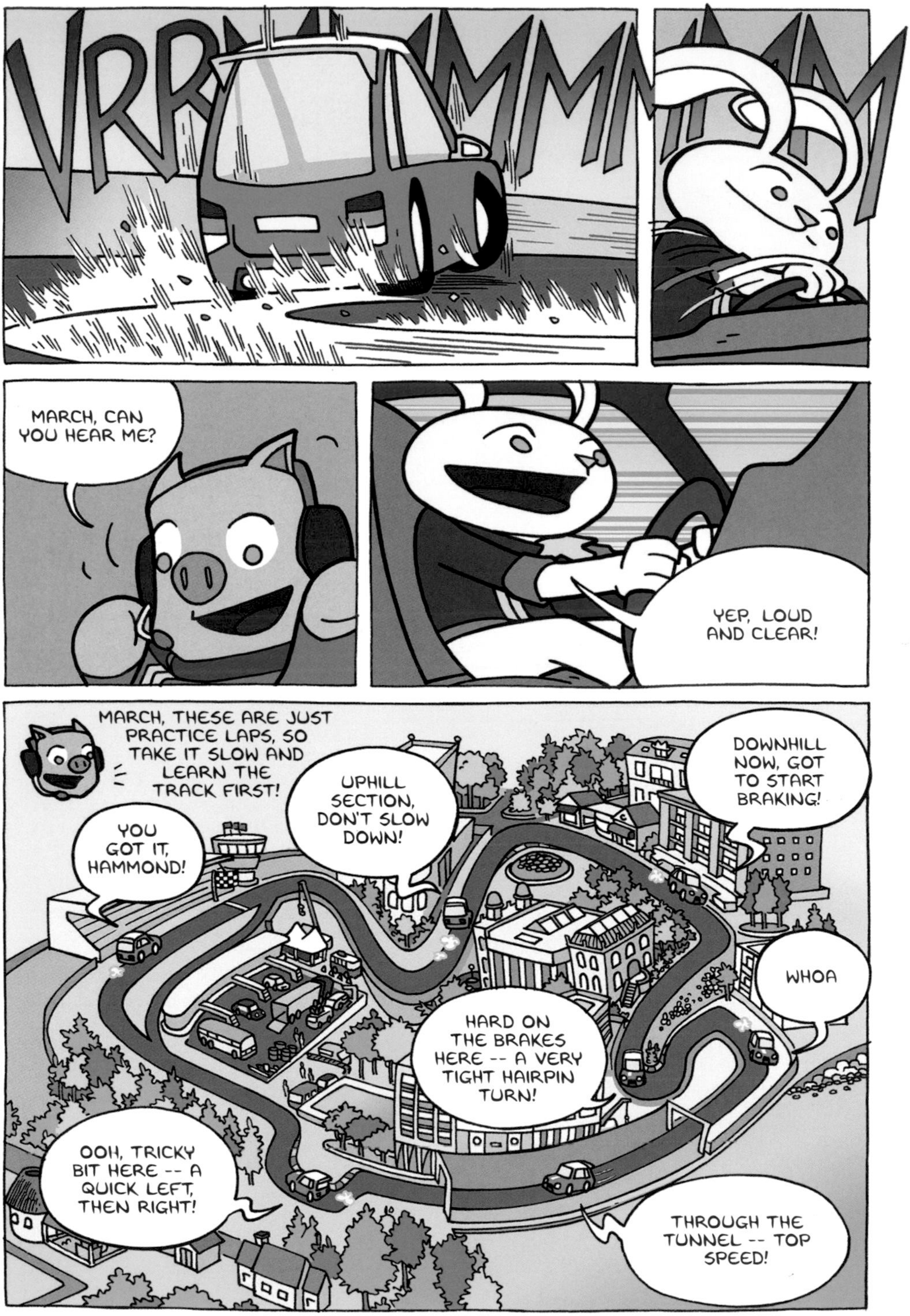

VRRMMMMMMMM
MARCH, CAN YOU HEAR ME?
YEP, LOUD AND CLEAR!
MARCH, THESE ARE JUST PRACTICE LAPS, SO TAKE IT SLOW AND LEARN THE TRACK FIRST!
YOU GOT IT, HAMMOND!
UPHILL SECTION, DON'T SLOW DOWN!
DOWNHILL NOW, GOT TO START BRAKING!
WHOA
HARD ON THE BRAKES HERE -- A VERY TIGHT HAIRPIN TURN!
OOH, TRICKY BIT HERE -- A QUICK LEFT, THEN RIGHT!
THROUGH THE TUNNEL -- TOP SPEED!

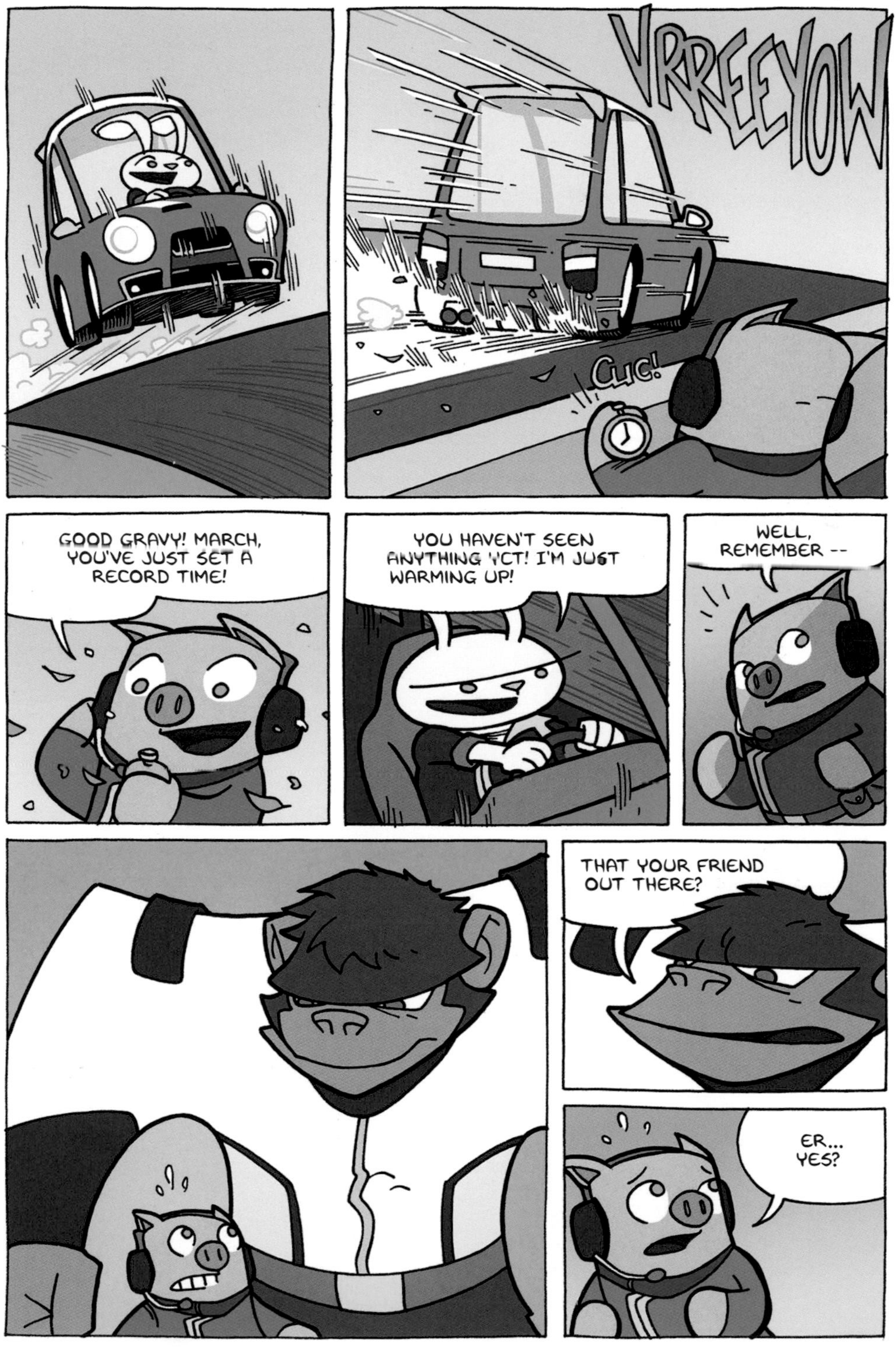
VRREEYOW
CLIC!
GOOD GRAVY! MARCH, YOU'VE JUST SET A RECORD TIME!
YOU HAVEN'T SEEN ANYTHING YET! I'M JUST WARMING UP!
WELL, REMEMBER --
THAT YOUR FRIEND OUT THERE?
ER... YES?

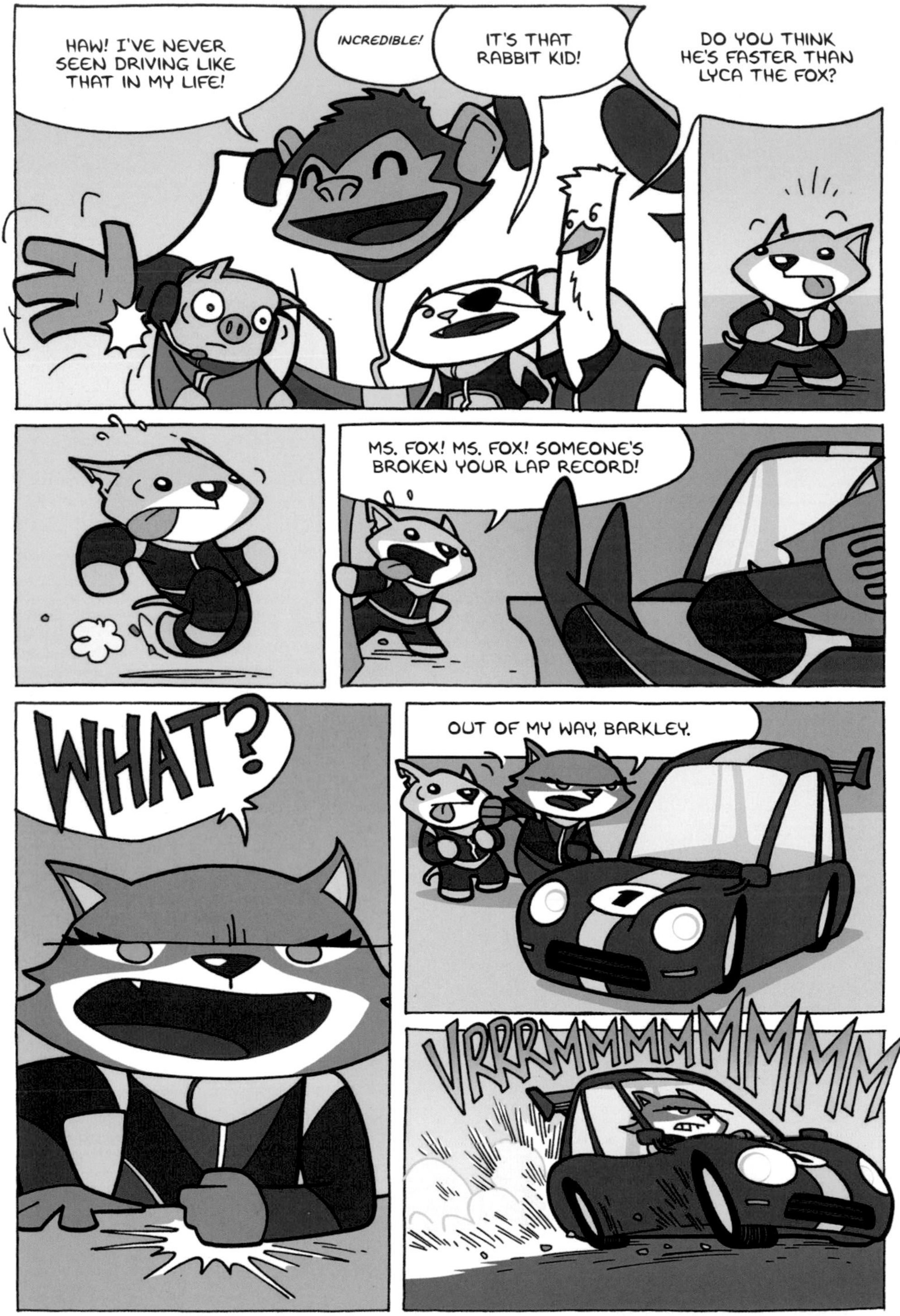
HAW! I'VE NEVER SEEN DRIVING LIKE THAT IN MY LIFE!
INCREDIBLE!
IT'S THAT RABBIT KID!
DO YOU THINK HE'S FASTER THAN LYCA THE FOX?
MS. FOX! MS. FOX! SOMEONE'S BROKEN YOUR LAP RECORD!
WHAT?
OUT OF MY WAY, BARKLEY.
VRRRMMMMMMMMMM

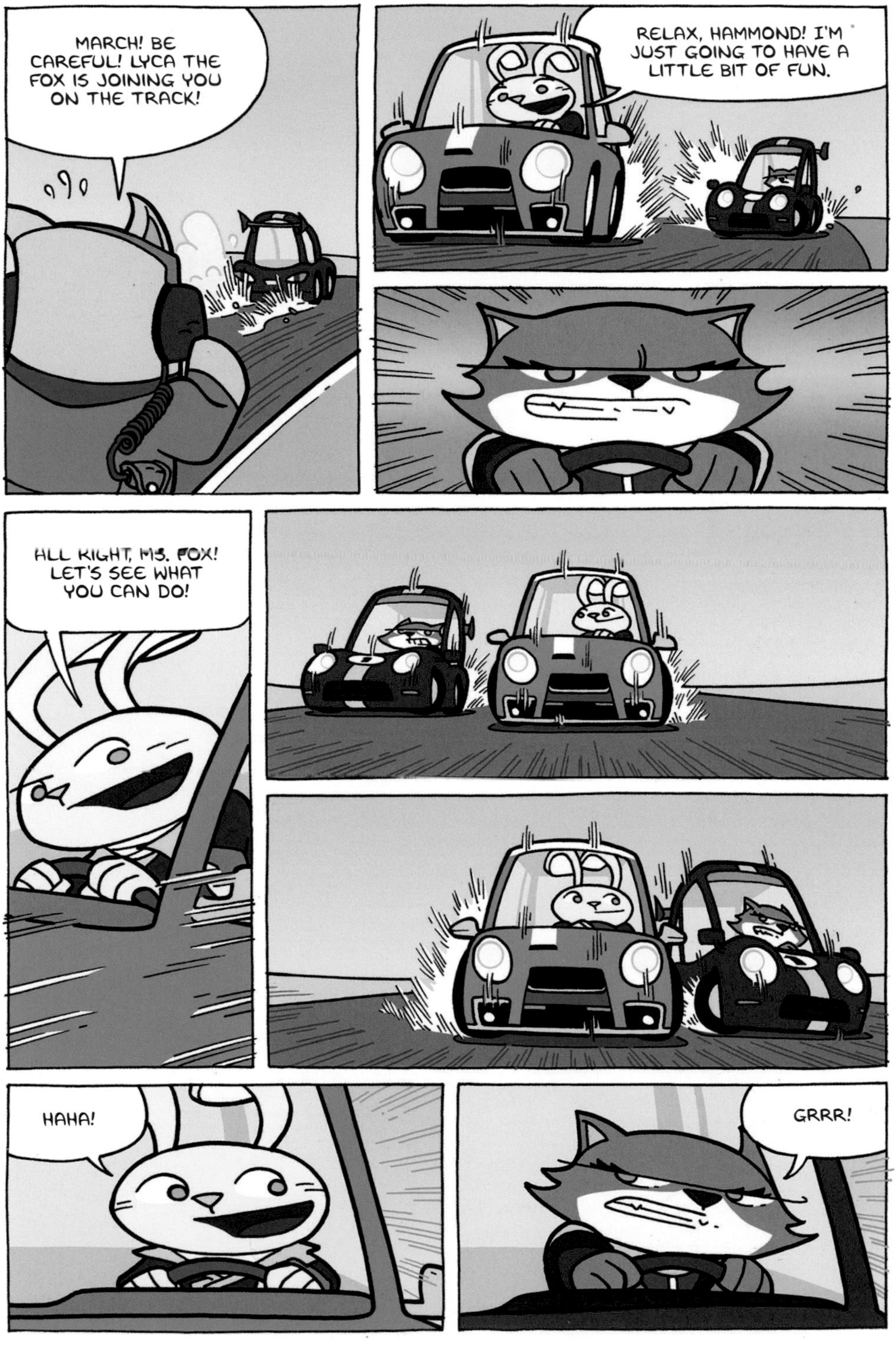
MARCH! BE CAREFUL! LYCA THE FOX IS JOINING YOU ON THE TRACK!
RELAX, HAMMOND! I'M JUST GOING TO HAVE A LITTLE BIT OF FUN.
ALL RIGHT, MS. FOX! LET'S SEE WHAT YOU CAN DO!
HAHA!
GRRR!

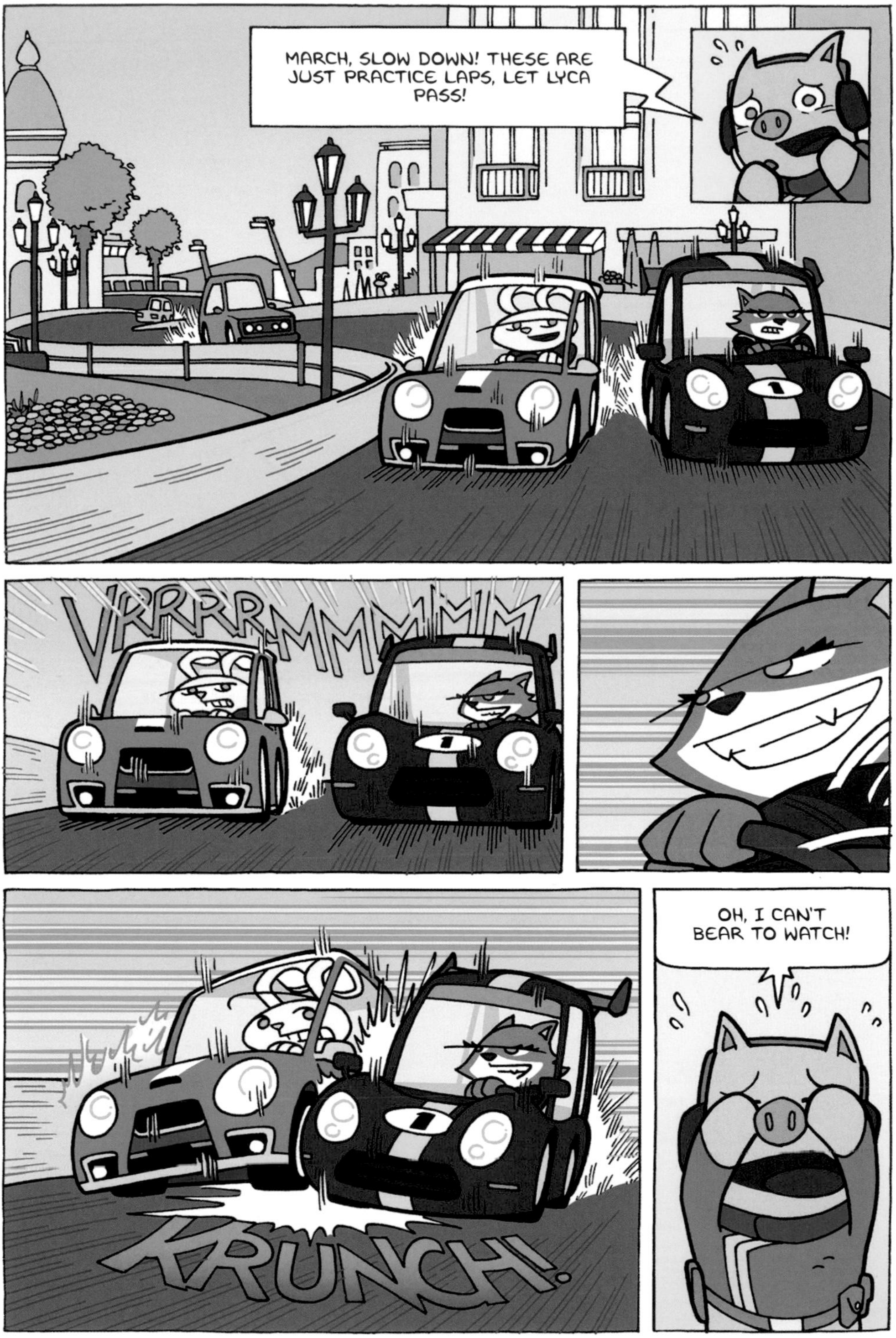
MARCH, SLOW DOWN! THESE ARE JUST PRACTICE LAPS, LET LYCA PASS!
VRRRRMMMMM
KRUNCH!
OH, I CAN'T BEAR TO WATCH!

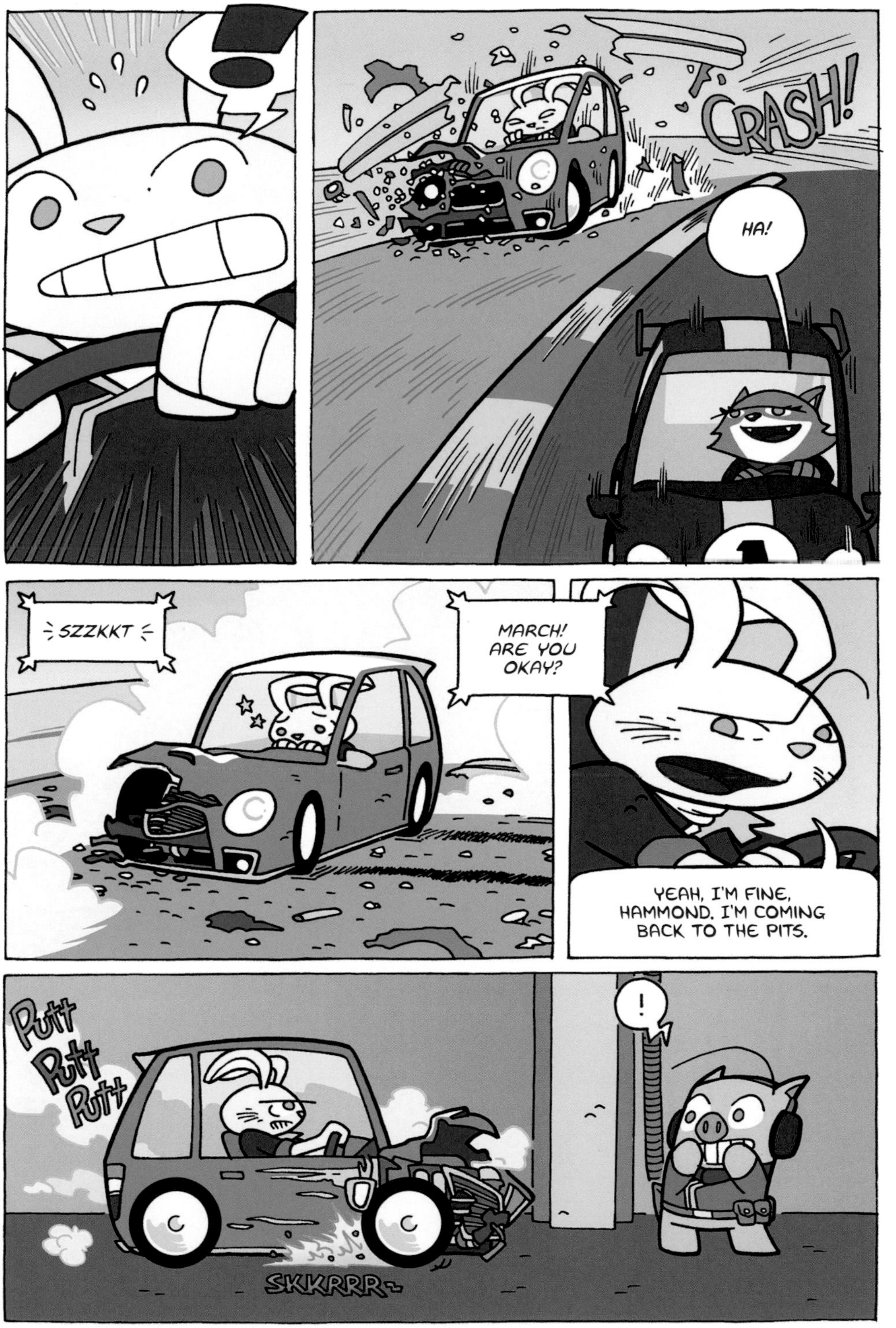
CRASH!
HA!
SZZKKT
MARCH! ARE YOU OKAY?
YEAH, I'M FINE, HAMMOND. I'M COMING BACK TO THE PITS.
Putt Putt Putt
!
SKKRRR

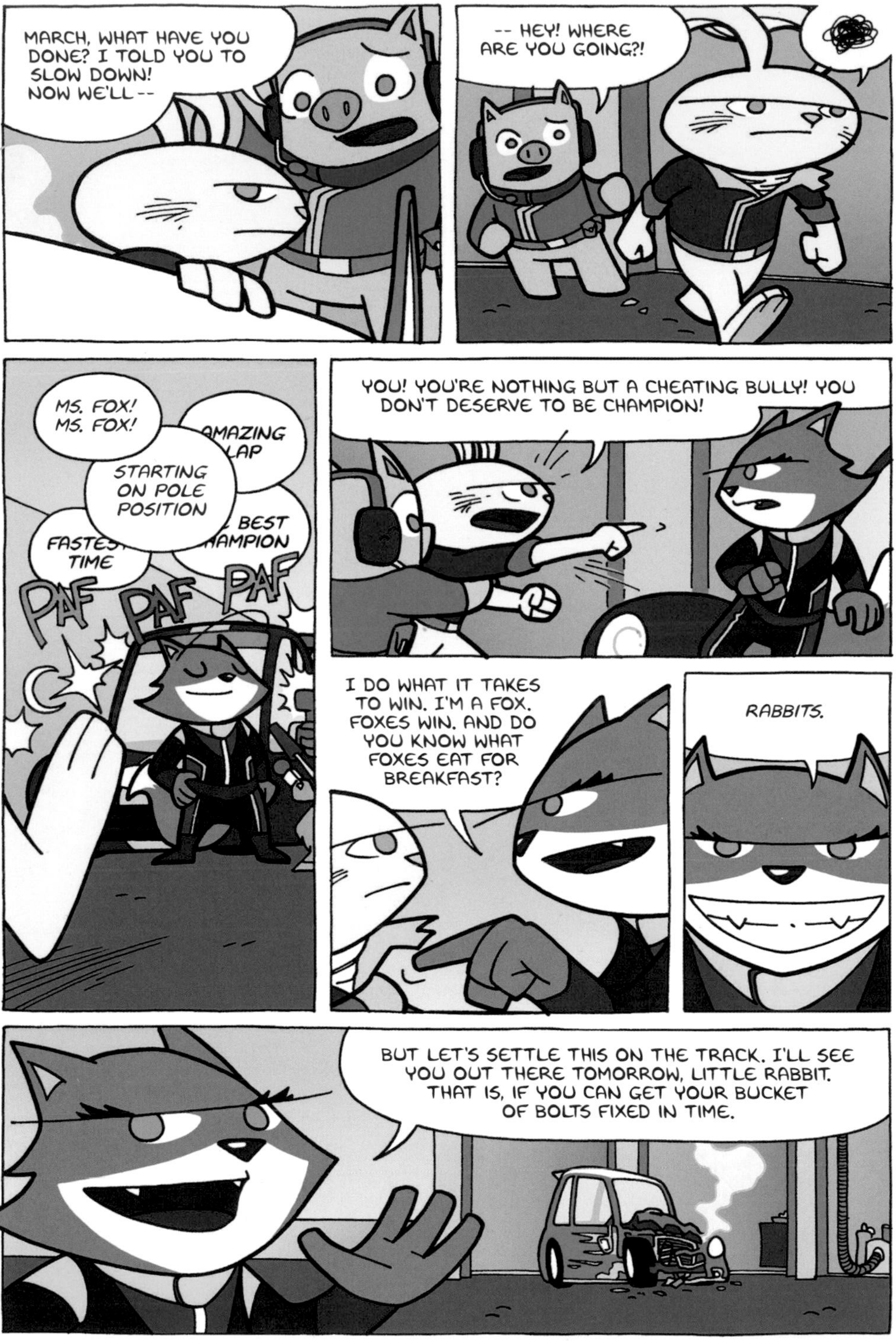
MARCH, WHAT HAVE YOU DONE? I TOLD YOU TO SLOW DOWN! NOW WE'LL--
-- HEY! WHERE ARE YOU GOING?!
MS. FOX! MS. FOX!
AMAZING LAP
STARTING ON POLE POSITION
BEST CHAMPION
FASTEST TIME
PAF PAF PAF
YOU! YOU'RE NOTHING BUT A CHEATING BULLY! YOU DON'T DESERVE TO BE CHAMPION!
I DO WHAT IT TAKES TO WIN. I'M A FOX. FOXES WIN. AND DO YOU KNOW WHAT FOXES EAT FOR BREAKFAST?
RABBITS.
BUT LET'S SETTLE THIS ON THE TRACK. I'LL SEE YOU OUT THERE TOMORROW, LITTLE RABBIT. THAT IS, IF YOU CAN GET YOUR BUCKET OF BOLTS FIXED IN TIME.

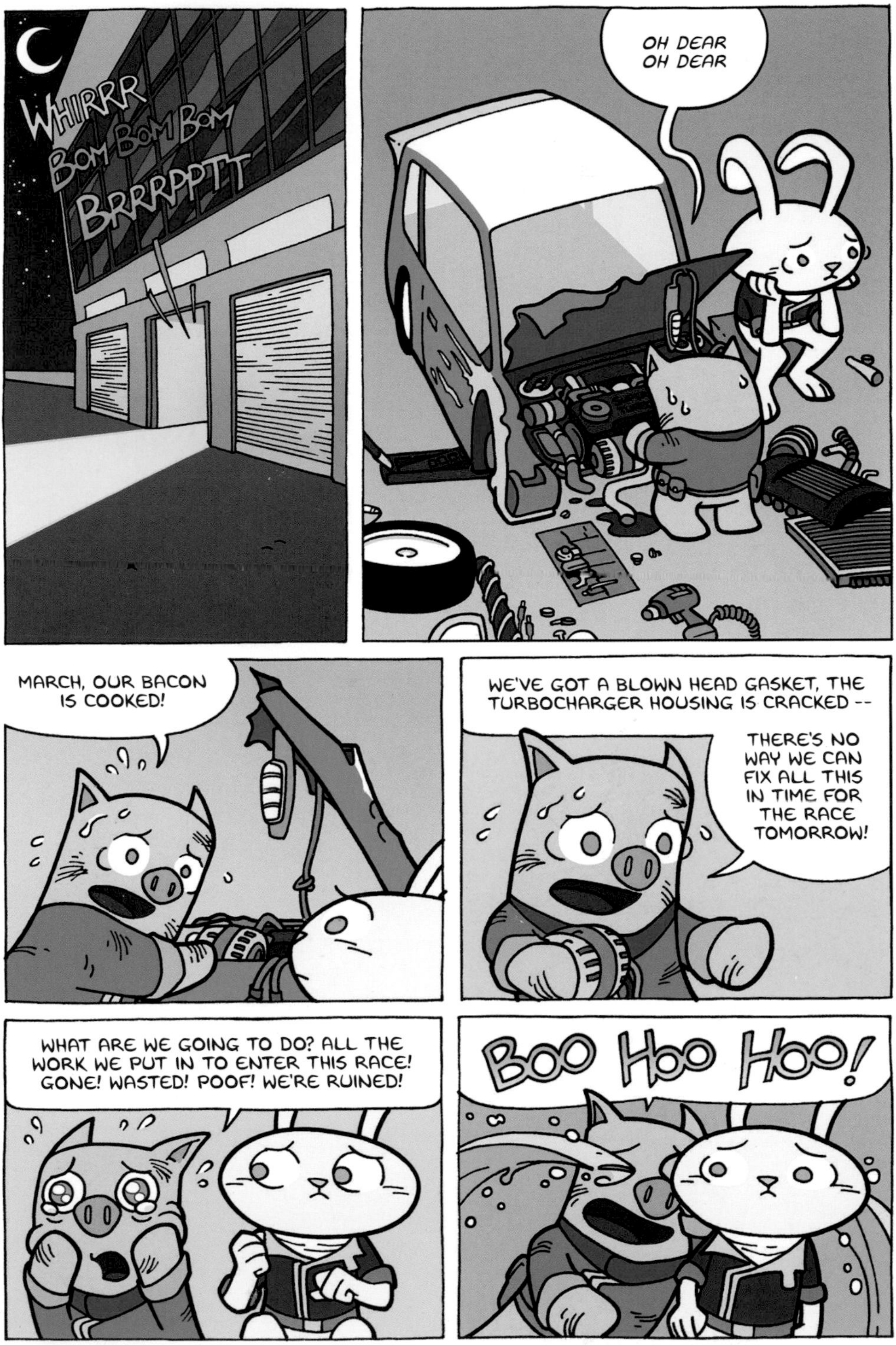
WHIRRR
BOM BOM BOM
BRRRPPTT
OH DEAR
OH DEAR
MARCH, OUR BACON IS COOKED!
WE'VE GOT A BLOWN HEAD GASKET, THE TURBOCHARGER HOUSING IS CRACKED --
THERE'S NO WAY WE CAN FIX ALL THIS IN TIME FOR THE RACE TOMORROW!
WHAT ARE WE GOING TO DO? ALL THE WORK WE PUT IN TO ENTER THIS RACE! GONE! WASTED! POOF! WE'RE RUINED!
BOO HOO HOO!

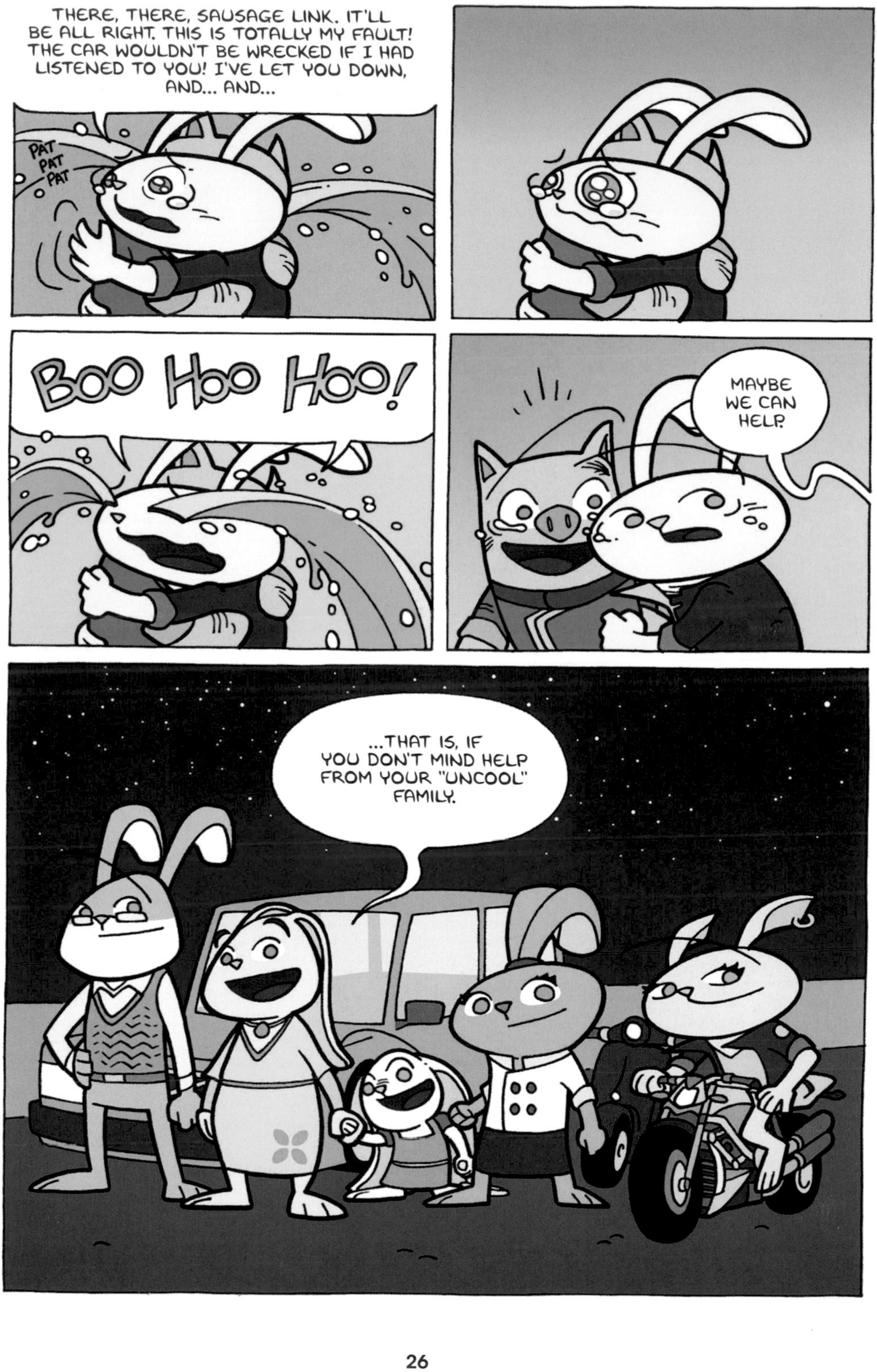
THERE, THERE, SAUSAGE LINK. IT'LL BE ALL RIGHT. THIS IS TOTALLY MY FAULT! THE CAR WOULDN'T BE WRECKED IF I HAD LISTENED TO YOU! I'VE LET YOU DOWN, AND... AND...
PAT PAT PAT
BOO HOO HOO!
MAYBE WE CAN HELP?
...THAT IS, IF YOU DON'T MIND HELP FROM YOUR "UNCOOL" FAMILY.

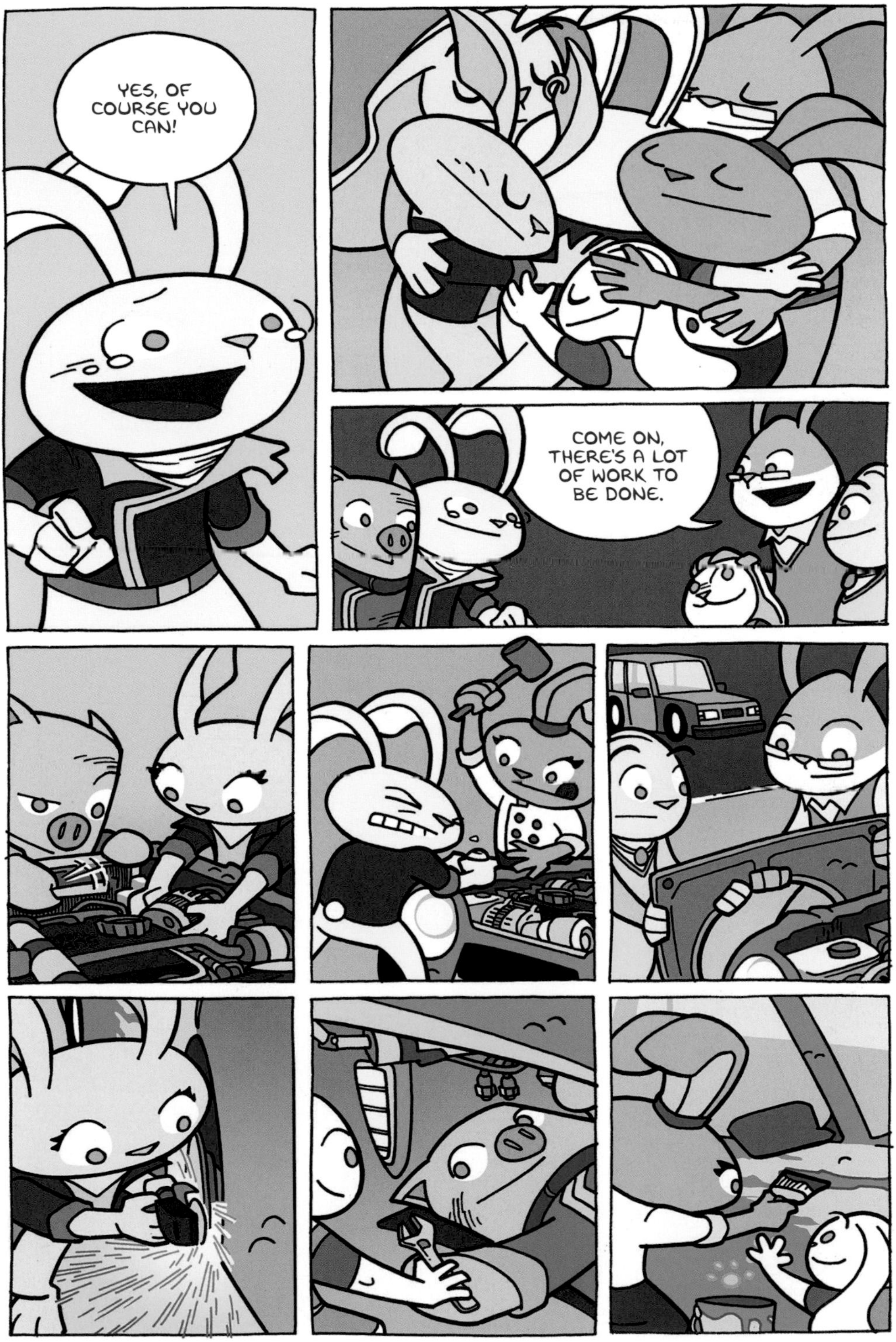
YES, OF COURSE YOU CAN!
COME ON, THERE'S A LOT OF WORK TO BE DONE.

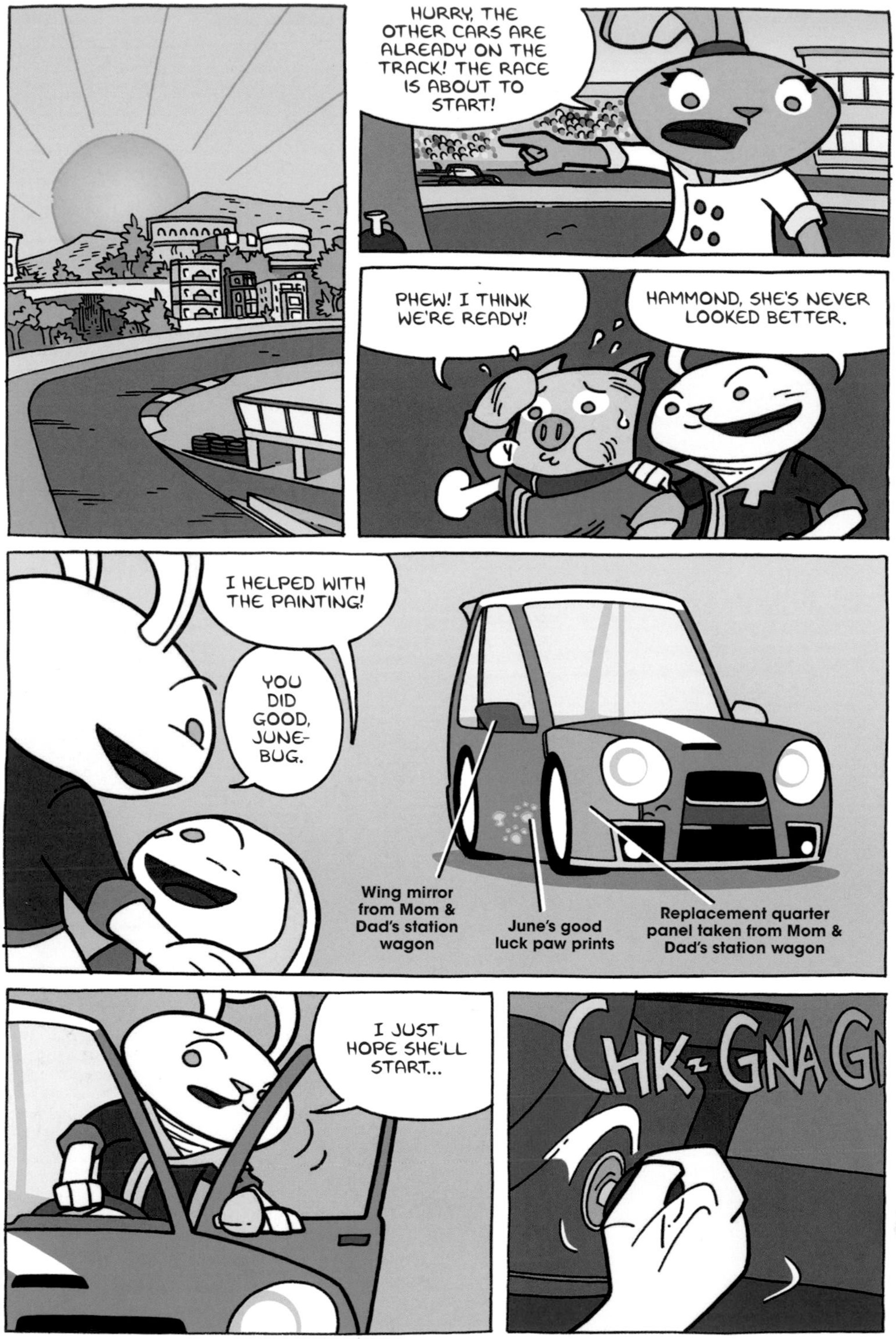
HURRY, THE OTHER CARS ARE ALREADY ON THE TRACK! THE RACE IS ABOUT TO START!
PHEW! I THINK WE'RE READY!
HAMMOND, SHE'S NEVER LOOKED BETTER.
I HELPED WITH THE PAINTING!
YOU DID GOOD, JUNE-BUG.
Wing mirror from Mom & Dad's station wagon
June's good luck paw prints
Replacement quarter panel taken from Mom & Dad's station wagon
I JUST HOPE SHE'LL START...
CHK-GNAGN

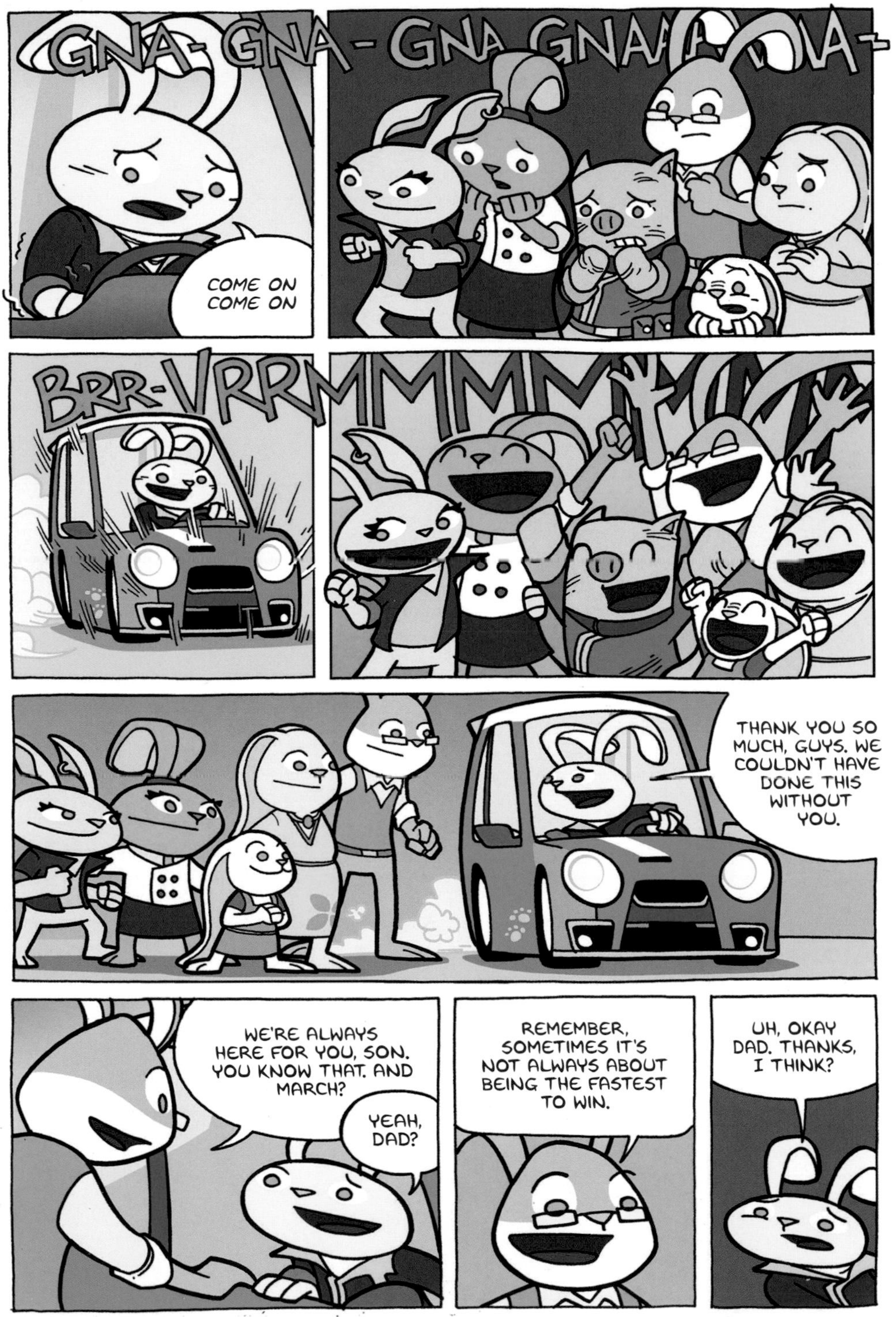
GNA-GNA-GNA GNAAAAAA-
COME ON COME ON
BRR-VRRMMMMMM
THANK YOU SO MUCH, GUYS. WE COULDN'T HAVE DONE THIS WITHOUT YOU.
WE'RE ALWAYS HERE FOR YOU, SON. YOU KNOW THAT. AND MARCH?
YEAH, DAD?
REMEMBER, SOMETIMES IT'S NOT ALWAYS ABOUT BEING THE FASTEST TO WIN.
UH, OKAY DAD. THANKS, I THINK?

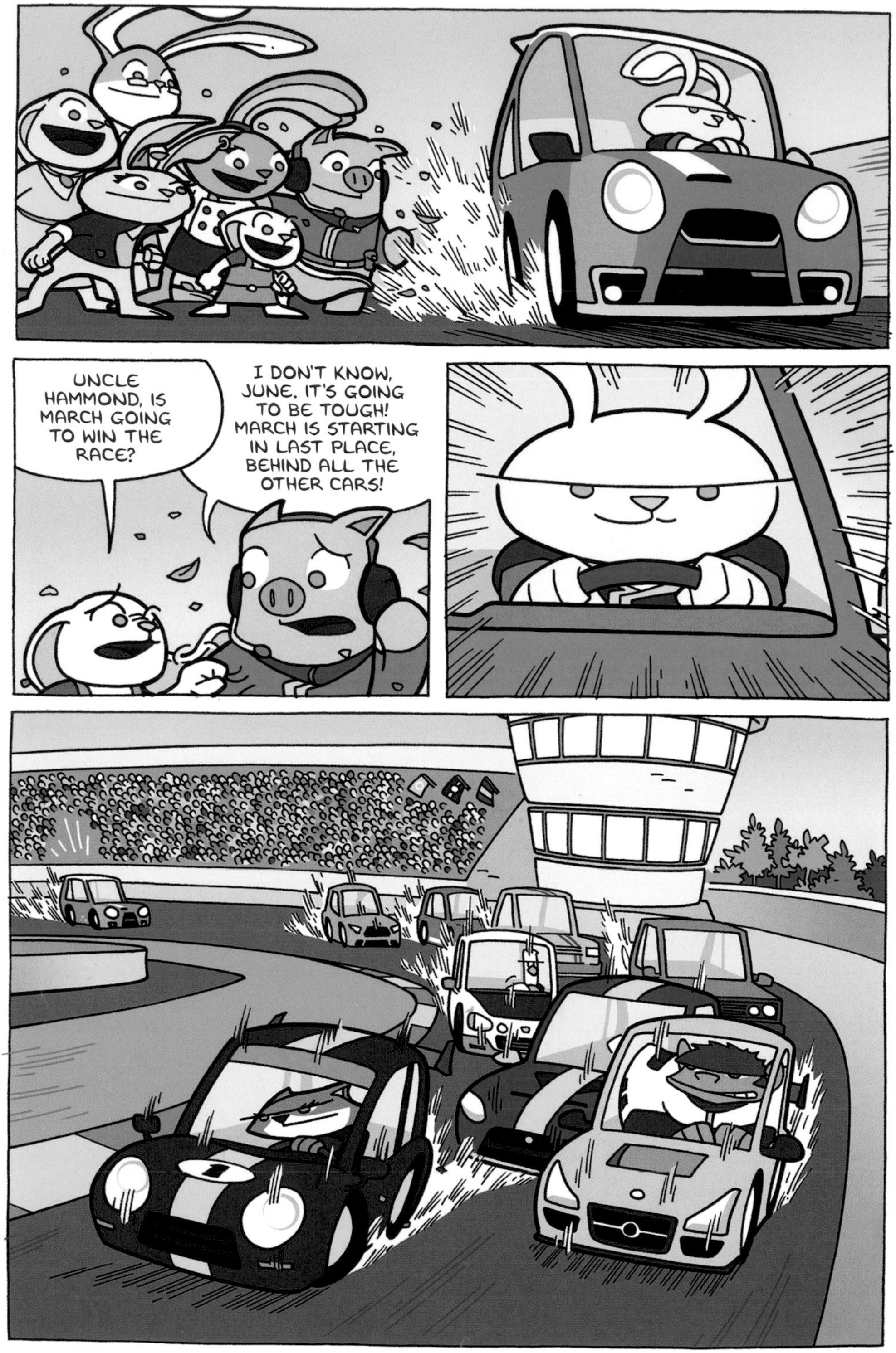
UNCLE HAMMOND, IS MARCH GOING TO WIN THE RACE?
I DON'T KNOW, JUNE. IT'S GOING TO BE TOUGH! MARCH IS STARTING IN LAST PLACE, BEHIND ALL THE OTHER CARS!

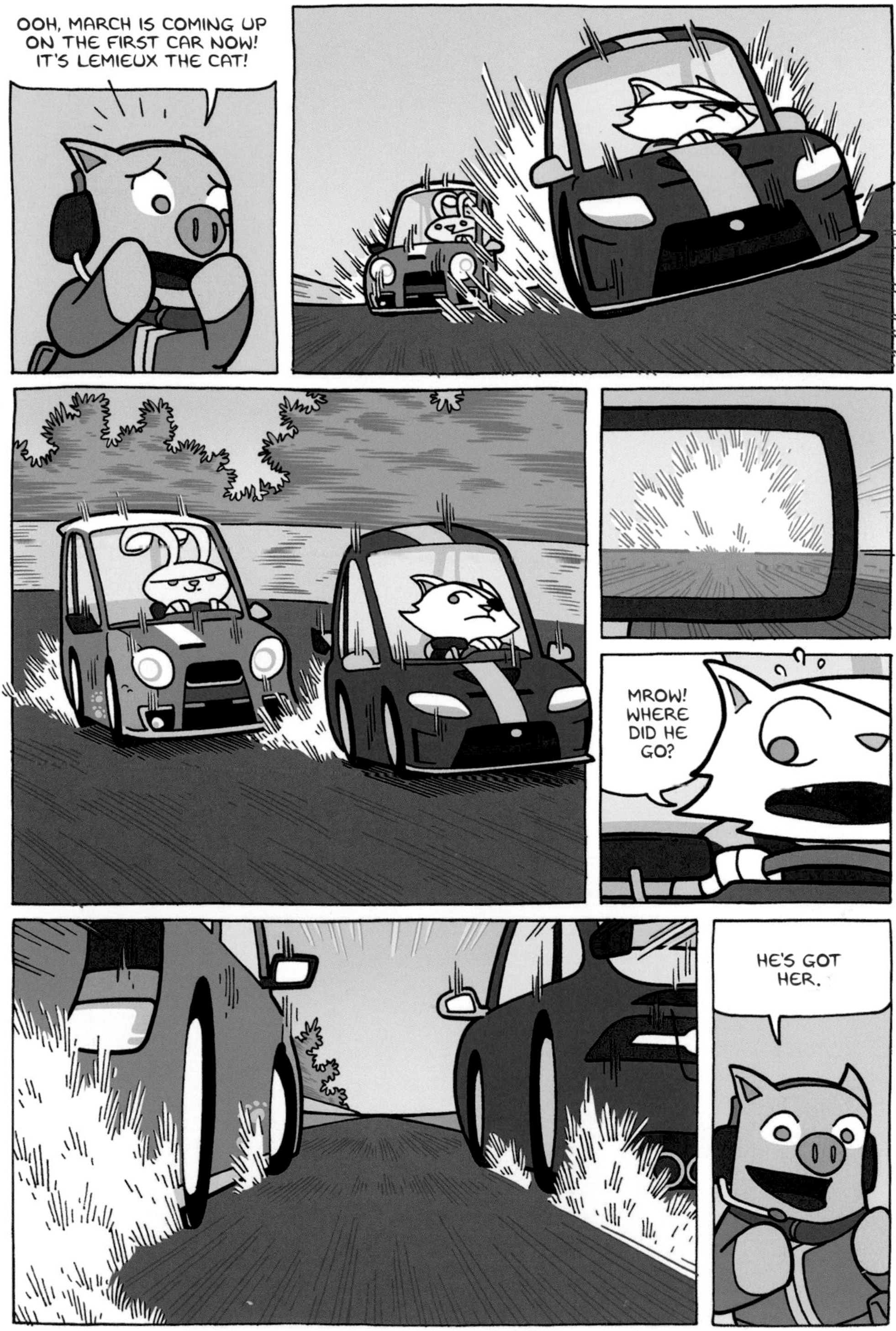
OOH, MARCH IS COMING UP ON THE FIRST CAR NOW! IT'S LEMIEUX THE CAT!
MROW! WHERE DID HE GO?
HE'S GOT HER.

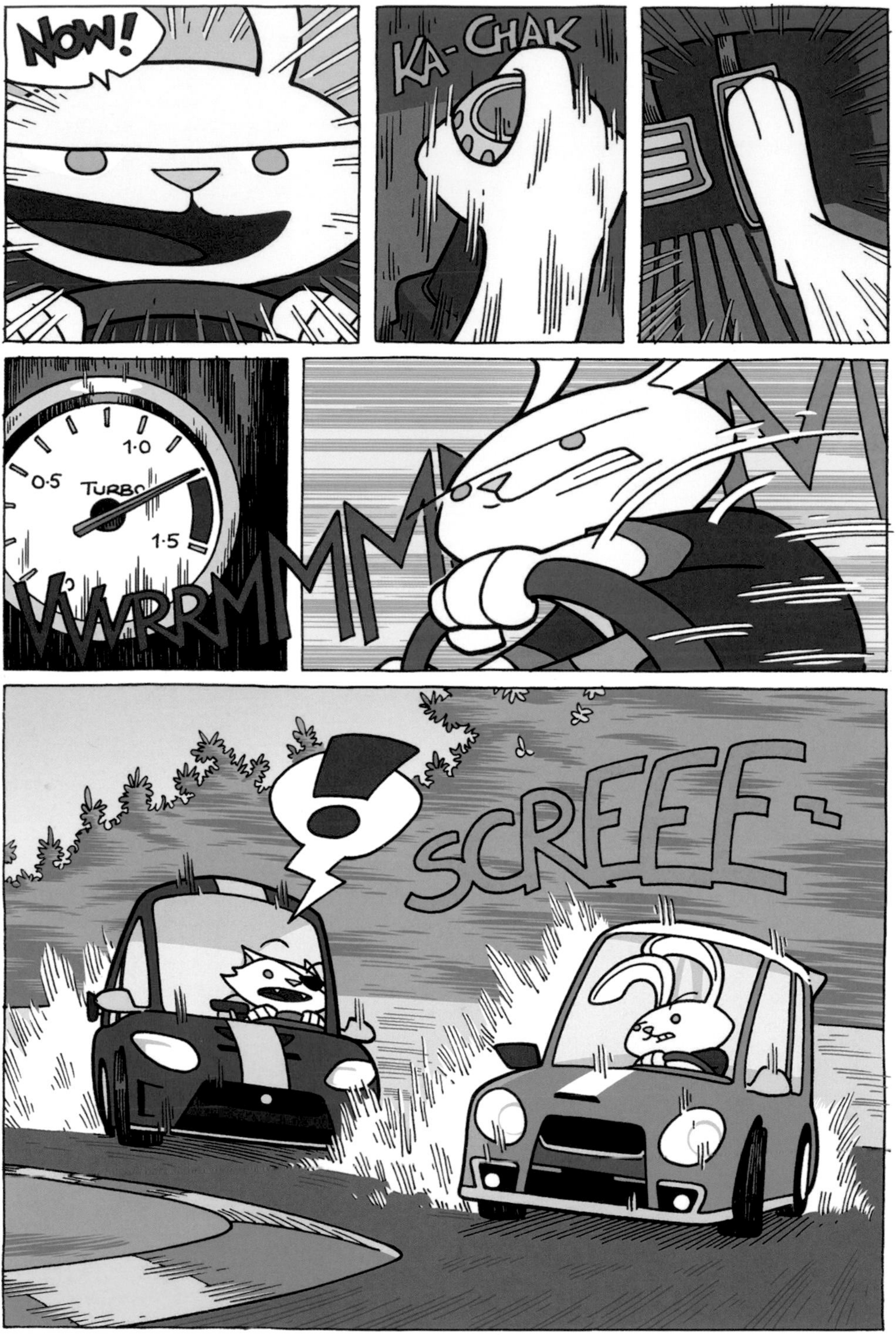
NOW!
KA-CHAK
1·0
0·5
TURBO
1·5
VWRRMMMMM
SCREEE-

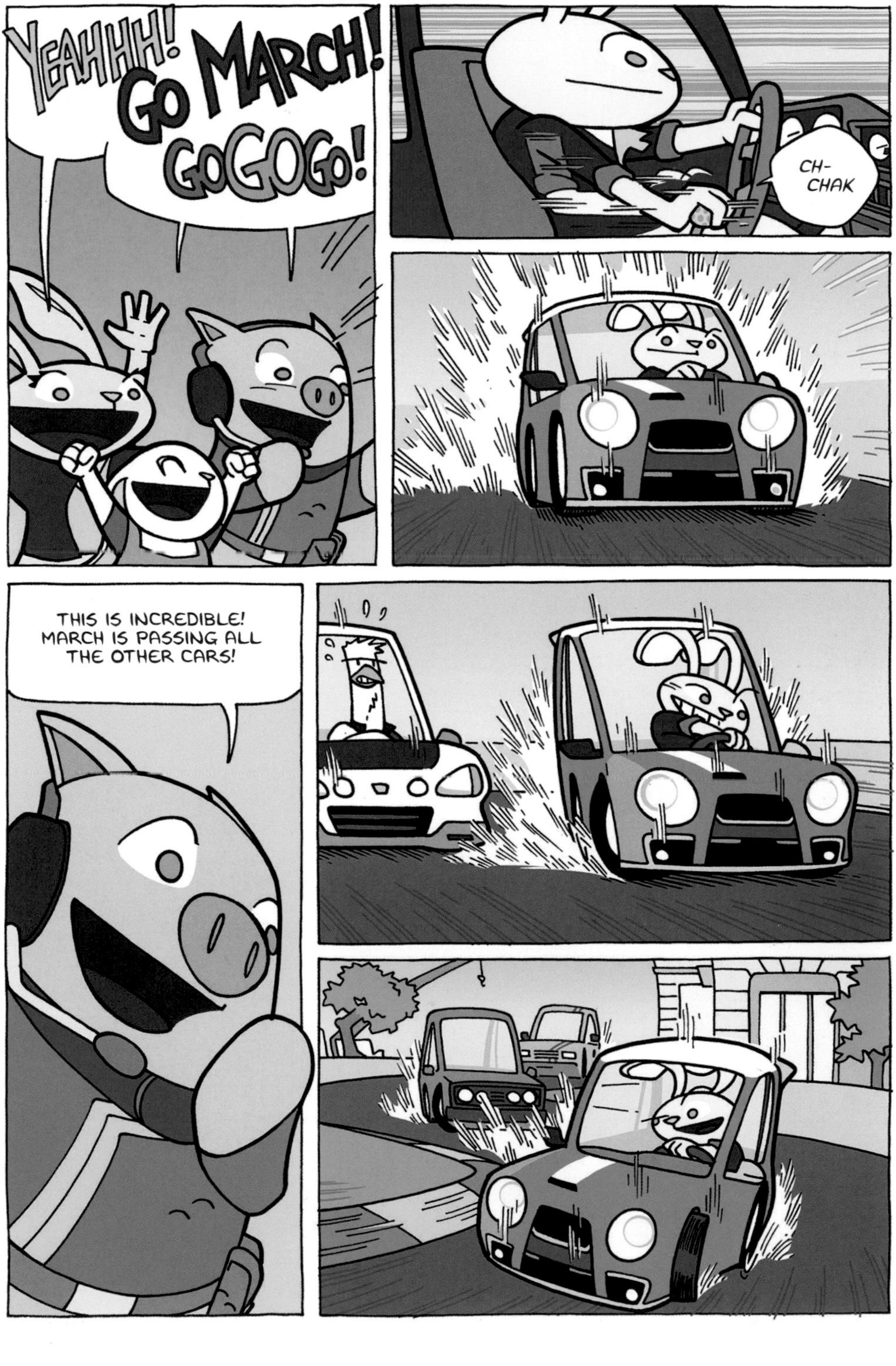
YEAHHH! GO MARCH! GOGOGO!
CH-CHAK
THIS IS INCREDIBLE! MARCH IS PASSING ALL THE OTHER CARS!

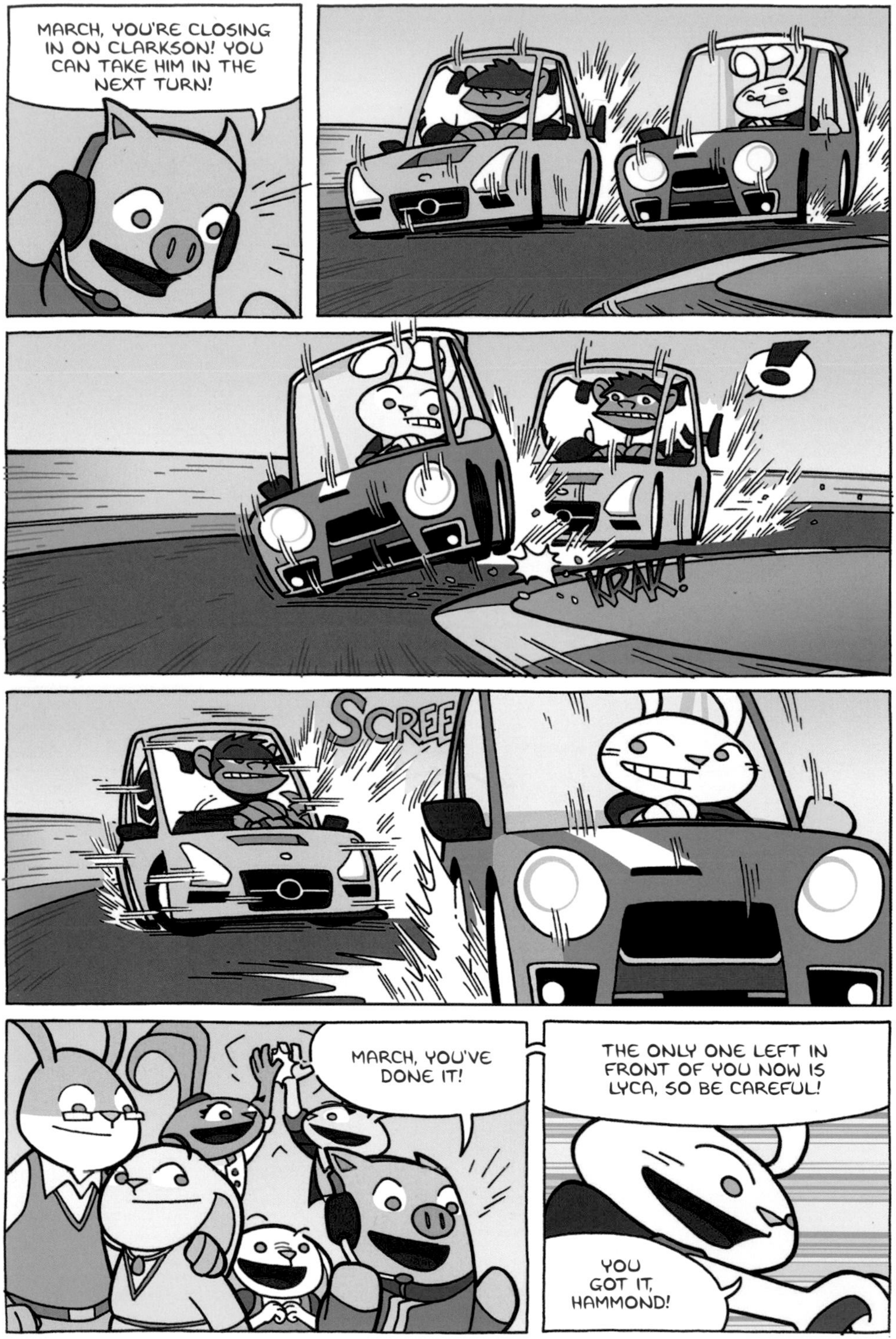
MARCH, YOU'RE CLOSING IN ON CLARKSON! YOU CAN TAKE HIM IN THE NEXT TURN!
KRAK!
SCREE
MARCH, YOU'VE DONE IT!
THE ONLY ONE LEFT IN FRONT OF YOU NOW IS LYCA, SO BE CAREFUL!
YOU GOT IT, HAMMOND!

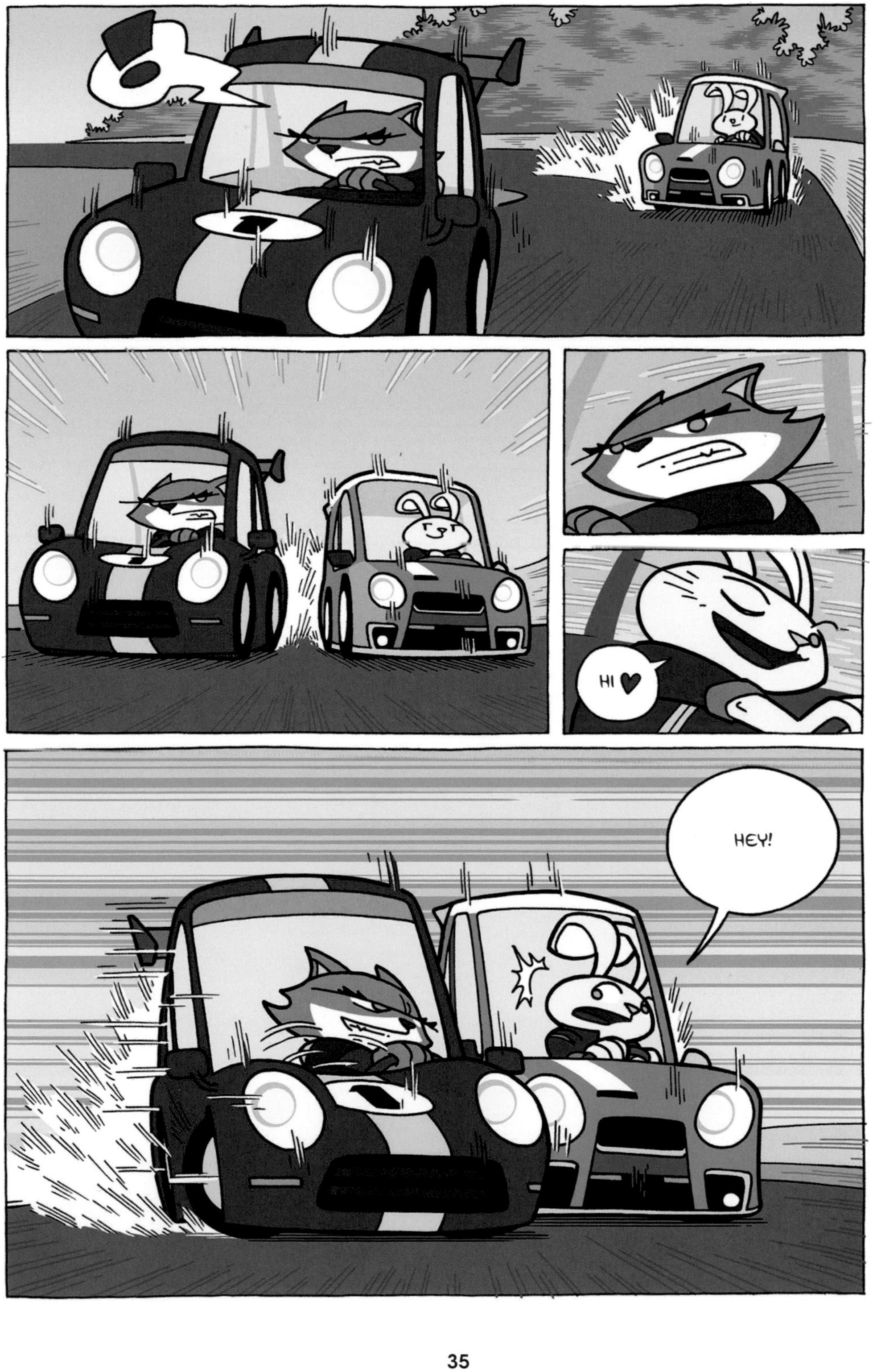
HI ♥
HEY!

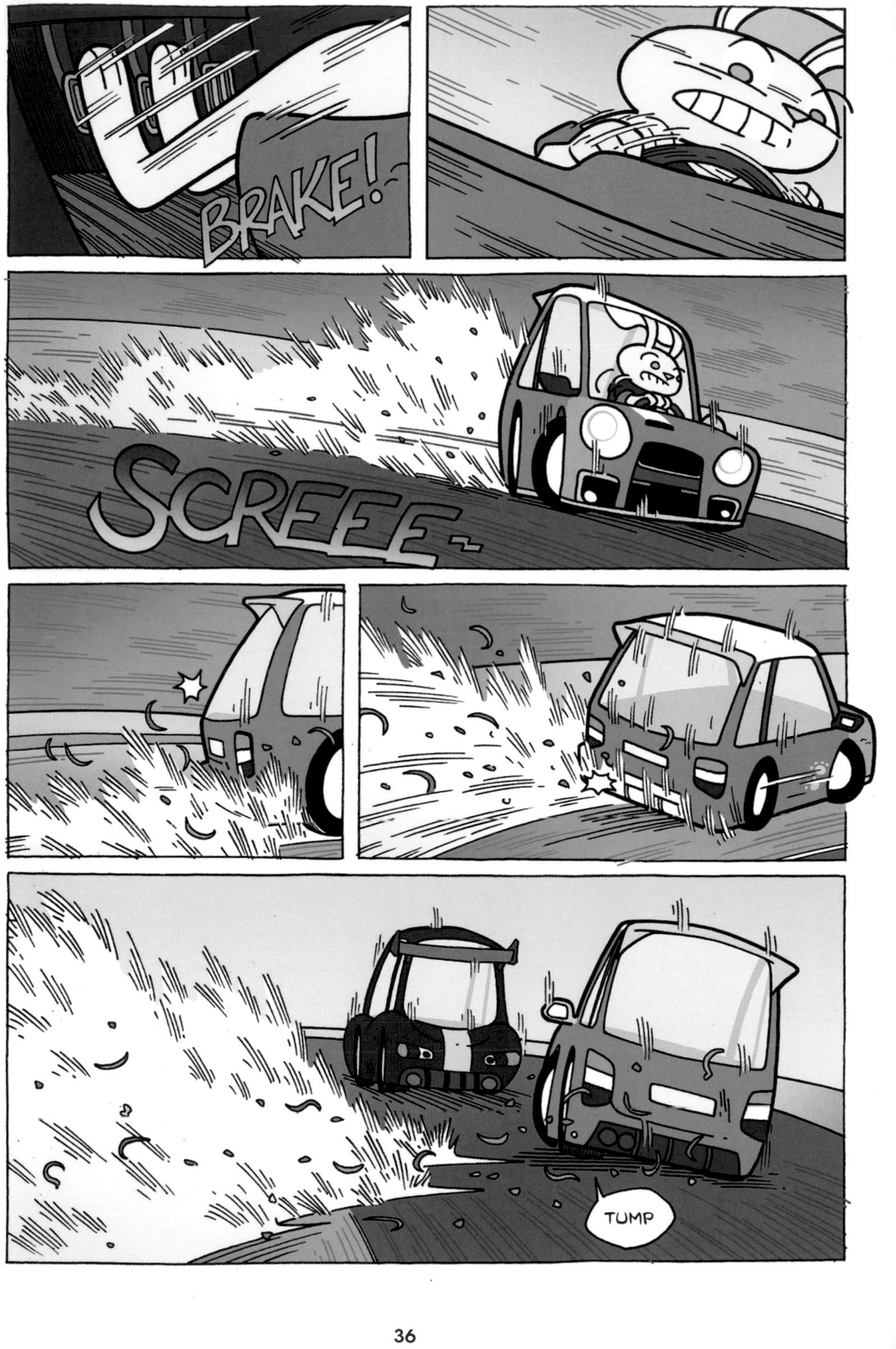
BRAKE!
SCREEE
TUMP

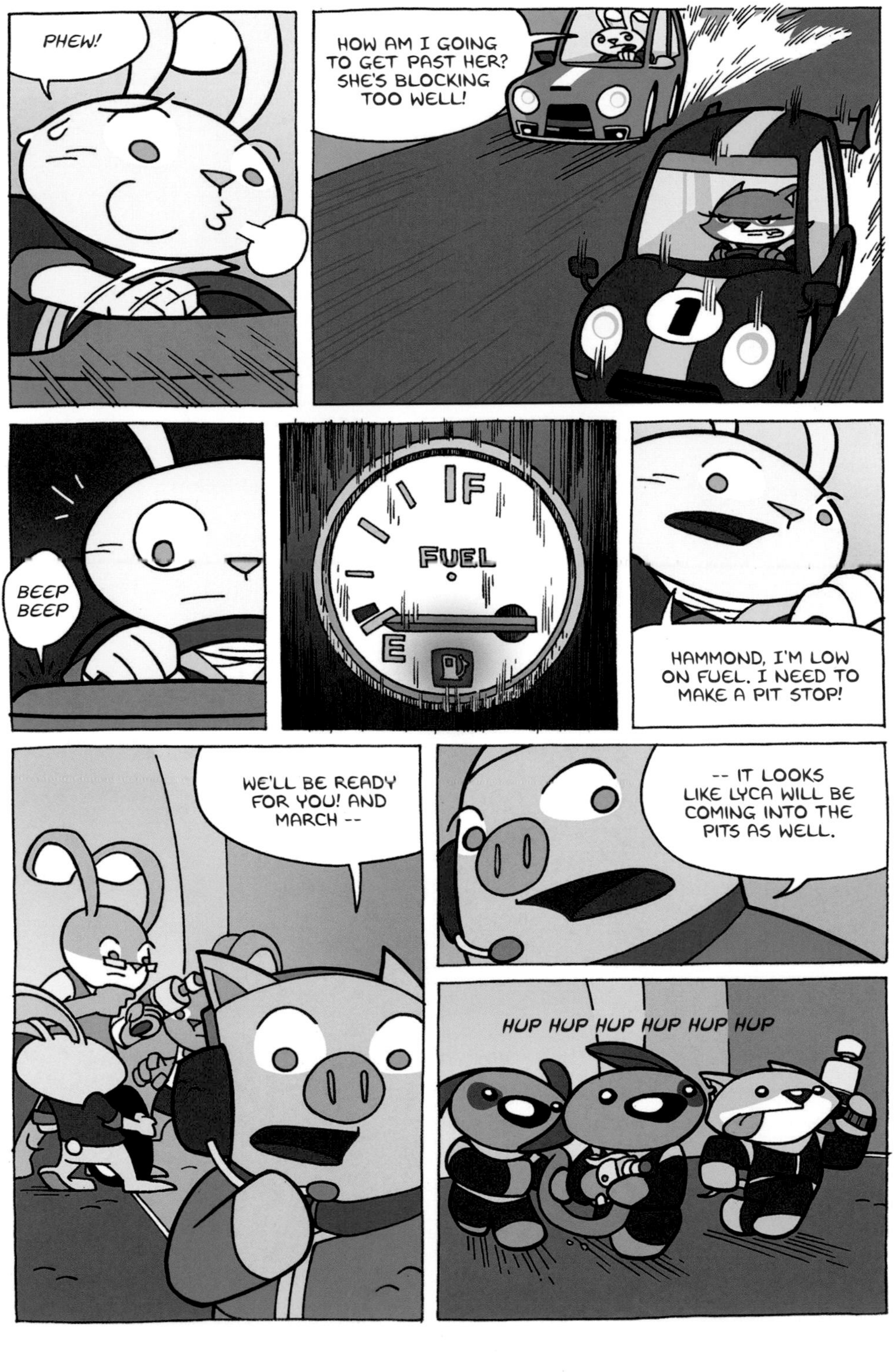
PHEW!
HOW AM I GOING TO GET PAST HER? SHE'S BLOCKING TOO WELL!
BEEP BEEP
F
FUEL
E
HAMMOND, I'M LOW ON FUEL. I NEED TO MAKE A PIT STOP!
WE'LL BE READY FOR YOU! AND MARCH --
-- IT LOOKS LIKE LYCA WILL BE COMING INTO THE PITS AS WELL.
HUP HUP HUP HUP HUP HUP

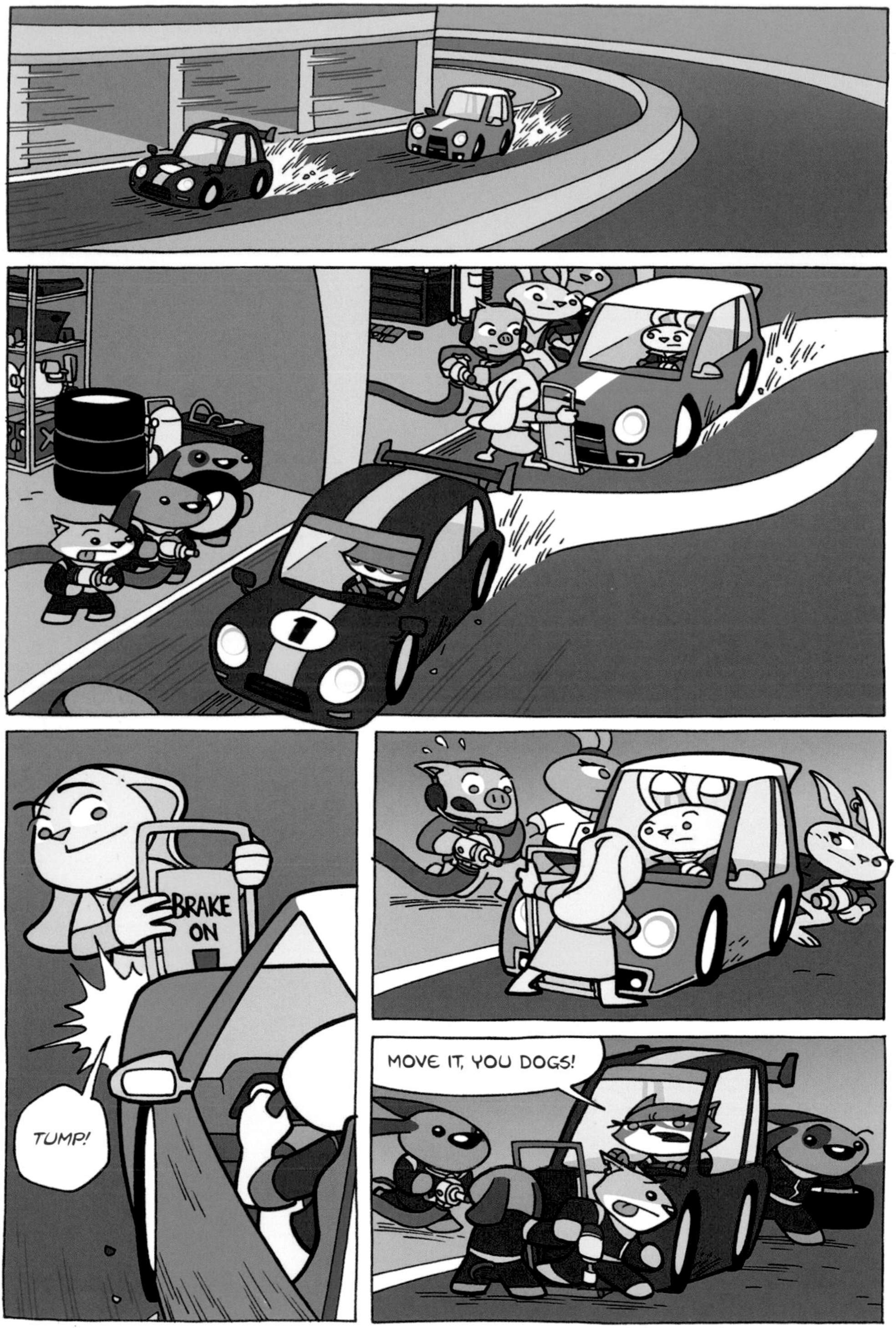
1
BRAKE ON
TUMP!
MOVE IT, YOU DOGS!

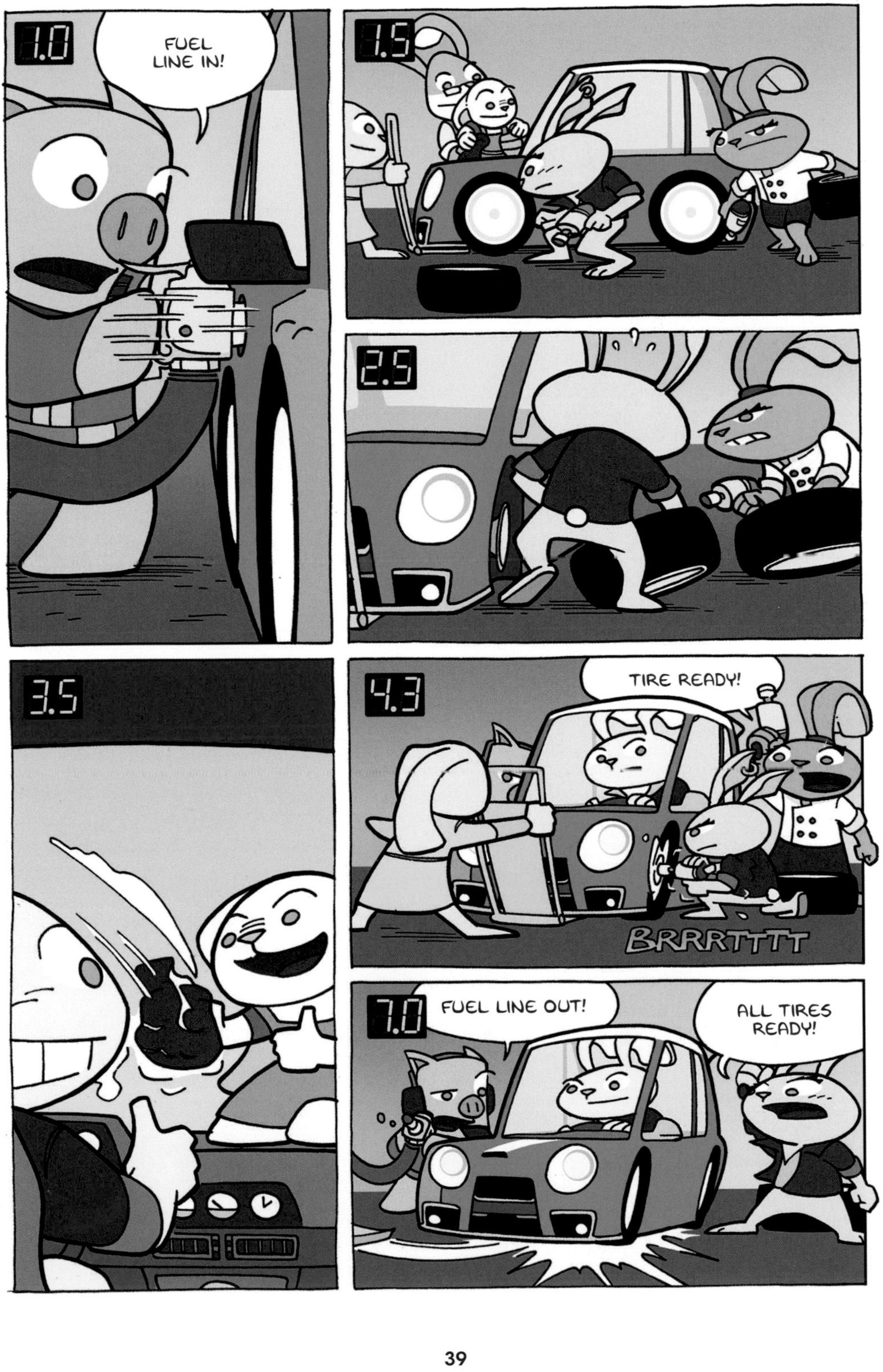
1.0
FUEL LINE IN!
1.5
2.5
3.5
4.3
TIRE READY!
BRRRTTTT
7.0
FUEL LINE OUT!
ALL TIRES READY!

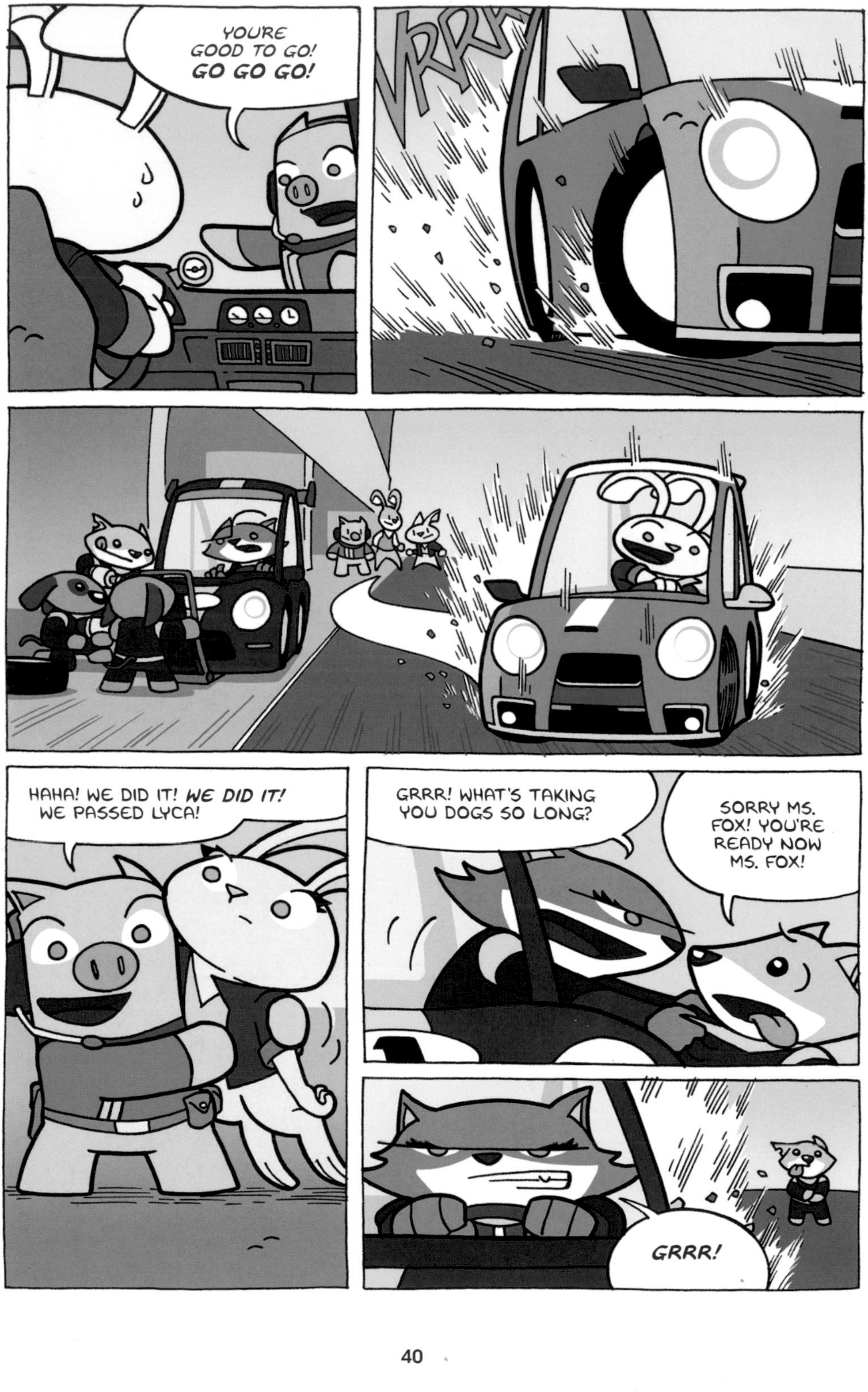
YOU'RE GOOD TO GO! GO GO GO!
VRRR
HAHA! WE DID IT! WE DID IT! WE PASSED LYCA!
GRRR! WHAT'S TAKING YOU DOGS SO LONG?
SORRY MS. FOX! YOU'RE READY NOW MS. FOX!
GRRR!

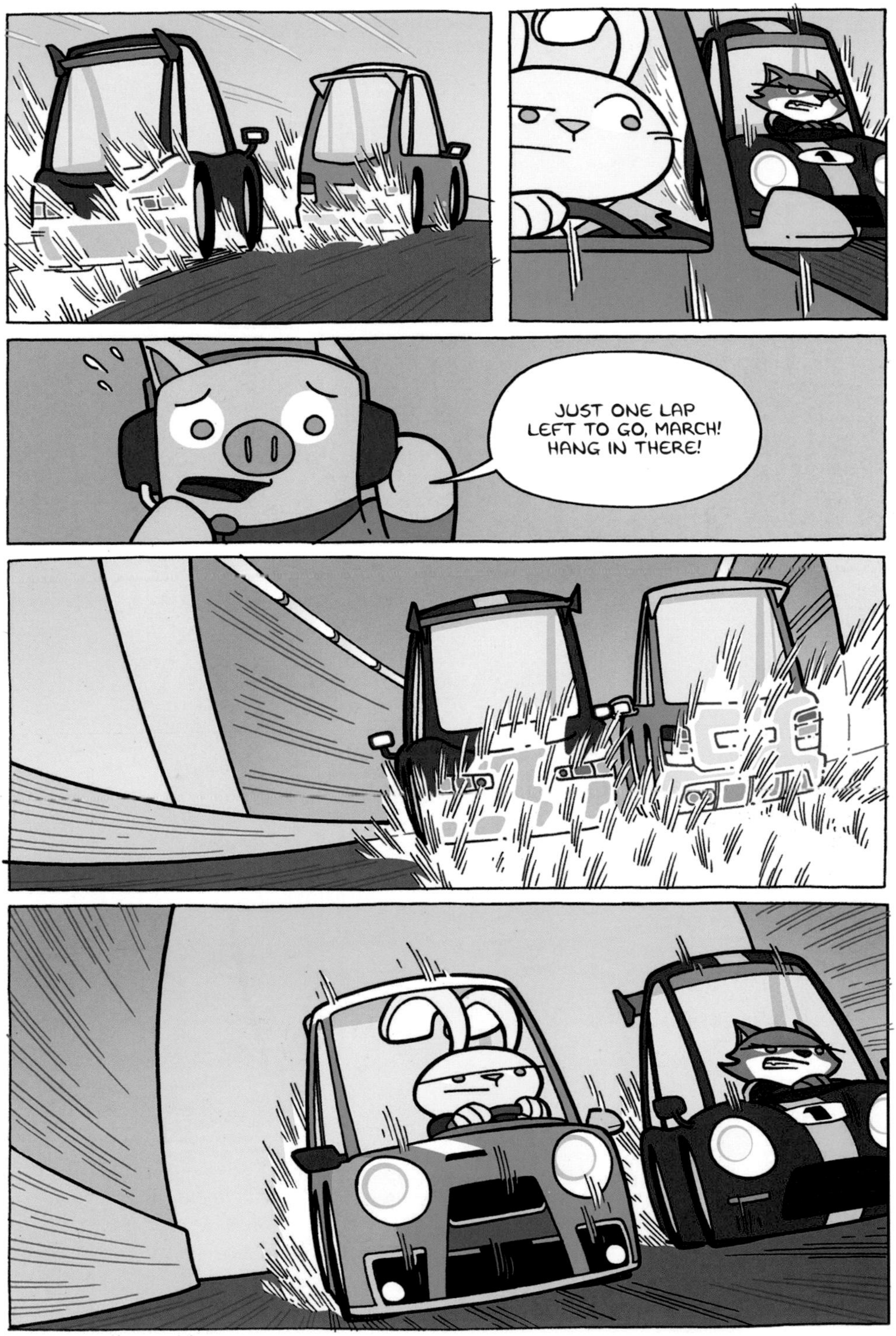
JUST ONE LAP LEFT TO GO, MARCH! HANG IN THERE!

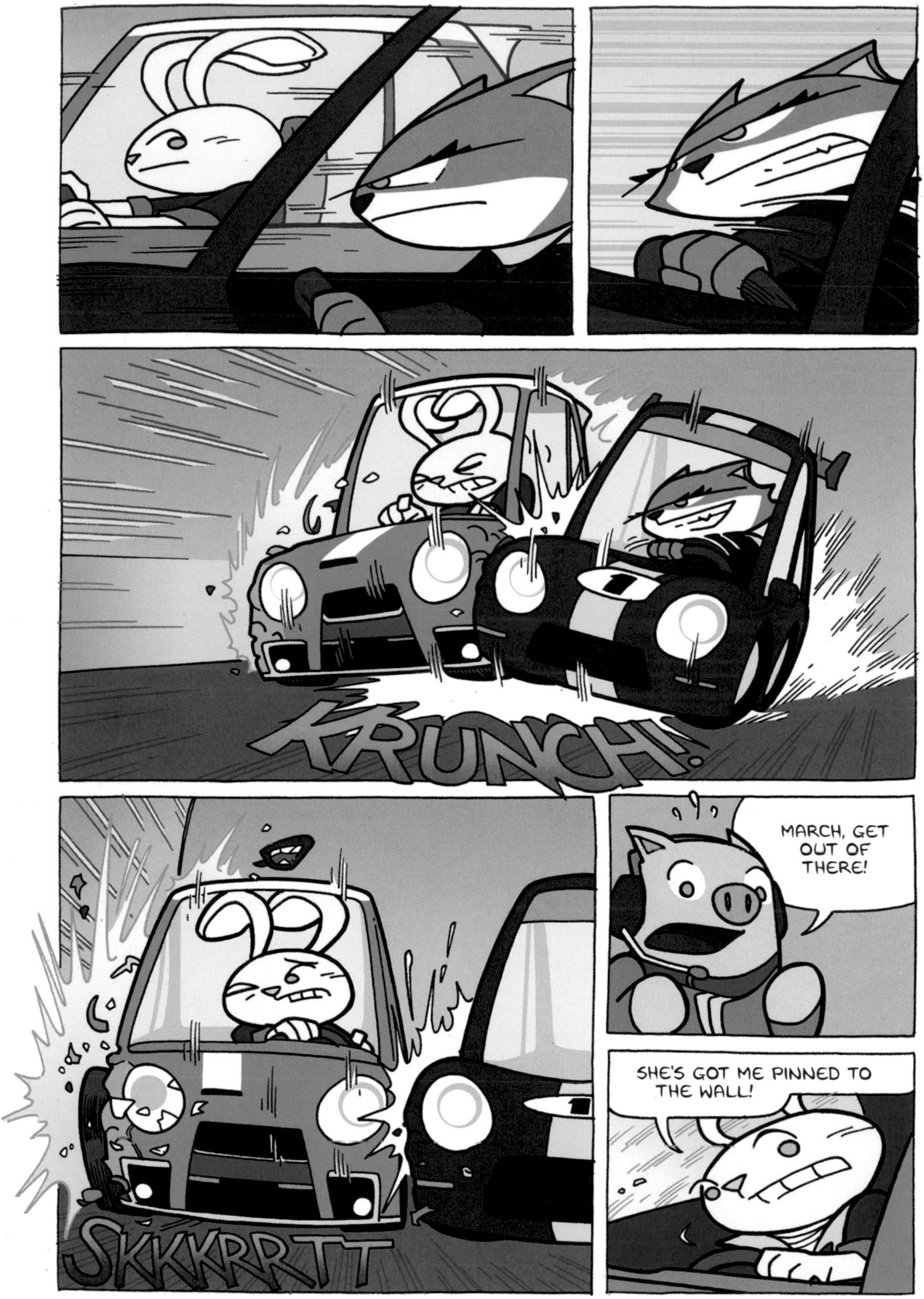
KRUNCH!
SKKRRTT
MARCH, GET OUT OF THERE!
SHE'S GOT ME PINNED TO THE WALL!

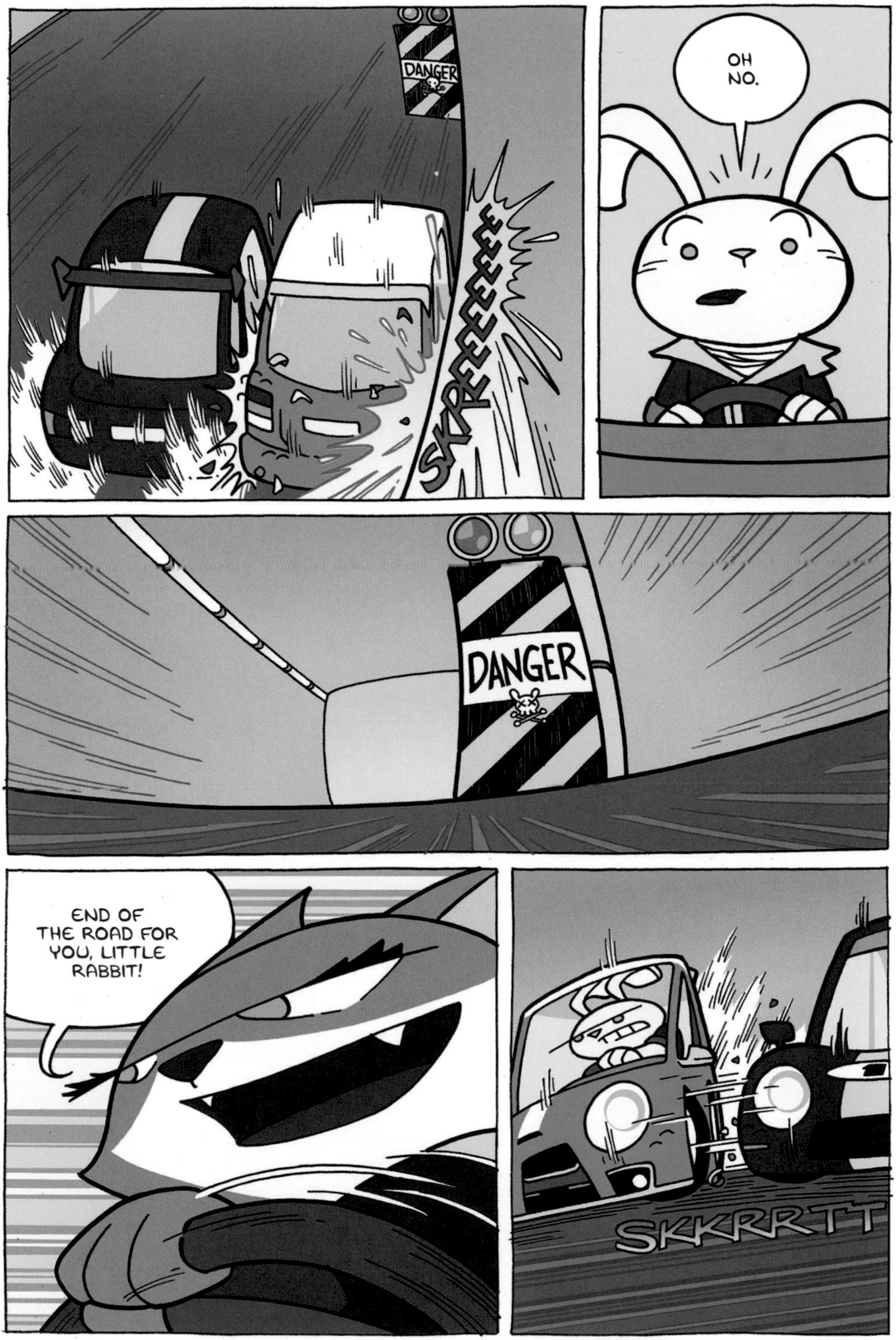
DANGER
SKREEEEEEE
OH NO.
DANGER
END OF THE ROAD FOR YOU, LITTLE RABBIT!
SKKRRTT

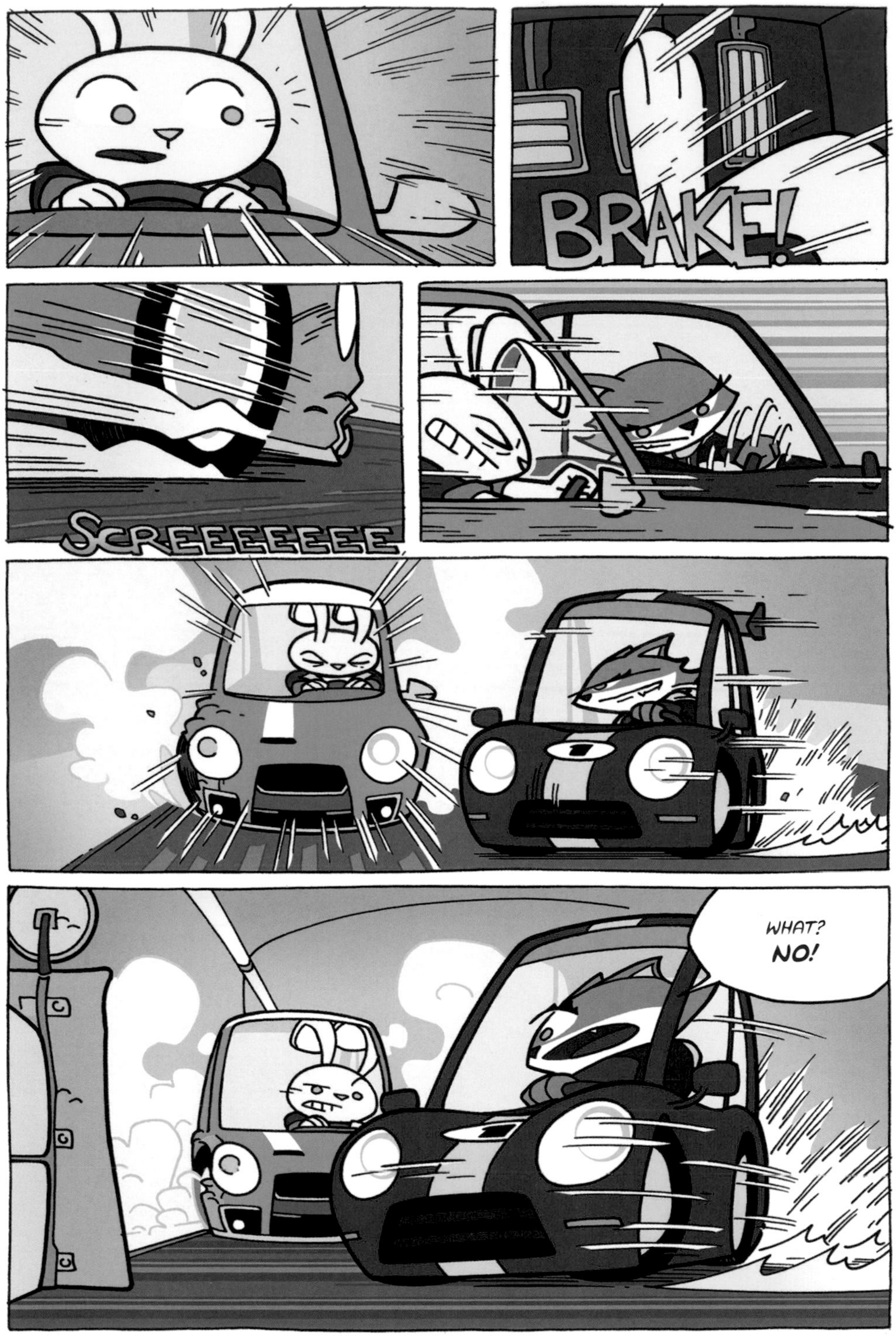
BRAKE!
SCREEEEEEEEE
WHAT?
NO!

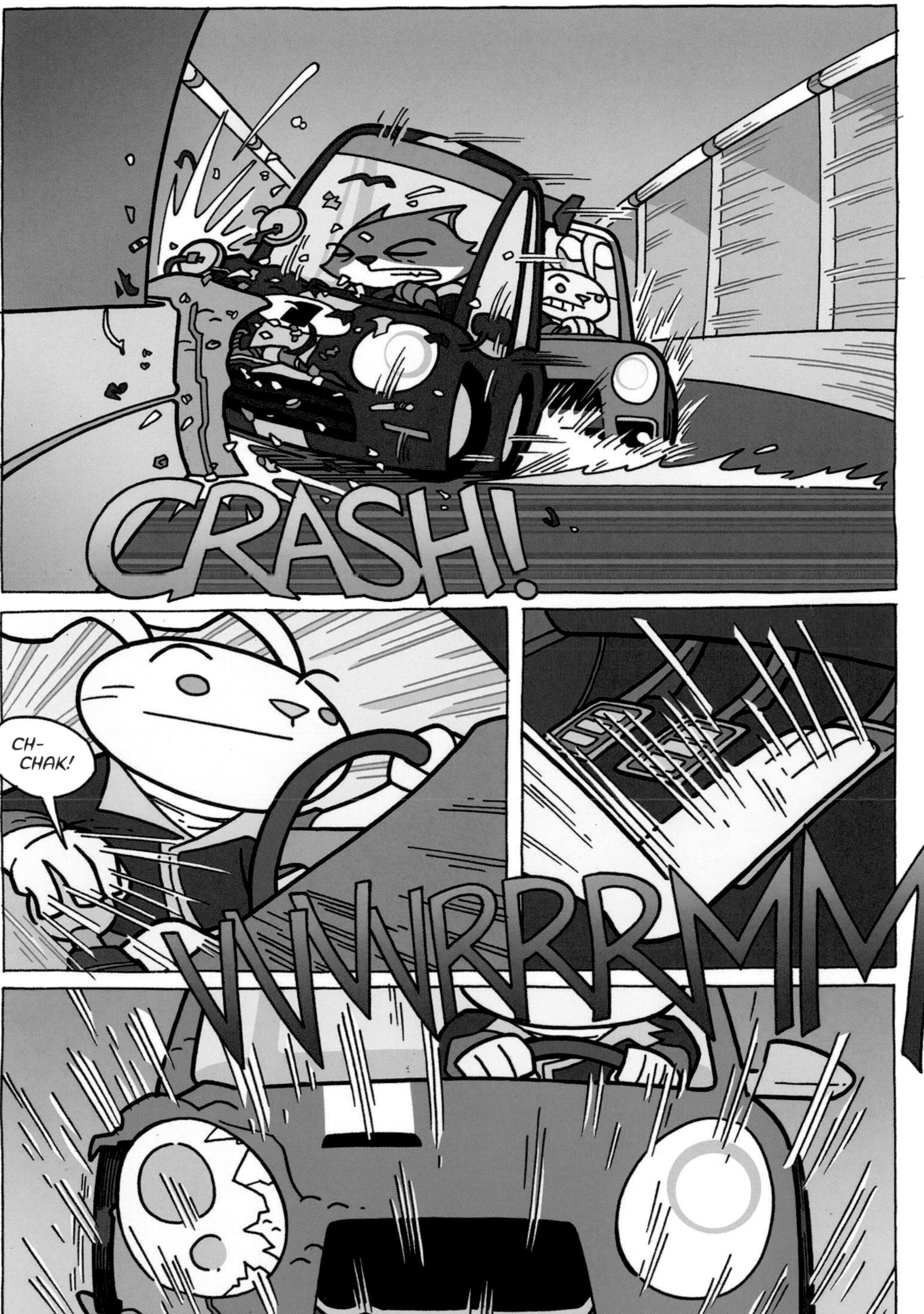
CRASH!
CH-CHAK!
VVVVRRRRMMM

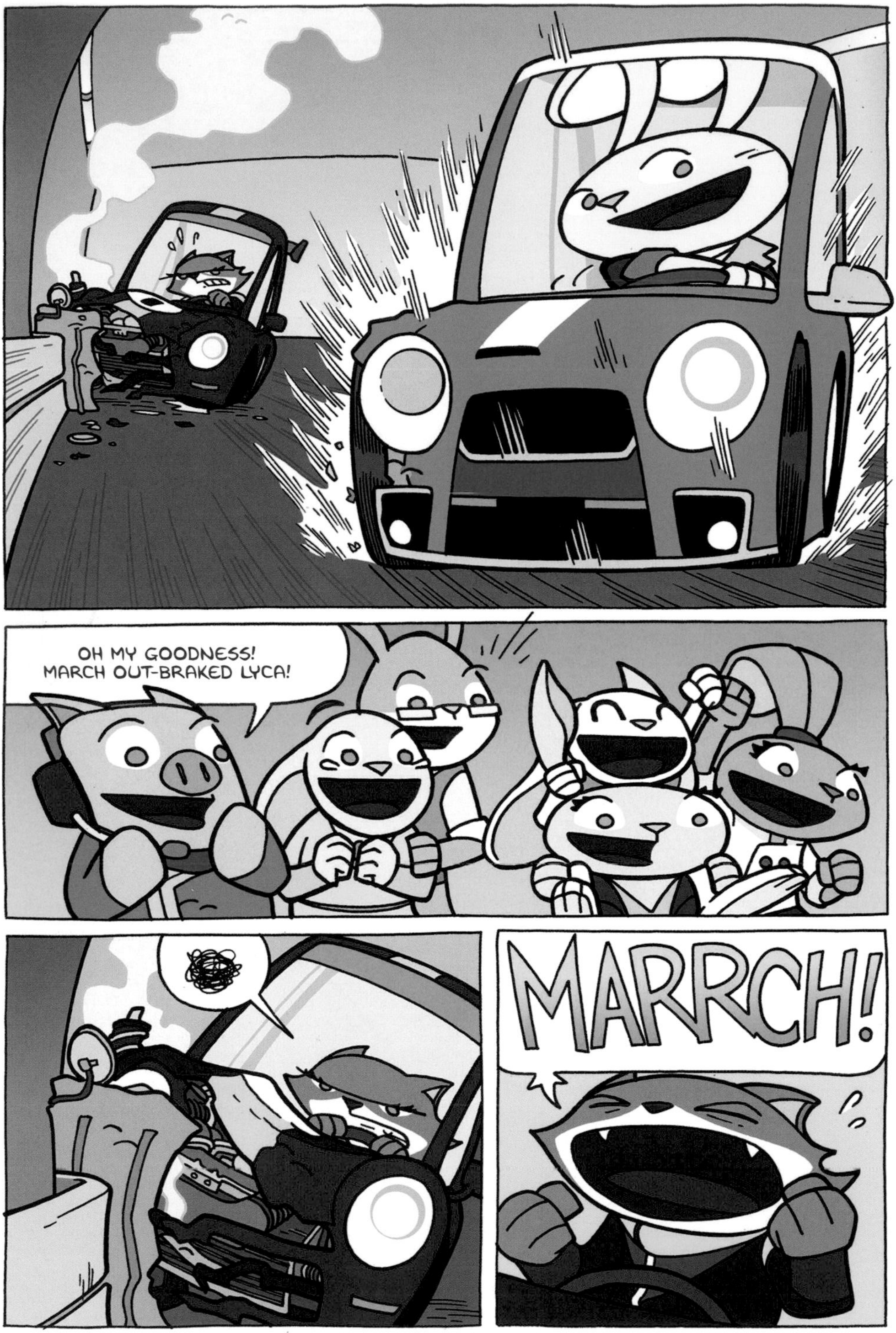
OH MY GOODNESS!
MARCH OUT-BRAKED LYCA!
MARRCH!

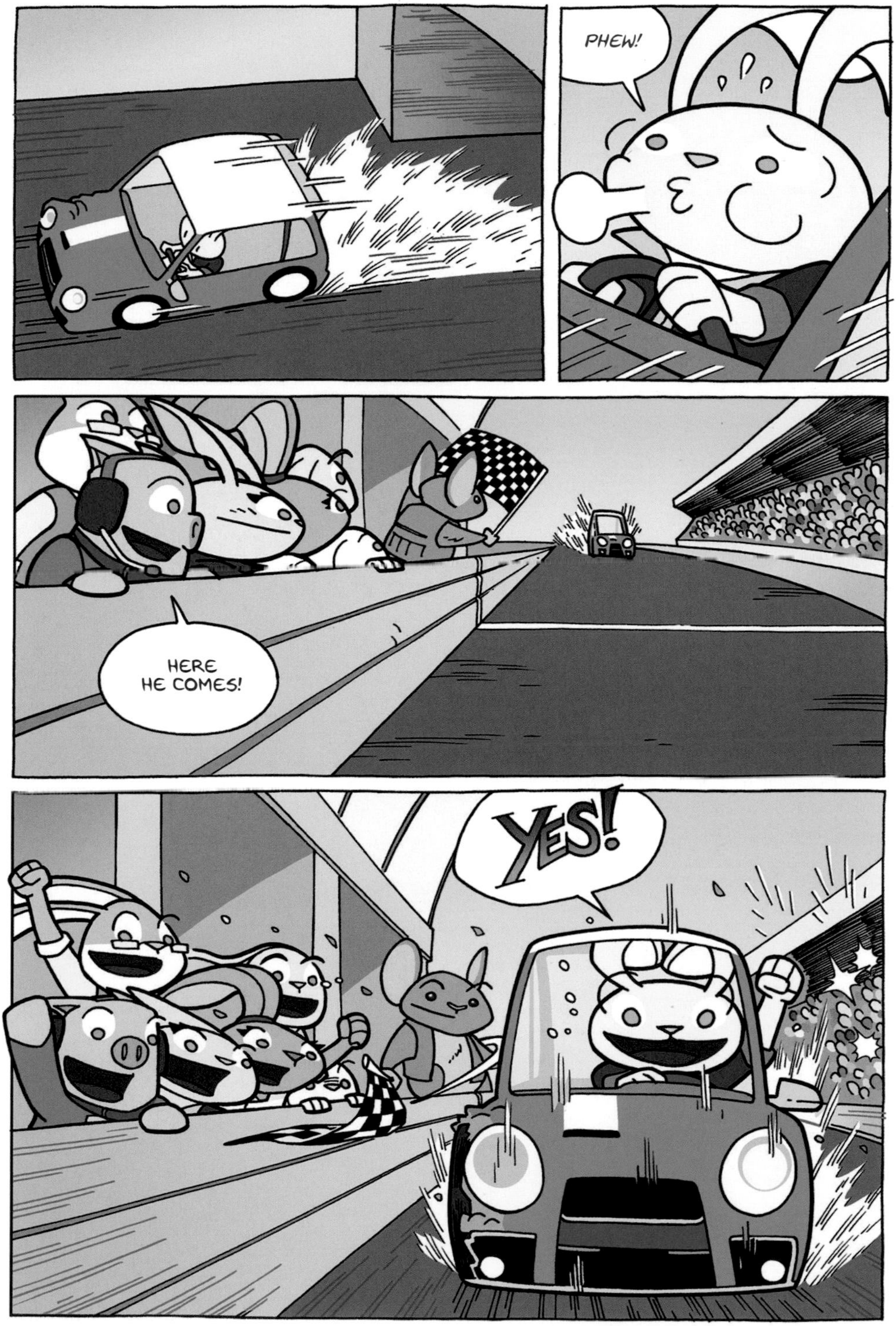
PHEW!
HERE HE COMES!
YES!

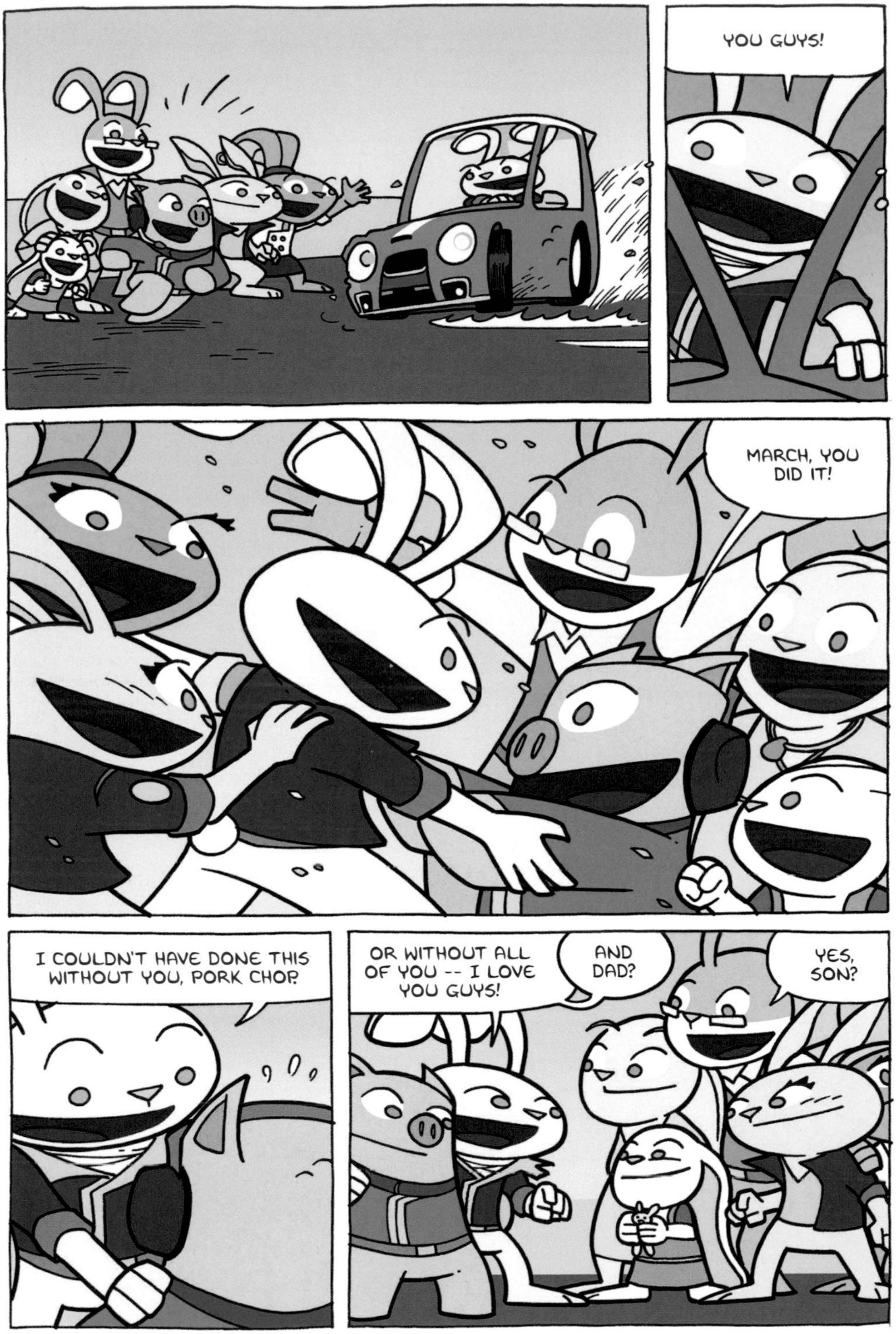
YOU GUYS!
MARCH, YOU DID IT!
I COULDN'T HAVE DONE THIS WITHOUT YOU, PORK CHOP.
OR WITHOUT ALL OF YOU -- I LOVE YOU GUYS!
AND DAD?
YES, SON?

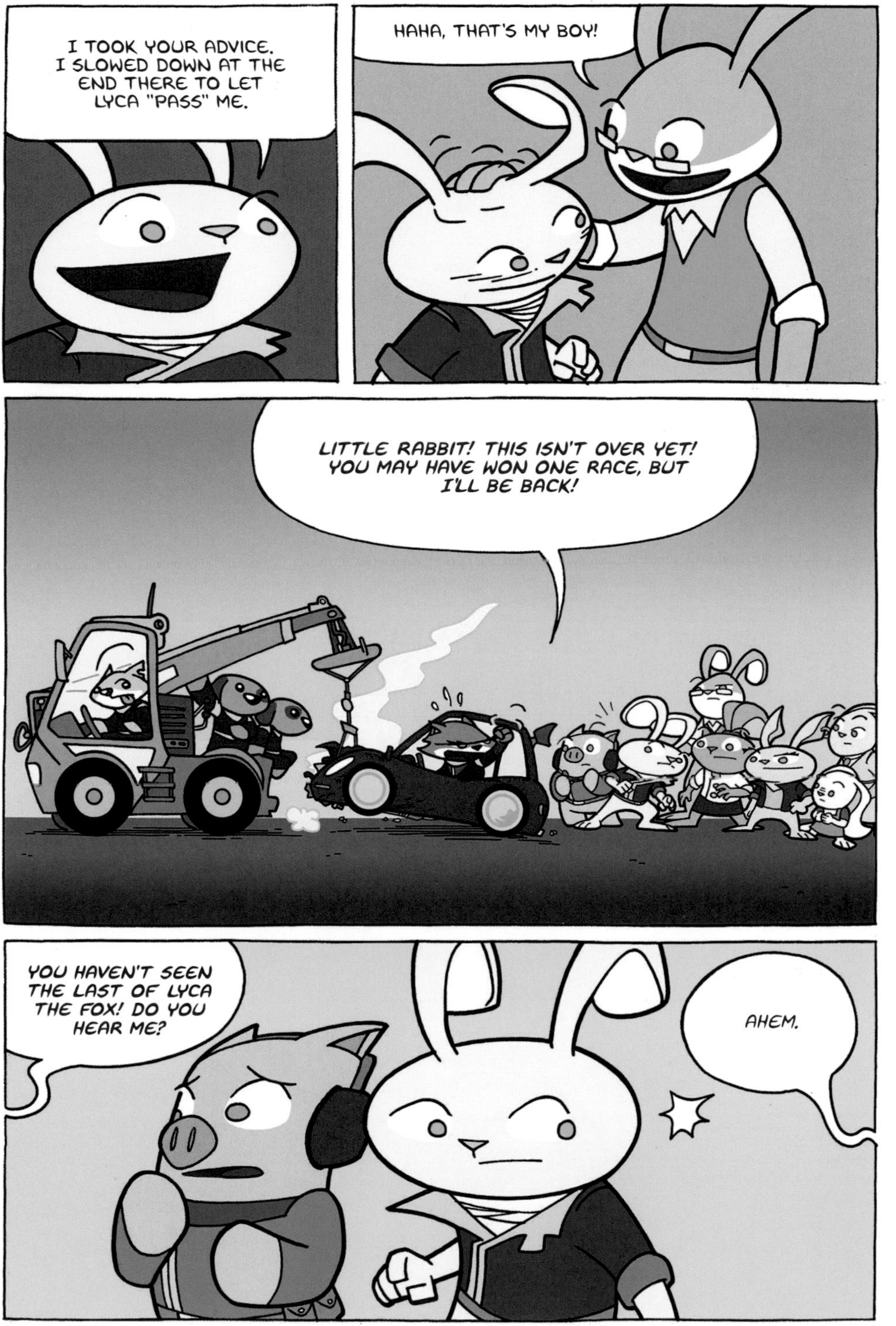
I TOOK YOUR ADVICE. I SLOWED DOWN AT THE END THERE TO LET LYCA "PASS" ME.
HAHA, THAT'S MY BOY!
LITTLE RABBIT! THIS ISN'T OVER YET! YOU MAY HAVE WON ONE RACE, BUT I'LL BE BACK!
YOU HAVEN'T SEEN THE LAST OF LYCA THE FOX! DO YOU HEAR ME?
AHEM.

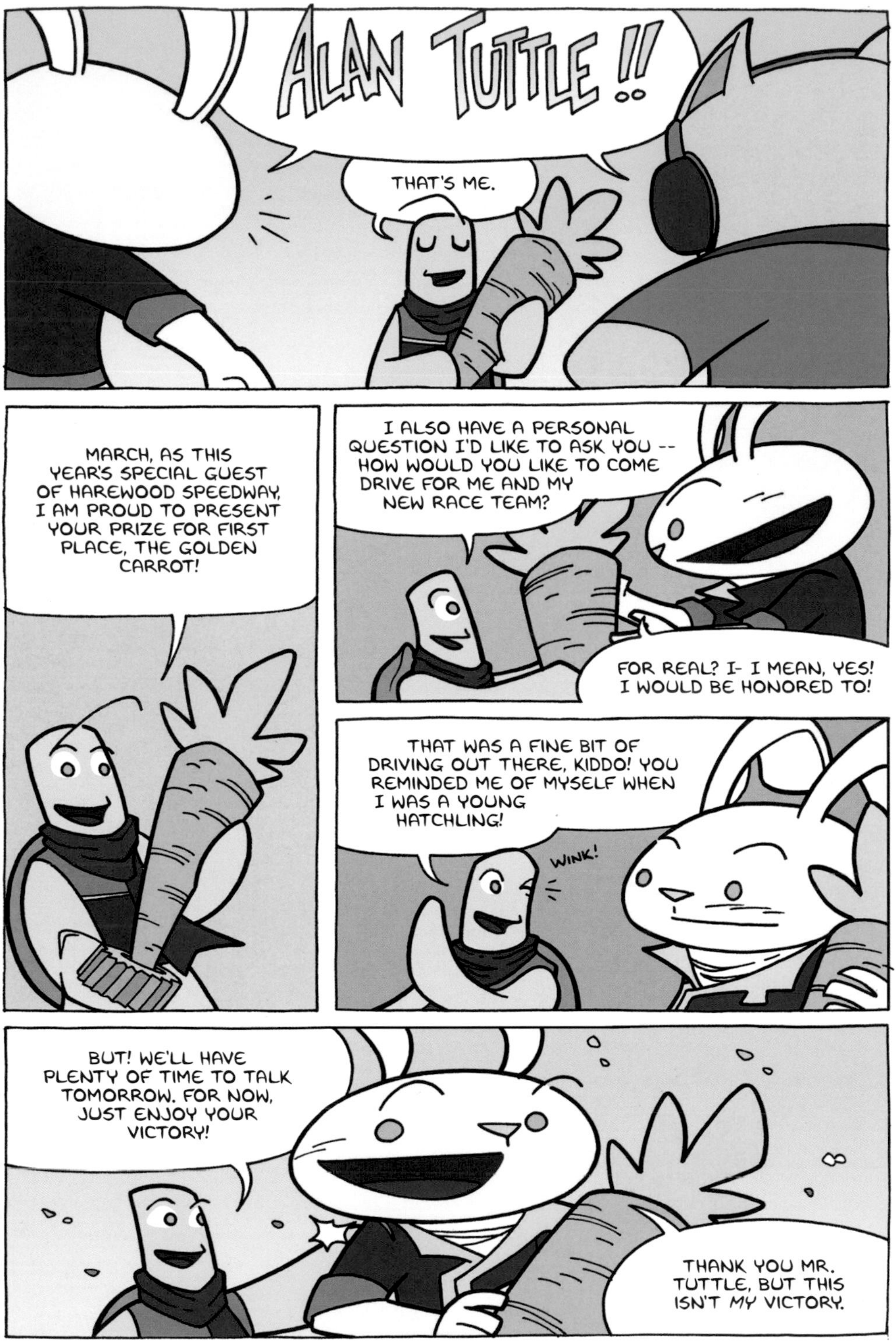
ALAN TUTTLE!!
THAT'S ME.
MARCH, AS THIS YEAR'S SPECIAL GUEST OF HAREWOOD SPEEDWAY, I AM PROUD TO PRESENT YOUR PRIZE FOR FIRST PLACE, THE GOLDEN CARROT!
I ALSO HAVE A PERSONAL QUESTION I'D LIKE TO ASK YOU -- HOW WOULD YOU LIKE TO COME DRIVE FOR ME AND MY NEW RACE TEAM?
FOR REAL? I- I MEAN, YES! I WOULD BE HONORED TO!
THAT WAS A FINE BIT OF DRIVING OUT THERE, KIDDO! YOU REMINDED ME OF MYSELF WHEN I WAS A YOUNG HATCHLING!
WINK!
BUT! WE'LL HAVE PLENTY OF TIME TO TALK TOMORROW. FOR NOW, JUST ENJOY YOUR VICTORY!
THANK YOU MR. TUTTLE, BUT THIS ISN'T *MY* VICTORY.

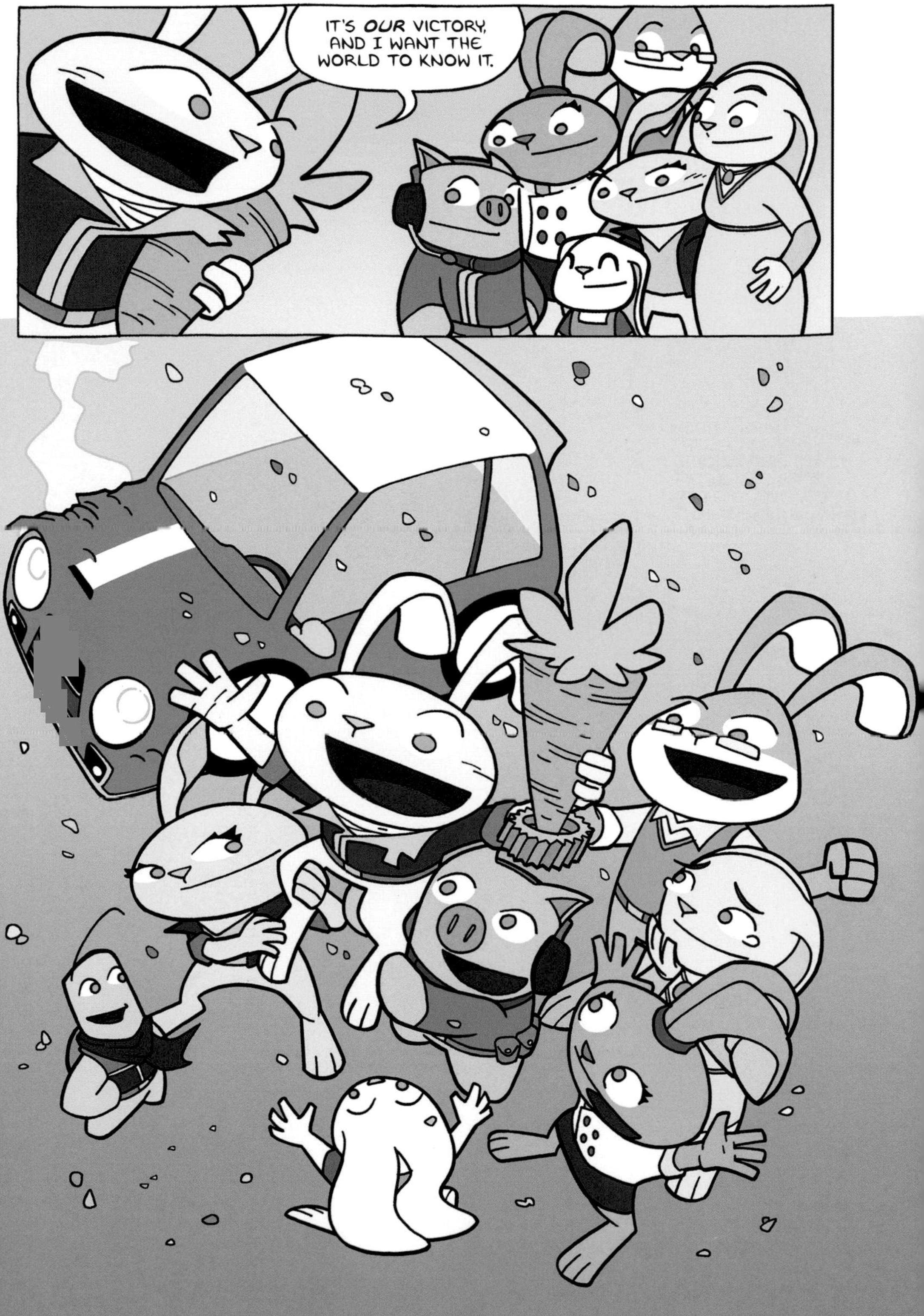
IT'S OUR VICTORY, AND I WANT THE WORLD TO KNOW IT.

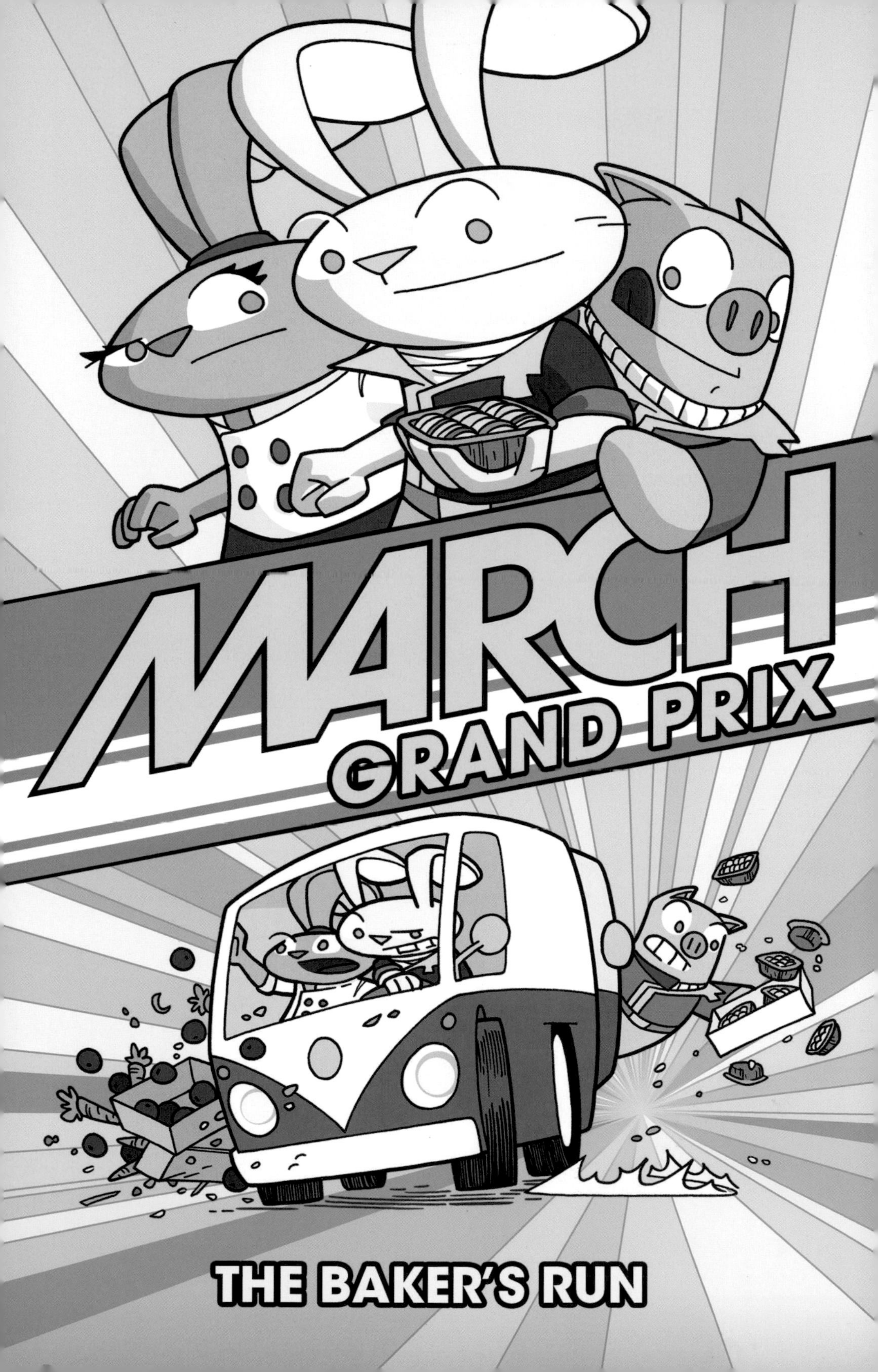
MARCH
GRAND PRIX
THE BAKER'S RUN

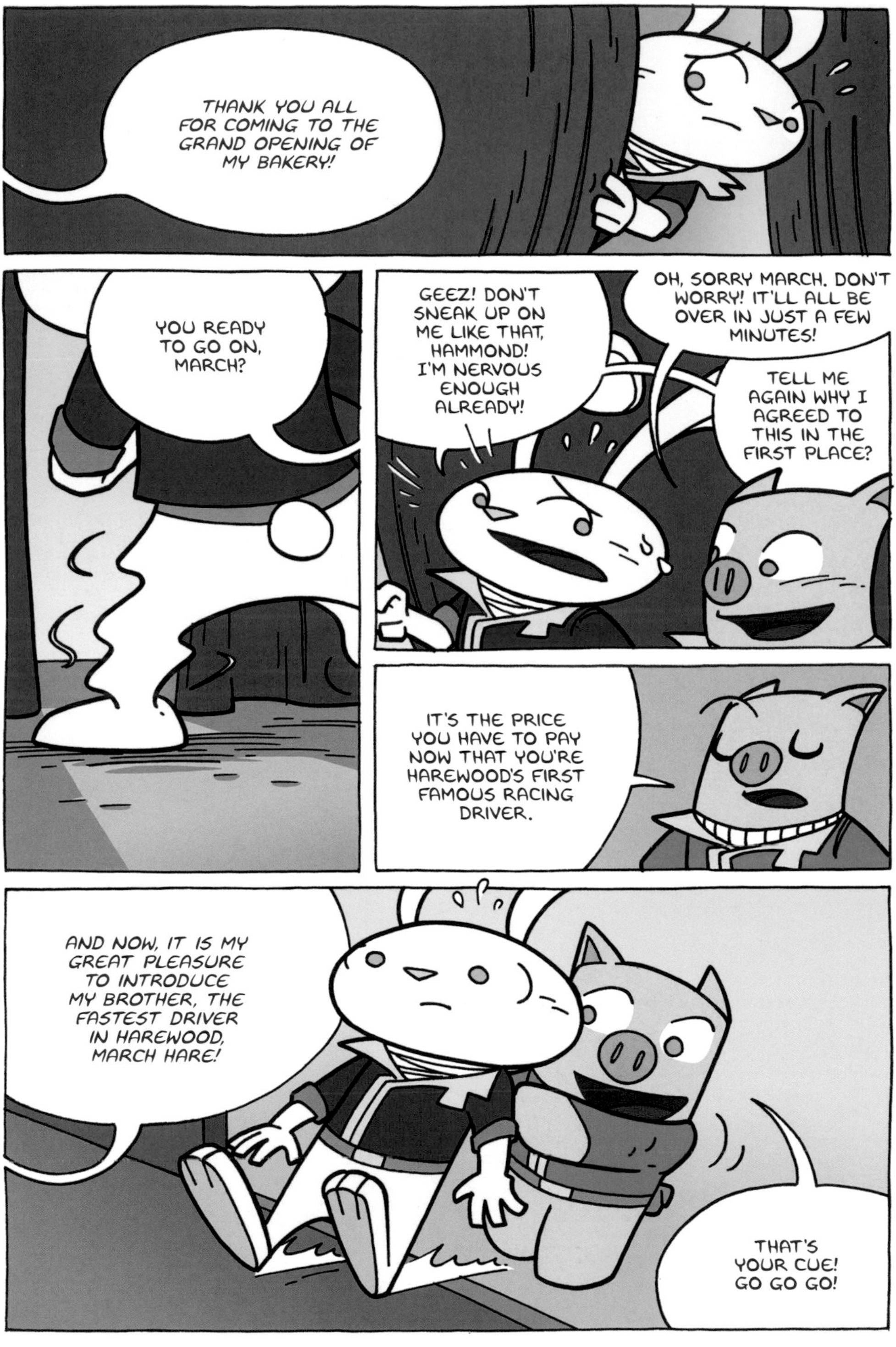
THANK YOU ALL FOR COMING TO THE GRAND OPENING OF MY BAKERY!
YOU READY TO GO ON, MARCH?
GEEZ! DON'T SNEAK UP ON ME LIKE THAT, HAMMOND! I'M NERVOUS ENOUGH ALREADY!
OH, SORRY MARCH. DON'T WORRY! IT'LL ALL BE OVER IN JUST A FEW MINUTES!
TELL ME AGAIN WHY I AGREED TO THIS IN THE FIRST PLACE?
IT'S THE PRICE YOU HAVE TO PAY NOW THAT YOU'RE HAREWOOD'S FIRST FAMOUS RACING DRIVER.
AND NOW, IT IS MY GREAT PLEASURE TO INTRODUCE MY BROTHER, THE FASTEST DRIVER IN HAREWOOD, MARCH HARE!
THAT'S YOUR CUE! GO GO GO!

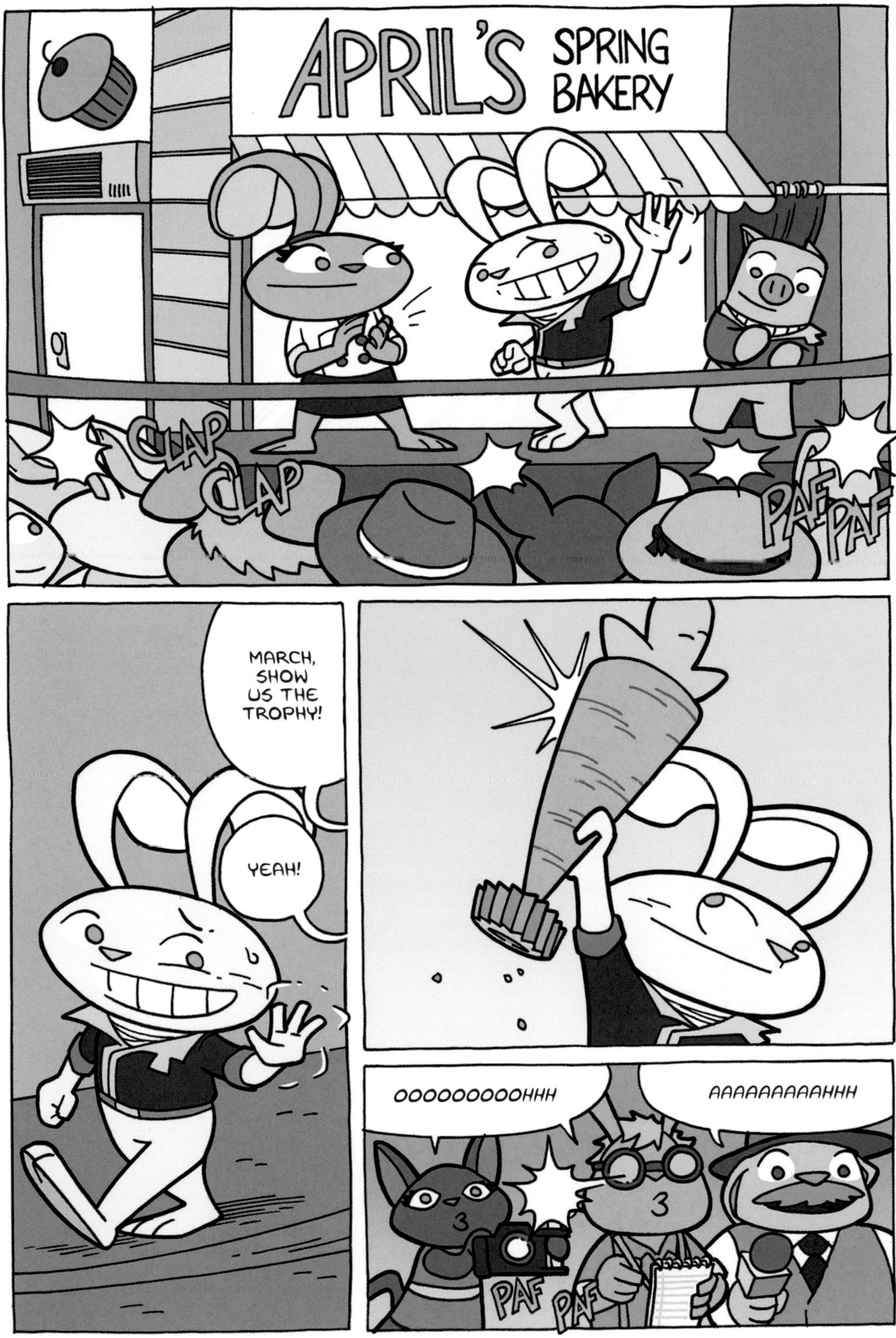
APRIL'S SPRING BAKERY
CLAP CLAP
PAF PAF
MARCH, SHOW US THE TROPHY!
YEAH!
OOOOOOOOOHHH
AAAAAAAAAHHH
PAF PAF

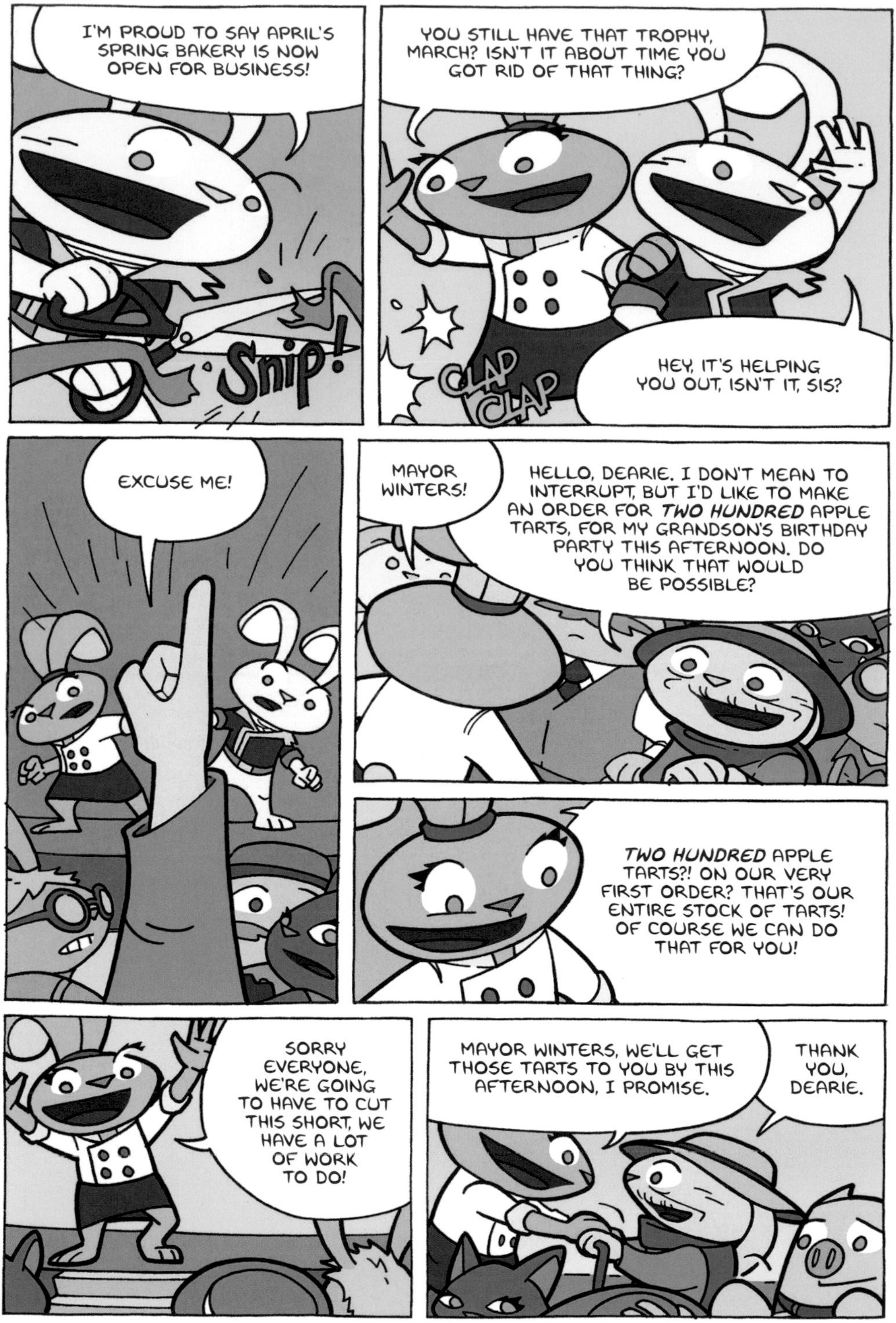

I'M PROUD TO SAY APRIL'S SPRING BAKERY IS NOW OPEN FOR BUSINESS!
SNIP!
YOU STILL HAVE THAT TROPHY, MARCH? ISN'T IT ABOUT TIME YOU GOT RID OF THAT THING?
CLAP CLAP
HEY, IT'S HELPING YOU OUT, ISN'T IT, SIS?
EXCUSE ME!
MAYOR WINTERS!
HELLO, DEARIE. I DON'T MEAN TO INTERRUPT, BUT I'D LIKE TO MAKE AN ORDER FOR *TWO HUNDRED* APPLE TARTS, FOR MY GRANDSON'S BIRTHDAY PARTY THIS AFTERNOON. DO YOU THINK THAT WOULD BE POSSIBLE?
TWO HUNDRED APPLE TARTS?! ON OUR VERY FIRST ORDER? THAT'S OUR ENTIRE STOCK OF TARTS! OF COURSE WE CAN DO THAT FOR YOU!
SORRY EVERYONE, WE'RE GOING TO HAVE TO CUT THIS SHORT, WE HAVE A LOT OF WORK TO DO!
MAYOR WINTERS, WE'LL GET THOSE TARTS TO YOU BY THIS AFTERNOON, I PROMISE.
THANK YOU, DEARIE.

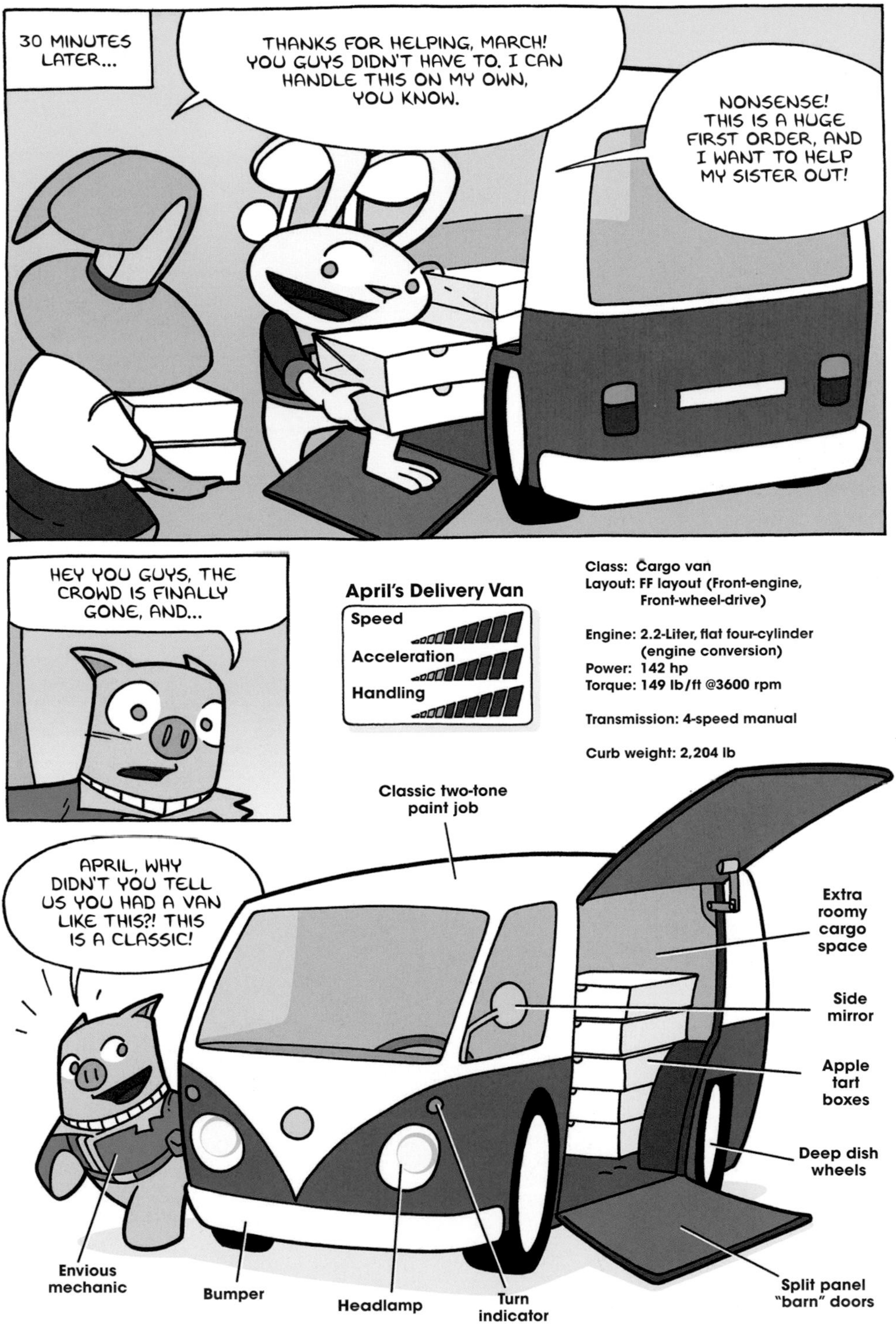
30 MINUTES LATER...
THANKS FOR HELPING, MARCH! YOU GUYS DIDN'T HAVE TO. I CAN HANDLE THIS ON MY OWN, YOU KNOW.
NONSENSE! THIS IS A HUGE FIRST ORDER, AND I WANT TO HELP MY SISTER OUT!
HEY YOU GUYS, THE CROWD IS FINALLY GONE, AND...
April's Delivery Van
Speed
Acceleration
Handling
Class: Cargo van
Layout: FF layout (Front-engine, Front-wheel-drive)
Engine: 2.2-Liter, flat four-cylinder (engine conversion)
Power: 142 hp
Torque: 149 lb/ft @3600 rpm
Transmission: 4-speed manual
Curb weight: 2,204 lb
Classic two-tone paint job
APRIL, WHY DIDN'T YOU TELL US YOU HAD A VAN LIKE THIS?! THIS IS A CLASSIC!
Extra roomy cargo space
Side mirror
Apple tart boxes
Deep dish wheels
Envious mechanic
Bumper
Headlamp
Turn indicator
Split panel "barn" doors

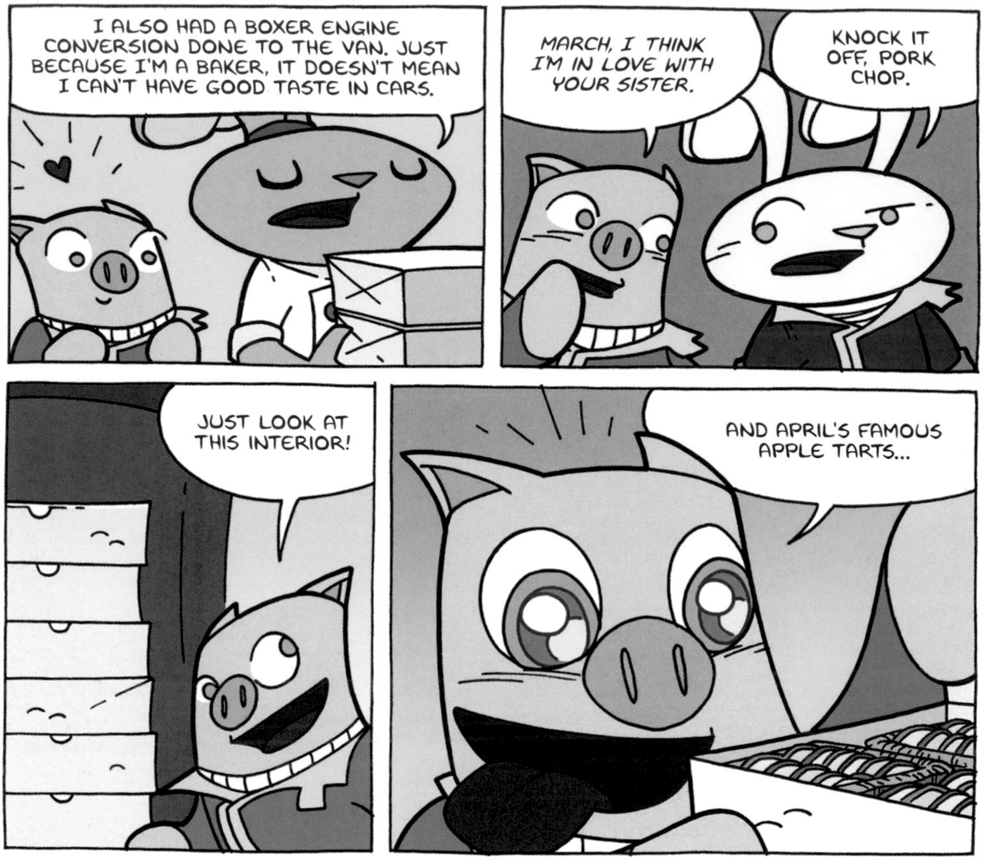
I ALSO HAD A BOXER ENGINE CONVERSION DONE TO THE VAN. JUST BECAUSE I'M A BAKER, IT DOESN'T MEAN I CAN'T HAVE GOOD TASTE IN CARS.
MARCH, I THINK I'M IN LOVE WITH YOUR SISTER.
KNOCK IT OFF, PORK CHOP.
JUST LOOK AT THIS INTERIOR!
AND APRIL'S FAMOUS APPLE TARTS...

April's Famous Apple Tart

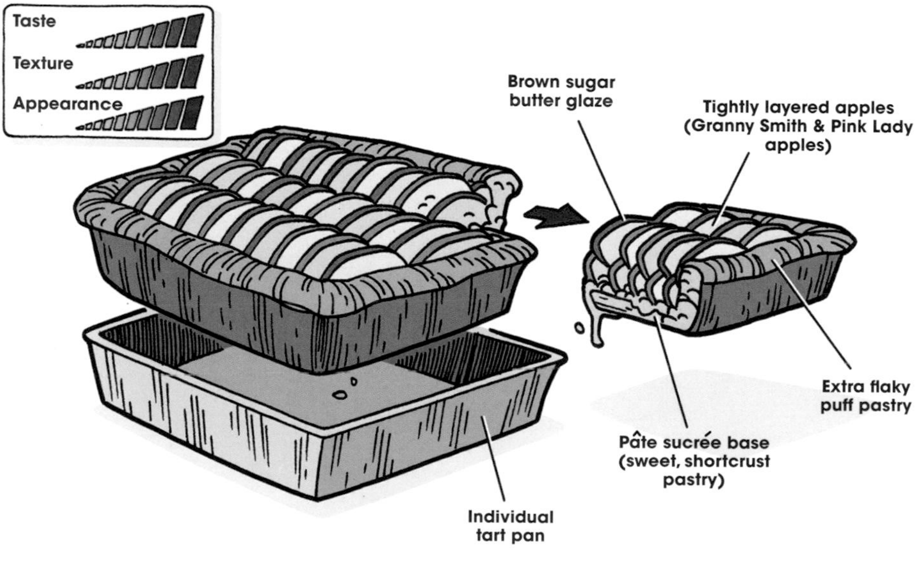
Taste
Texture
Appearance
Brown sugar butter glaze
Tightly layered apples (Granny Smith & Pink Lady apples)
Extra flaky puff pastry
Pâte sucrée base (sweet, shortcrust pastry)
Individual tart pan

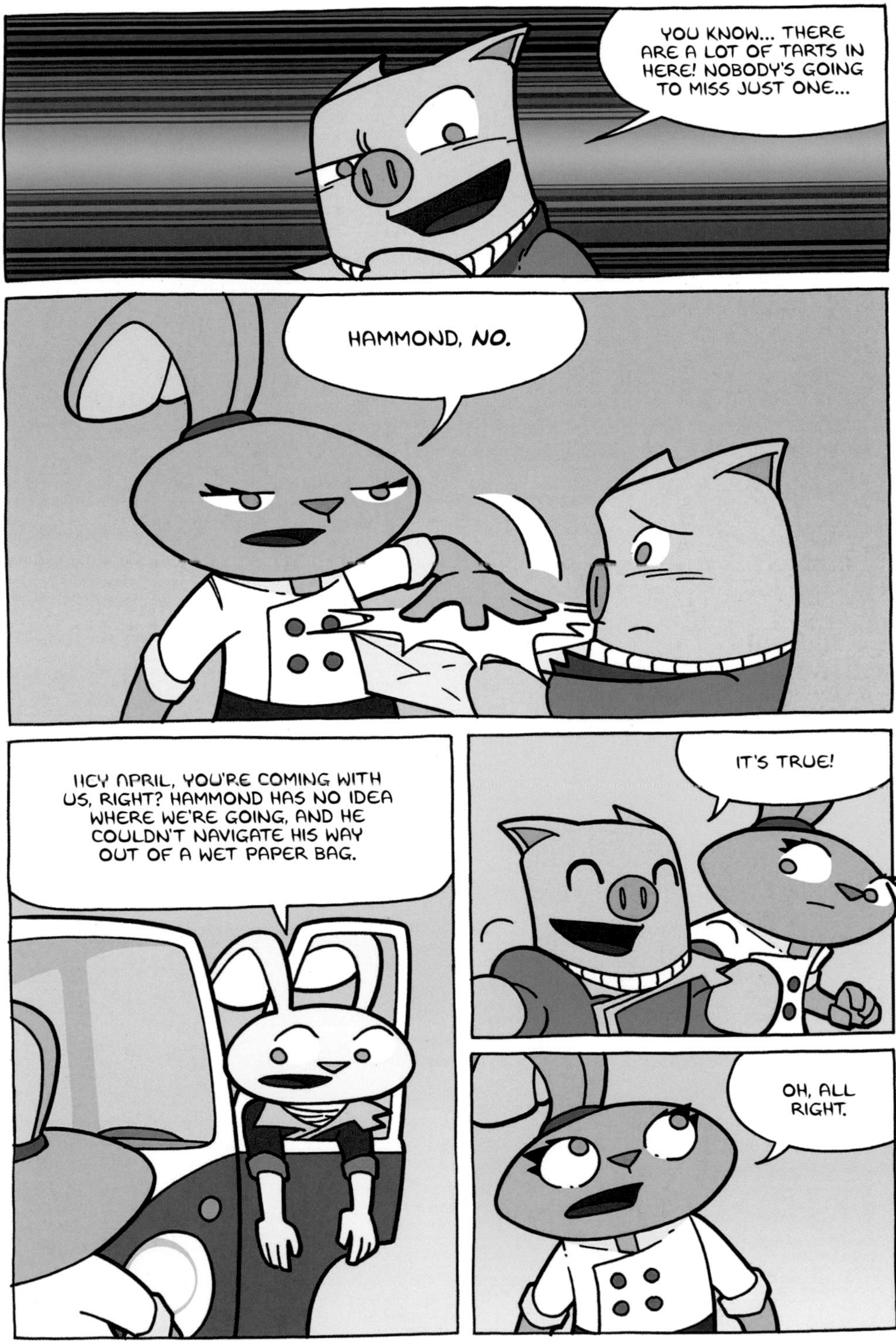
YOU KNOW... THERE ARE A LOT OF TARTS IN HERE! NOBODY'S GOING TO MISS JUST ONE...
HAMMOND, **NO.**
HEY APRIL, YOU'RE COMING WITH US, RIGHT? HAMMOND HAS NO IDEA WHERE WE'RE GOING, AND HE COULDN'T NAVIGATE HIS WAY OUT OF A WET PAPER BAG.
IT'S TRUE!
OH, ALL RIGHT.

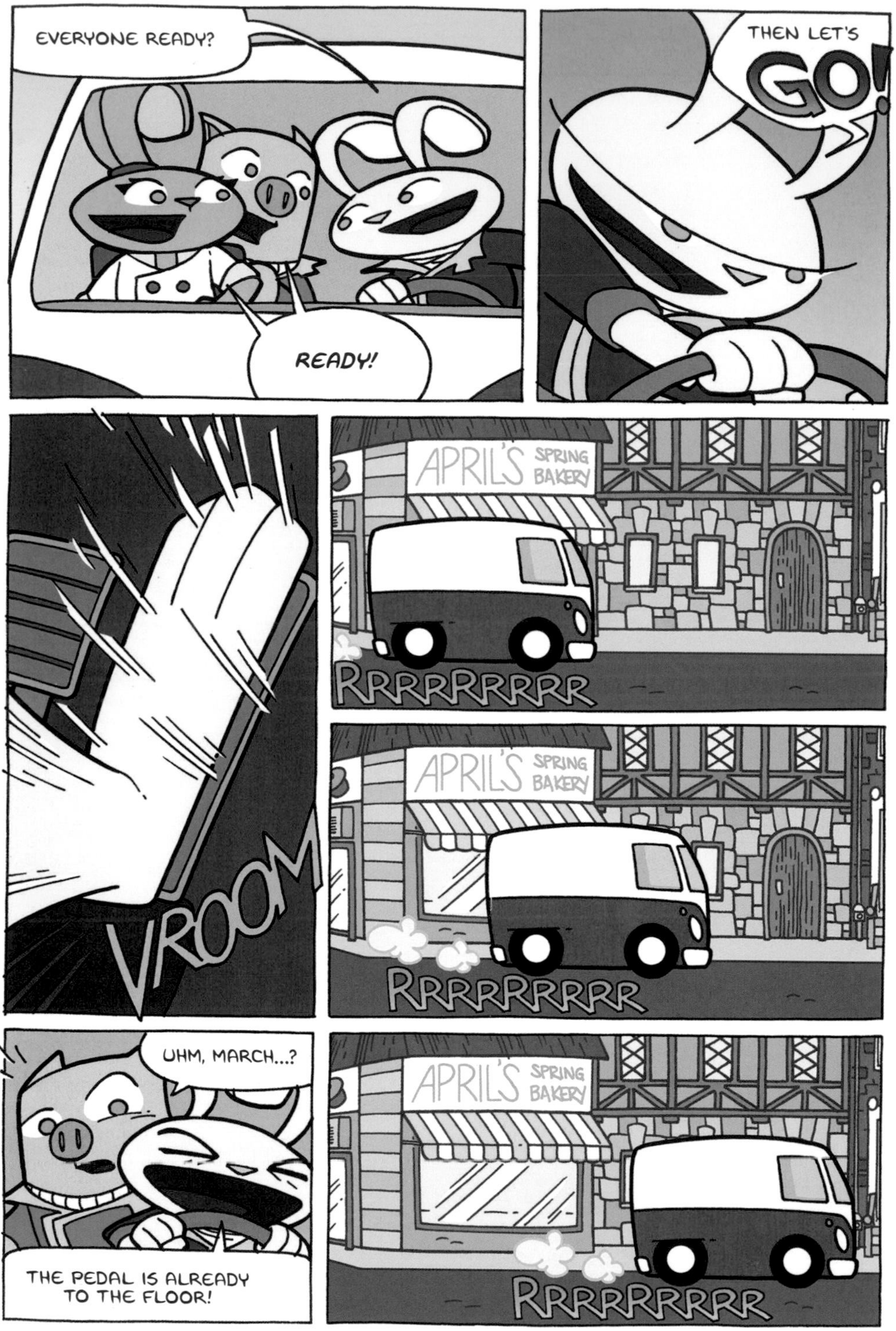
EVERYONE READY?
READY!
THEN LET'S
GO!
VROOM
APRIL'S SPRING BAKERY
RRRRRRRRRR
APRIL'S SPRING BAKERY
RRRRRRRRRR
UHM, MARCH...?
THE PEDAL IS ALREADY TO THE FLOOR!
APRIL'S SPRING BAKERY
RRRRRRRRRR

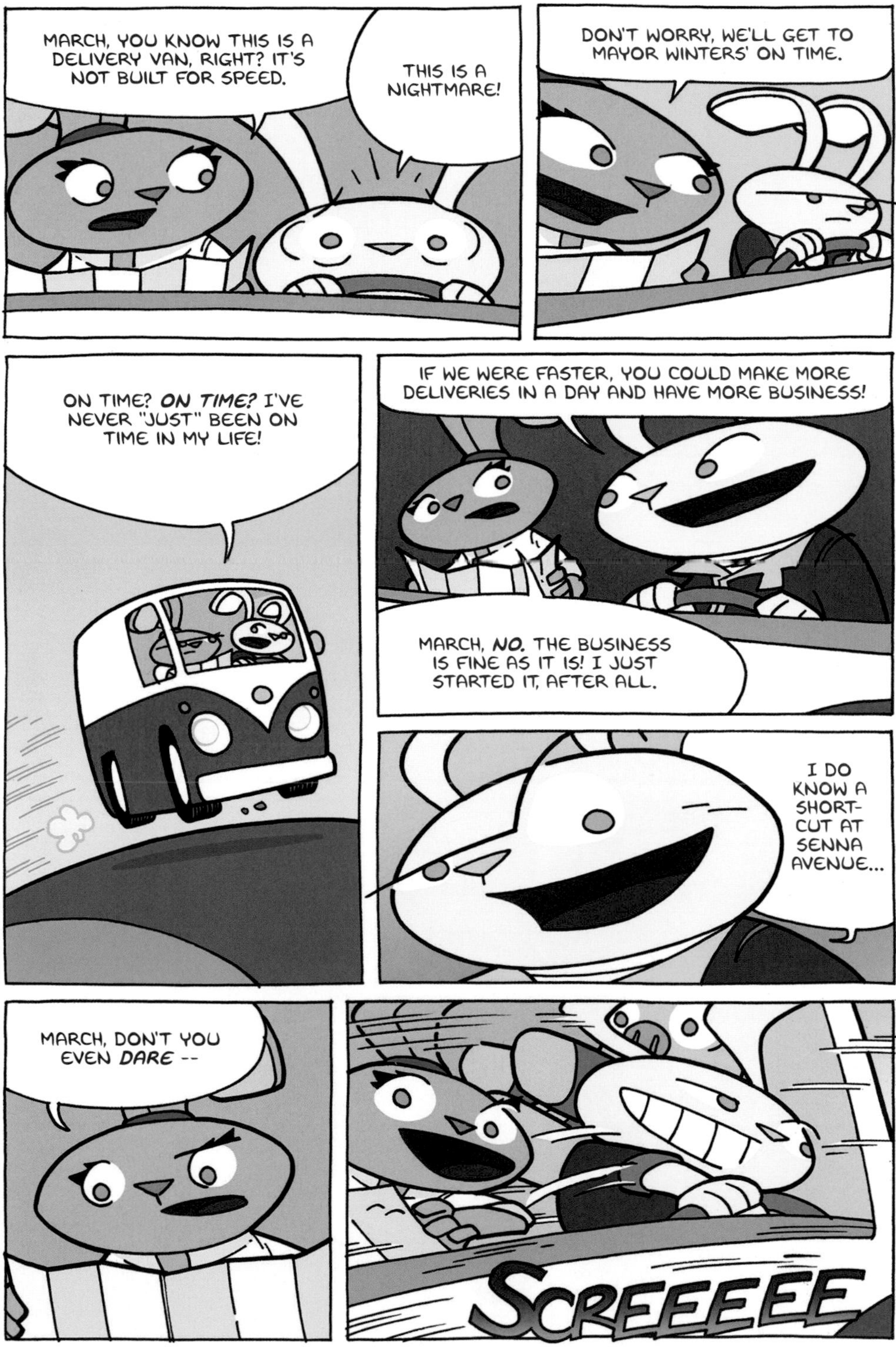
MARCH, YOU KNOW THIS IS A DELIVERY VAN, RIGHT? IT'S NOT BUILT FOR SPEED.
THIS IS A NIGHTMARE!
DON'T WORRY, WE'LL GET TO MAYOR WINTERS' ON TIME.
ON TIME? *ON TIME?* I'VE NEVER "JUST" BEEN ON TIME IN MY LIFE!
IF WE WERE FASTER, YOU COULD MAKE MORE DELIVERIES IN A DAY AND HAVE MORE BUSINESS!
MARCH, *NO.* THE BUSINESS IS FINE AS IT IS! I JUST STARTED IT, AFTER ALL.
I DO KNOW A SHORT-CUT AT SENNA AVENUE...
MARCH, DON'T YOU EVEN *DARE* --
SCREEEEE

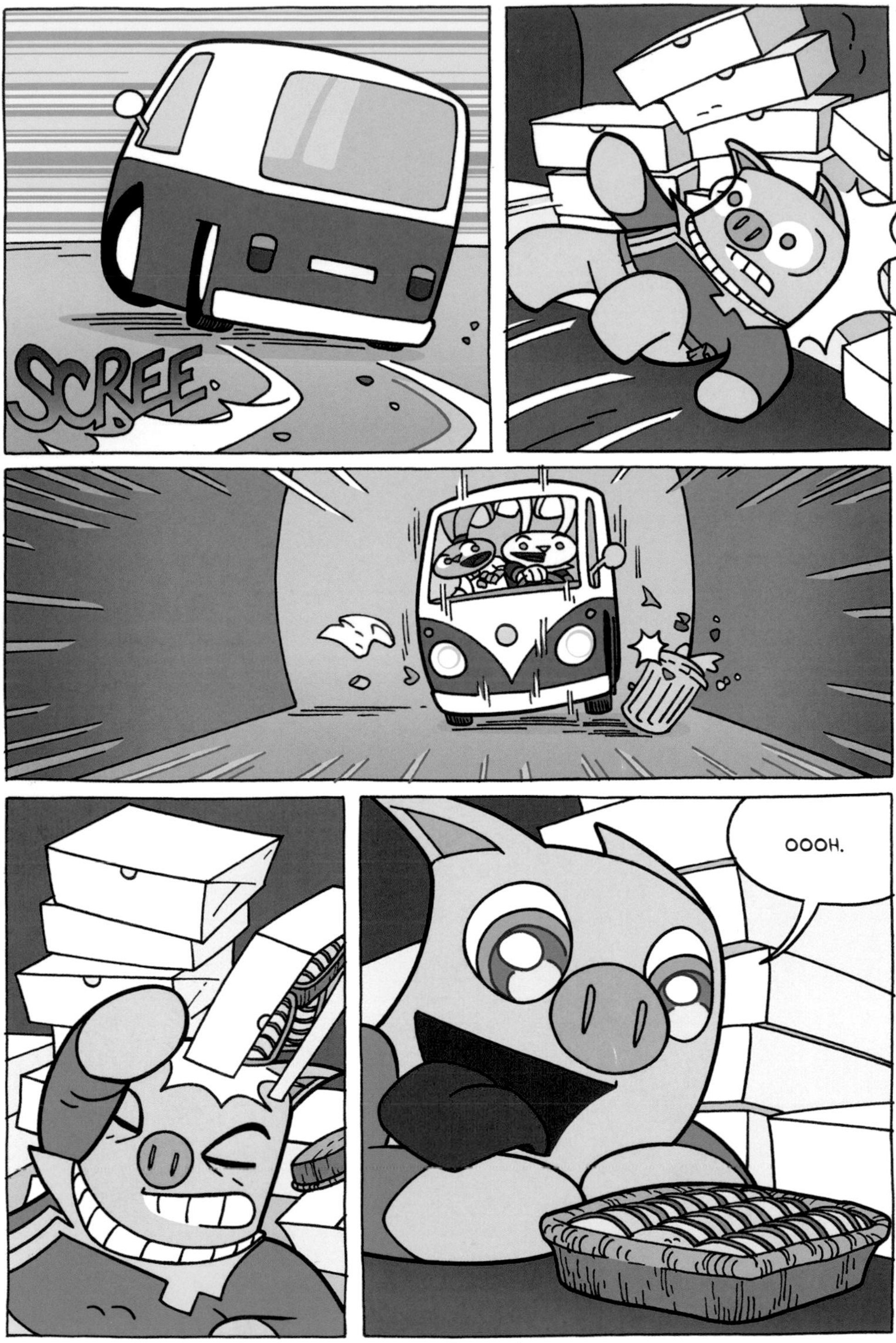
SCREE
OOOH.

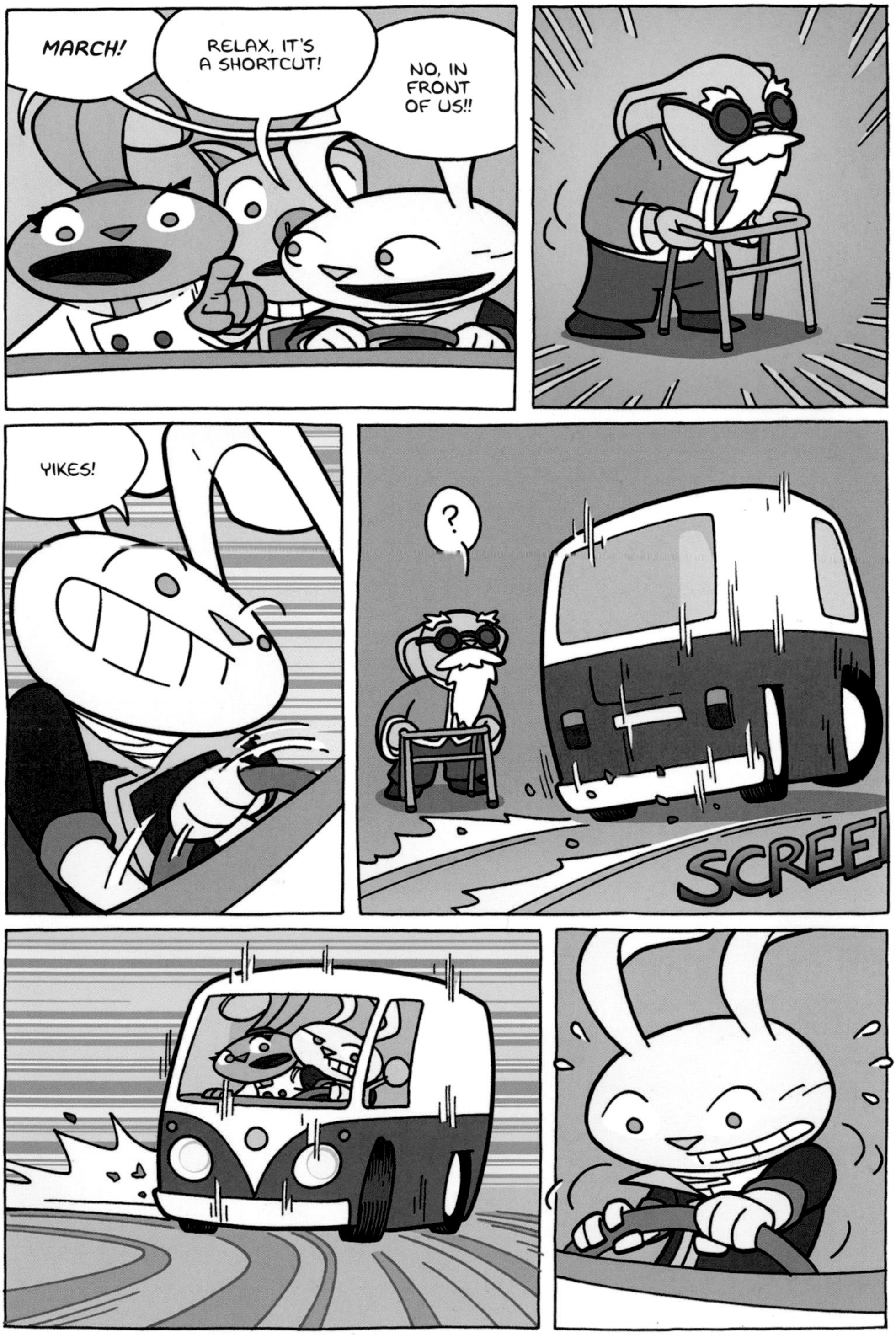
MARCH!
RELAX, IT'S A SHORTCUT!
NO, IN FRONT OF US!!
YIKES!
?
SCREE

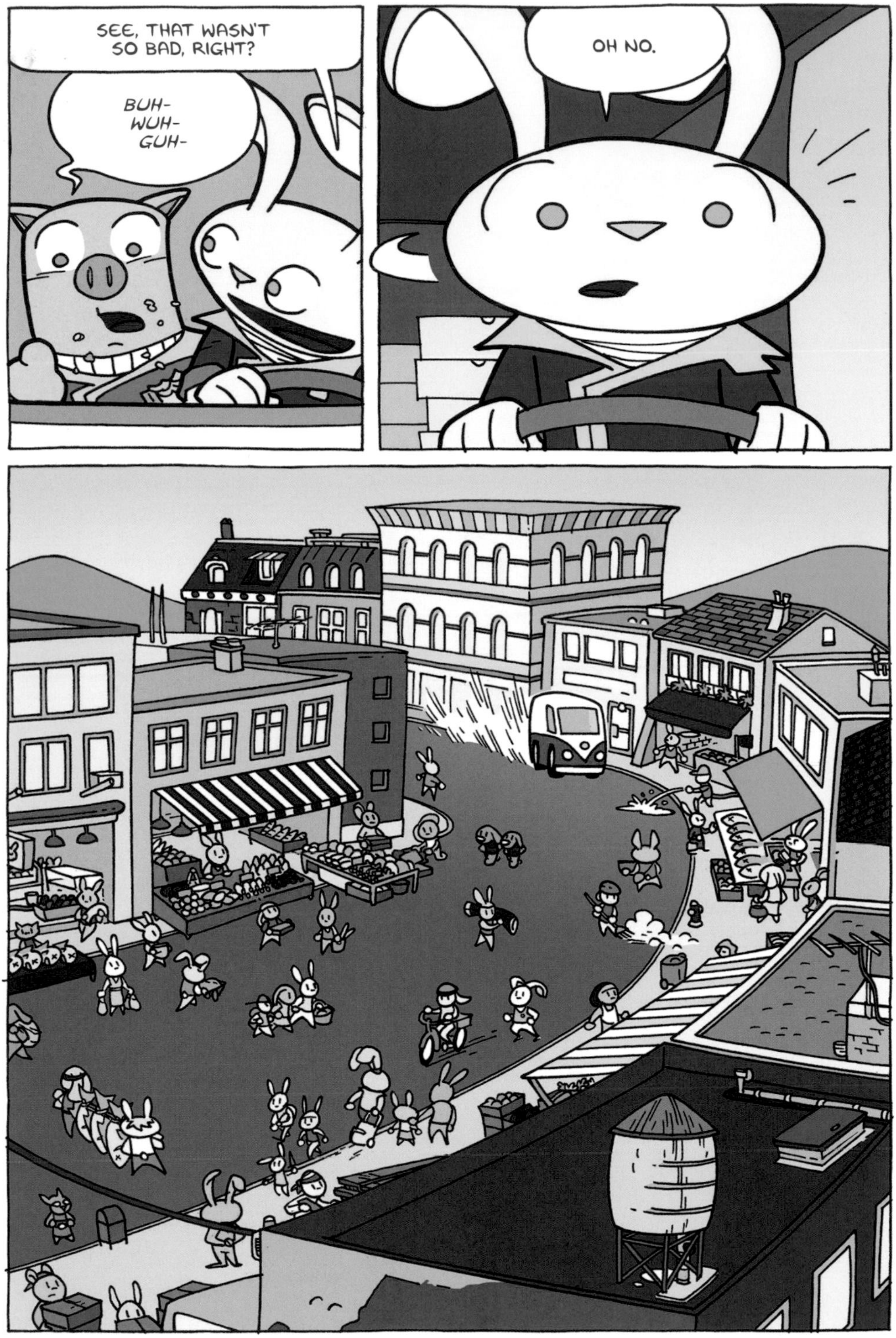
SEE, THAT WASN'T SO BAD, RIGHT?
BUH- WUH- GUH-
OH NO.

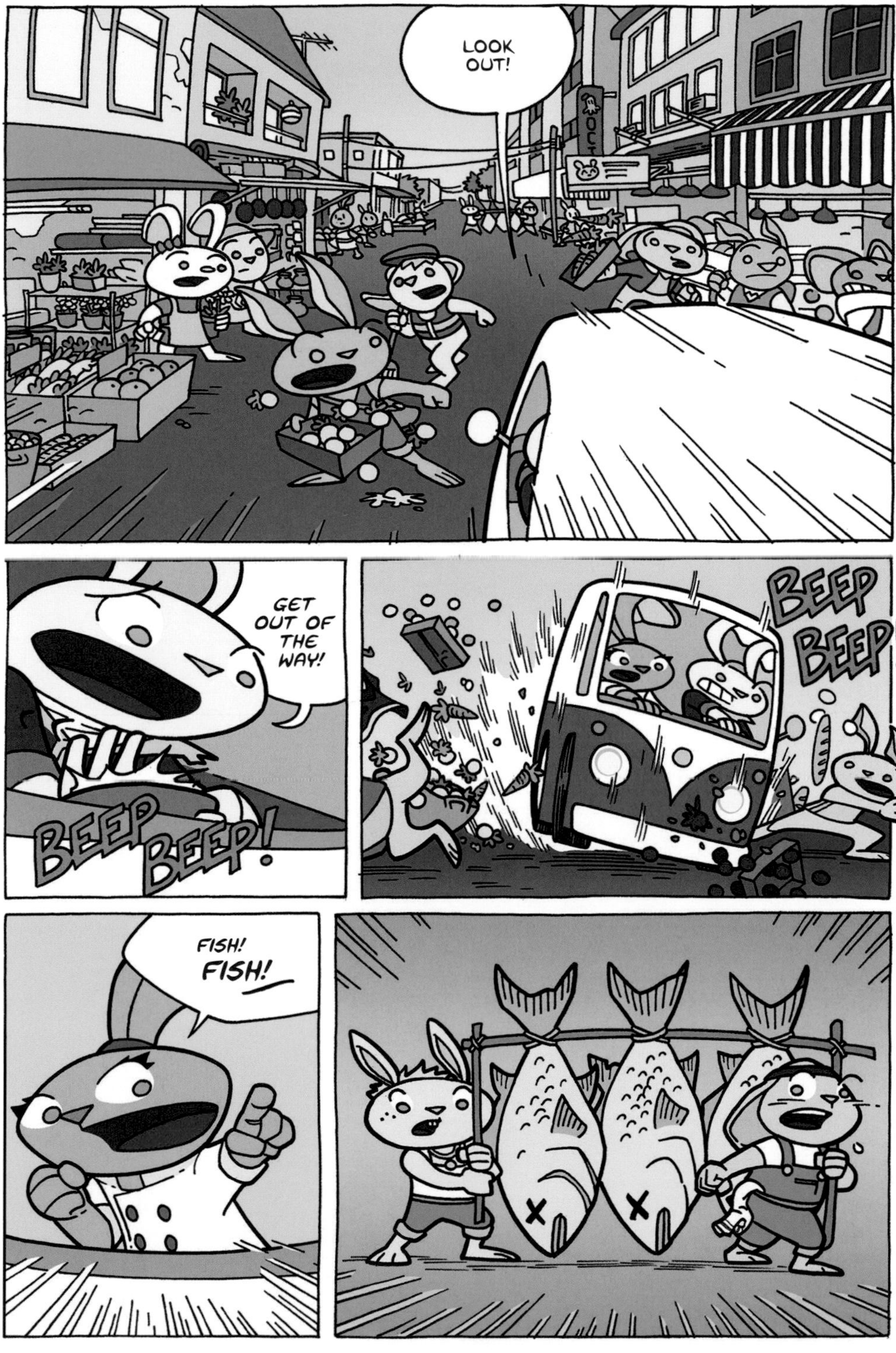
LOOK OUT!
GET OUT OF THE WAY!
BEEP BEEP!
BEEP BEEP!
FISH! FISH!

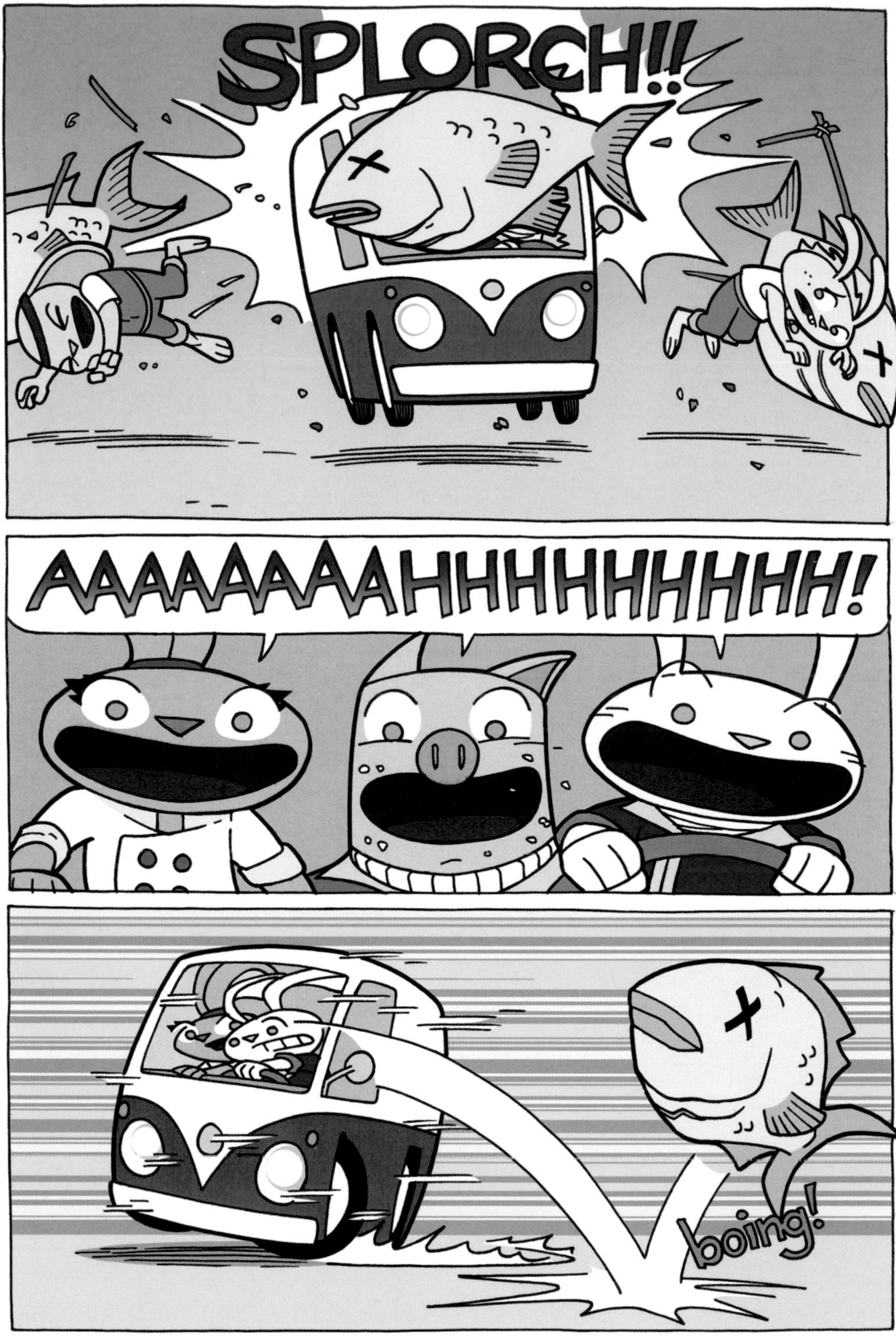
SPLORCH!!
AAAAAAAAHHHHHHHHHH!
boing!

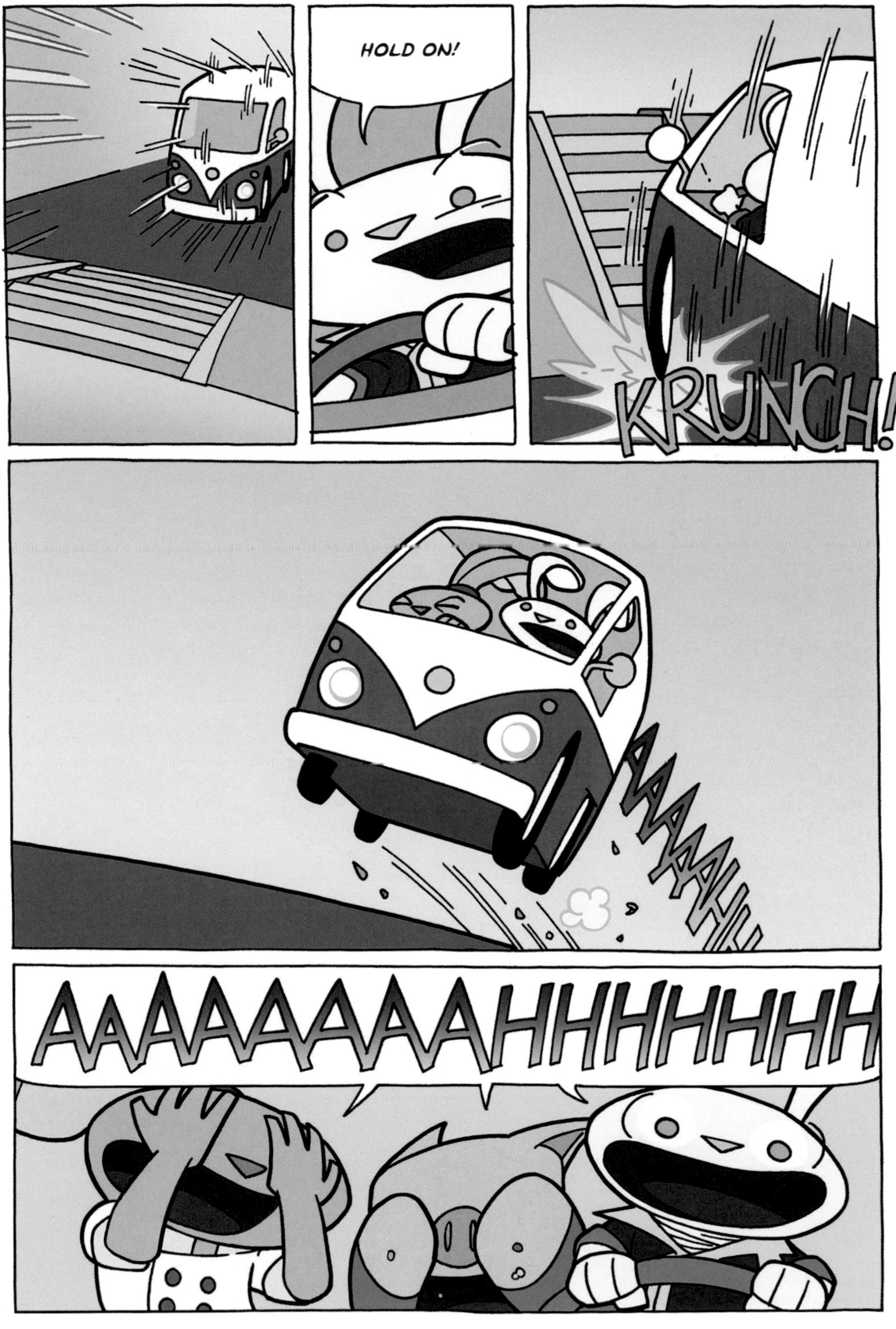
HOLD ON!
KRUNCH!
AAAAAAAAHHHHHHHH

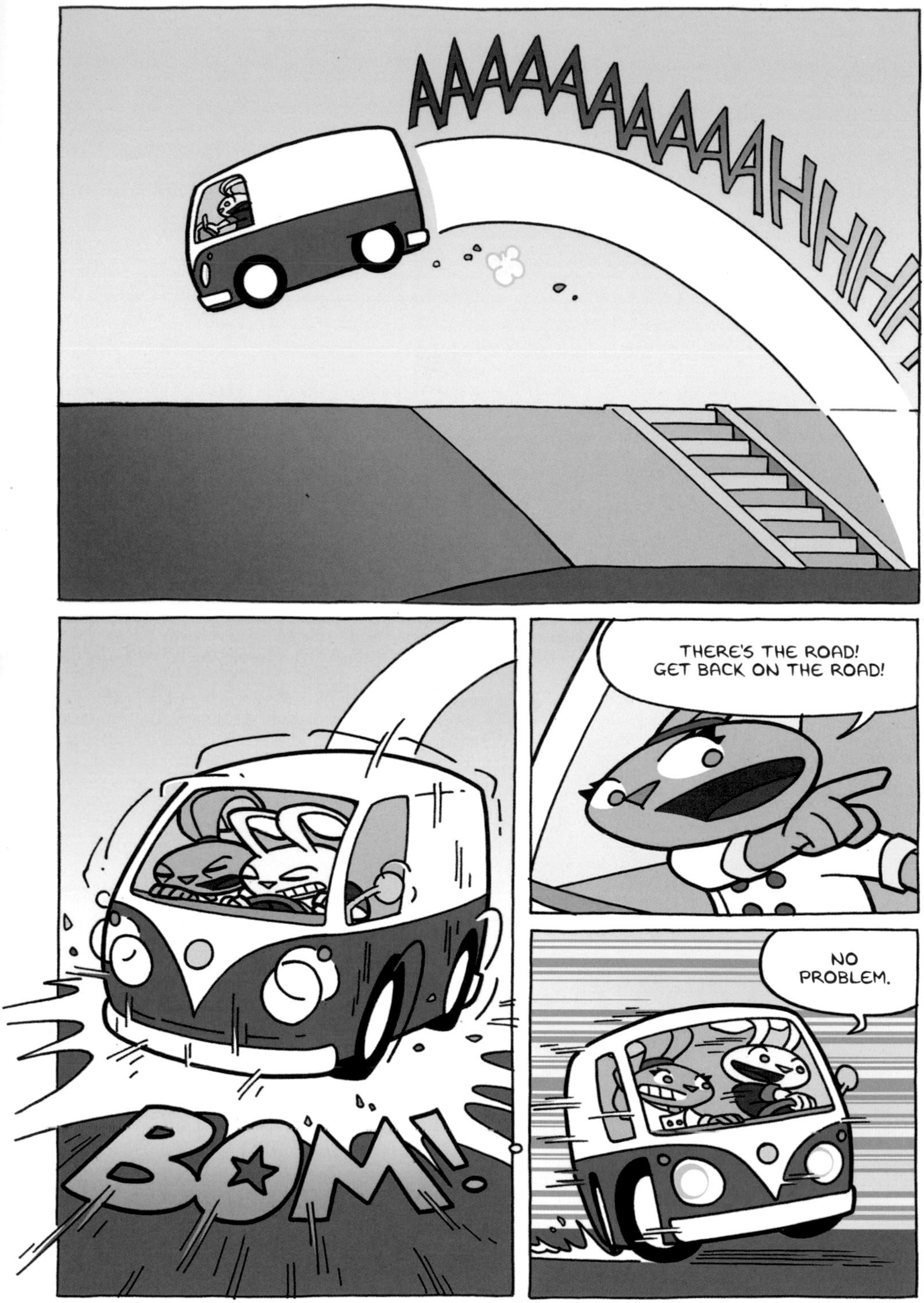
AAAAAAAAAAAAAHHHH
BOM!
THERE'S THE ROAD! GET BACK ON THE ROAD!
NO PROBLEM.

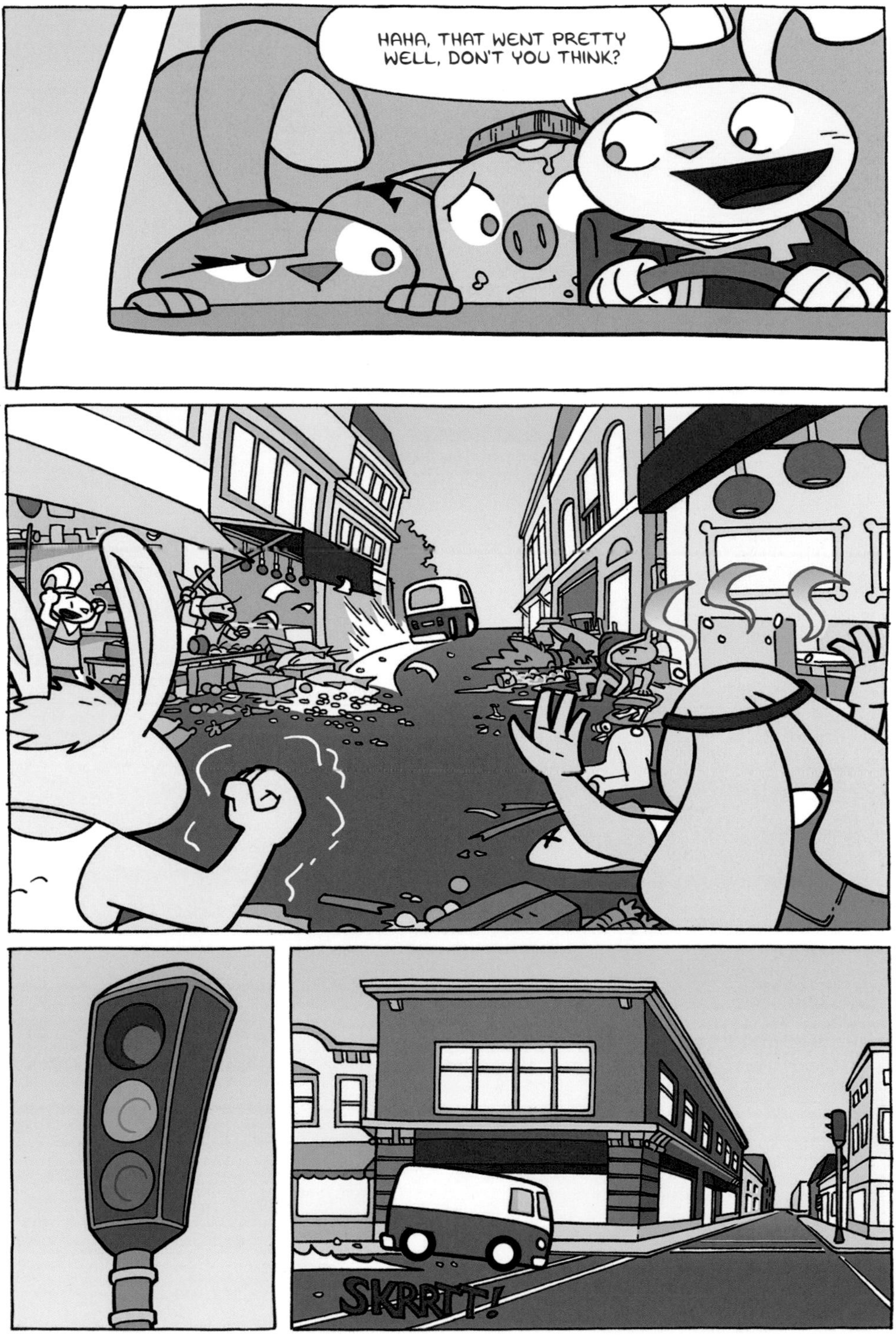
HAHA, THAT WENT PRETTY WELL, DON'T YOU THINK?
SKRRTT!

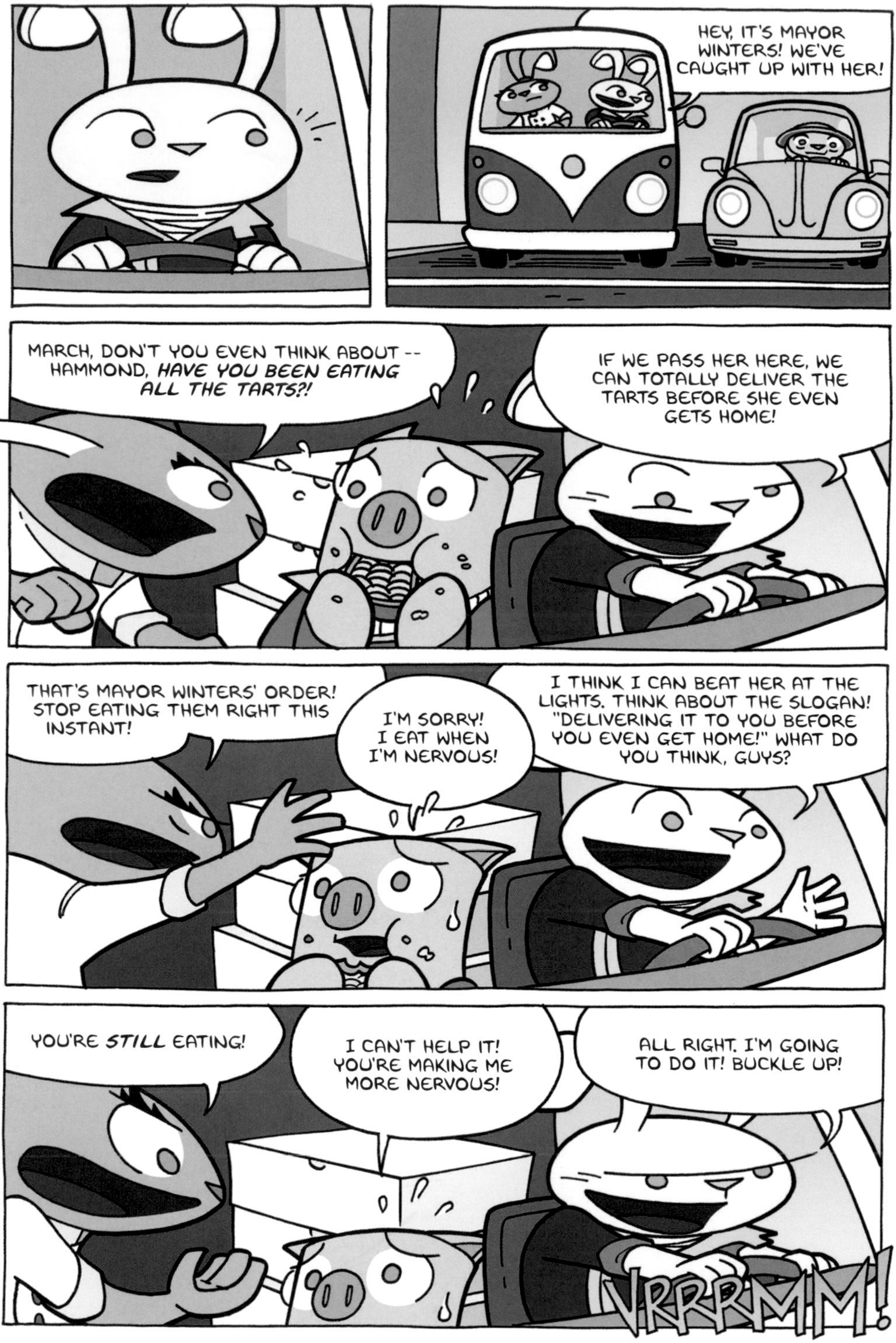
HEY, IT'S MAYOR WINTERS! WE'VE CAUGHT UP WITH HER!
MARCH, DON'T YOU EVEN THINK ABOUT -- HAMMOND, *HAVE YOU BEEN EATING ALL THE TARTS?!*
IF WE PASS HER HERE, WE CAN TOTALLY DELIVER THE TARTS BEFORE SHE EVEN GETS HOME!
THAT'S MAYOR WINTERS' ORDER! STOP EATING THEM RIGHT THIS INSTANT!
I'M SORRY! I EAT WHEN I'M NERVOUS!
I THINK I CAN BEAT HER AT THE LIGHTS. THINK ABOUT THE SLOGAN! "DELIVERING IT TO YOU BEFORE YOU EVEN GET HOME!" WHAT DO YOU THINK, GUYS?
YOU'RE *STILL* EATING!
I CAN'T HELP IT! YOU'RE MAKING ME MORE NERVOUS!
ALL RIGHT. I'M GOING TO DO IT! BUCKLE UP!
VRRRMMM!

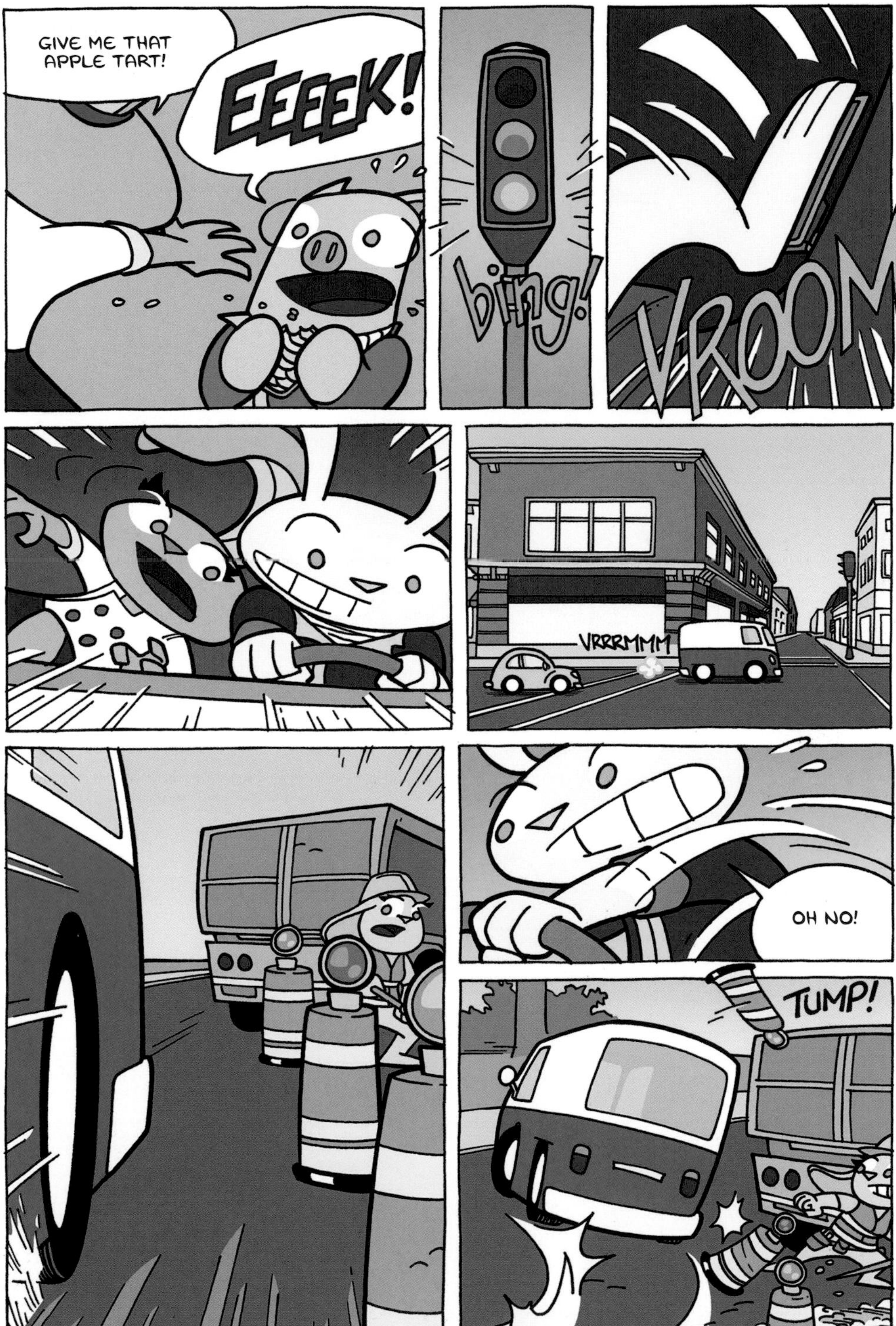
GIVE ME THAT APPLE TART!
EEEEK!
bing!
VROOM
VRRRMMM
OH NO!
TUMP!

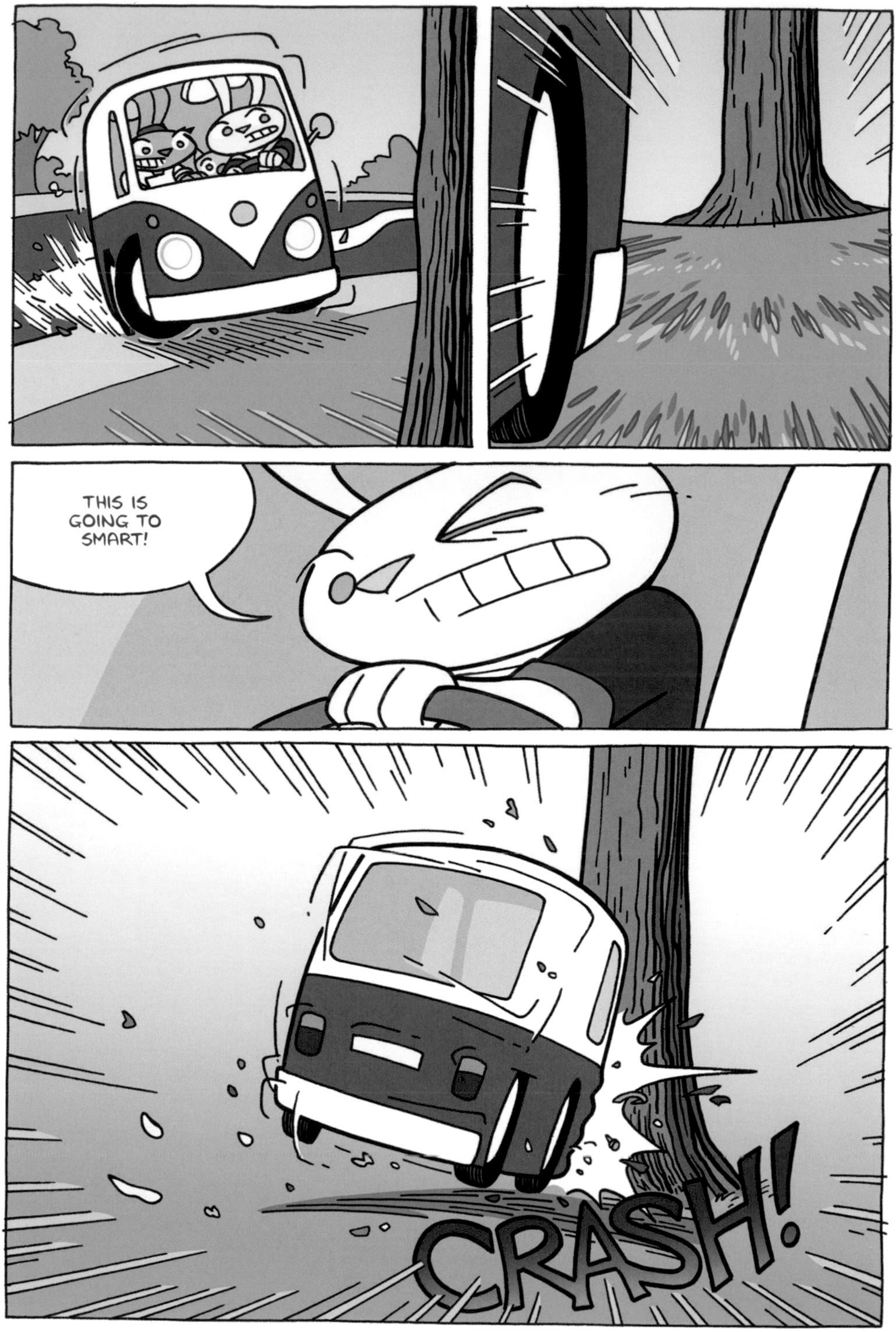
THIS IS GOING TO SMART!
CRASH!

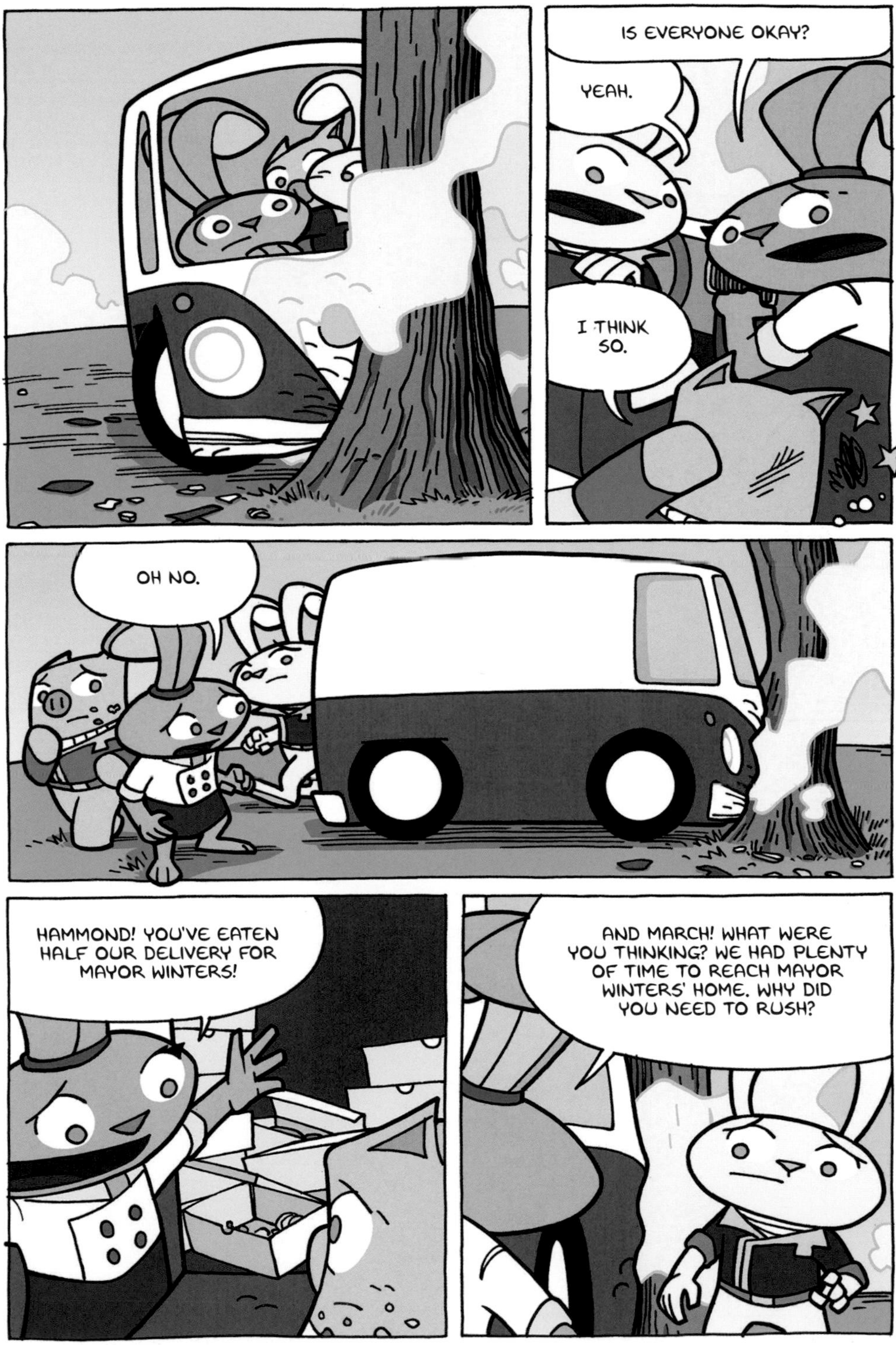
IS EVERYONE OKAY?
YEAH.
I THINK SO.
OH NO.
HAMMOND! YOU'VE EATEN HALF OUR DELIVERY FOR MAYOR WINTERS!
AND MARCH! WHAT WERE YOU THINKING? WE HAD PLENTY OF TIME TO REACH MAYOR WINTERS' HOME. WHY DID YOU NEED TO RUSH?

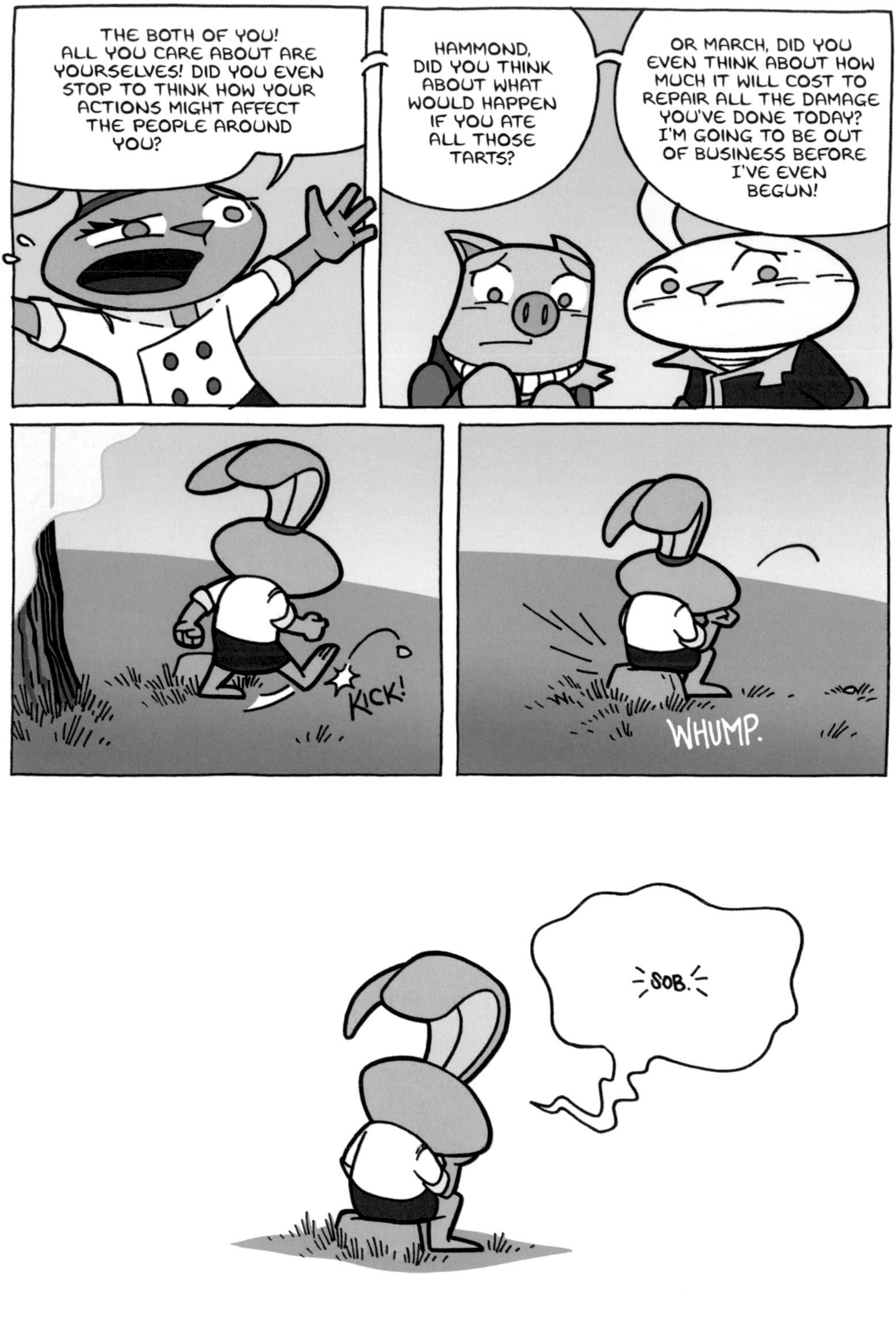
THE BOTH OF YOU! ALL YOU CARE ABOUT ARE YOURSELVES! DID YOU EVEN STOP TO THINK HOW YOUR ACTIONS MIGHT AFFECT THE PEOPLE AROUND YOU?
HAMMOND, DID YOU THINK ABOUT WHAT WOULD HAPPEN IF YOU ATE ALL THOSE TARTS?
OR MARCH, DID YOU EVEN THINK ABOUT HOW MUCH IT WILL COST TO REPAIR ALL THE DAMAGE YOU'VE DONE TODAY? I'M GOING TO BE OUT OF BUSINESS BEFORE I'VE EVEN BEGUN!
KICK!
WHUMP.
SOB.

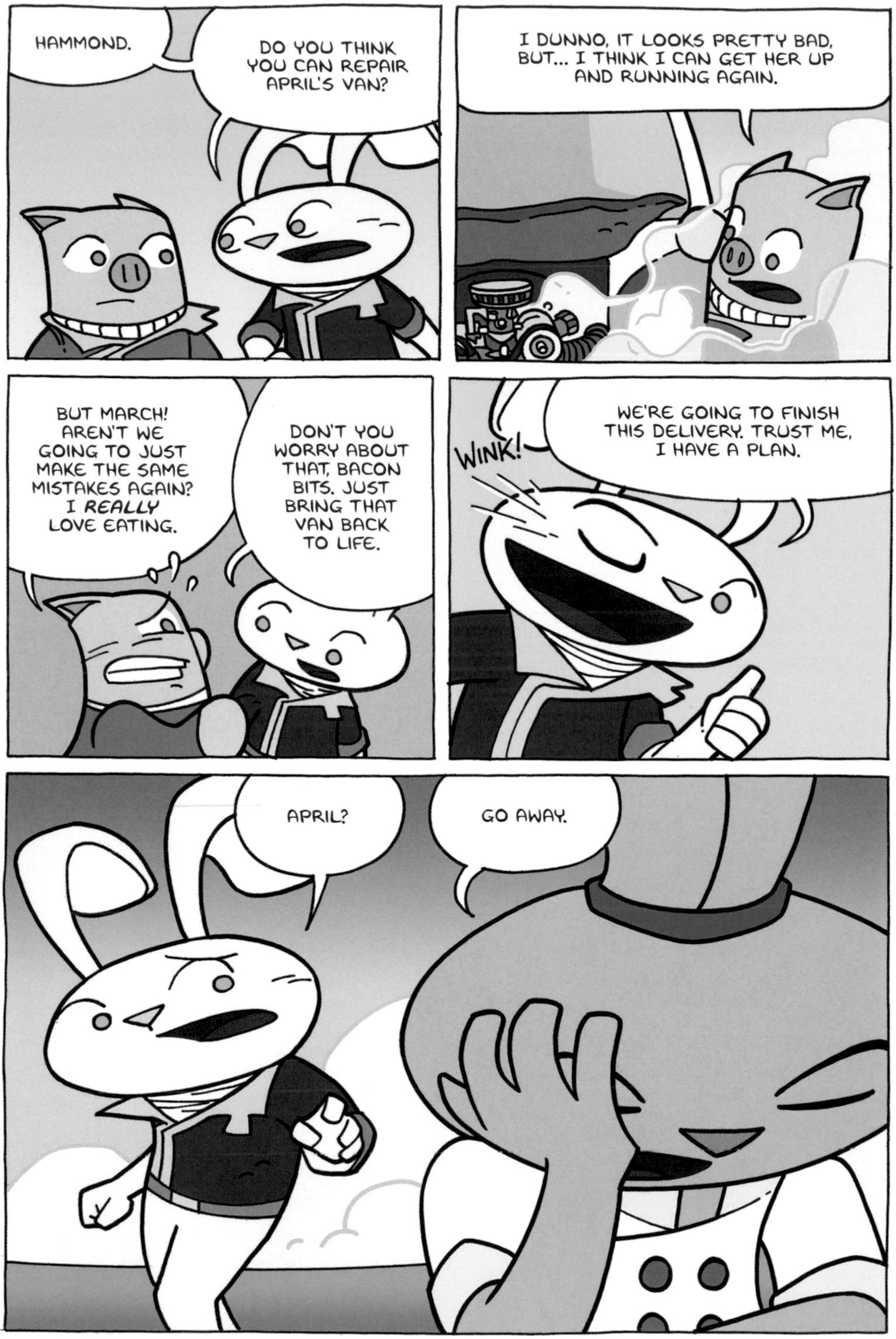
HAMMOND.
DO YOU THINK YOU CAN REPAIR APRIL'S VAN?
I DUNNO, IT LOOKS PRETTY BAD, BUT... I THINK I CAN GET HER UP AND RUNNING AGAIN.
BUT MARCH! AREN'T WE GOING TO JUST MAKE THE SAME MISTAKES AGAIN? I *REALLY* LOVE EATING.
DON'T YOU WORRY ABOUT THAT, BACON BITS. JUST BRING THAT VAN BACK TO LIFE.
WINK!
WE'RE GOING TO FINISH THIS DELIVERY. TRUST ME, I HAVE A PLAN.
APRIL?
GO AWAY.

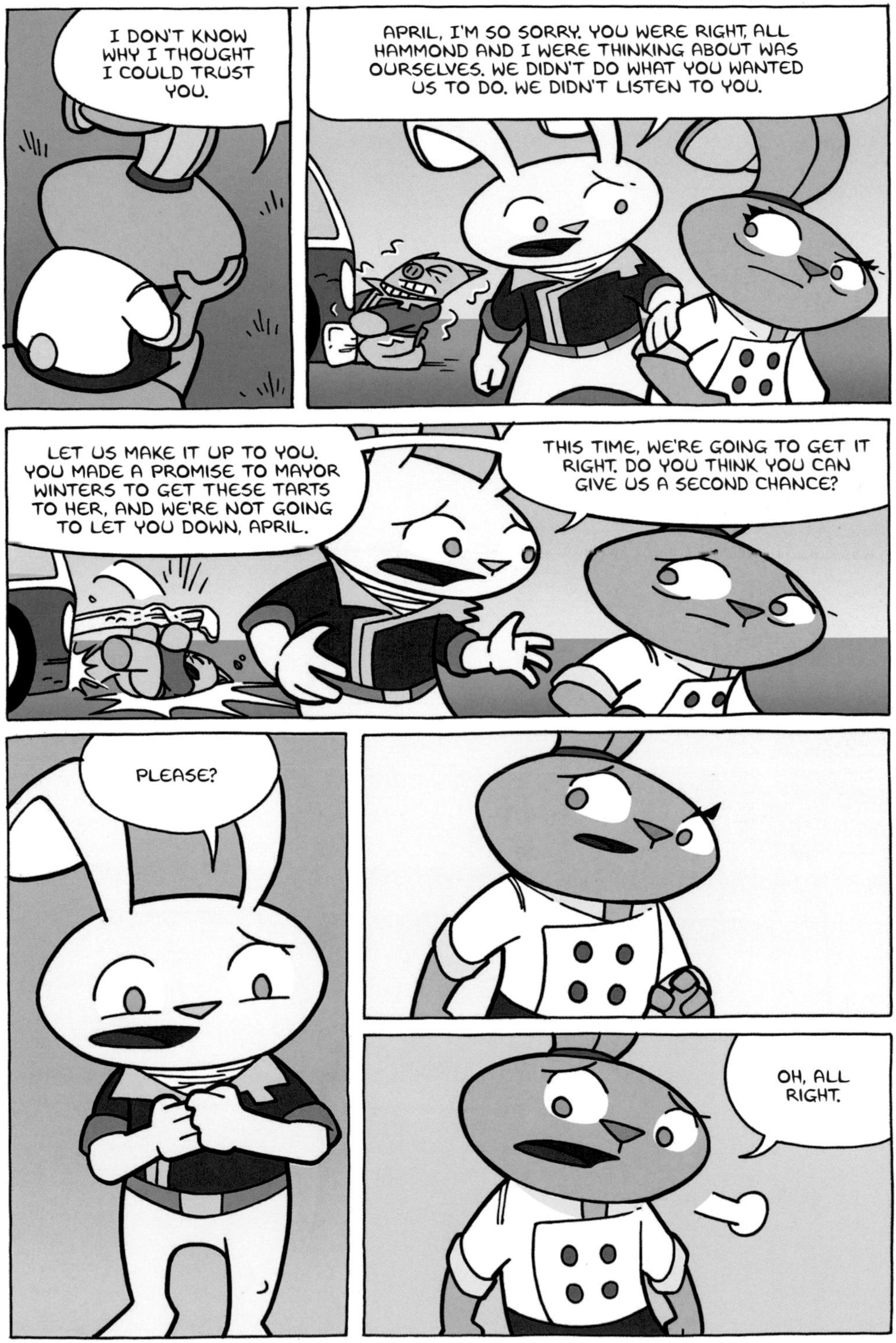
I DON'T KNOW WHY I THOUGHT I COULD TRUST YOU.
APRIL, I'M SO SORRY. YOU WERE RIGHT, ALL HAMMOND AND I WERE THINKING ABOUT WAS OURSELVES. WE DIDN'T DO WHAT YOU WANTED US TO DO. WE DIDN'T LISTEN TO YOU.
LET US MAKE IT UP TO YOU. YOU MADE A PROMISE TO MAYOR WINTERS TO GET THESE TARTS TO HER, AND WE'RE NOT GOING TO LET YOU DOWN, APRIL.
THIS TIME, WE'RE GOING TO GET IT RIGHT. DO YOU THINK YOU CAN GIVE US A SECOND CHANCE?
PLEASE?
OH, ALL RIGHT.

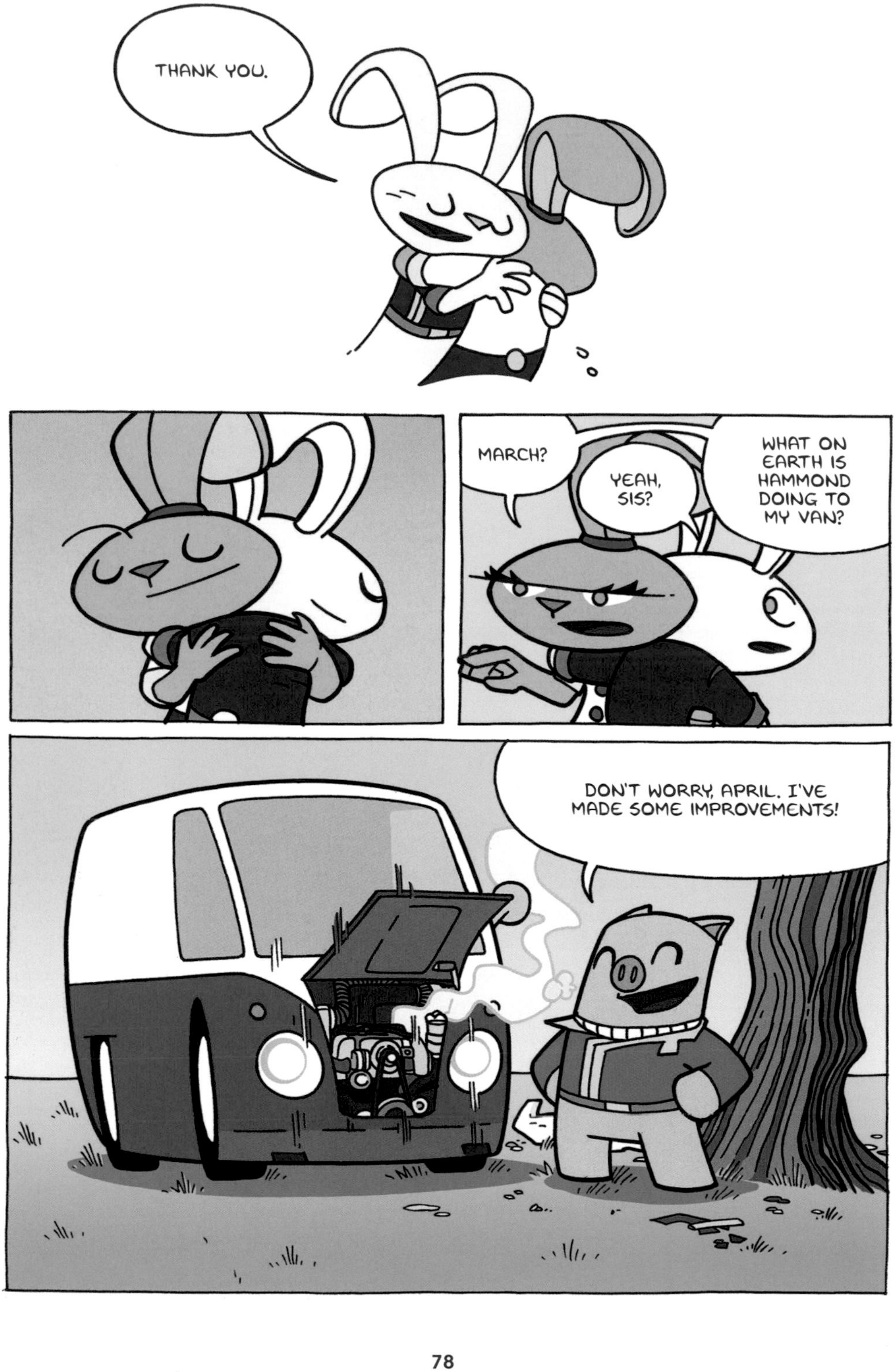
THANK YOU.
MARCH?
YEAH, SIS?
WHAT ON EARTH IS HAMMOND DOING TO MY VAN?
DON'T WORRY, APRIL. I'VE MADE SOME IMPROVEMENTS!

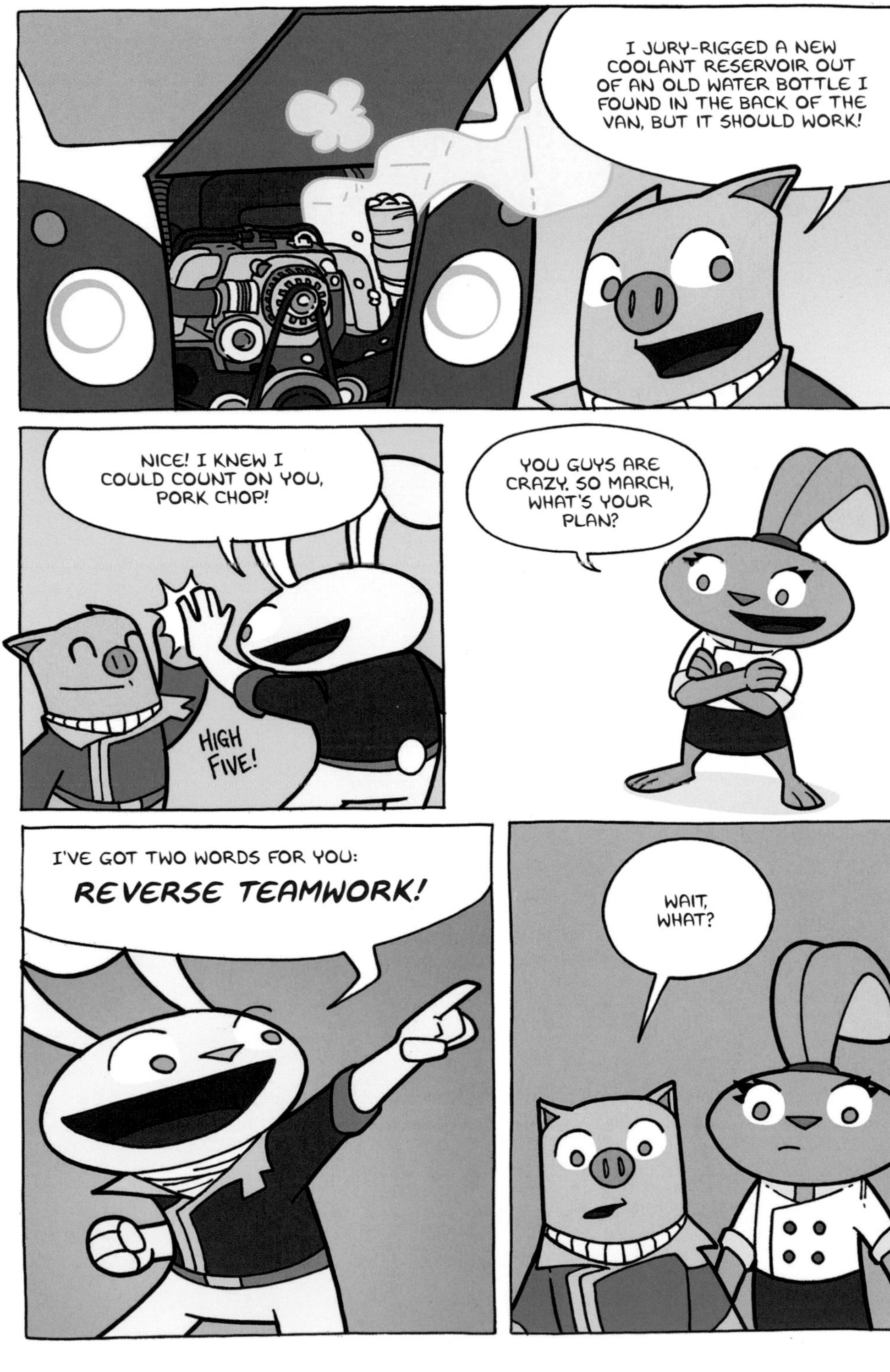
I JURY-RIGGED A NEW COOLANT RESERVOIR OUT OF AN OLD WATER BOTTLE I FOUND IN THE BACK OF THE VAN, BUT IT SHOULD WORK!
NICE! I KNEW I COULD COUNT ON YOU, PORK CHOP!
HIGH FIVE!
YOU GUYS ARE CRAZY. SO MARCH, WHAT'S YOUR PLAN?
I'VE GOT TWO WORDS FOR YOU:
REVERSE TEAMWORK!
WAIT, WHAT?

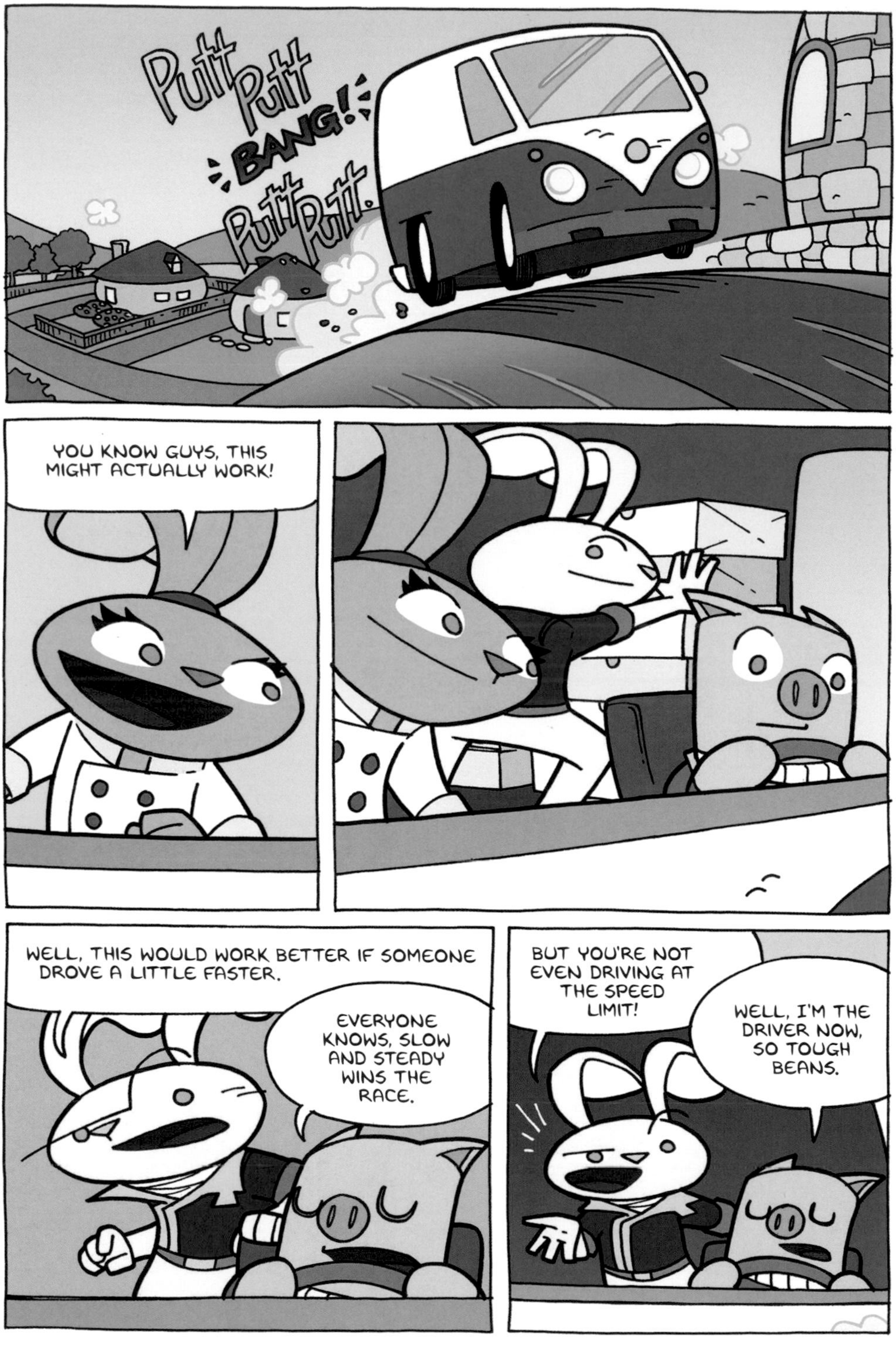
PUTT PUTT
BANG!
PUTT PUTT.
YOU KNOW GUYS, THIS MIGHT ACTUALLY WORK!
WELL, THIS WOULD WORK BETTER IF SOMEONE DROVE A LITTLE FASTER.
EVERYONE KNOWS, SLOW AND STEADY WINS THE RACE.
BUT YOU'RE NOT EVEN DRIVING AT THE SPEED LIMIT!
WELL, I'M THE DRIVER NOW, SO TOUGH BEANS.

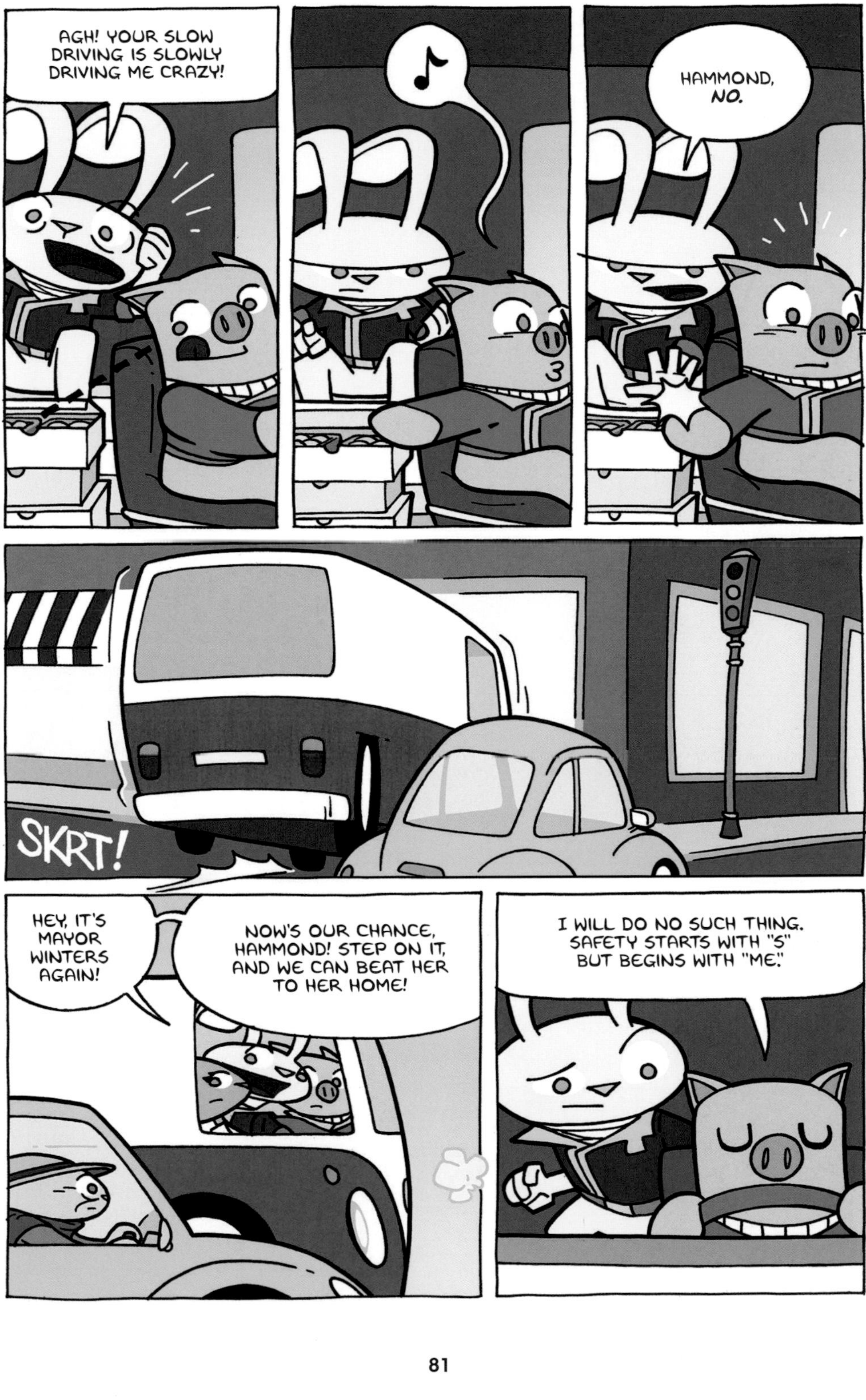
AGH! YOUR SLOW DRIVING IS SLOWLY DRIVING ME CRAZY!
♪
HAMMOND, NO.
SKRT!
HEY, IT'S MAYOR WINTERS AGAIN!
NOW'S OUR CHANCE, HAMMOND! STEP ON IT, AND WE CAN BEAT HER TO HER HOME!
I WILL DO NO SUCH THING. SAFETY STARTS WITH "S" BUT BEGINS WITH "ME."

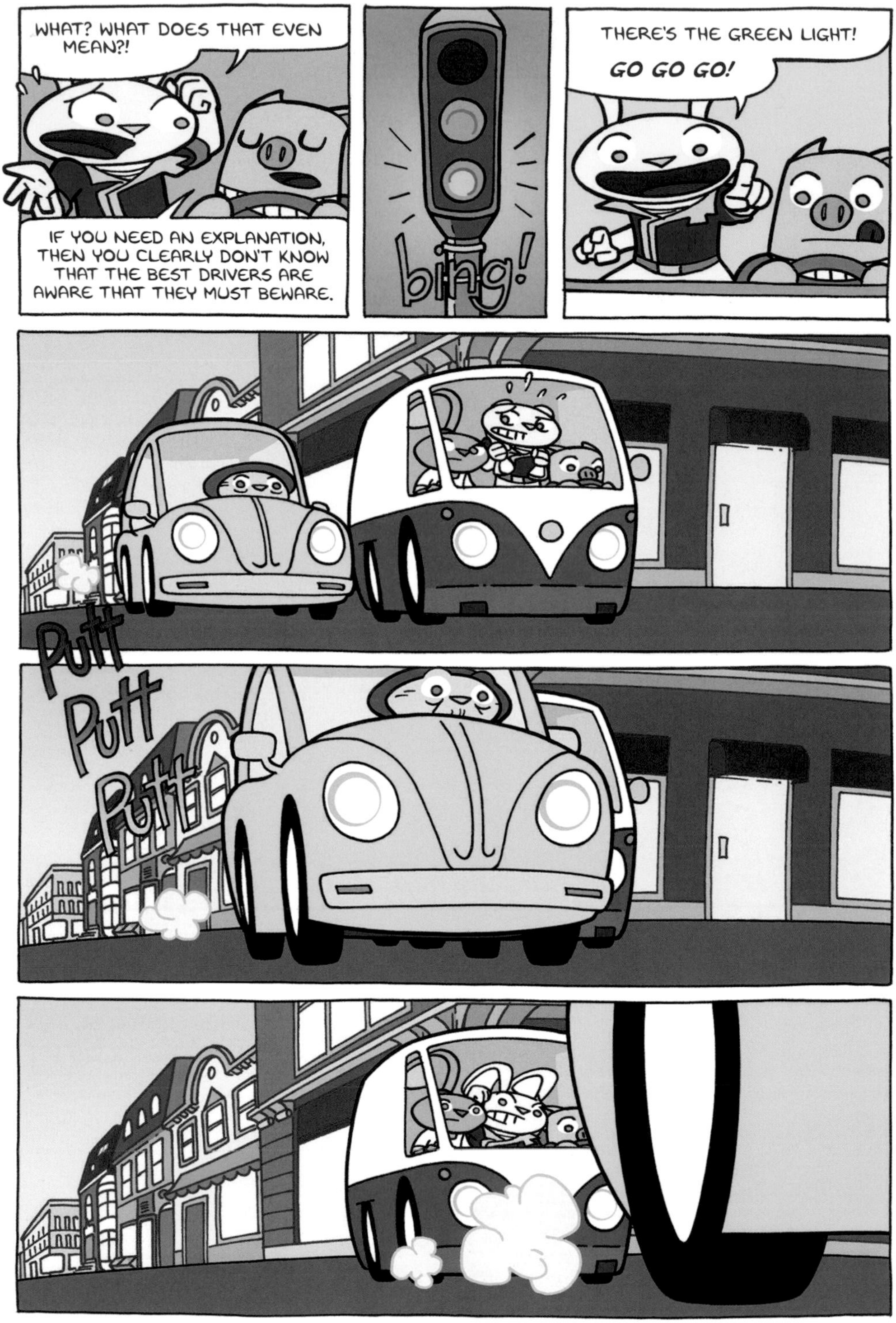
WHAT? WHAT DOES THAT EVEN MEAN?!
IF YOU NEED AN EXPLANATION, THEN YOU CLEARLY DON'T KNOW THAT THE BEST DRIVERS ARE AWARE THAT THEY MUST BEWARE.
bing!
THERE'S THE GREEN LIGHT!
GO GO GO!
Putt
Putt
Putt

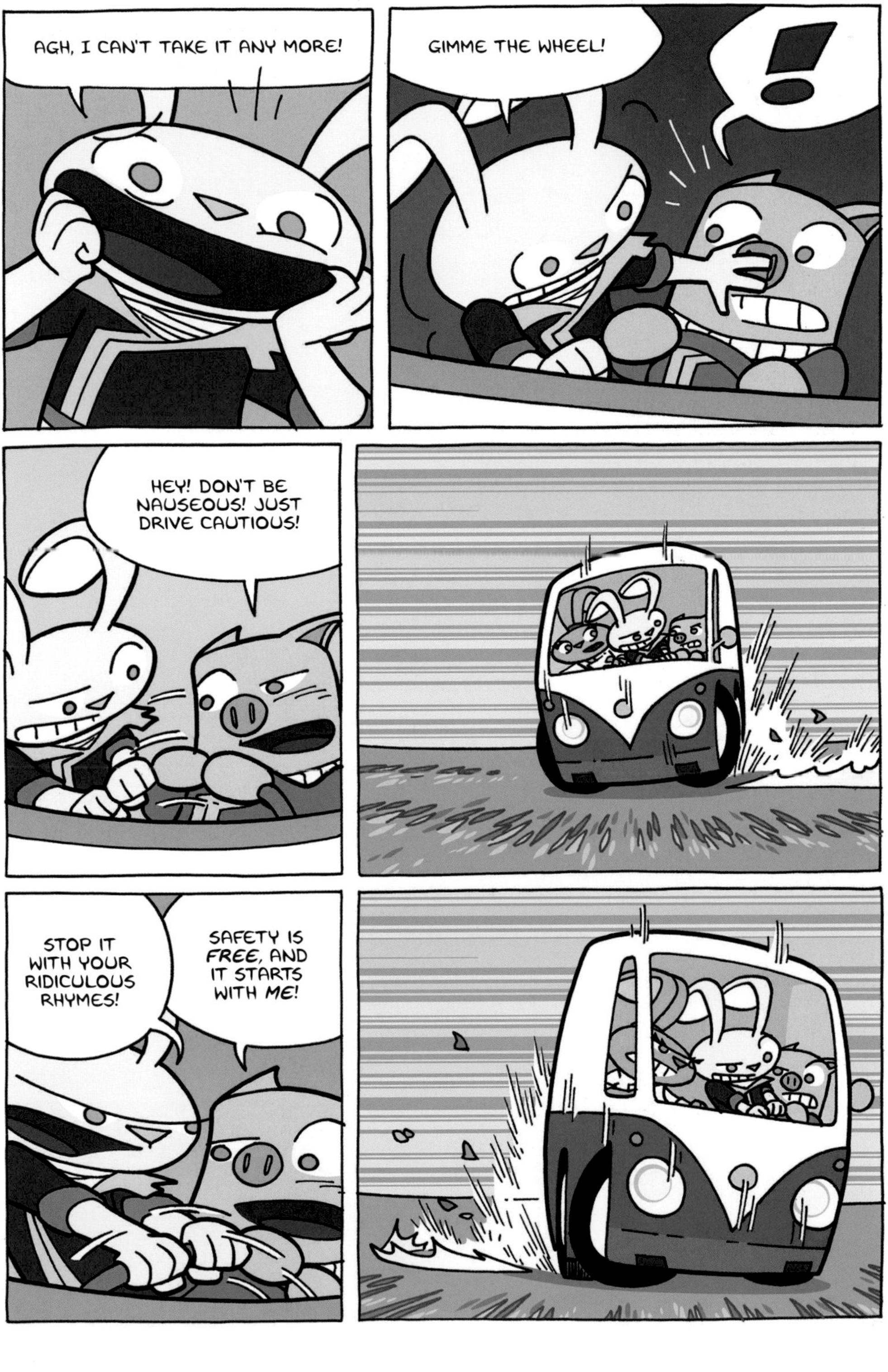
AGH, I CAN'T TAKE IT ANY MORE!
GIMME THE WHEEL!
!
HEY! DON'T BE NAUSEOUS! JUST DRIVE CAUTIOUS!
STOP IT WITH YOUR RIDICULOUS RHYMES!
SAFETY IS FREE, AND IT STARTS WITH ME!

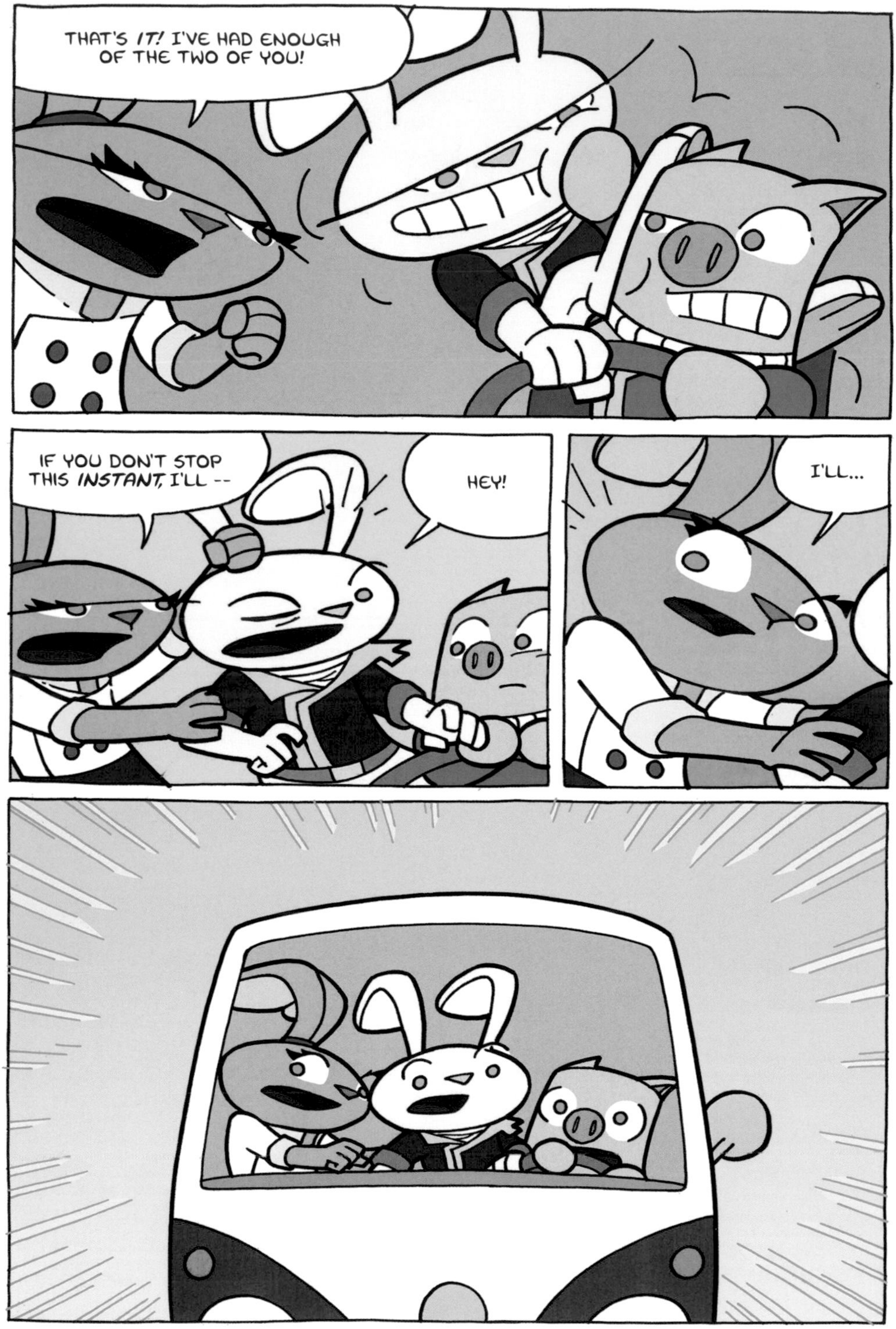
THAT'S *IT!* I'VE HAD ENOUGH OF THE TWO OF YOU!
IF YOU DON'T STOP THIS *INSTANT,* I'LL --
HEY!
I'LL...

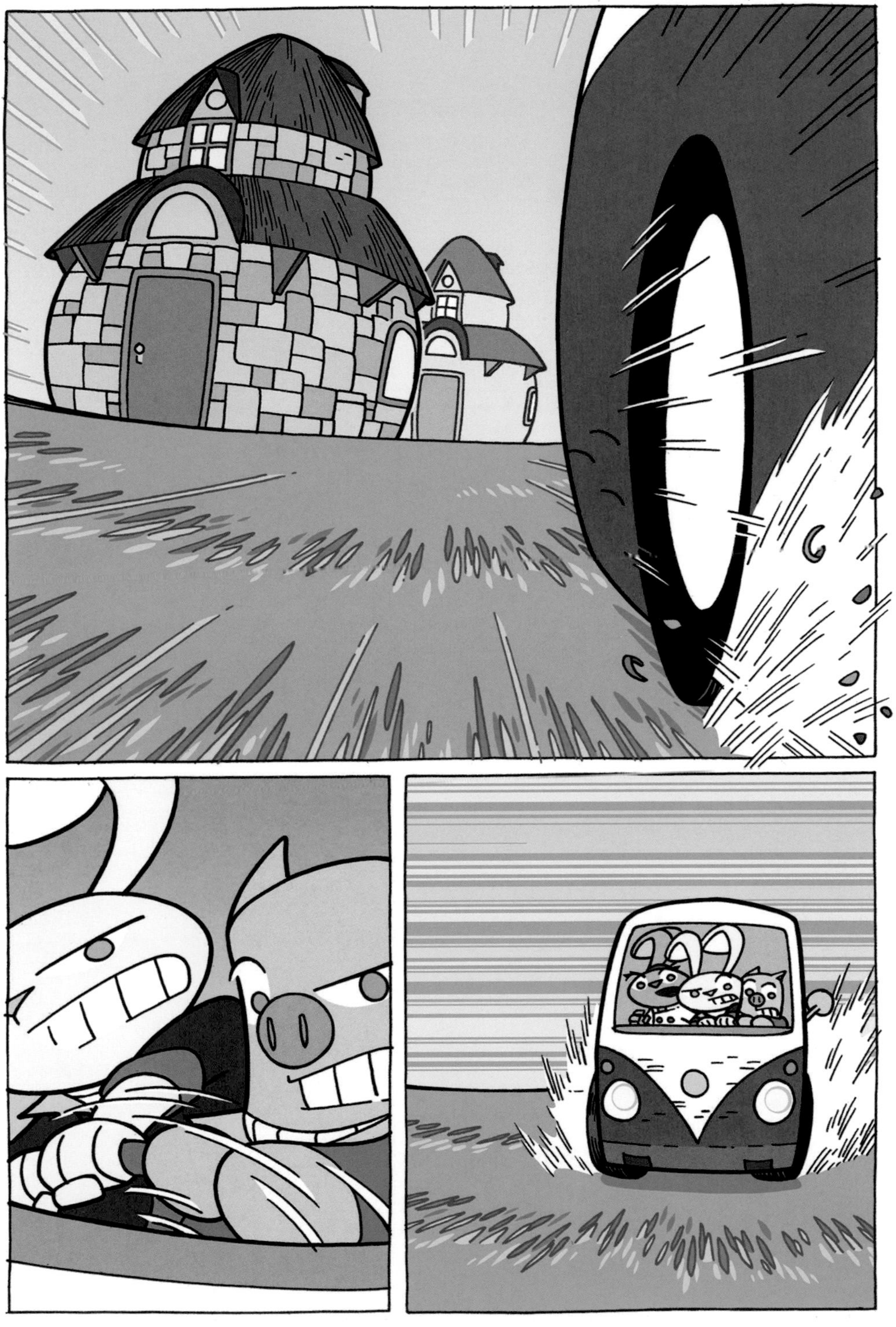

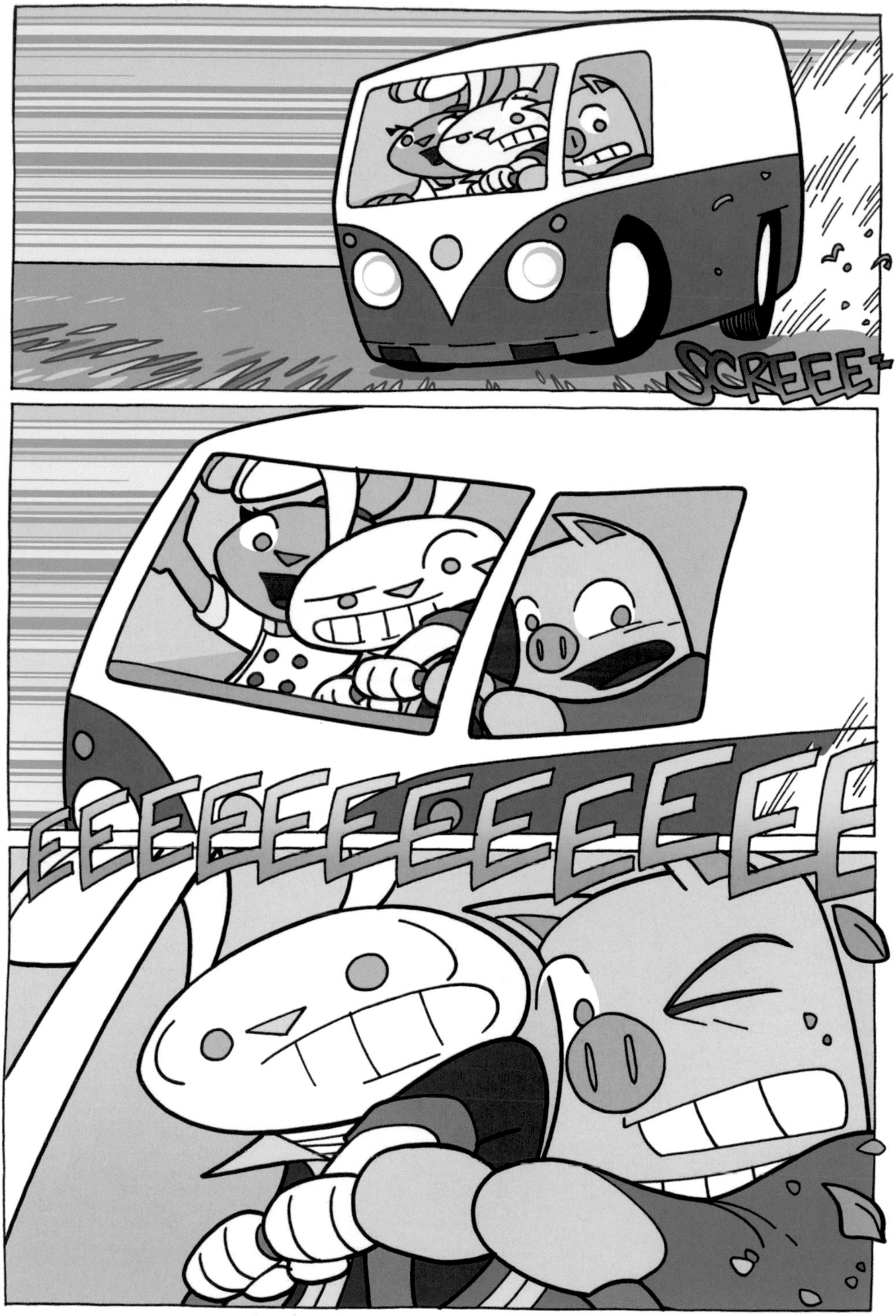
SCREEE-
EEEEEEEEEEEEEE

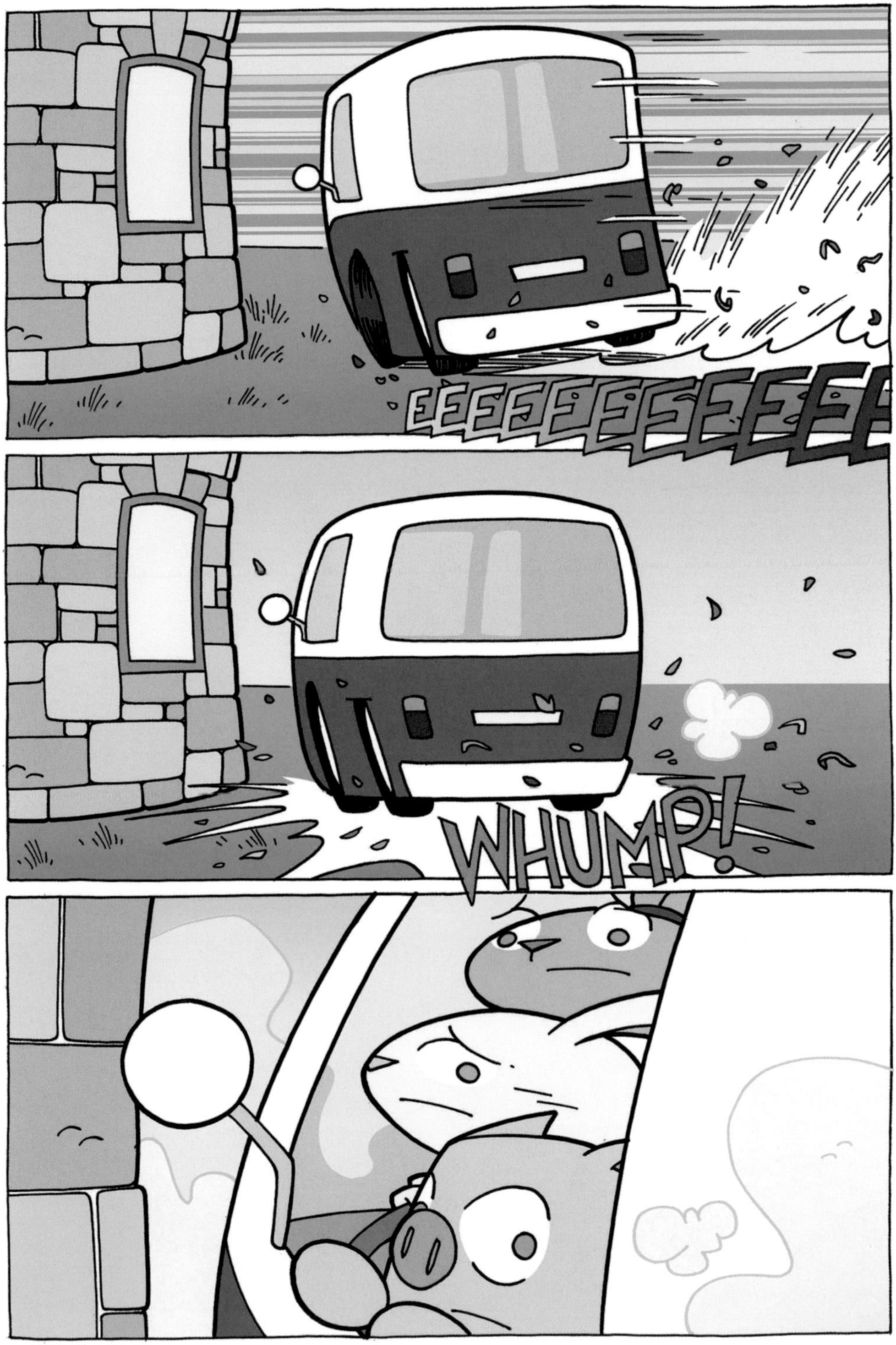
EEEEEEEEEEEE
WHUMP!

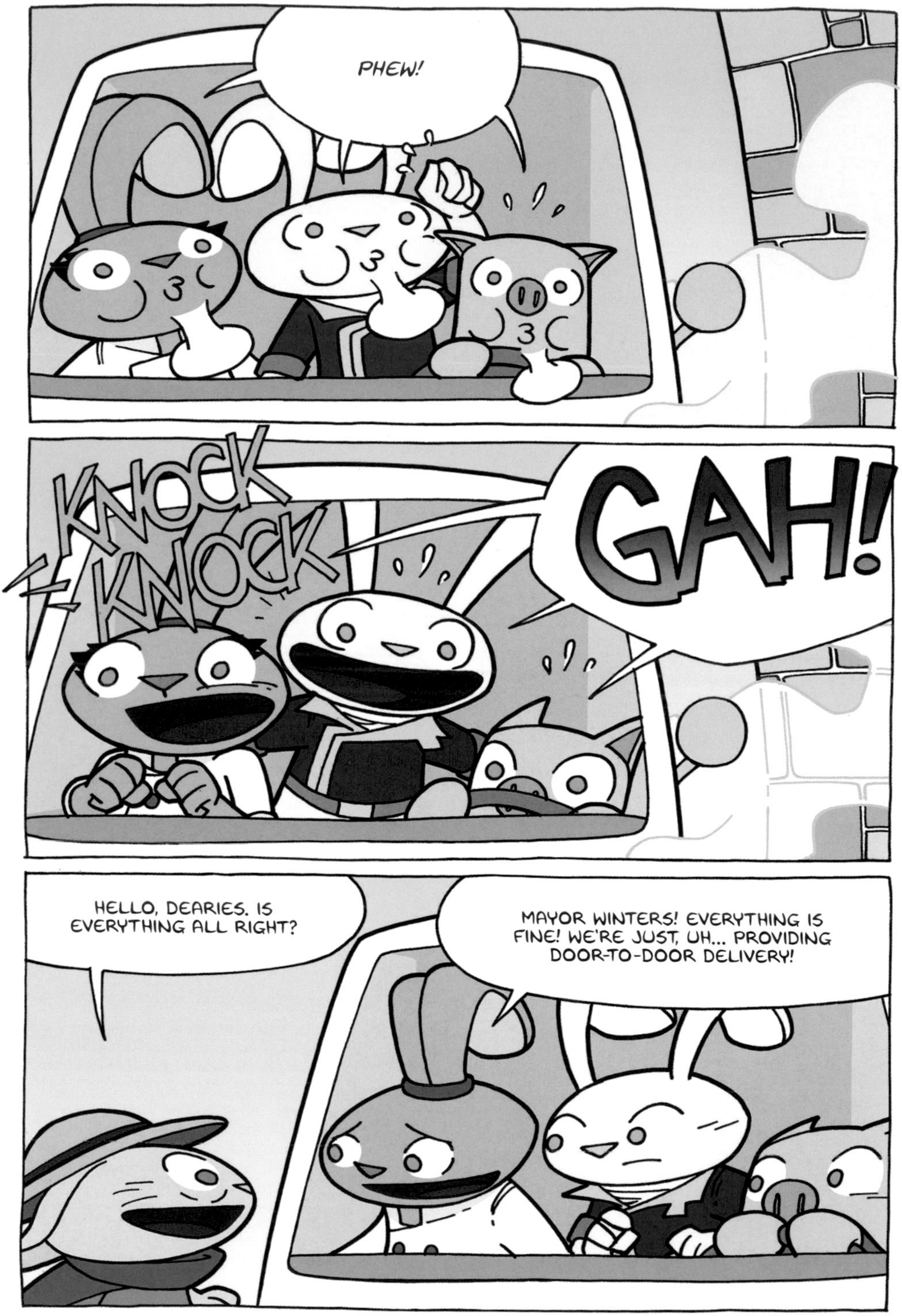
PHEW!
KNOCK KNOCK
GAH!
HELLO, DEARIES. IS EVERYTHING ALL RIGHT?
MAYOR WINTERS! EVERYTHING IS FINE! WE'RE JUST, UH... PROVIDING DOOR-TO-DOOR DELIVERY!

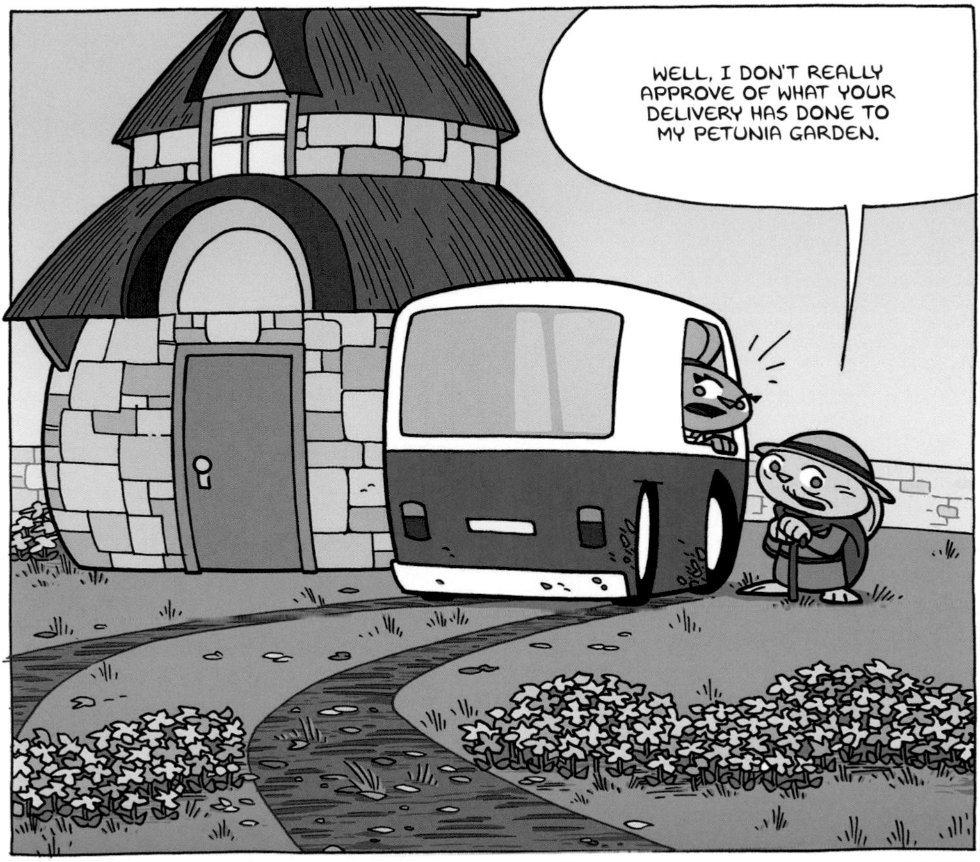
WELL, I DON'T REALLY APPROVE OF WHAT YOUR DELIVERY HAS DONE TO MY PETUNIA GARDEN.

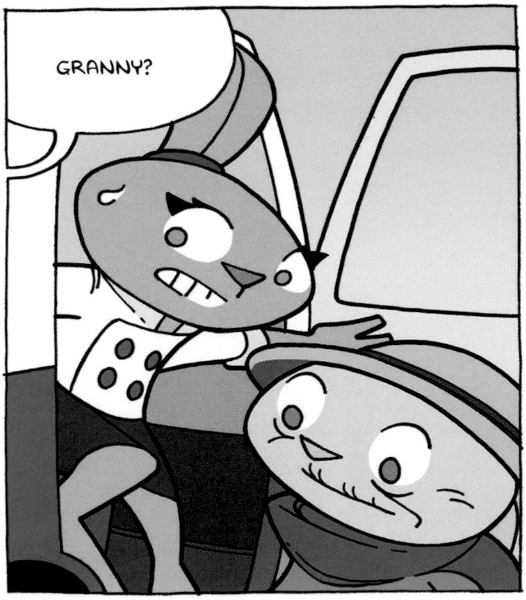
GRANNY?

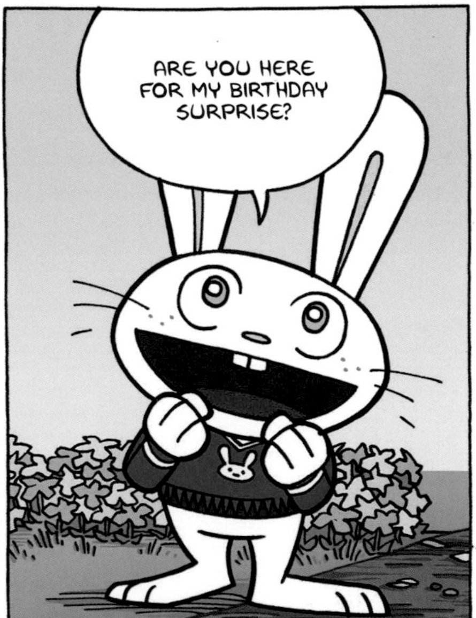
ARE YOU HERE FOR MY BIRTHDAY SURPRISE?

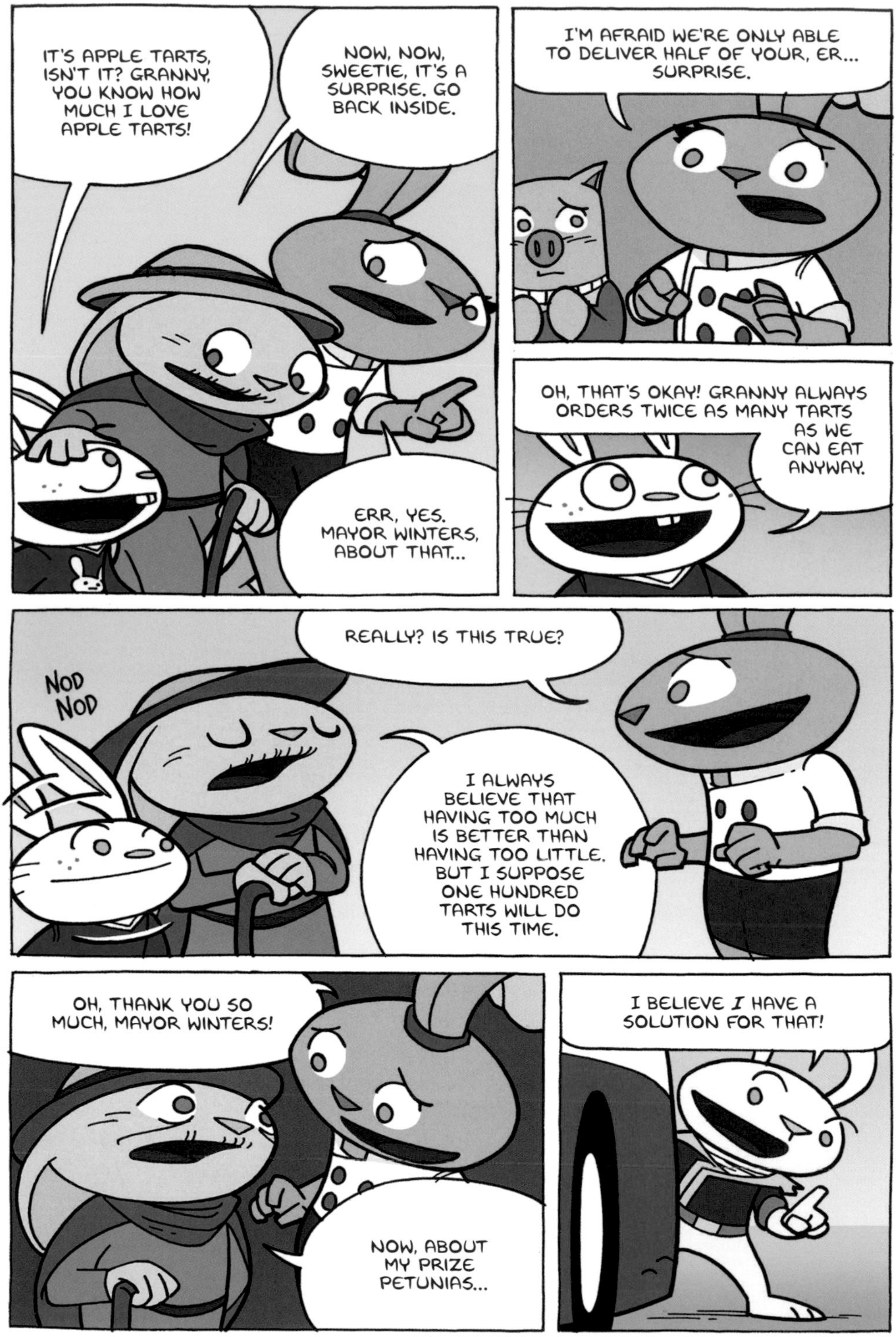
IT'S APPLE TARTS, ISN'T IT? GRANNY, YOU KNOW HOW MUCH I LOVE APPLE TARTS!
NOW, NOW, SWEETIE, IT'S A SURPRISE. GO BACK INSIDE.
ERR, YES. MAYOR WINTERS, ABOUT THAT...
I'M AFRAID WE'RE ONLY ABLE TO DELIVER HALF OF YOUR, ER... SURPRISE.
OH, THAT'S OKAY! GRANNY ALWAYS ORDERS TWICE AS MANY TARTS AS WE CAN EAT ANYWAY.
REALLY? IS THIS TRUE?
NOD NOD
I ALWAYS BELIEVE THAT HAVING TOO MUCH IS BETTER THAN HAVING TOO LITTLE. BUT I SUPPOSE ONE HUNDRED TARTS WILL DO THIS TIME.
OH, THANK YOU SO MUCH, MAYOR WINTERS!
NOW, ABOUT MY PRIZE PETUNIAS...
I BELIEVE *I* HAVE A SOLUTION FOR THAT!

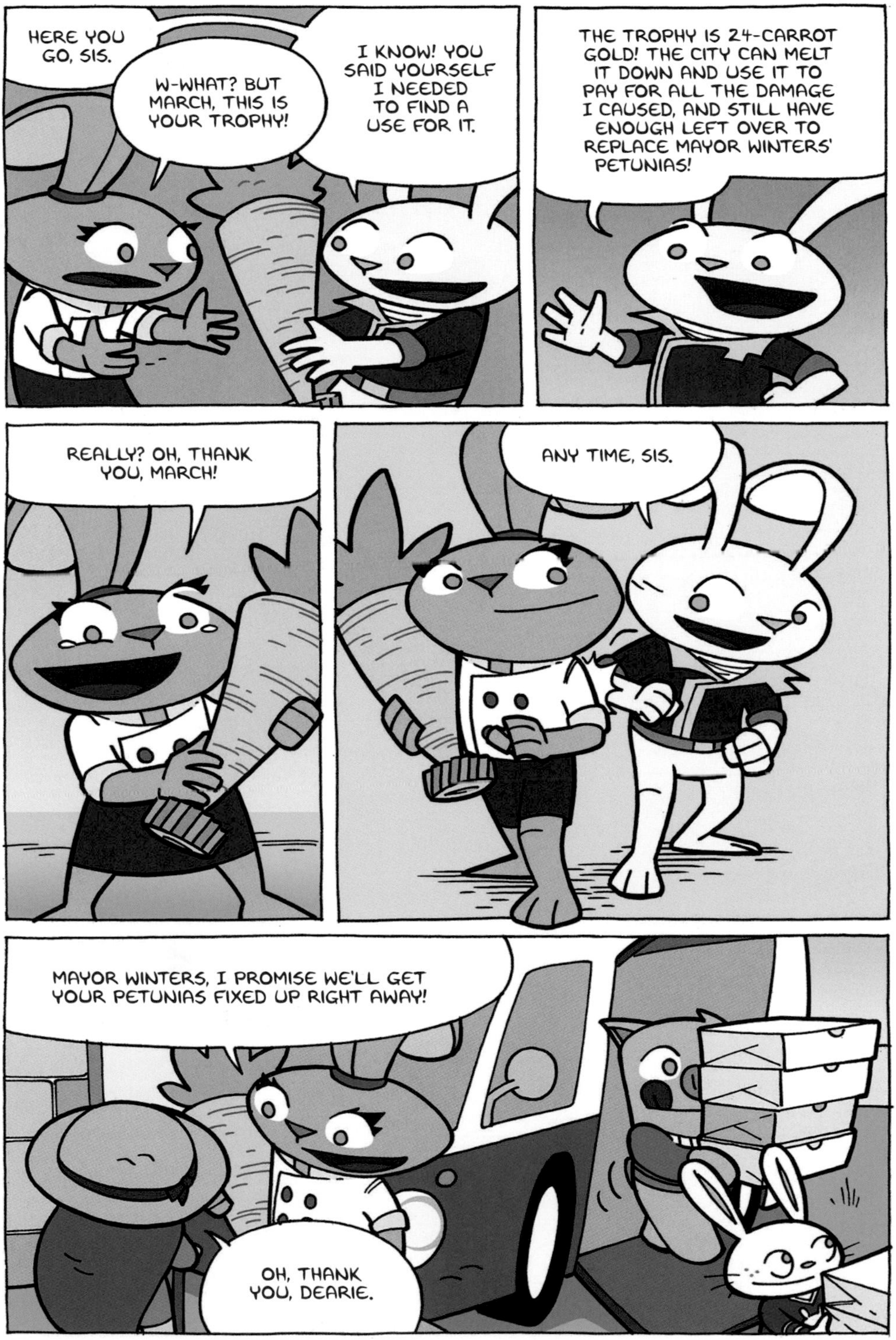
HERE YOU GO, SIS.
W-WHAT? BUT MARCH, THIS IS YOUR TROPHY!
I KNOW! YOU SAID YOURSELF I NEEDED TO FIND A USE FOR IT.
THE TROPHY IS 24-CARROT GOLD! THE CITY CAN MELT IT DOWN AND USE IT TO PAY FOR ALL THE DAMAGE I CAUSED, AND STILL HAVE ENOUGH LEFT OVER TO REPLACE MAYOR WINTERS' PETUNIAS!
REALLY? OH, THANK YOU, MARCH!
ANY TIME, SIS.
MAYOR WINTERS, I PROMISE WE'LL GET YOUR PETUNIAS FIXED UP RIGHT AWAY!
OH, THANK YOU, DEARIE.

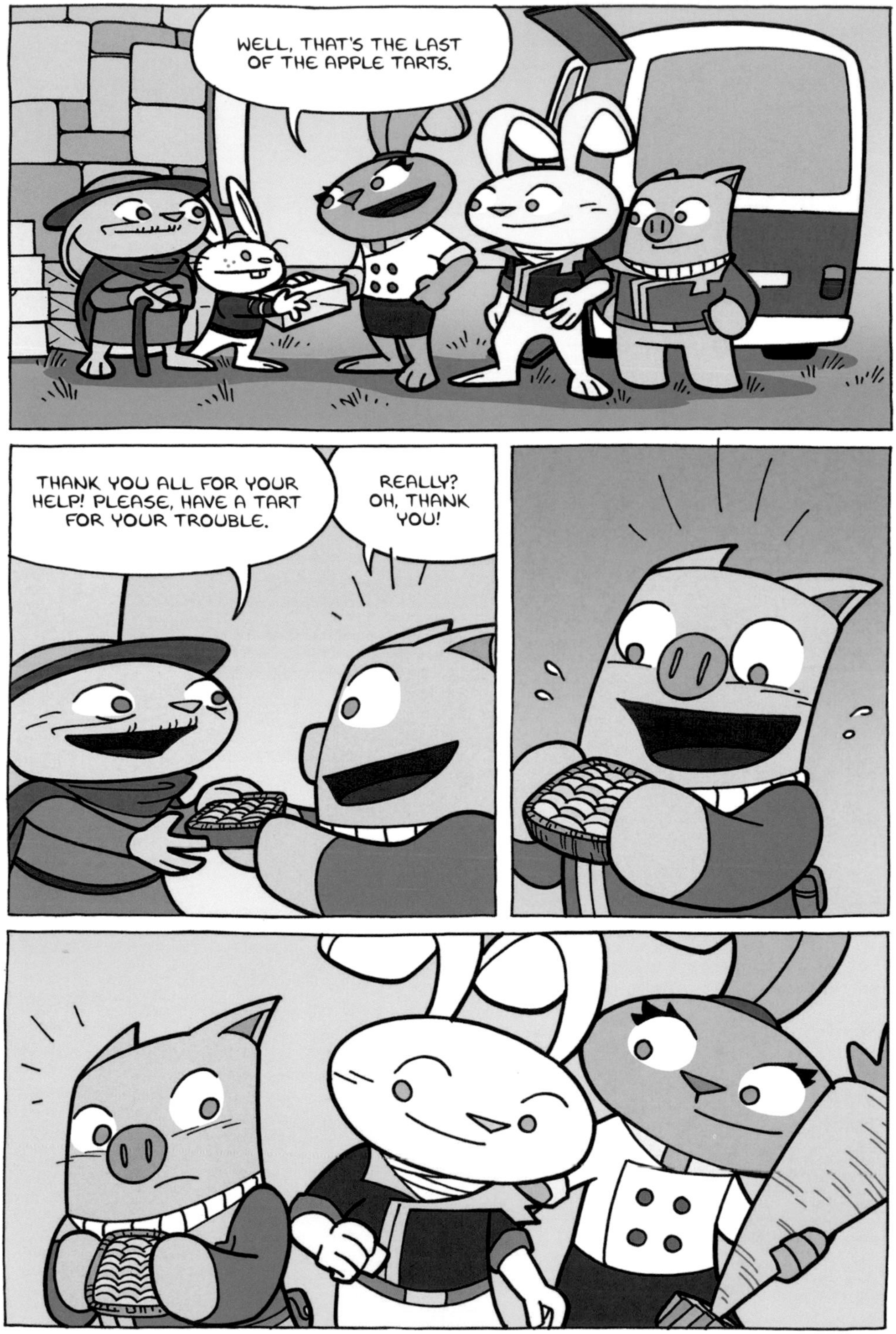
WELL, THAT'S THE LAST OF THE APPLE TARTS.
THANK YOU ALL FOR YOUR HELP! PLEASE, HAVE A TART FOR YOUR TROUBLE.
REALLY? OH, THANK YOU!

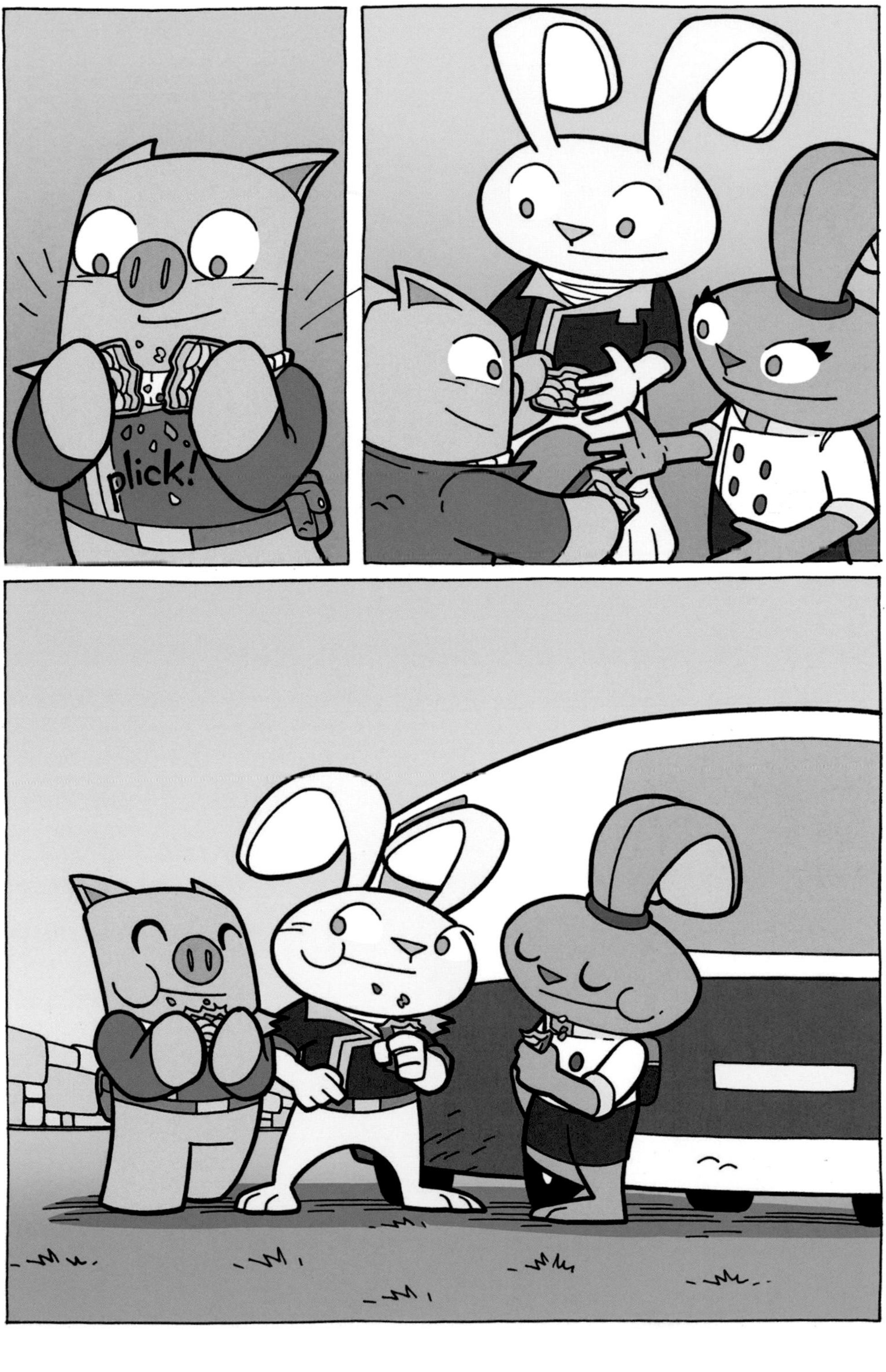
plick!

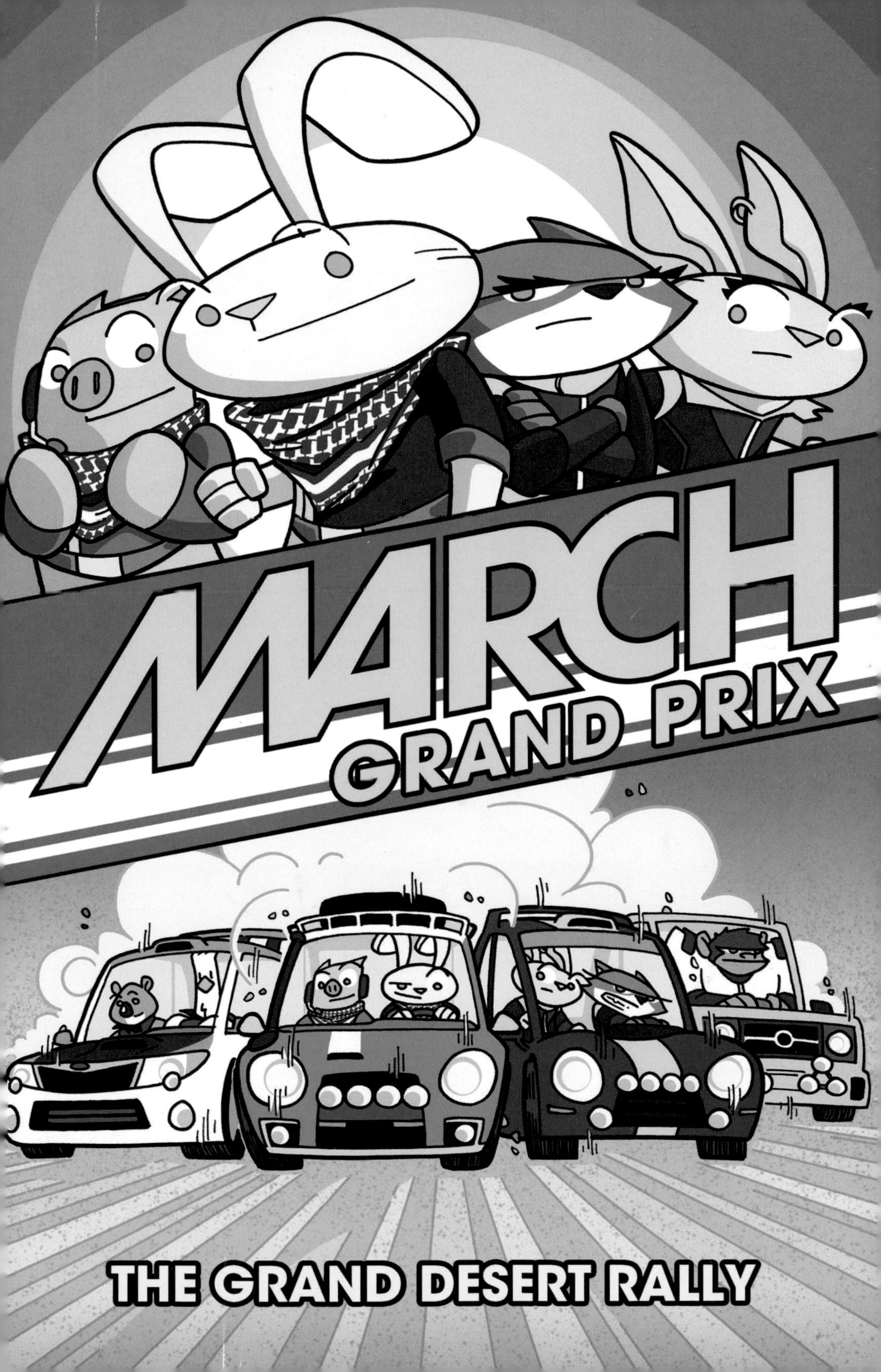
MARCH
GRAND PRIX
THE GRAND DESERT RALLY

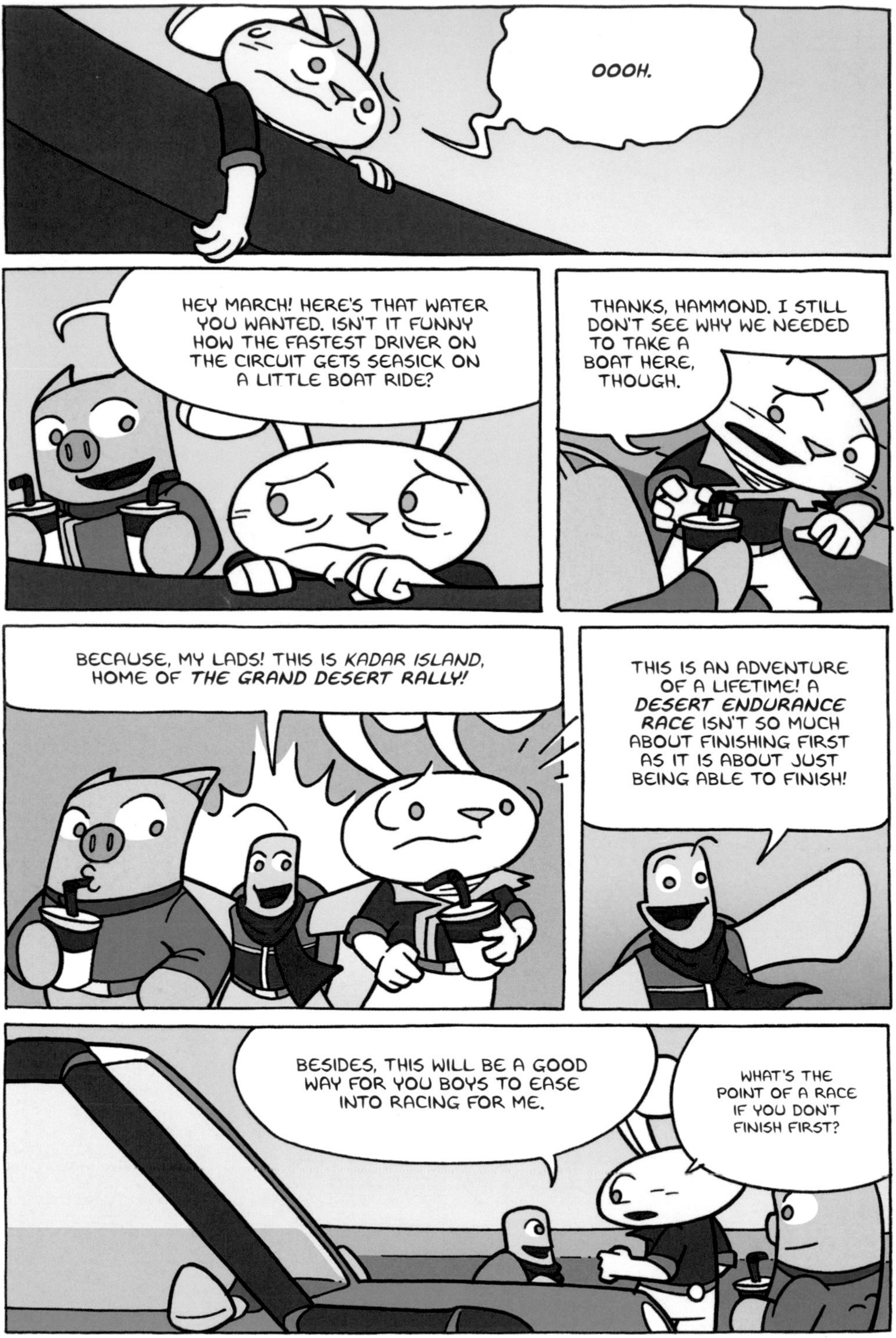
OOOH.
HEY MARCH! HERE'S THAT WATER YOU WANTED. ISN'T IT FUNNY HOW THE FASTEST DRIVER ON THE CIRCUIT GETS SEASICK ON A LITTLE BOAT RIDE?
THANKS, HAMMOND. I STILL DON'T SEE WHY WE NEEDED TO TAKE A BOAT HERE, THOUGH.
BECAUSE, MY LADS! THIS IS *KADAR ISLAND*, HOME OF ***THE GRAND DESERT RALLY!***
THIS IS AN ADVENTURE OF A LIFETIME! A ***DESERT ENDURANCE RACE*** ISN'T SO MUCH ABOUT FINISHING FIRST AS IT IS ABOUT JUST BEING ABLE TO FINISH!
BESIDES, THIS WILL BE A GOOD WAY FOR YOU BOYS TO EASE INTO RACING FOR ME.
WHAT'S THE POINT OF A RACE IF YOU DON'T FINISH FIRST?

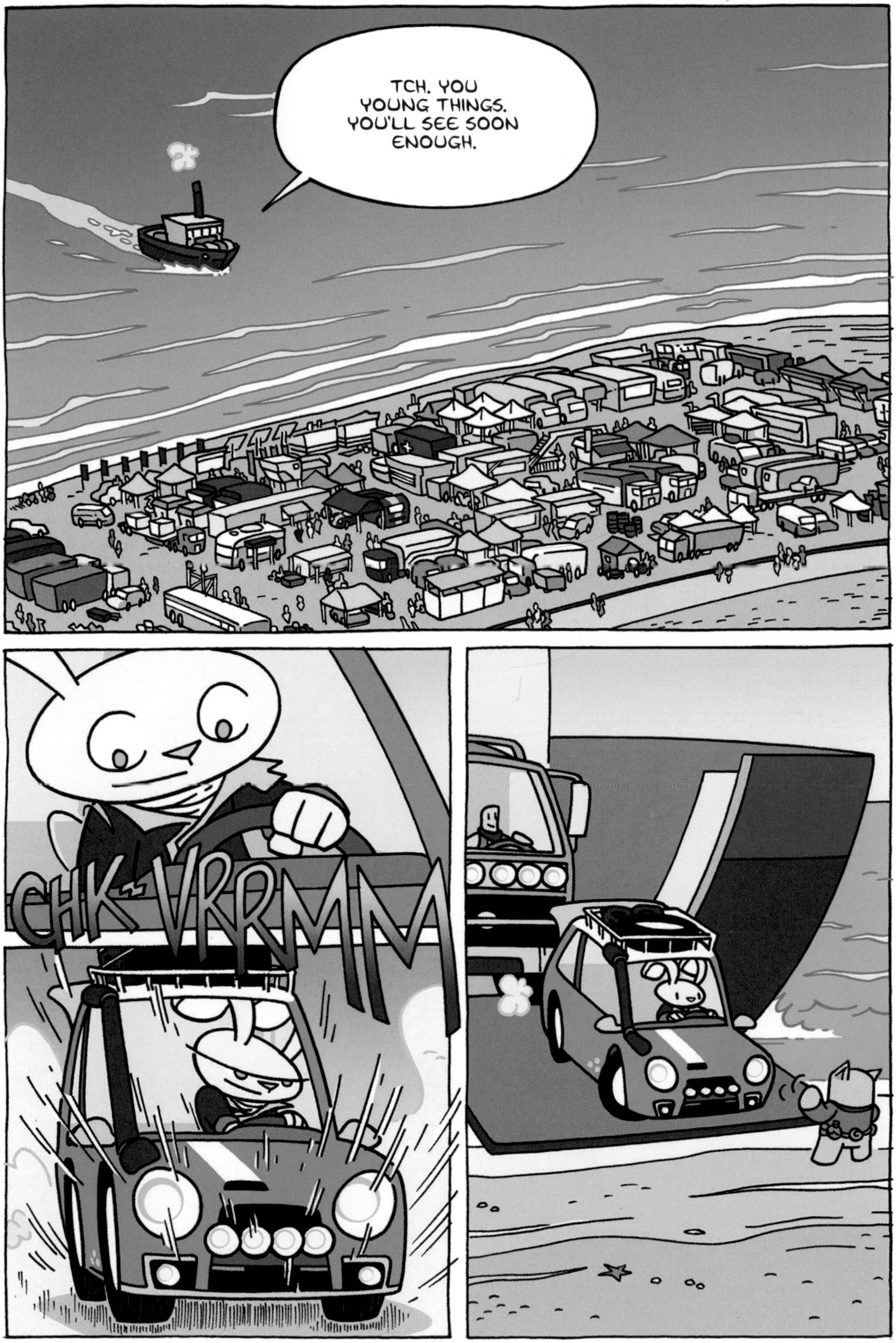
TCH. YOU YOUNG THINGS. YOU'LL SEE SOON ENOUGH.
CHK-VRRMM

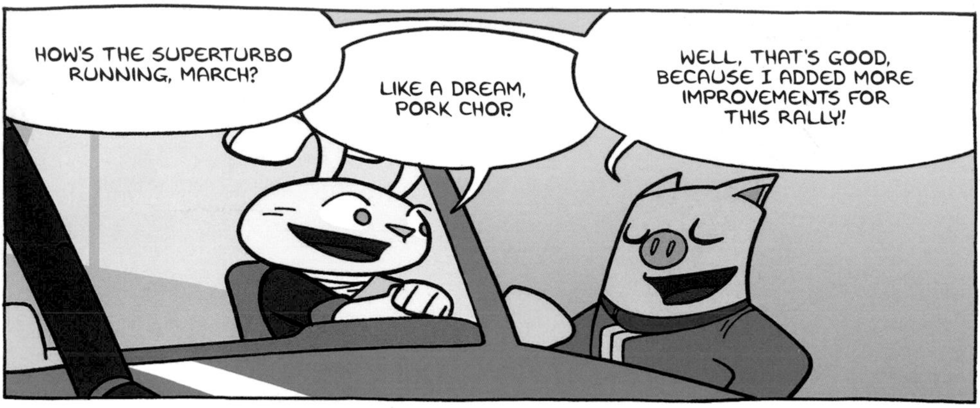
HOW'S THE SUPERTURBO RUNNING, MARCH?
LIKE A DREAM, PORK CHOP.
WELL, THAT'S GOOD, BECAUSE I ADDED MORE IMPROVEMENTS FOR THIS RALLY!

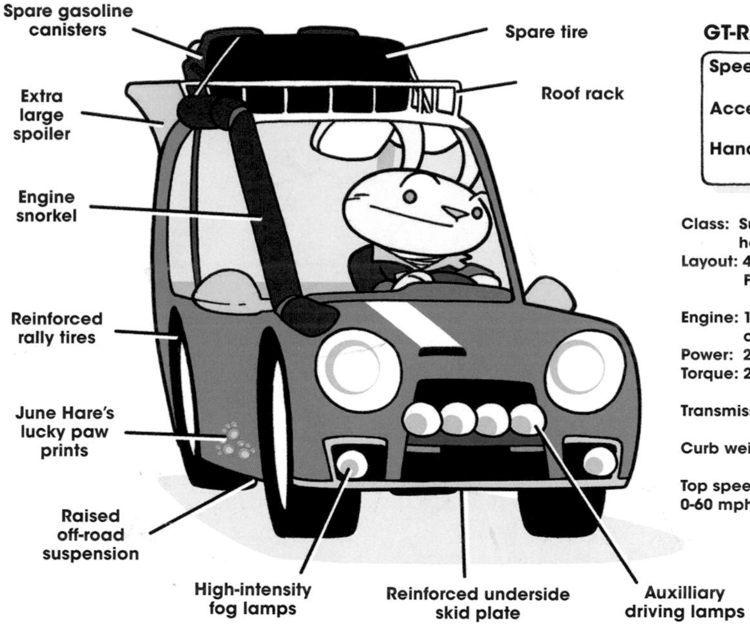
Spare gasoline canisters
Spare tire
Extra large spoiler
Roof rack
Engine snorkel
Reinforced rally tires
June Hare's lucky paw prints
Raised off-road suspension
High-intensity fog lamps
Reinforced underside skid plate
Auxilliary driving lamps

GT-RX Superturbo

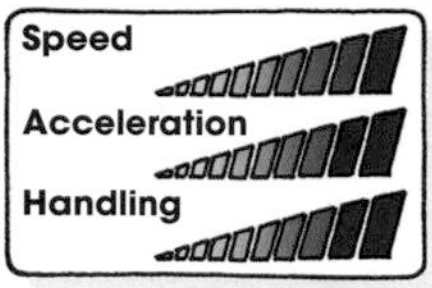
Speed
Acceleration
Handling

Class: Subcompact 3-door rally hatchback
Layout: 4WD layout (Front-engine, Four-wheel-drive)

Engine: 1.4-Liter, 16-valve twin charged inline four-cylinder
Power: 276 hp
Torque: 295 lb/ft @ 5000 rpm

Transmission: 6-speed manual

Curb weight: 1,488 lb

Top speed: 135 mph
0-60 mph: 4.2 seconds

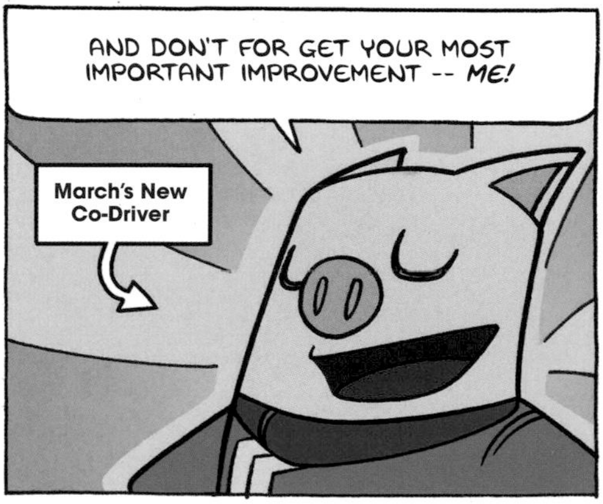
AND DON'T FOR GET YOUR MOST IMPORTANT IMPROVEMENT -- *ME!*
March's New Co-Driver

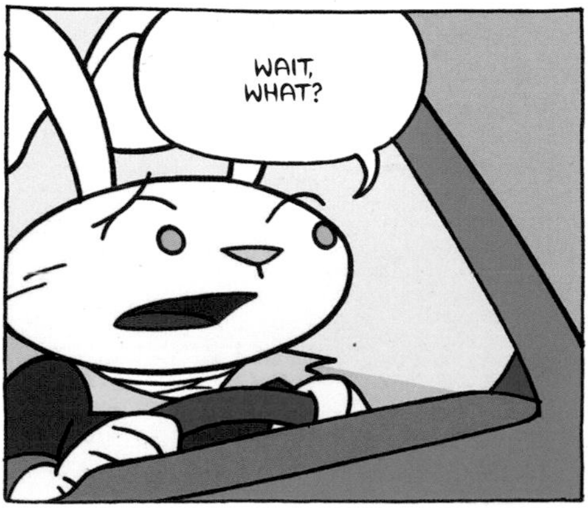
WAIT, WHAT?

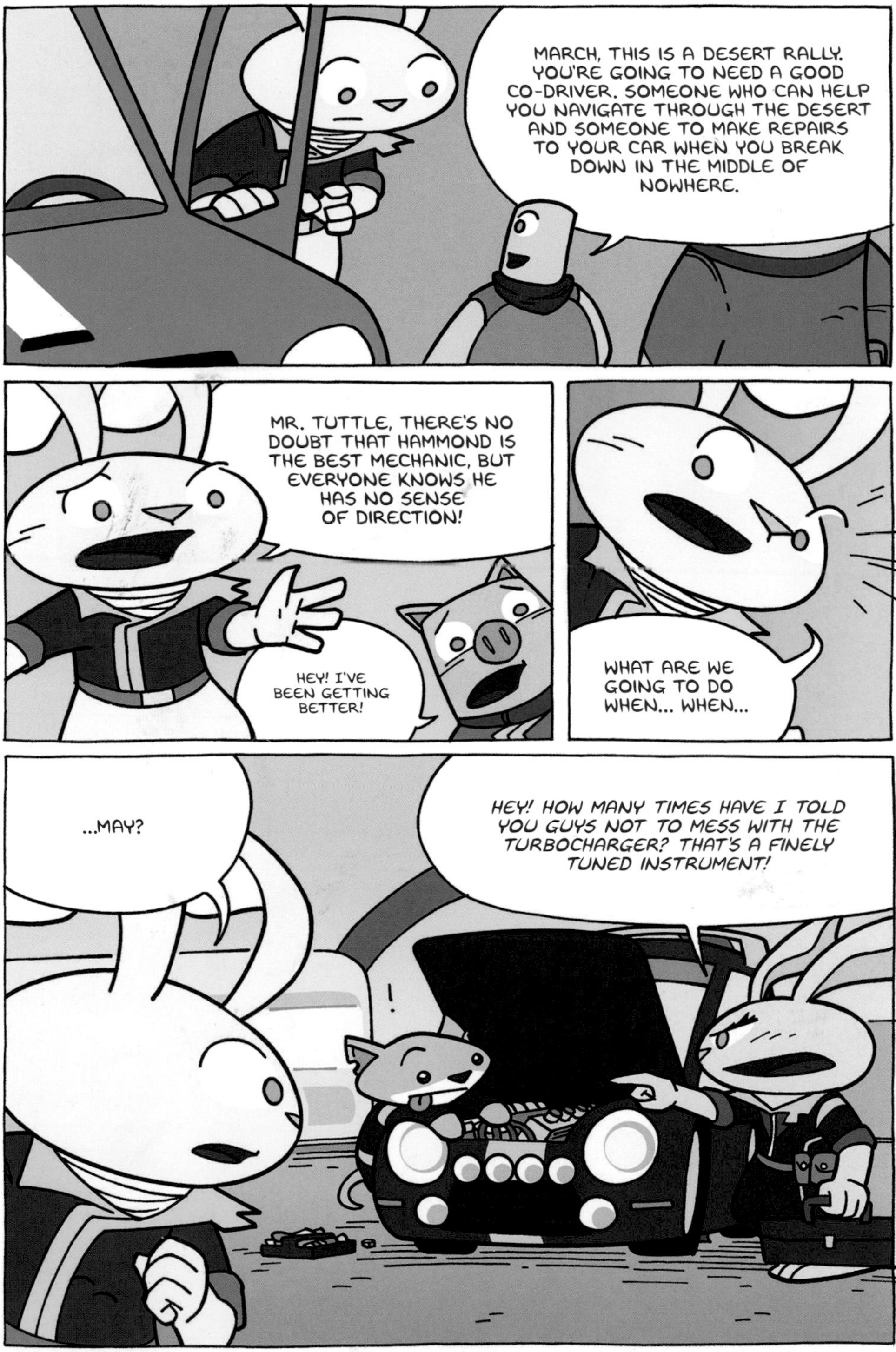
MARCH, THIS IS A DESERT RALLY. YOU'RE GOING TO NEED A GOOD CO-DRIVER. SOMEONE WHO CAN HELP YOU NAVIGATE THROUGH THE DESERT AND SOMEONE TO MAKE REPAIRS TO YOUR CAR WHEN YOU BREAK DOWN IN THE MIDDLE OF NOWHERE.
MR. TUTTLE, THERE'S NO DOUBT THAT HAMMOND IS THE BEST MECHANIC, BUT EVERYONE KNOWS HE HAS NO SENSE OF DIRECTION!
HEY! I'VE BEEN GETTING BETTER!
WHAT ARE WE GOING TO DO WHEN... WHEN...
...MAY?
!
HEY! HOW MANY TIMES HAVE I TOLD YOU GUYS NOT TO MESS WITH THE TURBOCHARGER? THAT'S A FINELY TUNED INSTRUMENT!

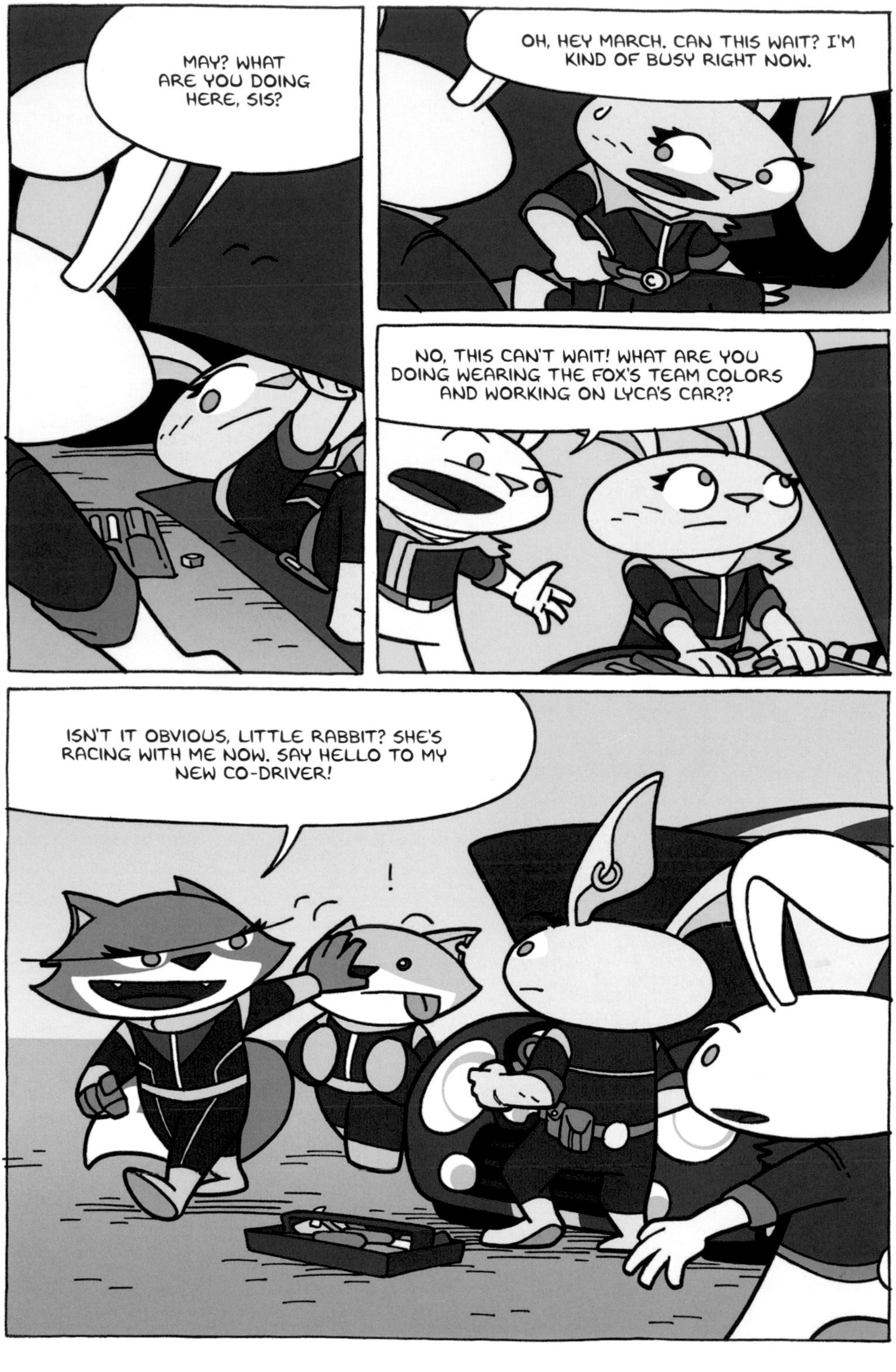
MAY? WHAT ARE YOU DOING HERE, SIS?
OH, HEY MARCH. CAN THIS WAIT? I'M KIND OF BUSY RIGHT NOW.
NO, THIS CAN'T WAIT! WHAT ARE YOU DOING WEARING THE FOX'S TEAM COLORS AND WORKING ON LYCA'S CAR??
ISN'T IT OBVIOUS, LITTLE RABBIT? SHE'S RACING WITH ME NOW. SAY HELLO TO MY NEW CO-DRIVER!
!

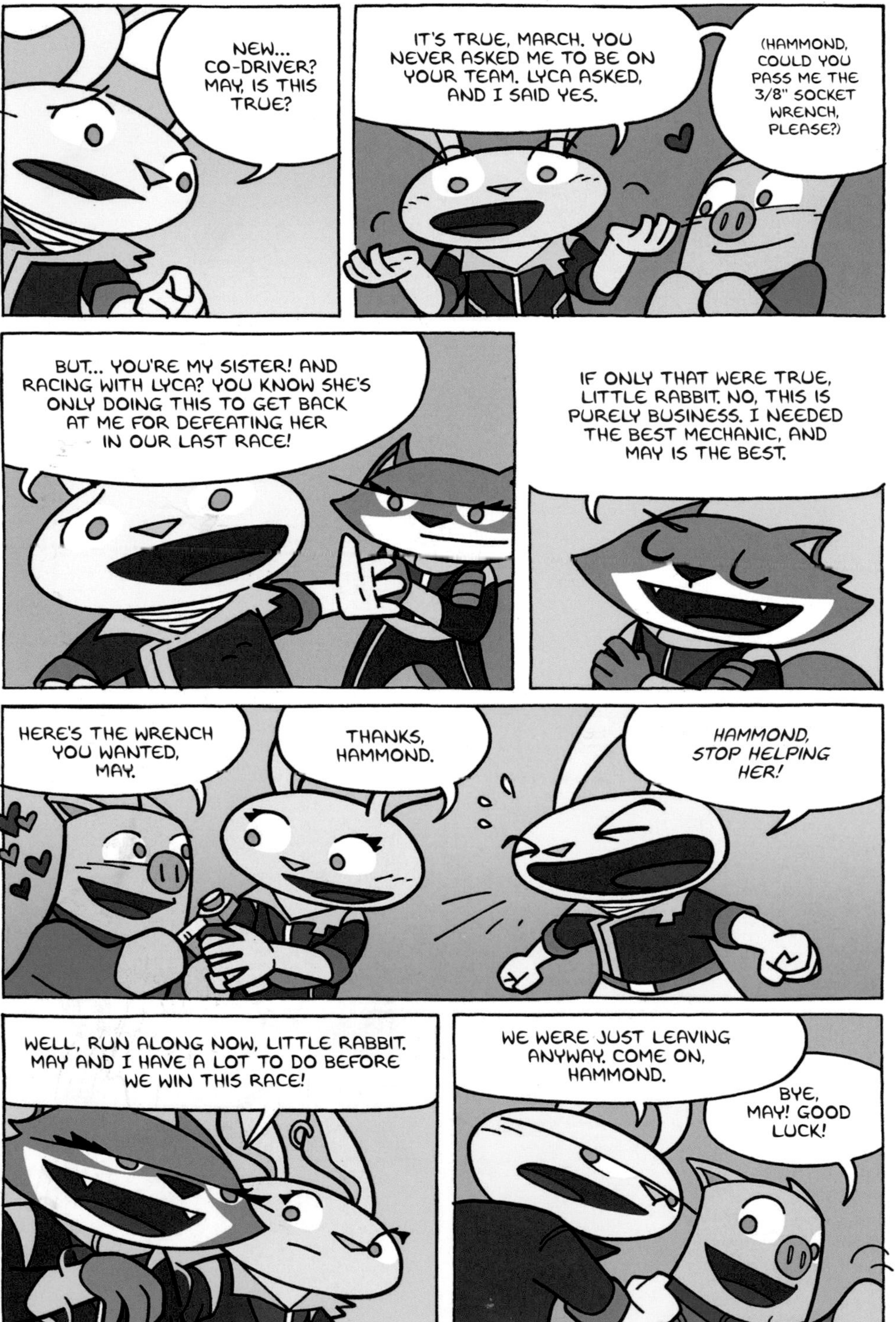
NEW... CO-DRIVER? MAY, IS THIS TRUE?
IT'S TRUE, MARCH. YOU NEVER ASKED ME TO BE ON YOUR TEAM. LYCA ASKED, AND I SAID YES.
(HAMMOND, COULD YOU PASS ME THE 3/8" SOCKET WRENCH, PLEASE?)
BUT... YOU'RE MY SISTER! AND RACING WITH LYCA? YOU KNOW SHE'S ONLY DOING THIS TO GET BACK AT ME FOR DEFEATING HER IN OUR LAST RACE!
IF ONLY THAT WERE TRUE, LITTLE RABBIT. NO, THIS IS PURELY BUSINESS. I NEEDED THE BEST MECHANIC, AND MAY IS THE BEST.
HERE'S THE WRENCH YOU WANTED, MAY.
THANKS, HAMMOND.
HAMMOND, STOP HELPING HER!
WELL, RUN ALONG NOW, LITTLE RABBIT. MAY AND I HAVE A LOT TO DO BEFORE WE WIN THIS RACE!
WE WERE JUST LEAVING ANYWAY. COME ON, HAMMOND.
BYE, MAY! GOOD LUCK!

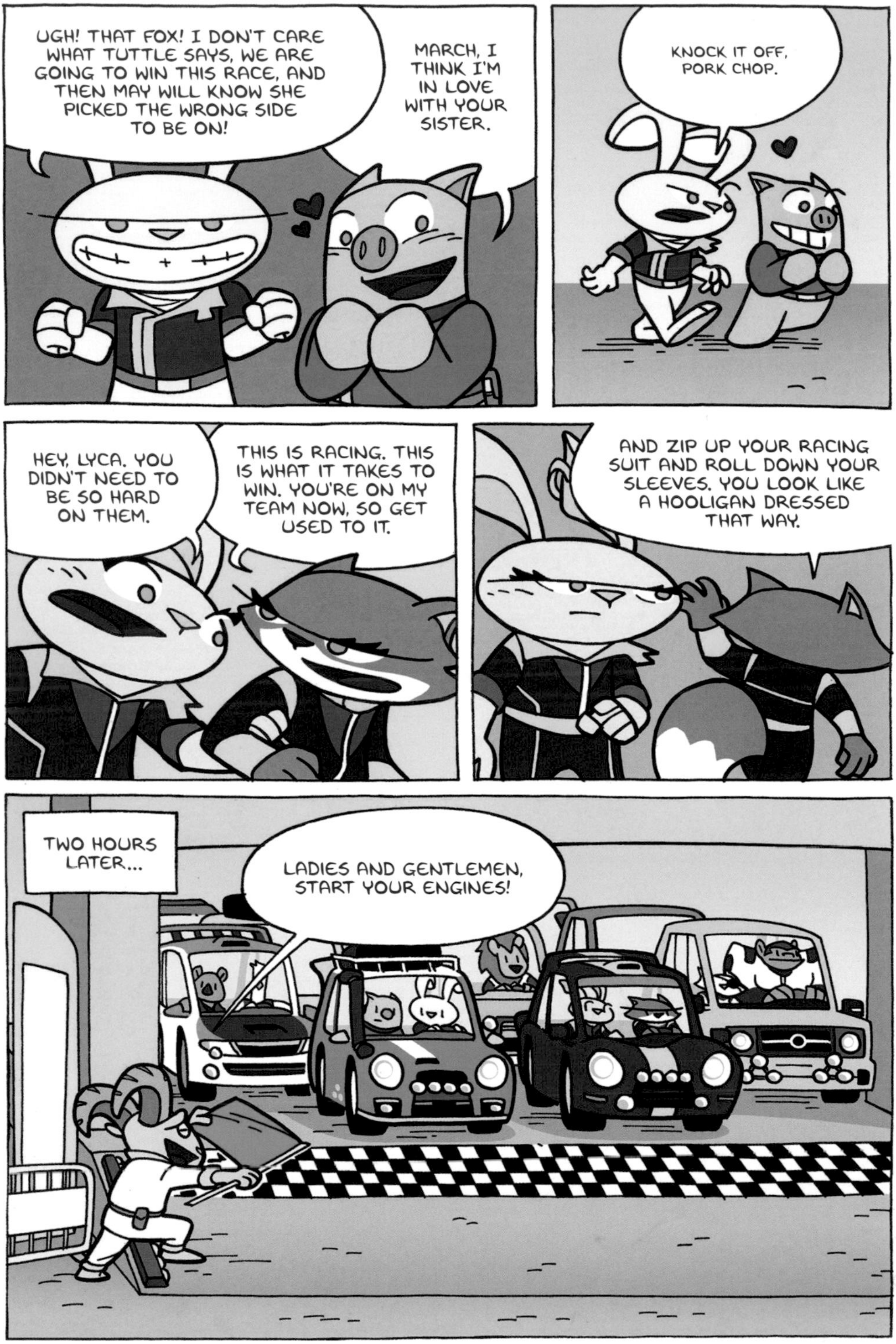
UGH! THAT FOX! I DON'T CARE WHAT TUTTLE SAYS, WE ARE GOING TO WIN THIS RACE, AND THEN MAY WILL KNOW SHE PICKED THE WRONG SIDE TO BE ON!
MARCH, I THINK I'M IN LOVE WITH YOUR SISTER.
KNOCK IT OFF, PORK CHOP.
HEY, LYCA. YOU DIDN'T NEED TO BE SO HARD ON THEM.
THIS IS RACING. THIS IS WHAT IT TAKES TO WIN. YOU'RE ON MY TEAM NOW, SO GET USED TO IT.
AND ZIP UP YOUR RACING SUIT AND ROLL DOWN YOUR SLEEVES. YOU LOOK LIKE A HOOLIGAN DRESSED THAT WAY.
TWO HOURS LATER...
LADIES AND GENTLEMEN, START YOUR ENGINES!

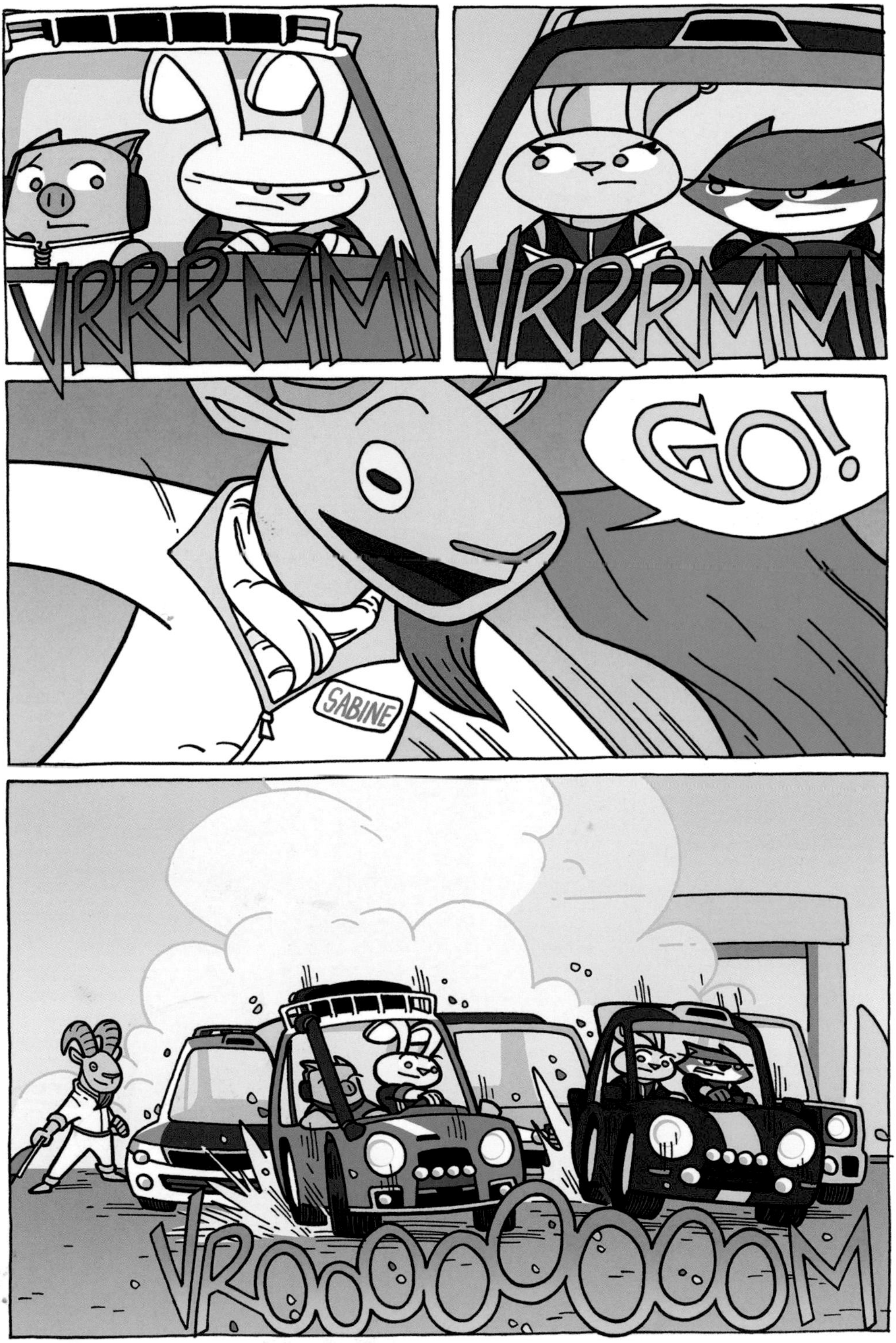
VRRRMMM
VRRRMMM
GO!
SABINE
VROOOOOOOOM

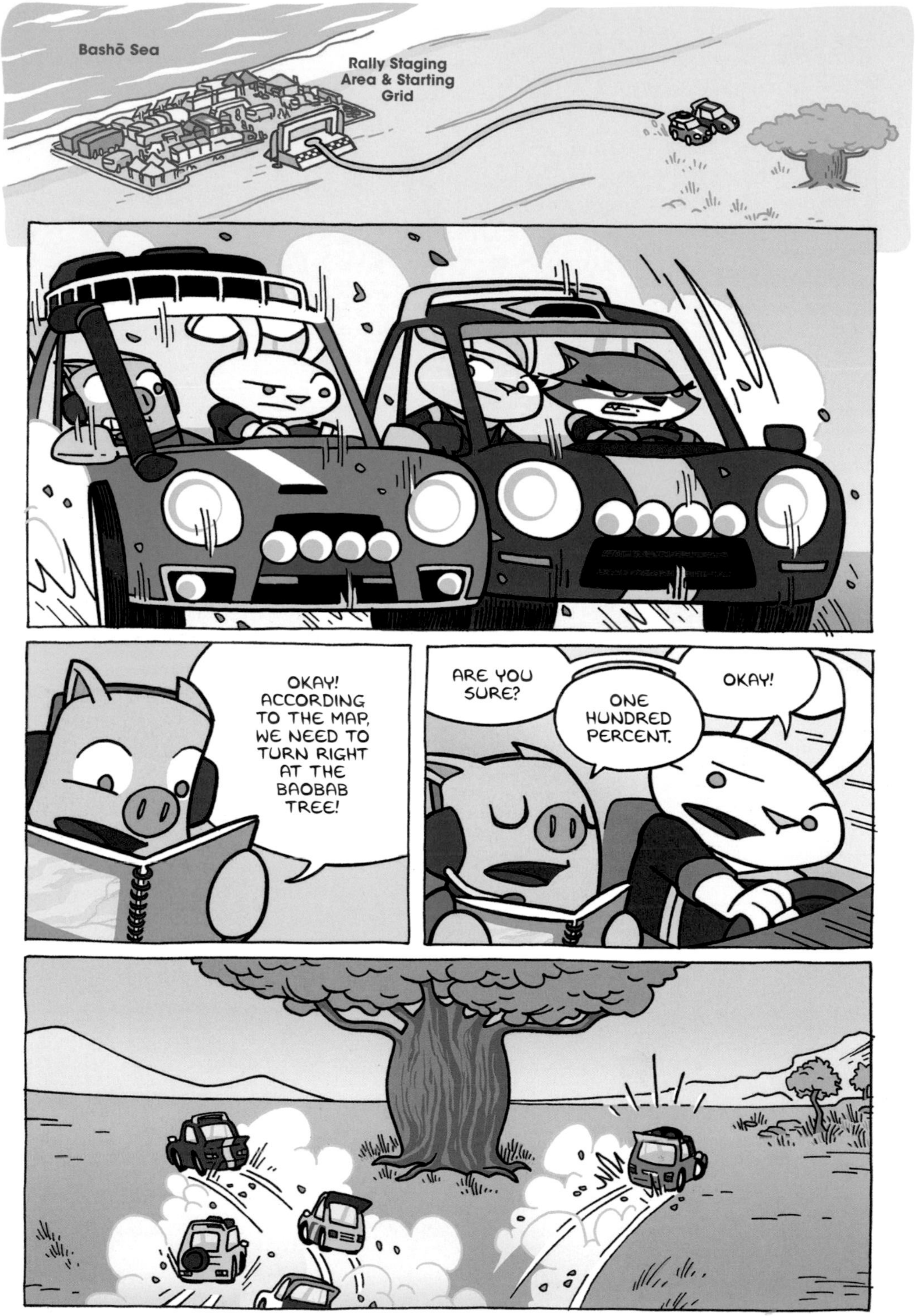
Bashō Sea
Rally Staging Area & Starting Grid
OKAY! ACCORDING TO THE MAP, WE NEED TO TURN RIGHT AT THE BAOBAB TREE!
ARE YOU SURE?
ONE HUNDRED PERCENT.
OKAY!

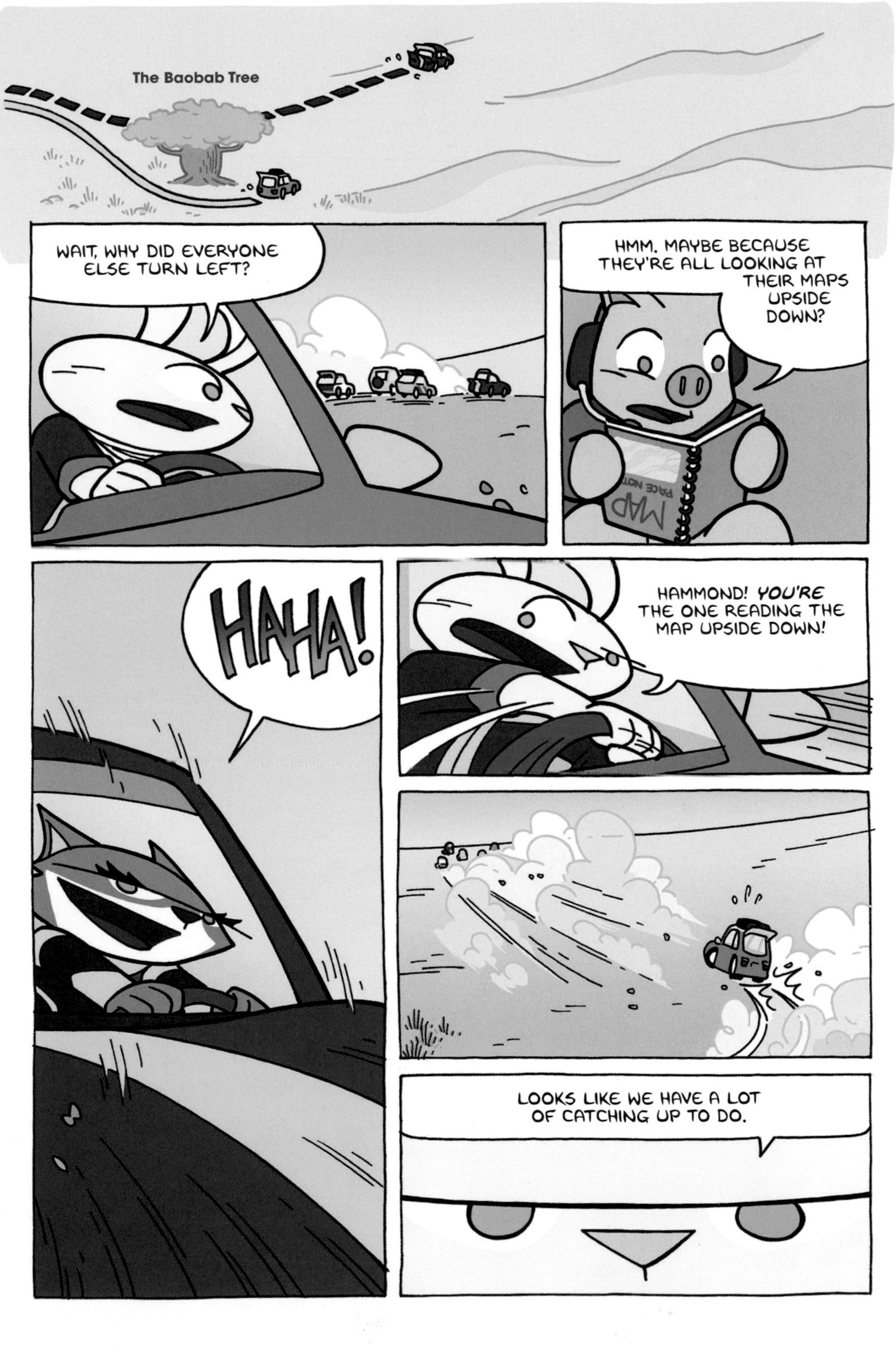
The Baobab Tree
WAIT, WHY DID EVERYONE ELSE TURN LEFT?
HMM. MAYBE BECAUSE THEY'RE ALL LOOKING AT THEIR MAPS UPSIDE DOWN?
MAP
PACE NOT
HAHA!
HAMMOND! *YOU'RE* THE ONE READING THE MAP UPSIDE DOWN!
LOOKS LIKE WE HAVE A LOT OF CATCHING UP TO DO.

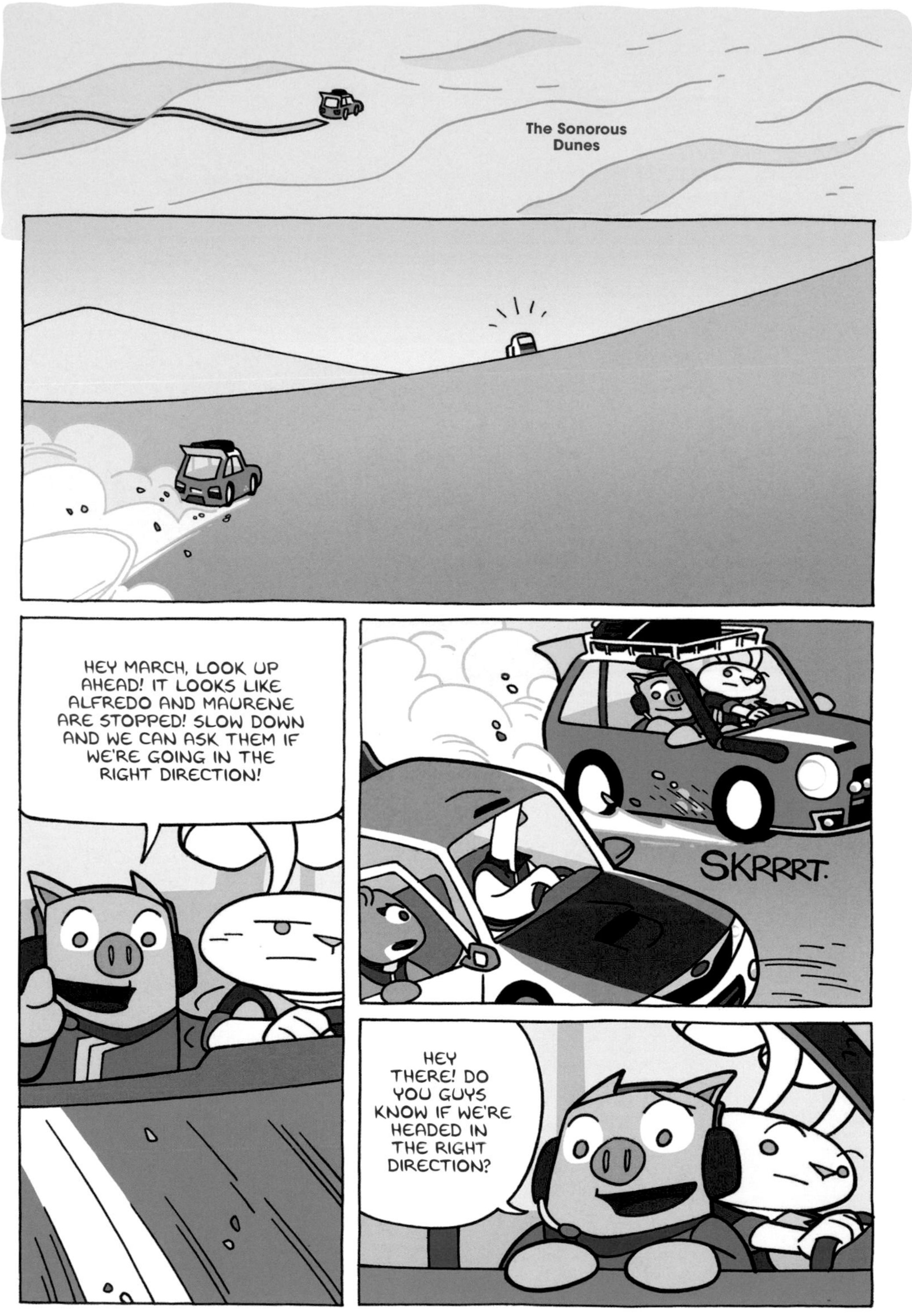
The Sonorous Dunes
HEY MARCH, LOOK UP AHEAD! IT LOOKS LIKE ALFREDO AND MAURENE ARE STOPPED! SLOW DOWN AND WE CAN ASK THEM IF WE'RE GOING IN THE RIGHT DIRECTION!
SKRRRT.
HEY THERE! DO YOU GUYS KNOW IF WE'RE HEADED IN THE RIGHT DIRECTION?

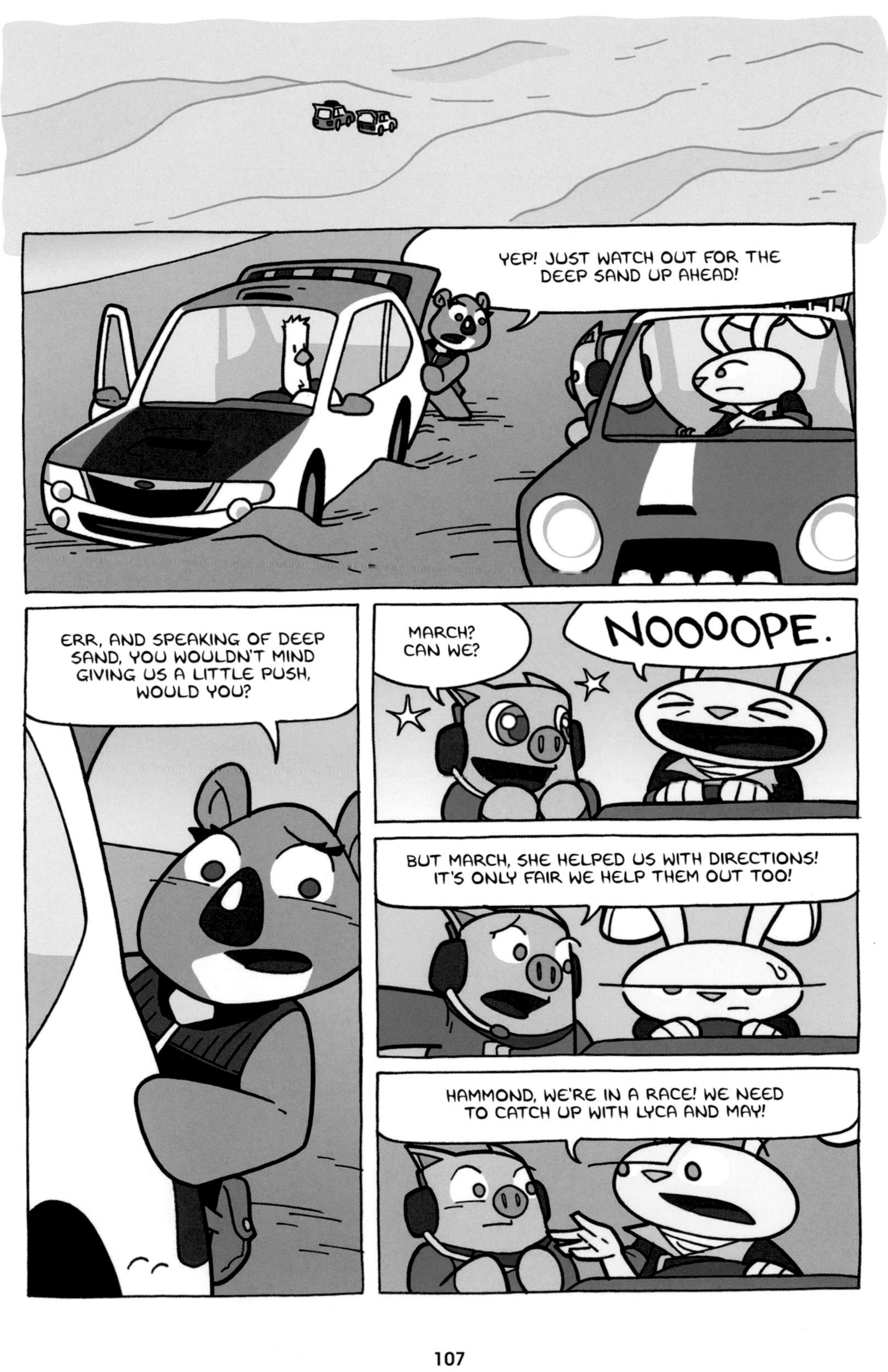
YEP! JUST WATCH OUT FOR THE DEEP SAND UP AHEAD!
ERR, AND SPEAKING OF DEEP SAND, YOU WOULDN'T MIND GIVING US A LITTLE PUSH, WOULD YOU?
MARCH? CAN WE?
NOOOOPE.
BUT MARCH, SHE HELPED US WITH DIRECTIONS! IT'S ONLY FAIR WE HELP THEM OUT TOO!
HAMMOND, WE'RE IN A RACE! WE NEED TO CATCH UP WITH LYCA AND MAY!

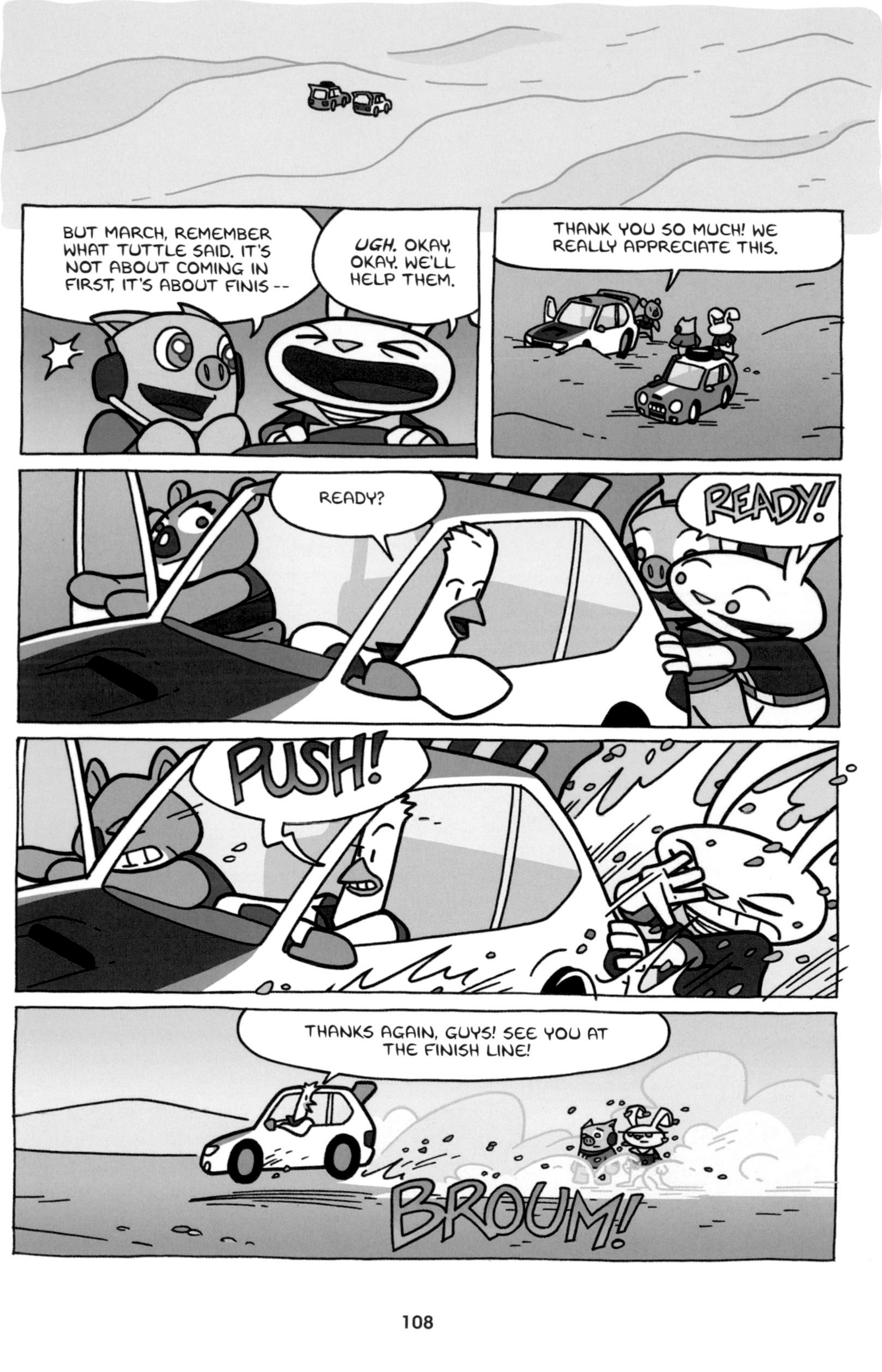
BUT MARCH, REMEMBER WHAT TUTTLE SAID. IT'S NOT ABOUT COMING IN FIRST, IT'S ABOUT FINIS --
UGH. OKAY, OKAY. WE'LL HELP THEM.
THANK YOU SO MUCH! WE REALLY APPRECIATE THIS.
READY?
READY!
PUSH!
THANKS AGAIN, GUYS! SEE YOU AT THE FINISH LINE!
BROUM!

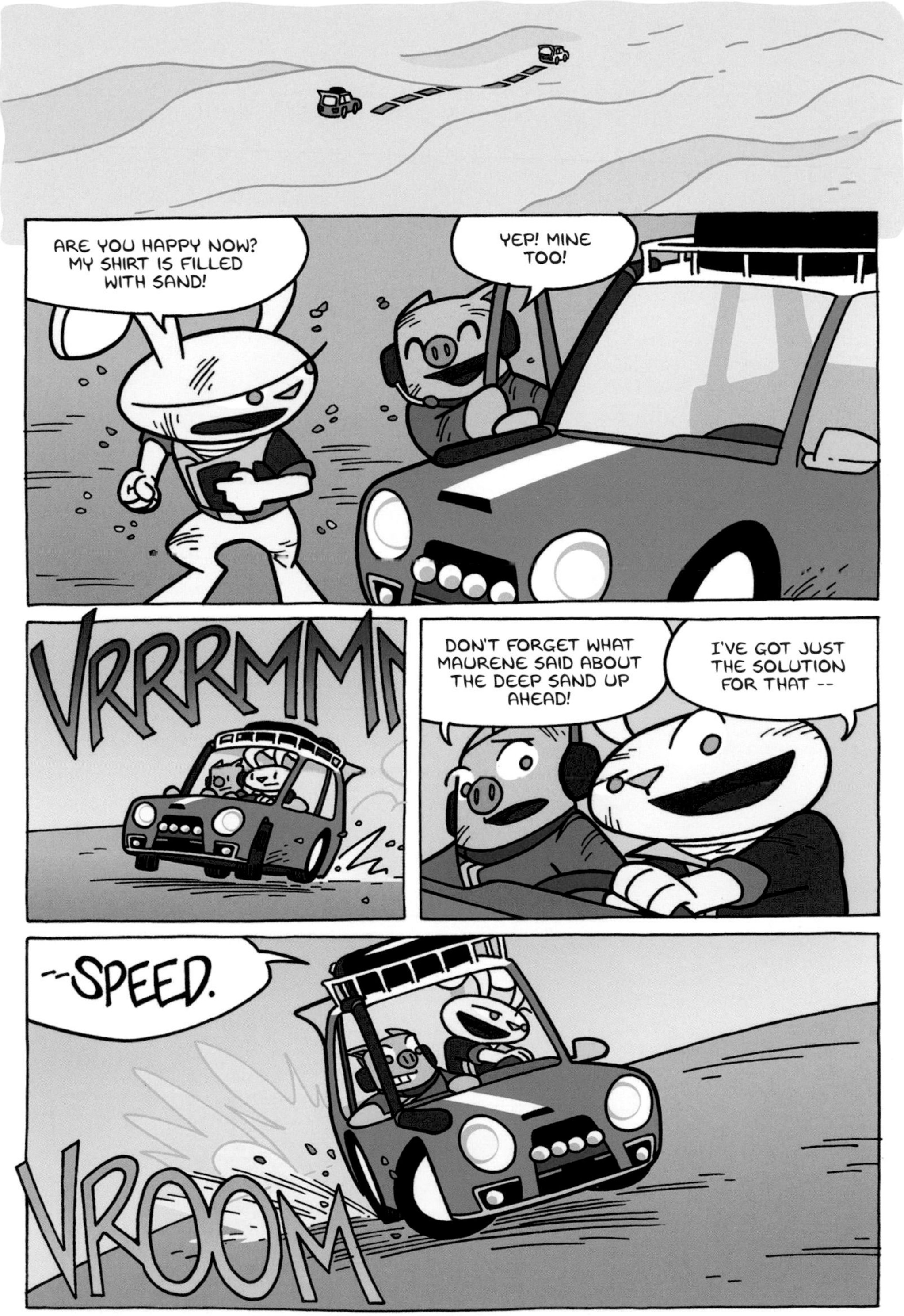
ARE YOU HAPPY NOW? MY SHIRT IS FILLED WITH SAND!
YEP! MINE TOO!
VRRRMMM
DON'T FORGET WHAT MAURENE SAID ABOUT THE DEEP SAND UP AHEAD!
I'VE GOT JUST THE SOLUTION FOR THAT --
--SPEED.
VROOM

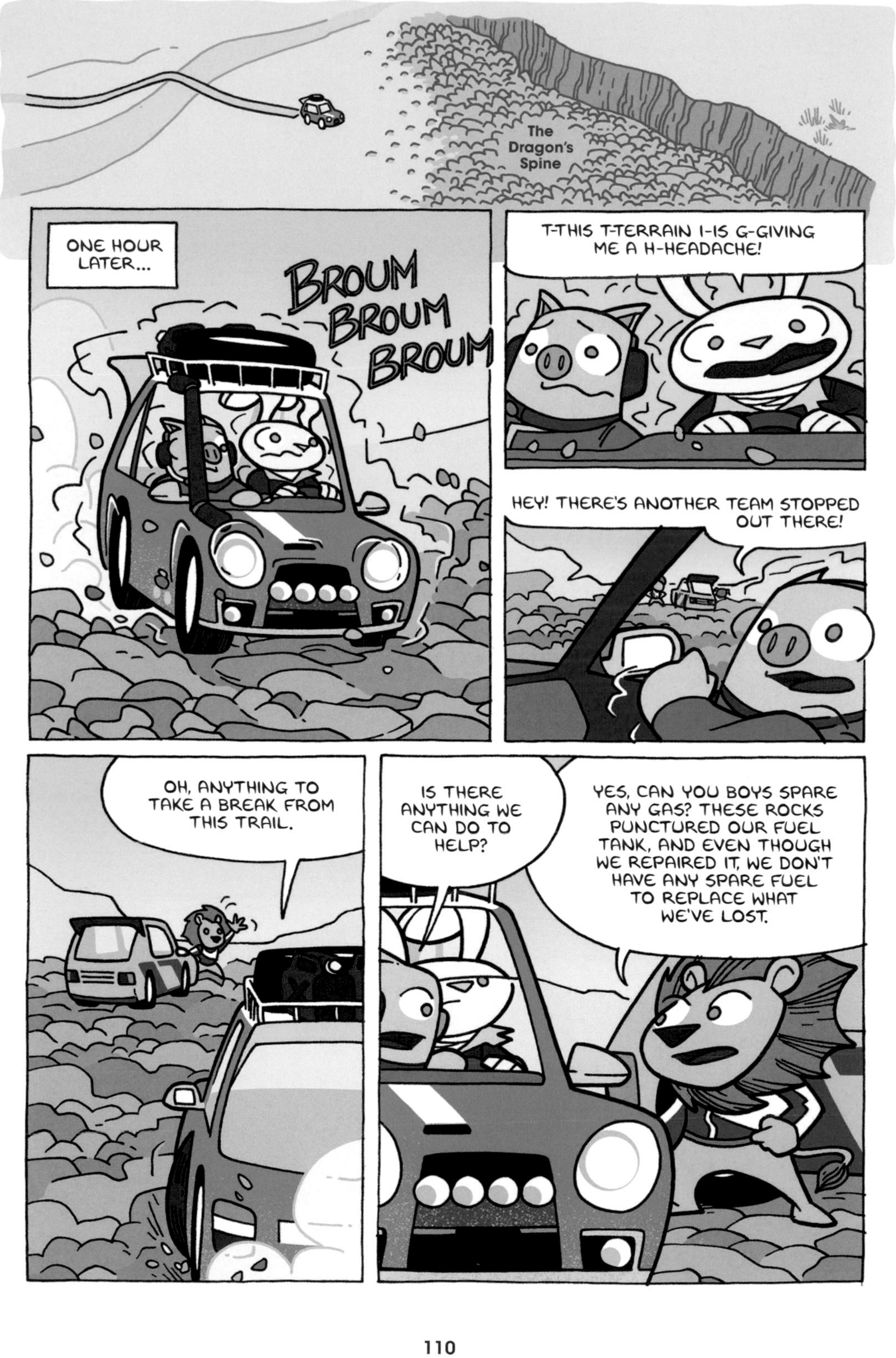
The Dragon's Spine
ONE HOUR LATER...
BROUM BROUM BROUM
T-THIS T-TERRAIN I-IS G-GIVING ME A H-HEADACHE!
HEY! THERE'S ANOTHER TEAM STOPPED OUT THERE!
OH, ANYTHING TO TAKE A BREAK FROM THIS TRAIL.
IS THERE ANYTHING WE CAN DO TO HELP?
YES, CAN YOU BOYS SPARE ANY GAS? THESE ROCKS PUNCTURED OUR FUEL TANK, AND EVEN THOUGH WE REPAIRED IT, WE DON'T HAVE ANY SPARE FUEL TO REPLACE WHAT WE'VE LOST.

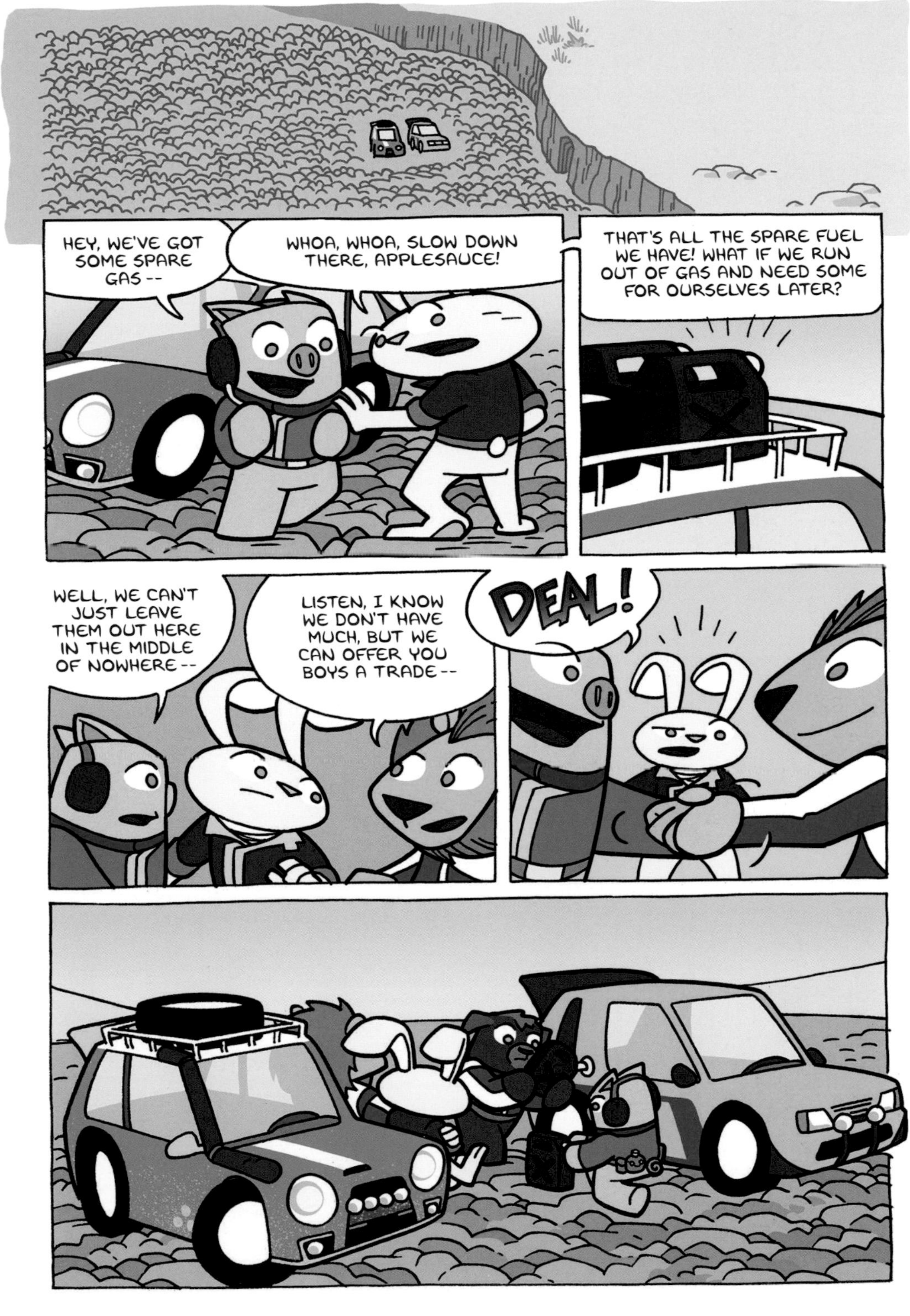
HEY, WE'VE GOT SOME SPARE GAS --
WHOA, WHOA, SLOW DOWN THERE, APPLESAUCE!
THAT'S ALL THE SPARE FUEL WE HAVE! WHAT IF WE RUN OUT OF GAS AND NEED SOME FOR OURSELVES LATER?
WELL, WE CAN'T JUST LEAVE THEM OUT HERE IN THE MIDDLE OF NOWHERE --
LISTEN, I KNOW WE DON'T HAVE MUCH, BUT WE CAN OFFER YOU BOYS A TRADE --
DEAL!

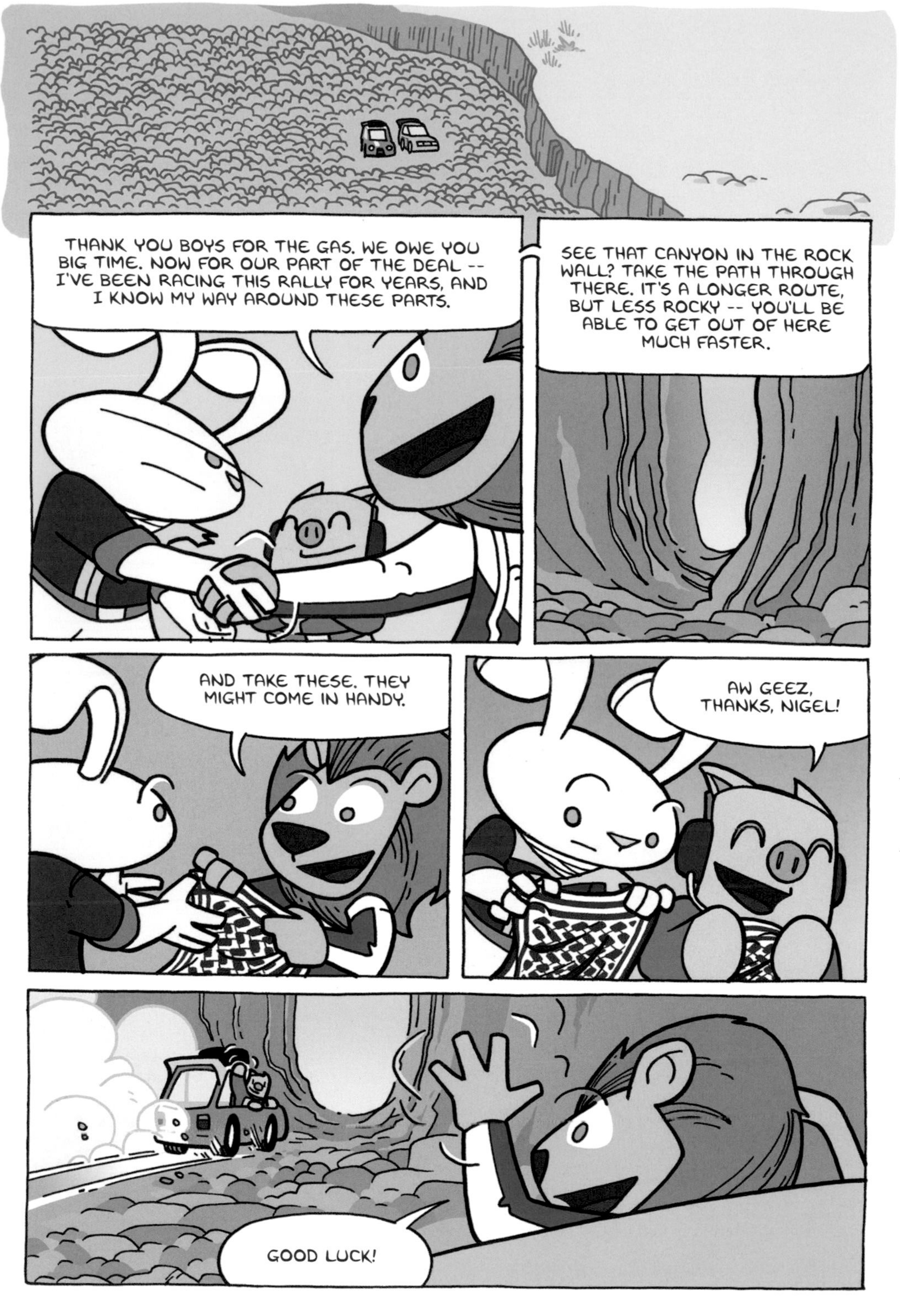
THANK YOU BOYS FOR THE GAS. WE OWE YOU BIG TIME. NOW FOR OUR PART OF THE DEAL -- I'VE BEEN RACING THIS RALLY FOR YEARS, AND I KNOW MY WAY AROUND THESE PARTS.
SEE THAT CANYON IN THE ROCK WALL? TAKE THE PATH THROUGH THERE. IT'S A LONGER ROUTE, BUT LESS ROCKY -- YOU'LL BE ABLE TO GET OUT OF HERE MUCH FASTER.
AND TAKE THESE. THEY MIGHT COME IN HANDY.
AW GEEZ, THANKS, NIGEL!
GOOD LUCK!

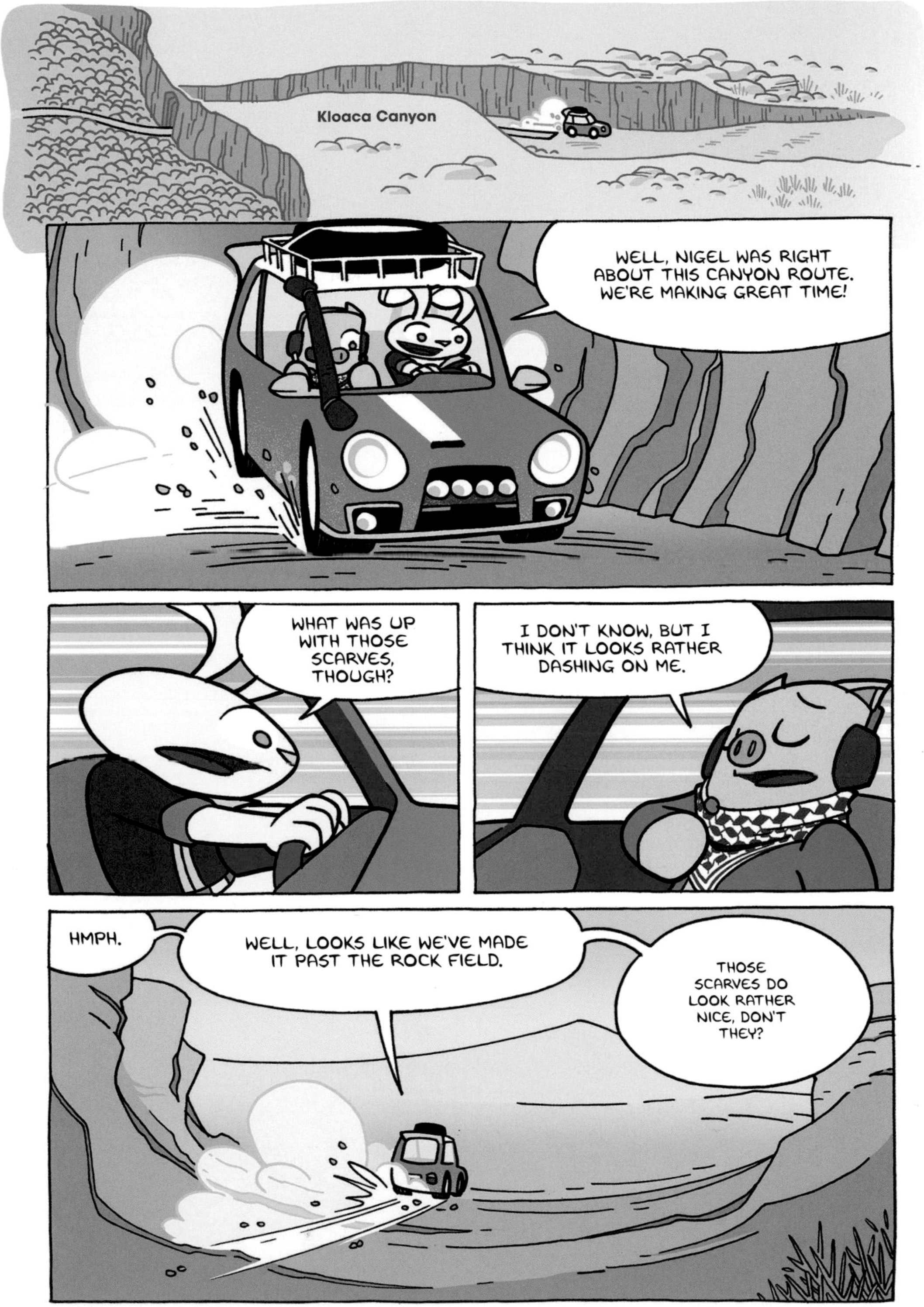
Kloaca Canyon
WELL, NIGEL WAS RIGHT ABOUT THIS CANYON ROUTE. WE'RE MAKING GREAT TIME!
WHAT WAS UP WITH THOSE SCARVES, THOUGH?
I DON'T KNOW, BUT I THINK IT LOOKS RATHER DASHING ON ME.
HMPH.
WELL, LOOKS LIKE WE'VE MADE IT PAST THE ROCK FIELD.
THOSE SCARVES DO LOOK RATHER NICE, DON'T THEY?

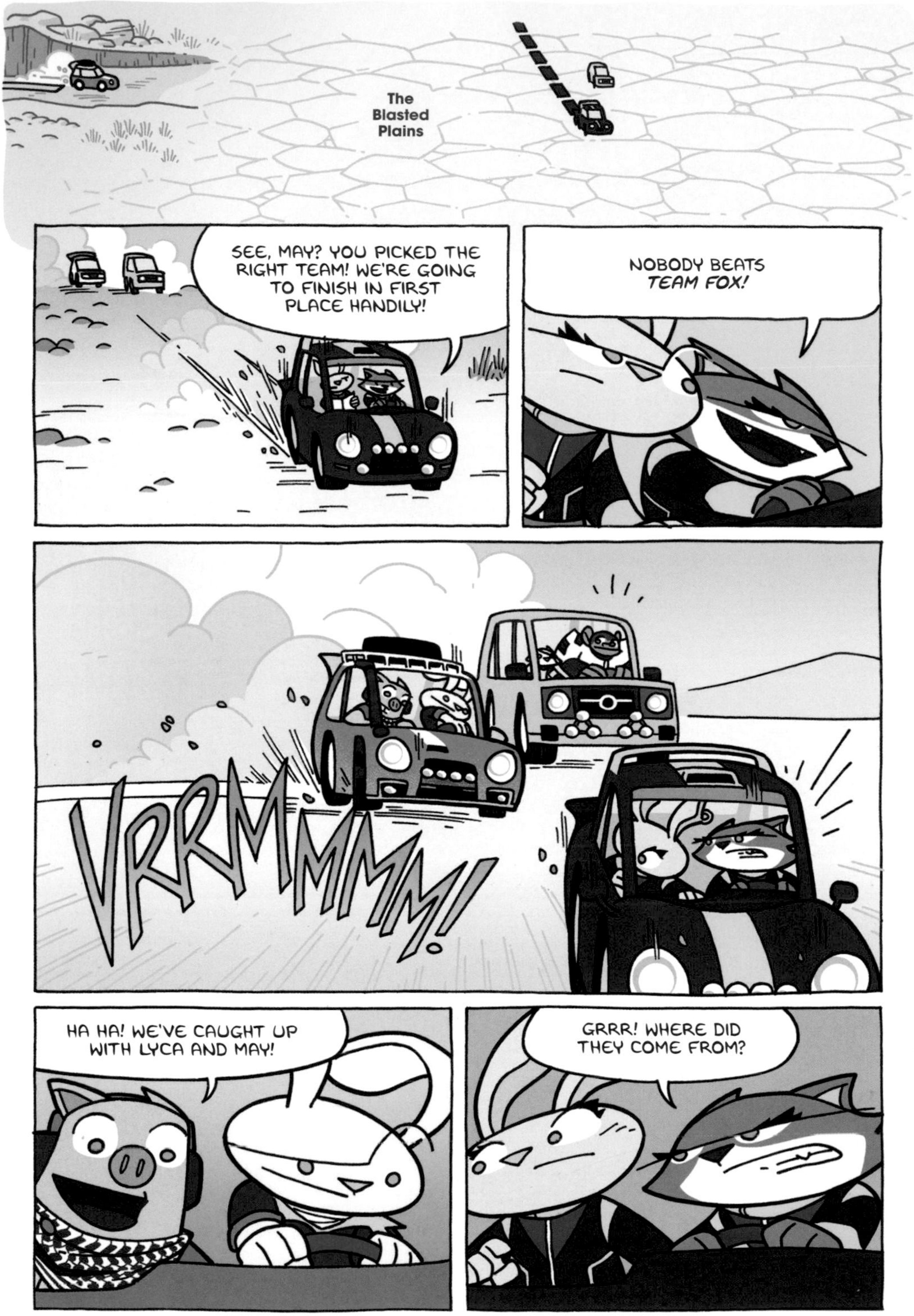
The Blasted Plains
SEE, MAY? YOU PICKED THE RIGHT TEAM! WE'RE GOING TO FINISH IN FIRST PLACE HANDILY!
NOBODY BEATS *TEAM FOX!*
VRRMMMM!
HA HA! WE'VE CAUGHT UP WITH LYCA AND MAY!
GRRR! WHERE DID THEY COME FROM?

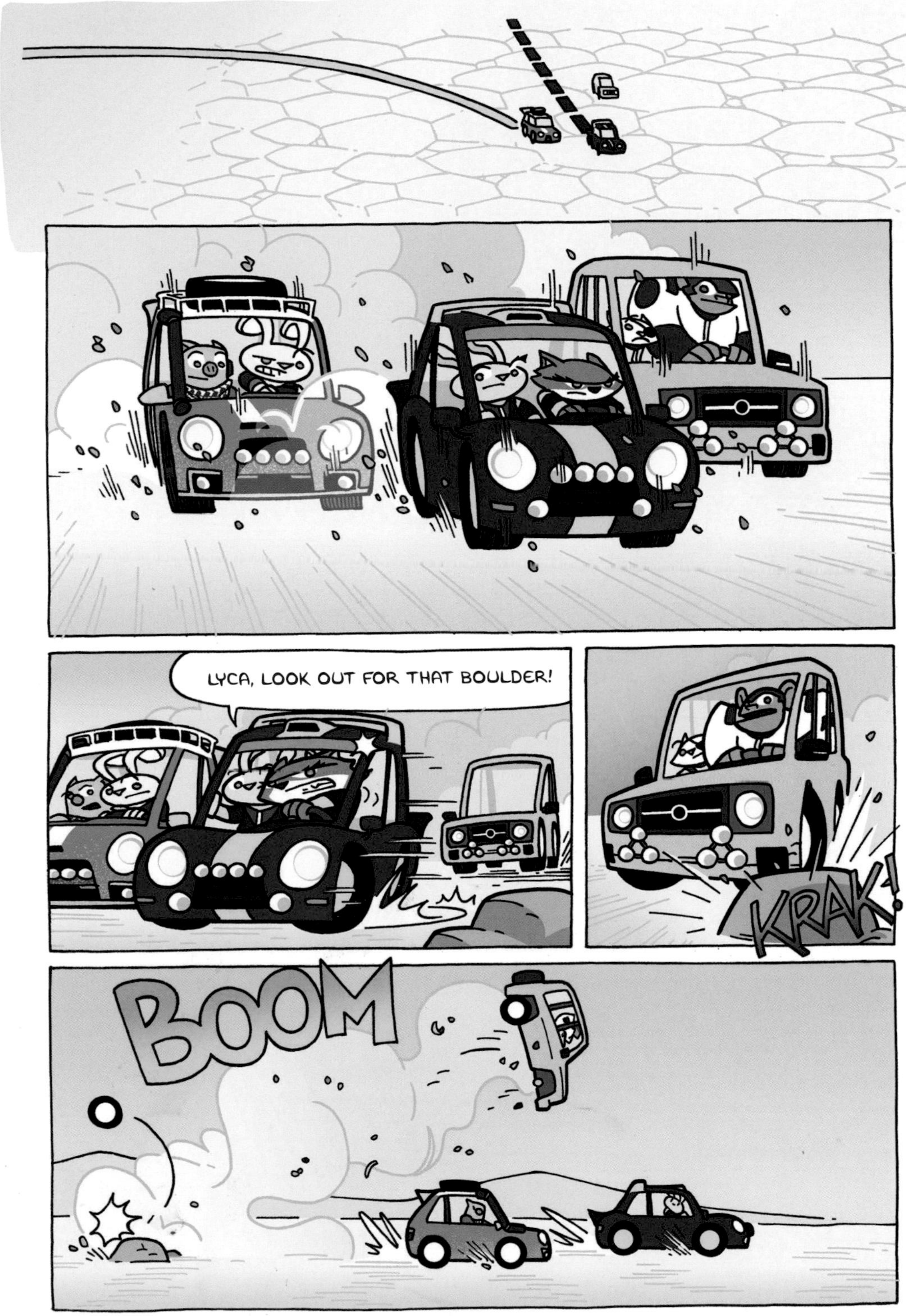
LYCA, LOOK OUT FOR THAT BOULDER!
KRAK!
BOOM

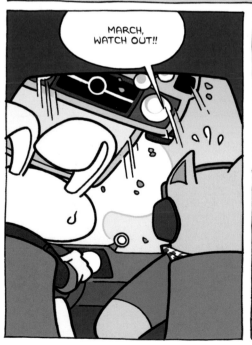

MARCH, WATCH OUT!!

BRAKE!

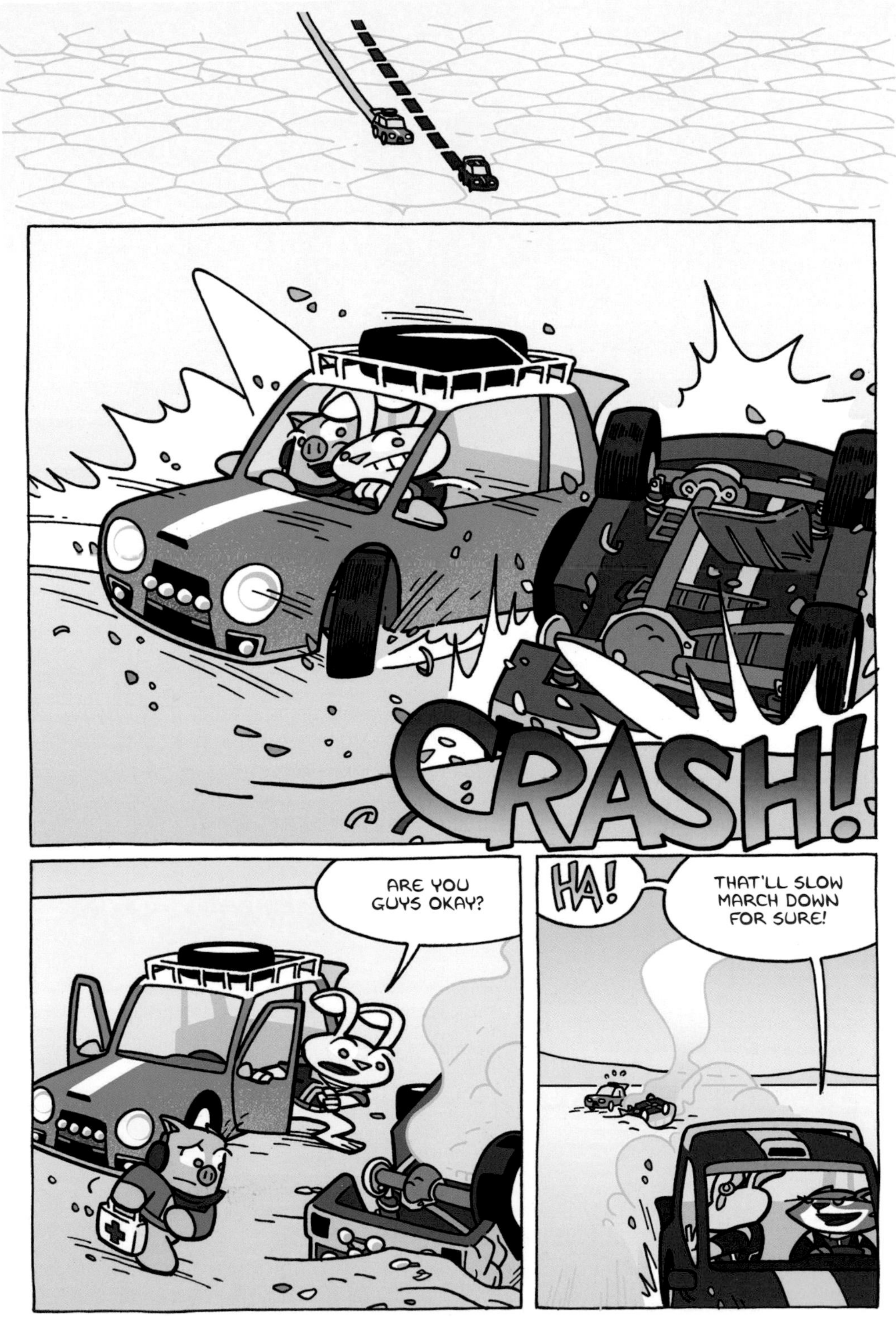
CRASH!
ARE YOU GUYS OKAY?
HA!
THAT'LL SLOW MARCH DOWN FOR SURE!

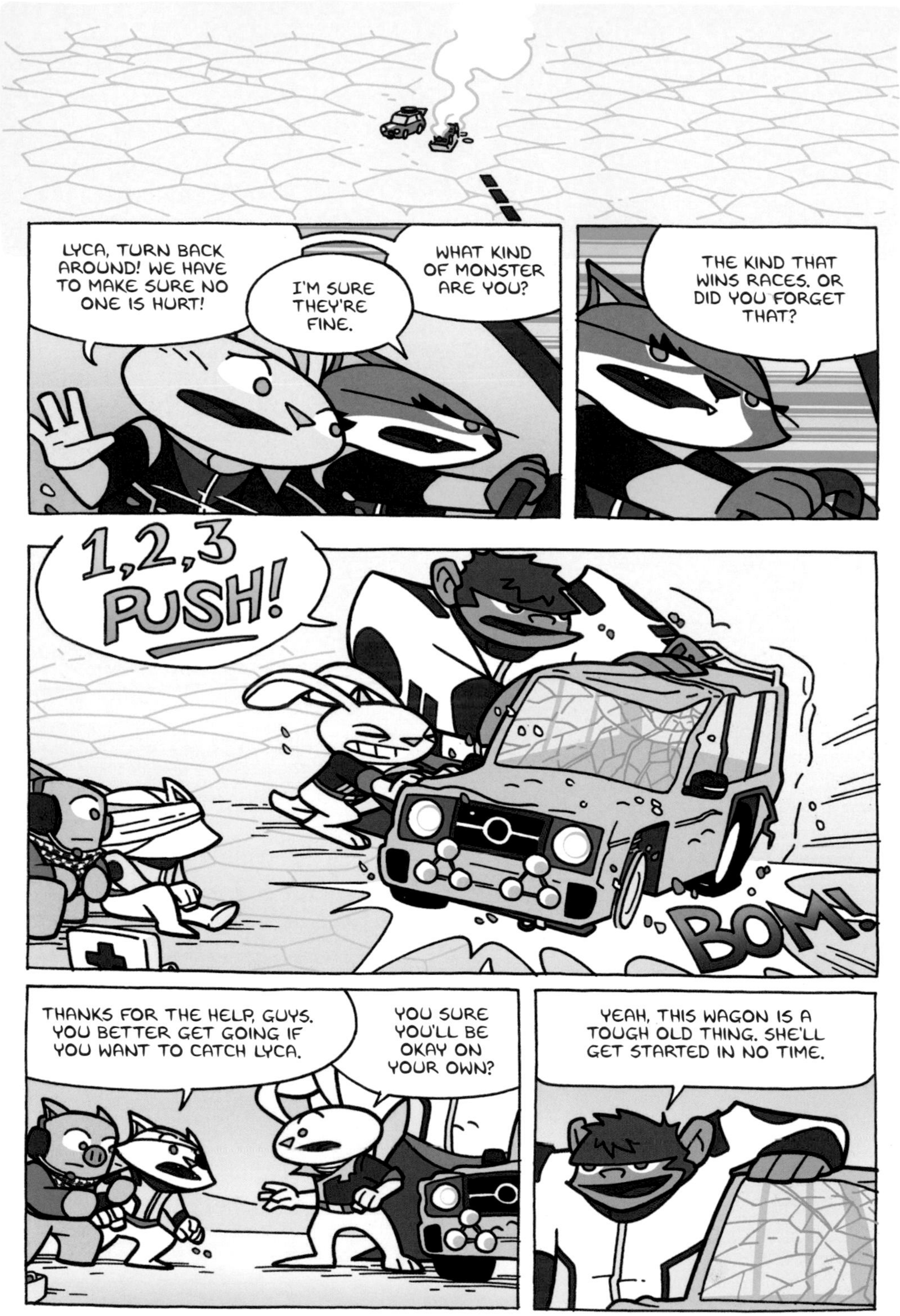

LYCA, TURN BACK AROUND! WE HAVE TO MAKE SURE NO ONE IS HURT!
I'M SURE THEY'RE FINE.
WHAT KIND OF MONSTER ARE YOU?
THE KIND THAT WINS RACES. OR DID YOU FORGET THAT?
1,2,3 PUSH!
BOM!
THANKS FOR THE HELP, GUYS. YOU BETTER GET GOING IF YOU WANT TO CATCH LYCA.
YOU SURE YOU'LL BE OKAY ON YOUR OWN?
YEAH, THIS WAGON IS A TOUGH OLD THING. SHE'LL GET STARTED IN NO TIME.

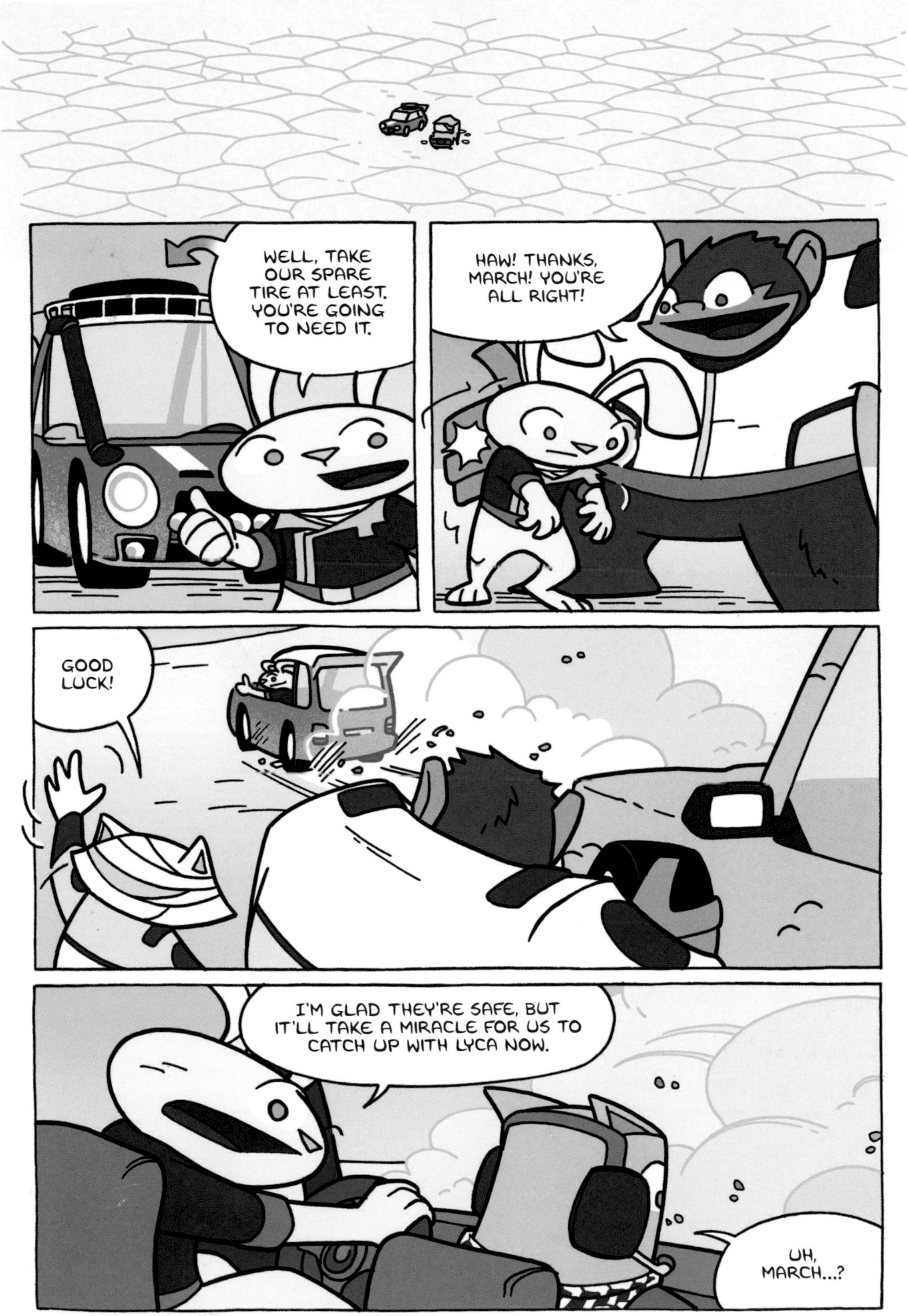
WELL, TAKE OUR SPARE TIRE AT LEAST. YOU'RE GOING TO NEED IT.
HAW! THANKS, MARCH! YOU'RE ALL RIGHT!
GOOD LUCK!
I'M GLAD THEY'RE SAFE, BUT IT'LL TAKE A MIRACLE FOR US TO CATCH UP WITH LYCA NOW.
UH, MARCH...?

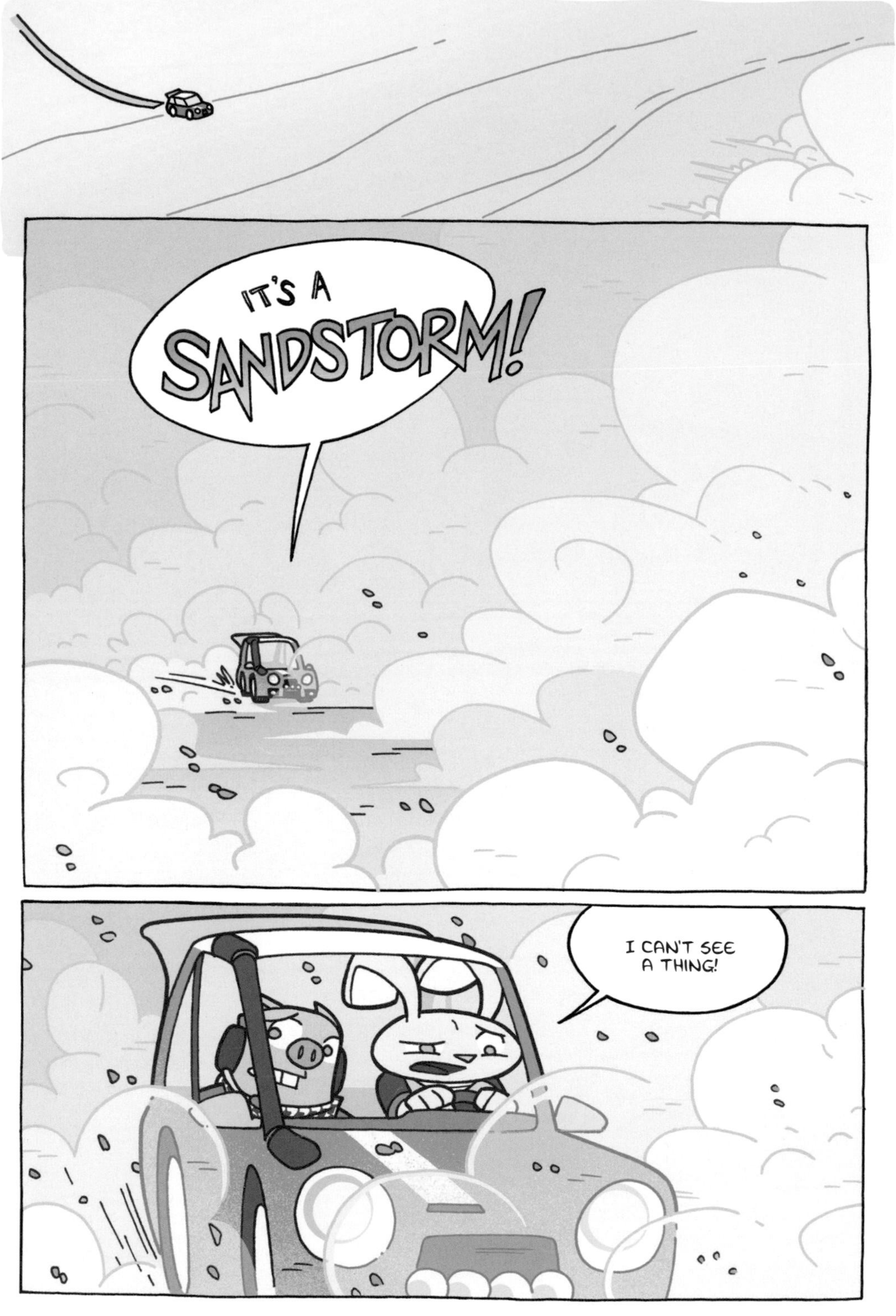
IT'S A SANDSTORM!
I CAN'T SEE A THING!

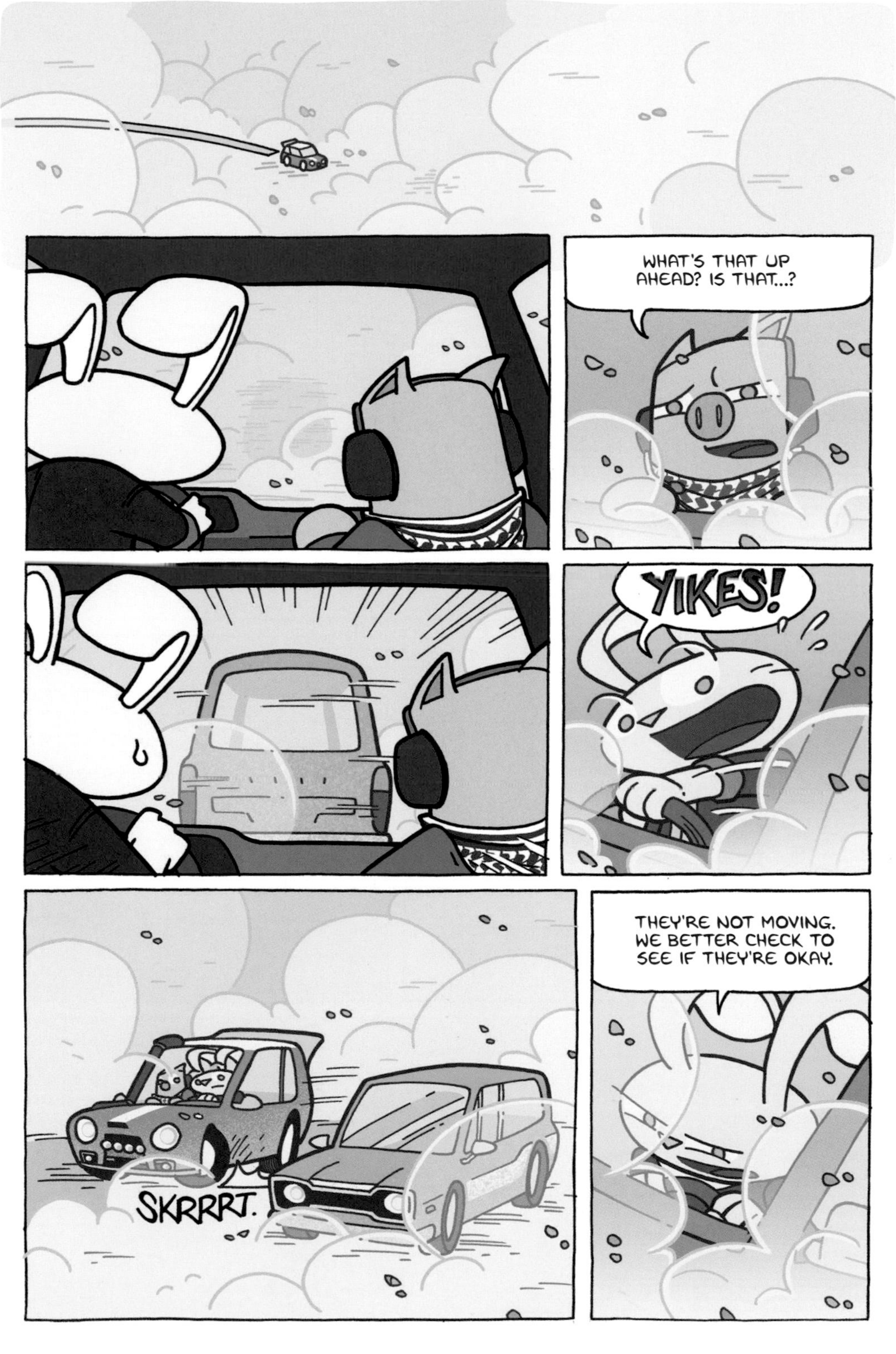
WHAT'S THAT UP AHEAD? IS THAT...?
YIKES!
SKRRRT.
THEY'RE NOT MOVING. WE BETTER CHECK TO SEE IF THEY'RE OKAY.

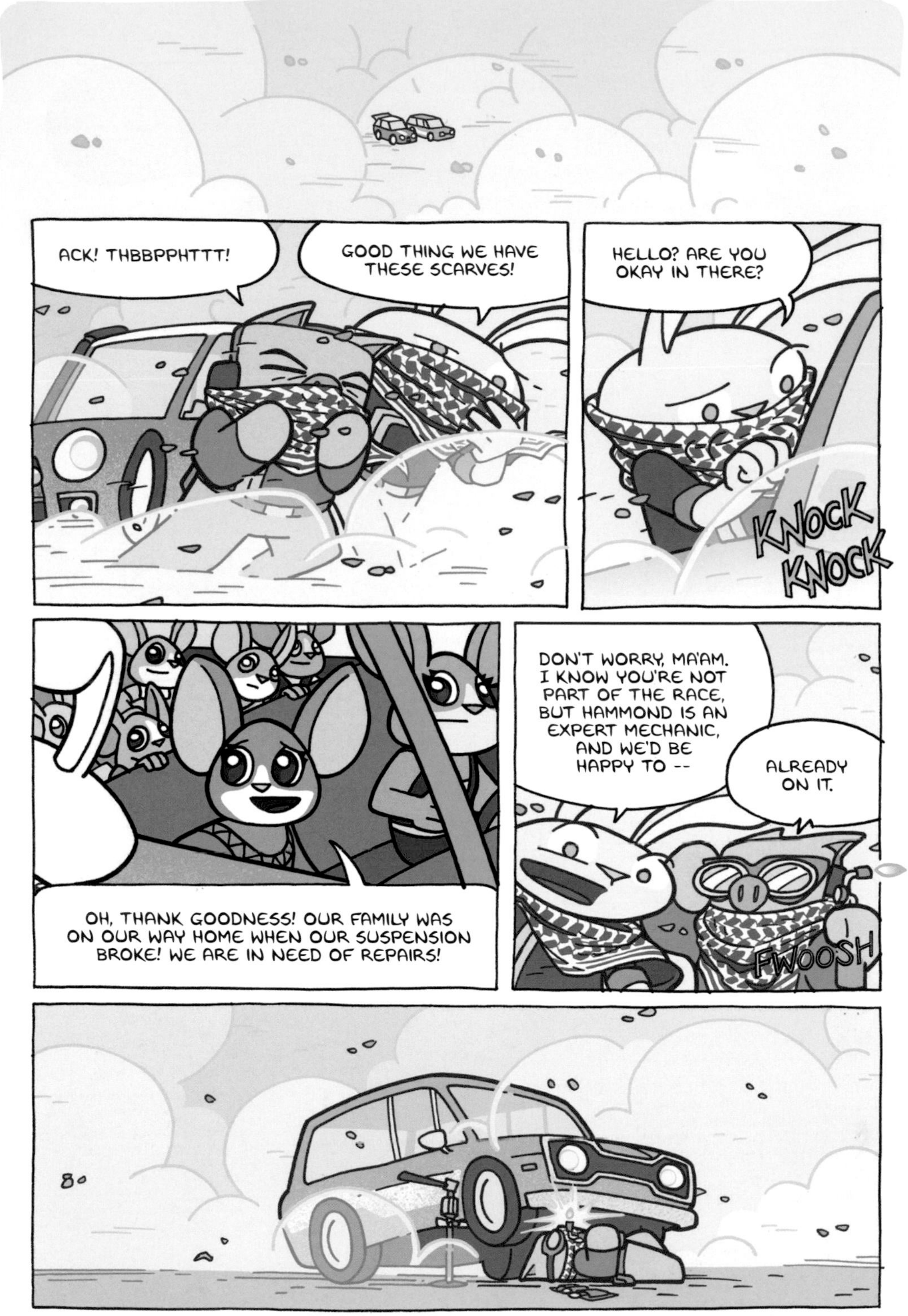
ACK! THBBPPHTTT!
GOOD THING WE HAVE THESE SCARVES!
HELLO? ARE YOU OKAY IN THERE?
KNOCK KNOCK
OH, THANK GOODNESS! OUR FAMILY WAS ON OUR WAY HOME WHEN OUR SUSPENSION BROKE! WE ARE IN NEED OF REPAIRS!
DON'T WORRY, MA'AM. I KNOW YOU'RE NOT PART OF THE RACE, BUT HAMMOND IS AN EXPERT MECHANIC, AND WE'D BE HAPPY TO --
ALREADY ON IT.
FWOOSH

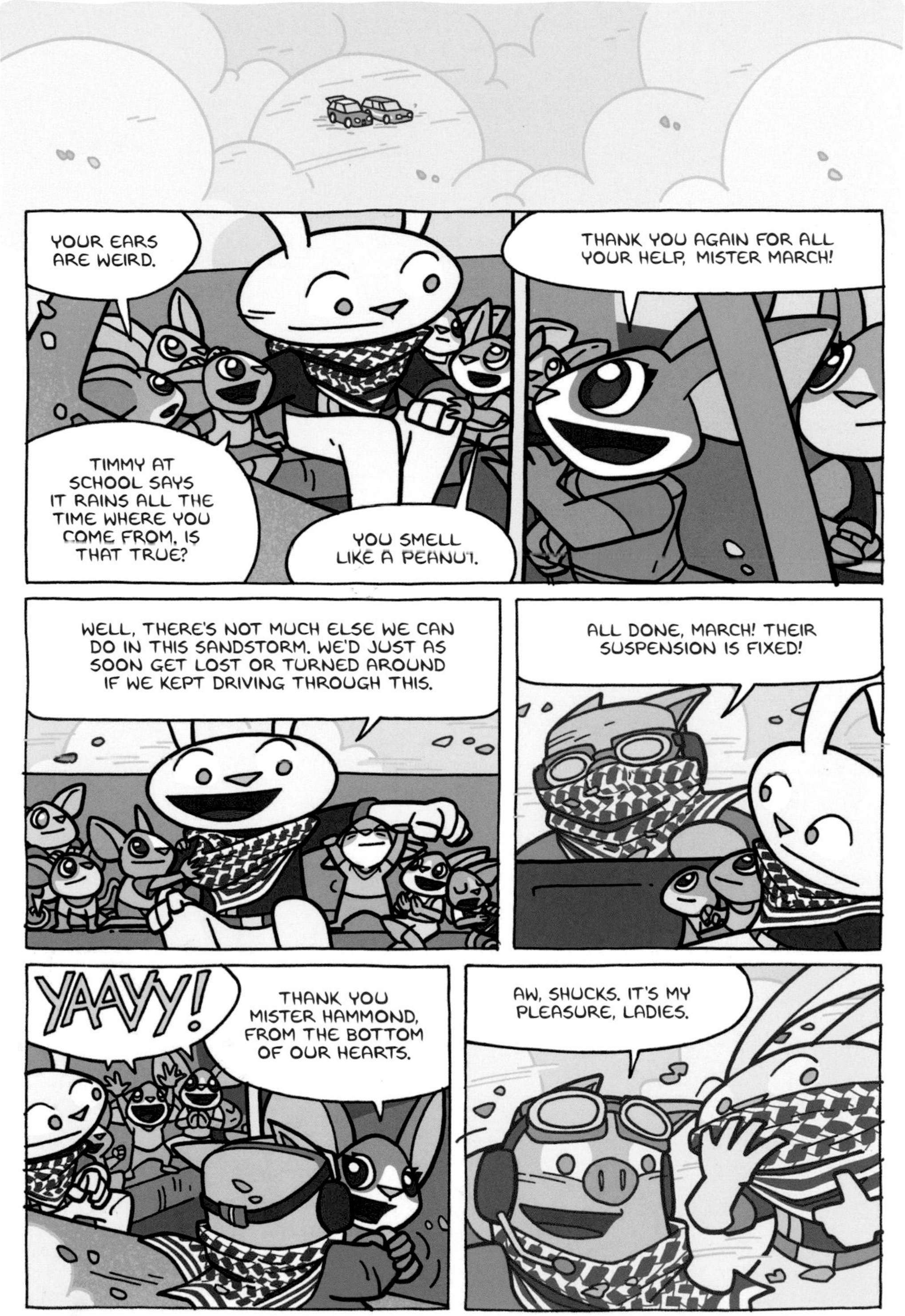
YOUR EARS ARE WEIRD.
TIMMY AT SCHOOL SAYS IT RAINS ALL THE TIME WHERE YOU COME FROM. IS THAT TRUE?
YOU SMELL LIKE A PEANUT.
THANK YOU AGAIN FOR ALL YOUR HELP, MISTER MARCH!
WELL, THERE'S NOT MUCH ELSE WE CAN DO IN THIS SANDSTORM. WE'D JUST AS SOON GET LOST OR TURNED AROUND IF WE KEPT DRIVING THROUGH THIS.
ALL DONE, MARCH! THEIR SUSPENSION IS FIXED!
YAAYY!
THANK YOU MISTER HAMMOND, FROM THE BOTTOM OF OUR HEARTS.
AW, SHUCKS. IT'S MY PLEASURE, LADIES.

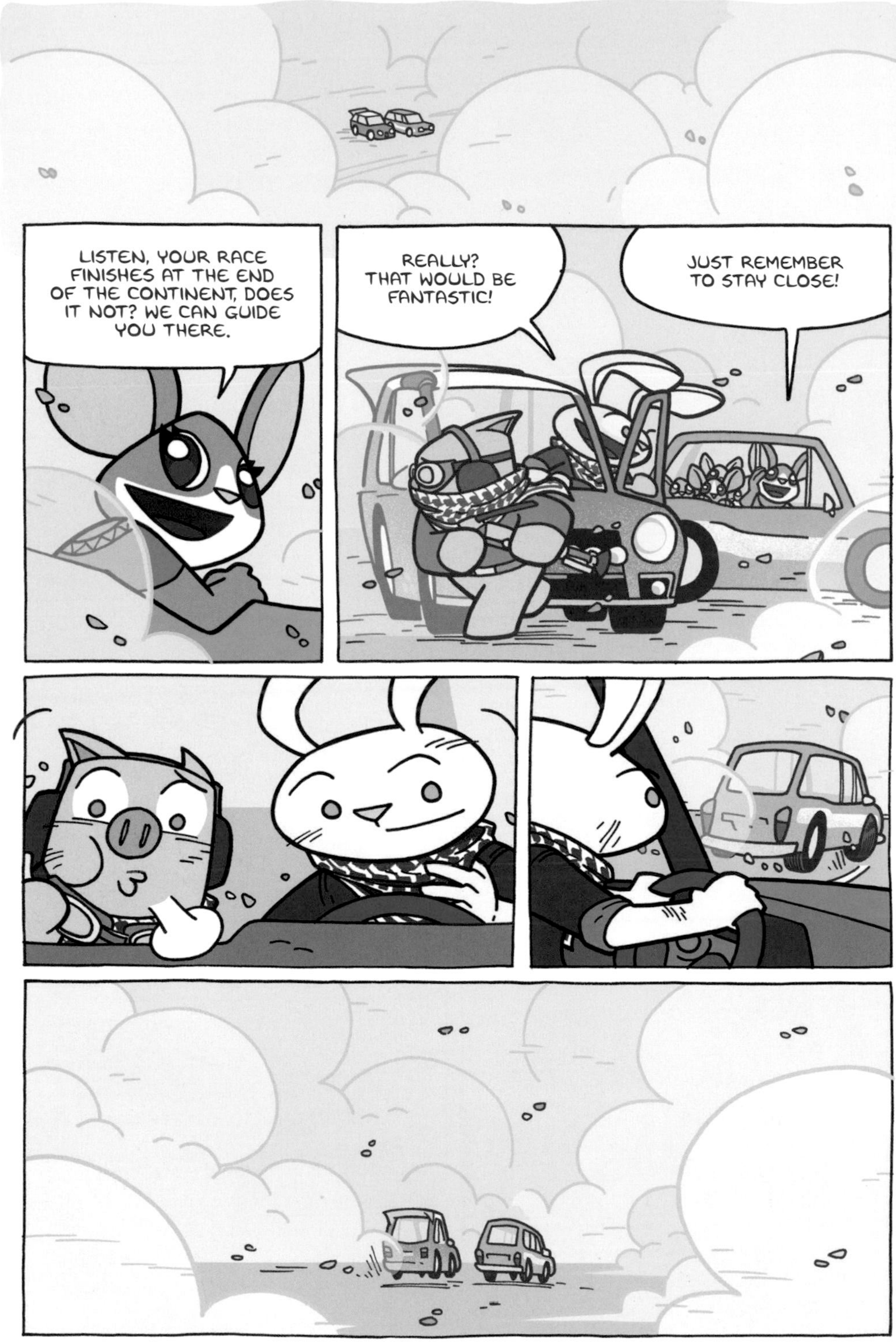
LISTEN, YOUR RACE FINISHES AT THE END OF THE CONTINENT, DOES IT NOT? WE CAN GUIDE YOU THERE.
REALLY? THAT WOULD BE FANTASTIC!
JUST REMEMBER TO STAY CLOSE!

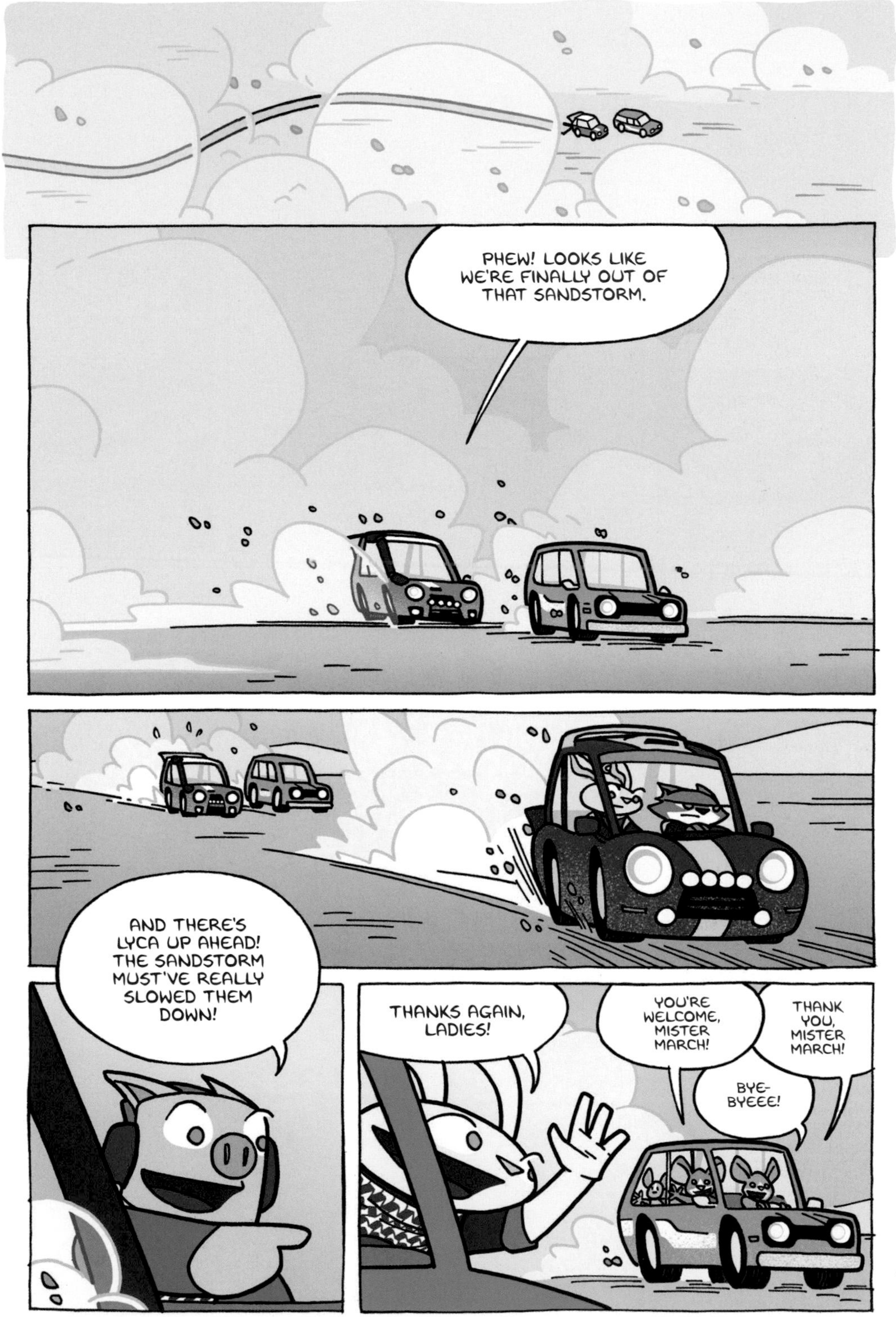

PHEW! LOOKS LIKE WE'RE FINALLY OUT OF THAT SANDSTORM.
AND THERE'S LYCA UP AHEAD! THE SANDSTORM MUST'VE REALLY SLOWED THEM DOWN!
THANKS AGAIN, LADIES!
YOU'RE WELCOME, MISTER MARCH!
THANK YOU, MISTER MARCH!
BYE-BYEEE!

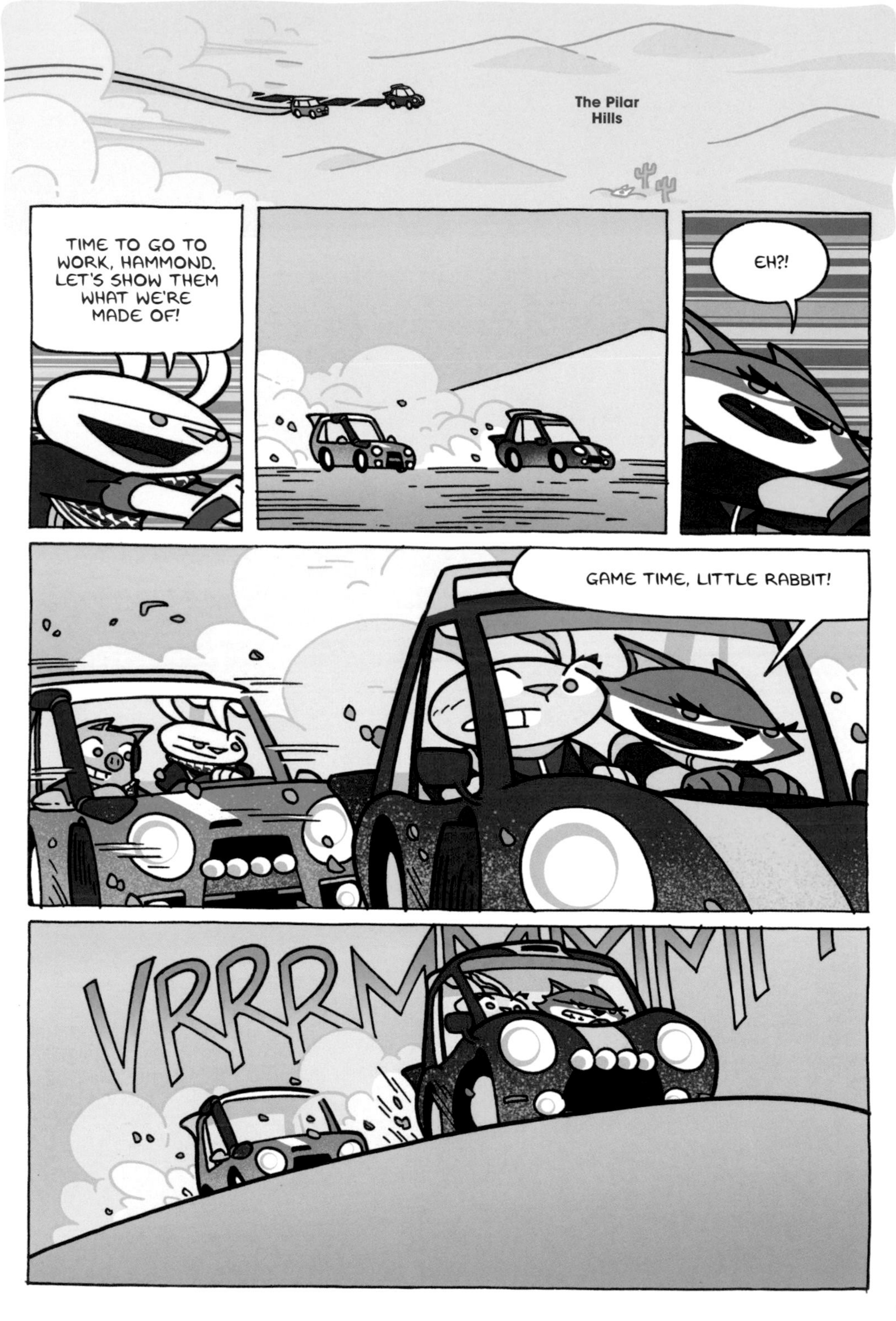
The Pilar Hills
TIME TO GO TO WORK, HAMMOND. LET'S SHOW THEM WHAT WE'RE MADE OF!
EH?!
GAME TIME, LITTLE RABBIT!
VRRRMMMM

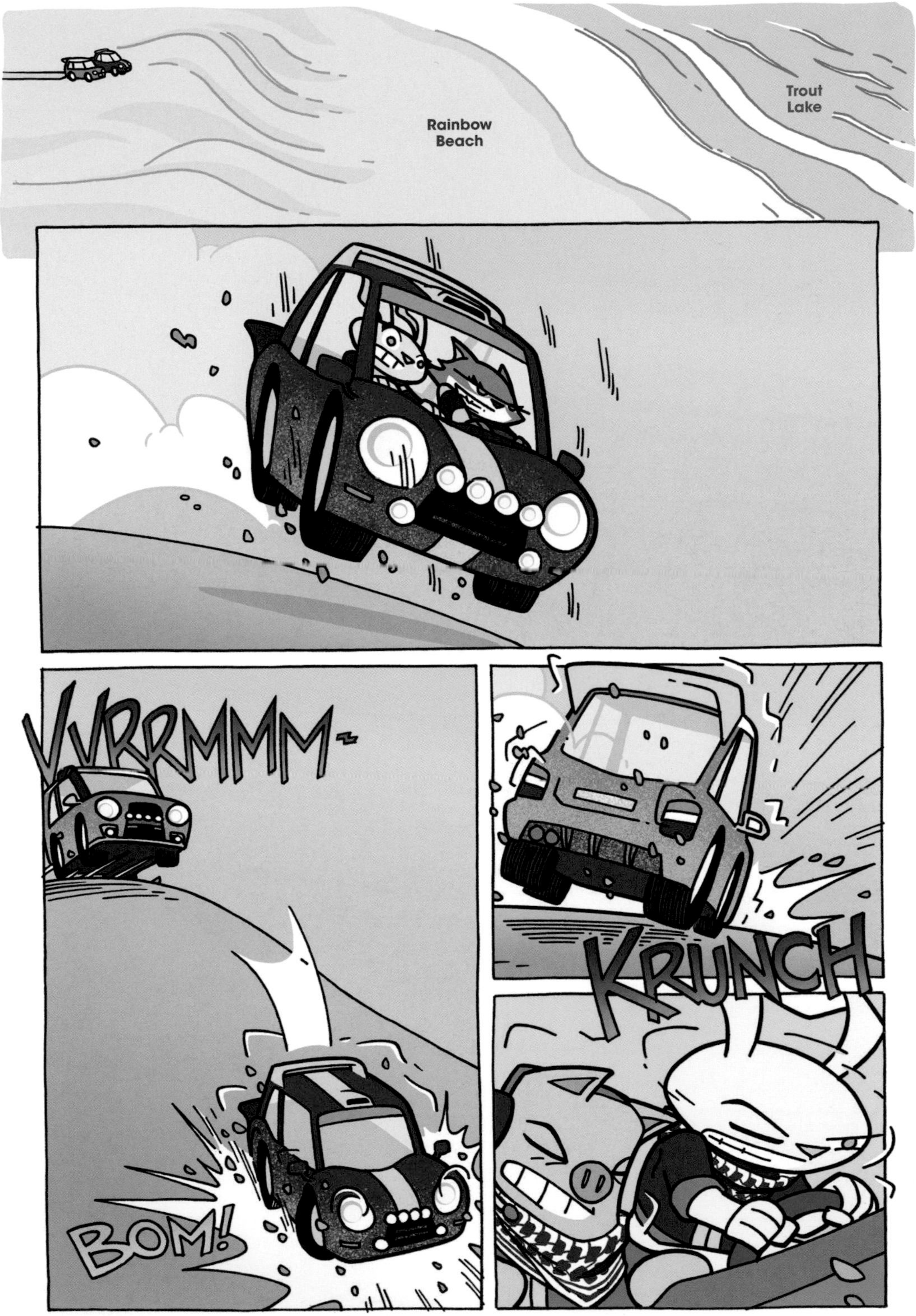

Rainbow Beach
Trout Lake
VVRRMMM
BOM!
KRUNCH

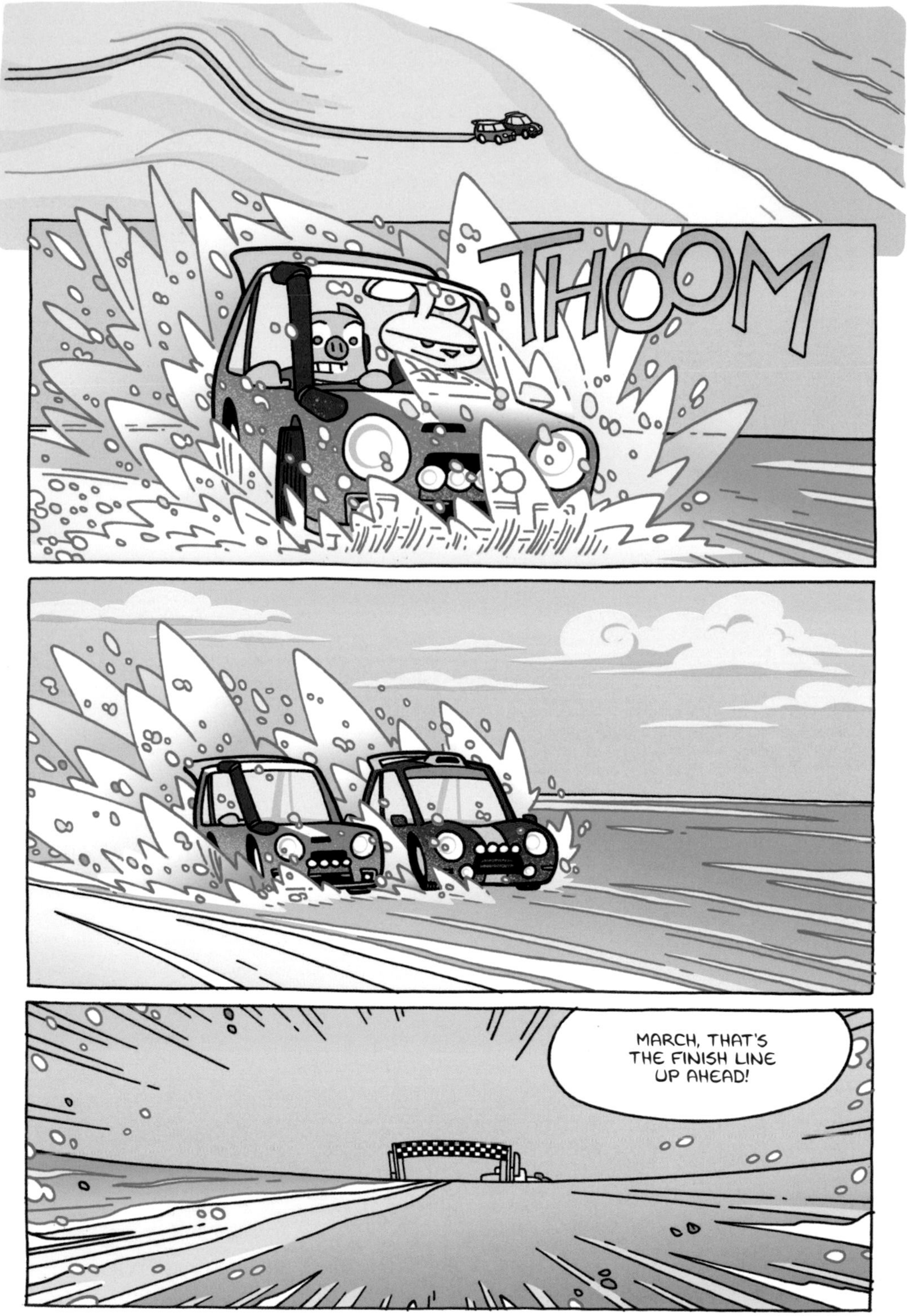
THOOM
MARCH, THAT'S THE FINISH LINE UP AHEAD!

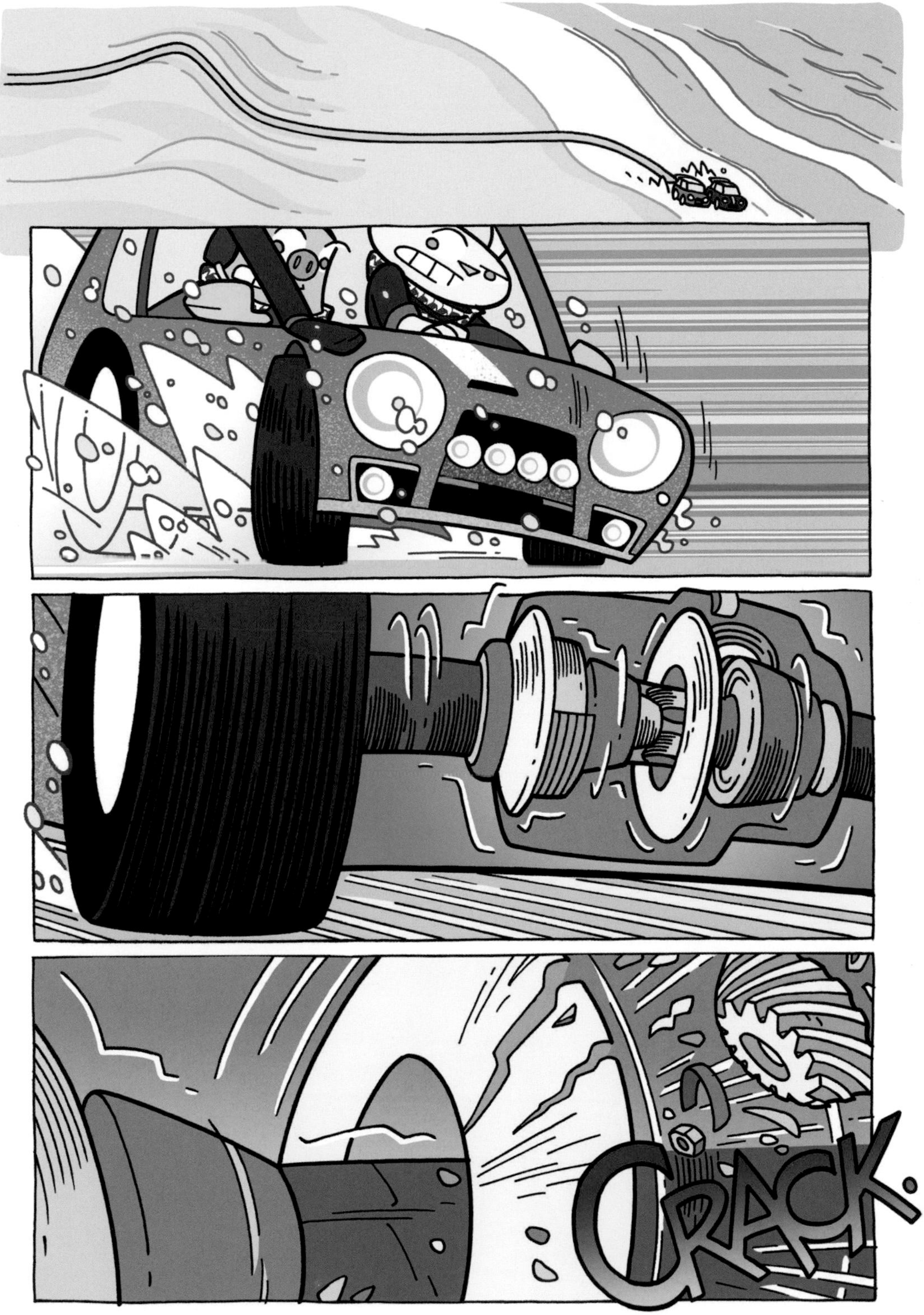
CRACK

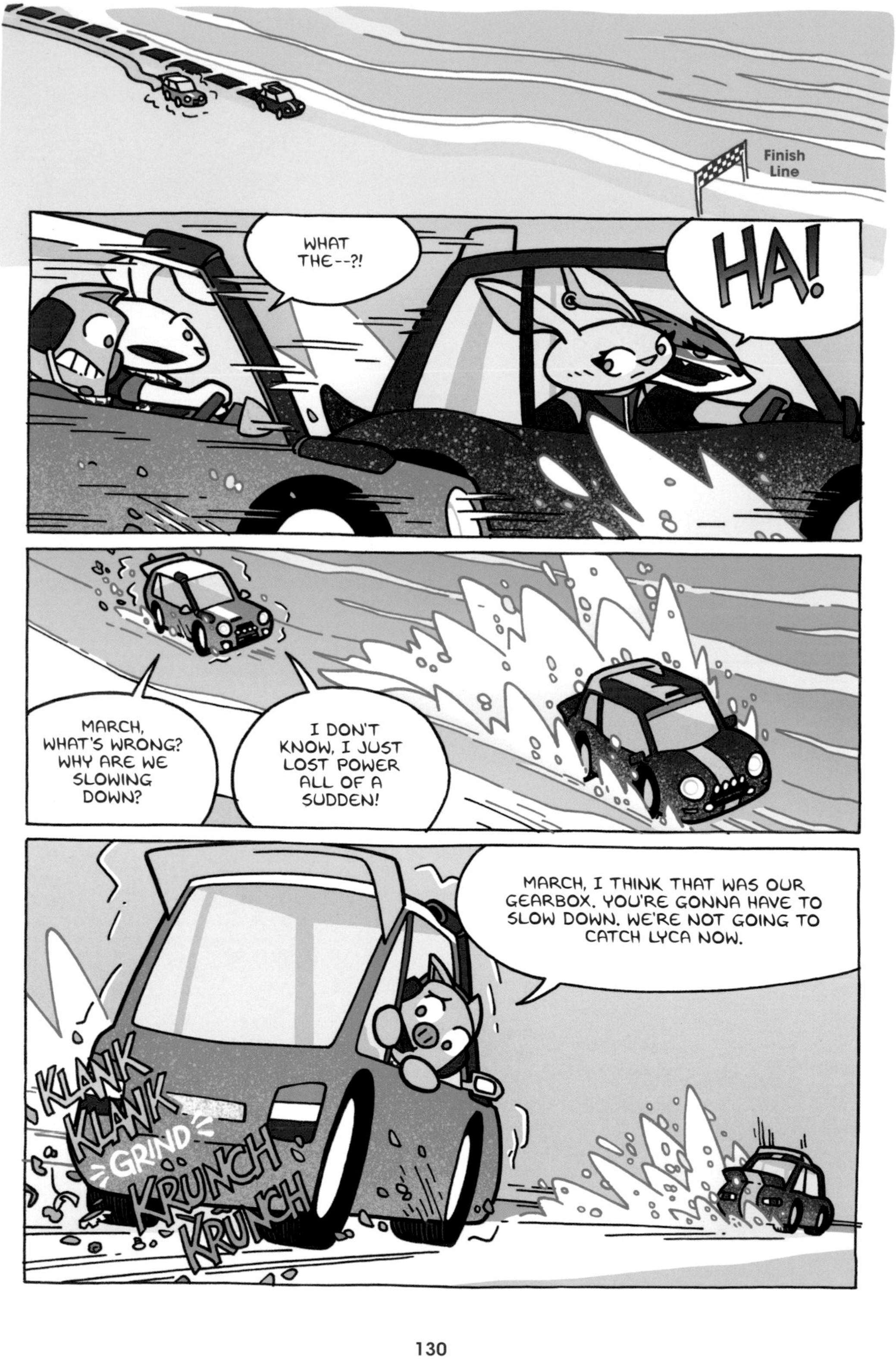
Finish Line
WHAT THE--?!
HA!
MARCH, WHAT'S WRONG? WHY ARE WE SLOWING DOWN?
I DON'T KNOW, I JUST LOST POWER ALL OF A SUDDEN!
MARCH, I THINK THAT WAS OUR GEARBOX. YOU'RE GONNA HAVE TO SLOW DOWN. WE'RE NOT GOING TO CATCH LYCA NOW.
KLANK
KLANK
GRIND
KRUNCH
KRUNCH

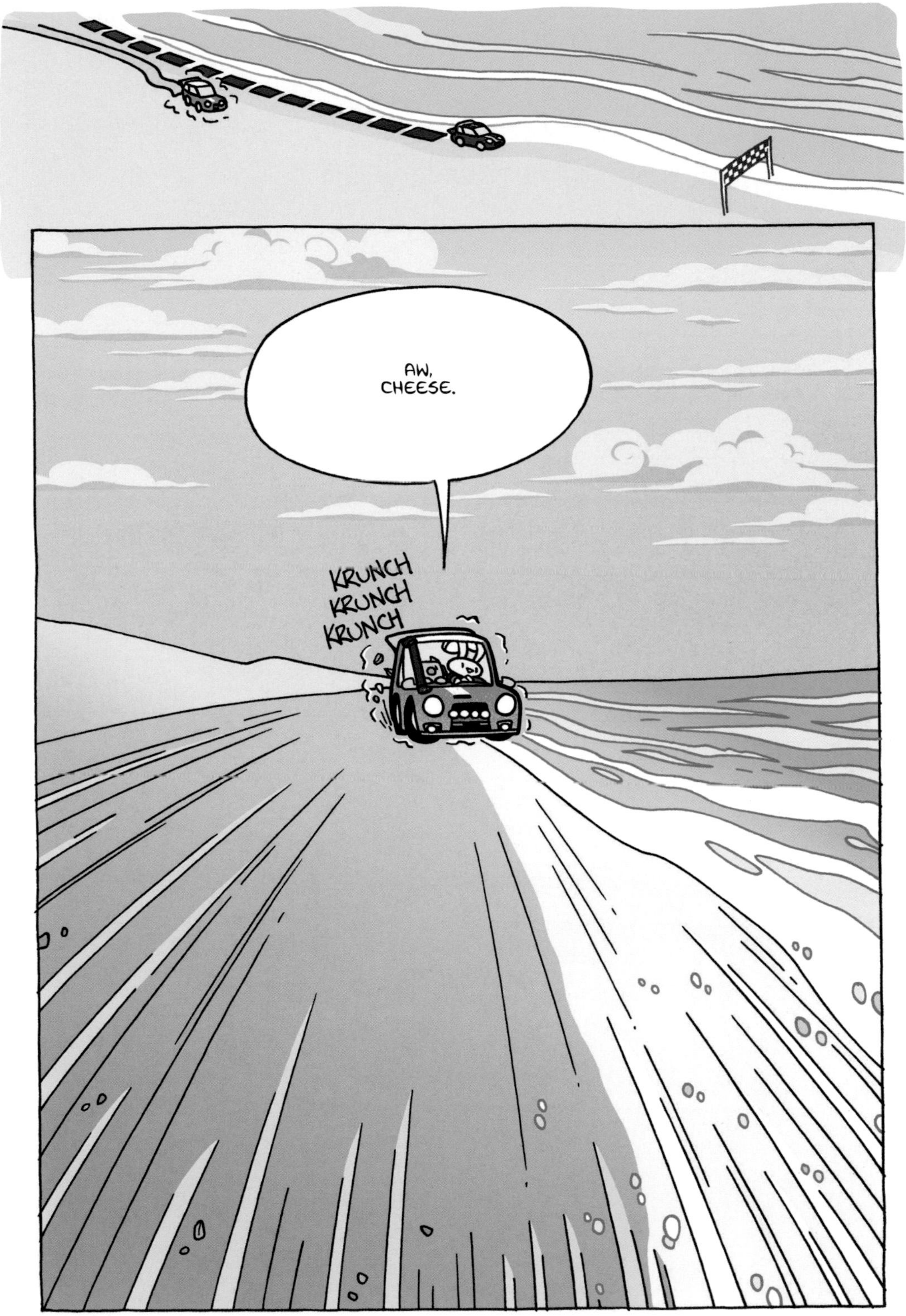
AW, CHEESE.
KRUNCH
KRUNCH
KRUNCH

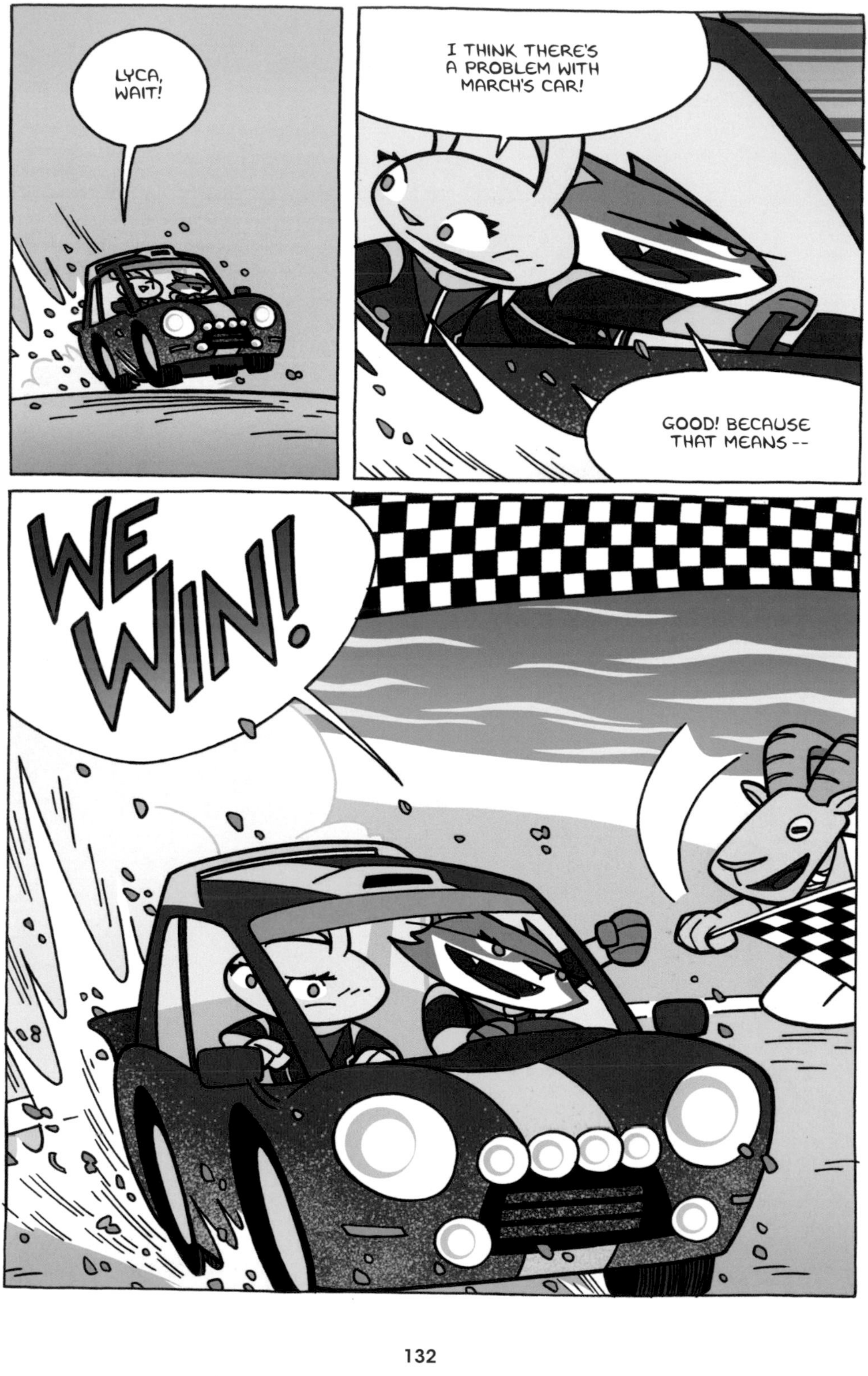
LYCA, WAIT!
I THINK THERE'S A PROBLEM WITH MARCH'S CAR!
GOOD! BECAUSE THAT MEANS --
WE WIN!

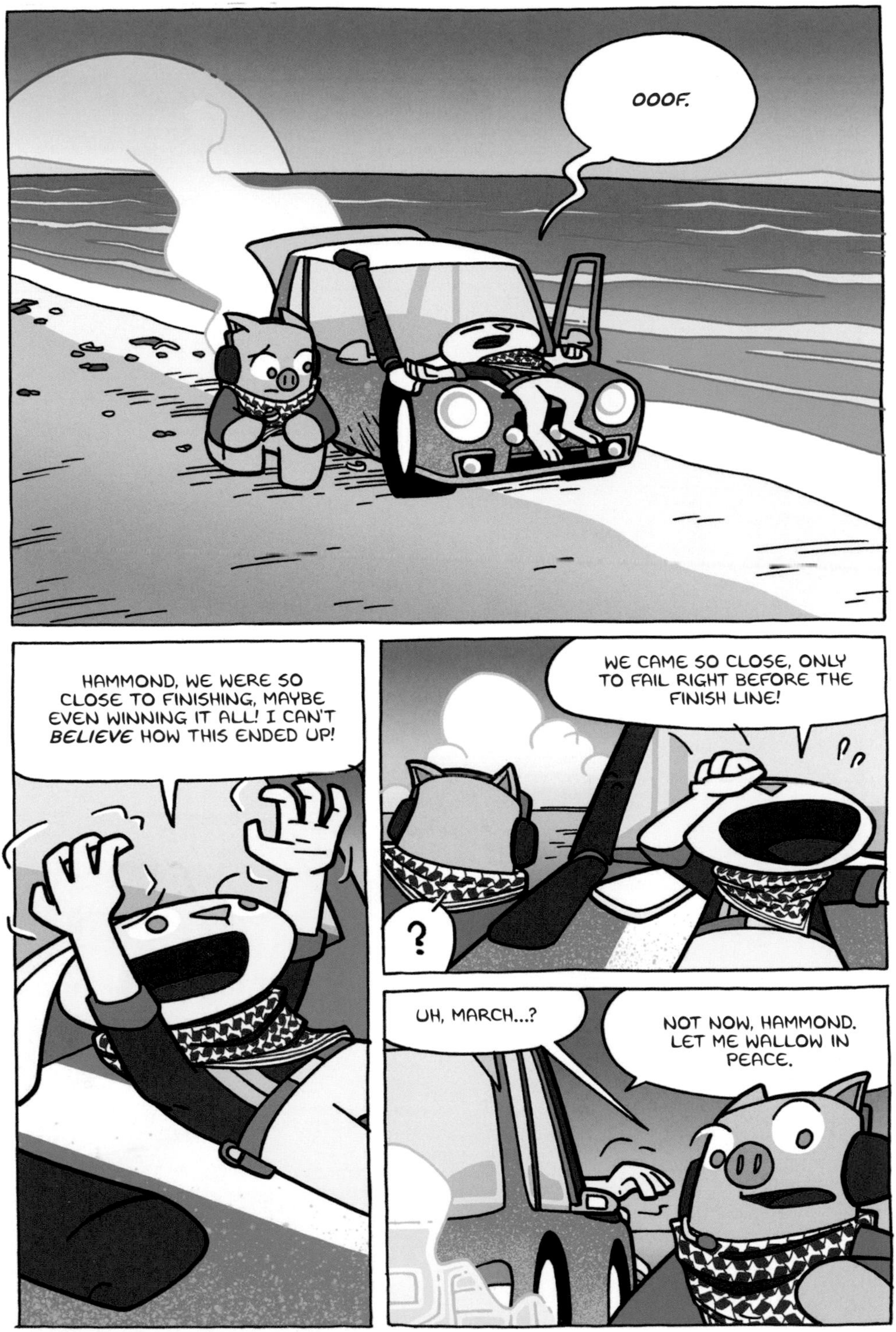
OOOF.
HAMMOND, WE WERE SO CLOSE TO FINISHING, MAYBE EVEN WINNING IT ALL! I CAN'T *BELIEVE* HOW THIS ENDED UP!
WE CAME SO CLOSE, ONLY TO FAIL RIGHT BEFORE THE FINISH LINE!
?
UH, MARCH...?
NOT NOW, HAMMOND. LET ME WALLOW IN PEACE.

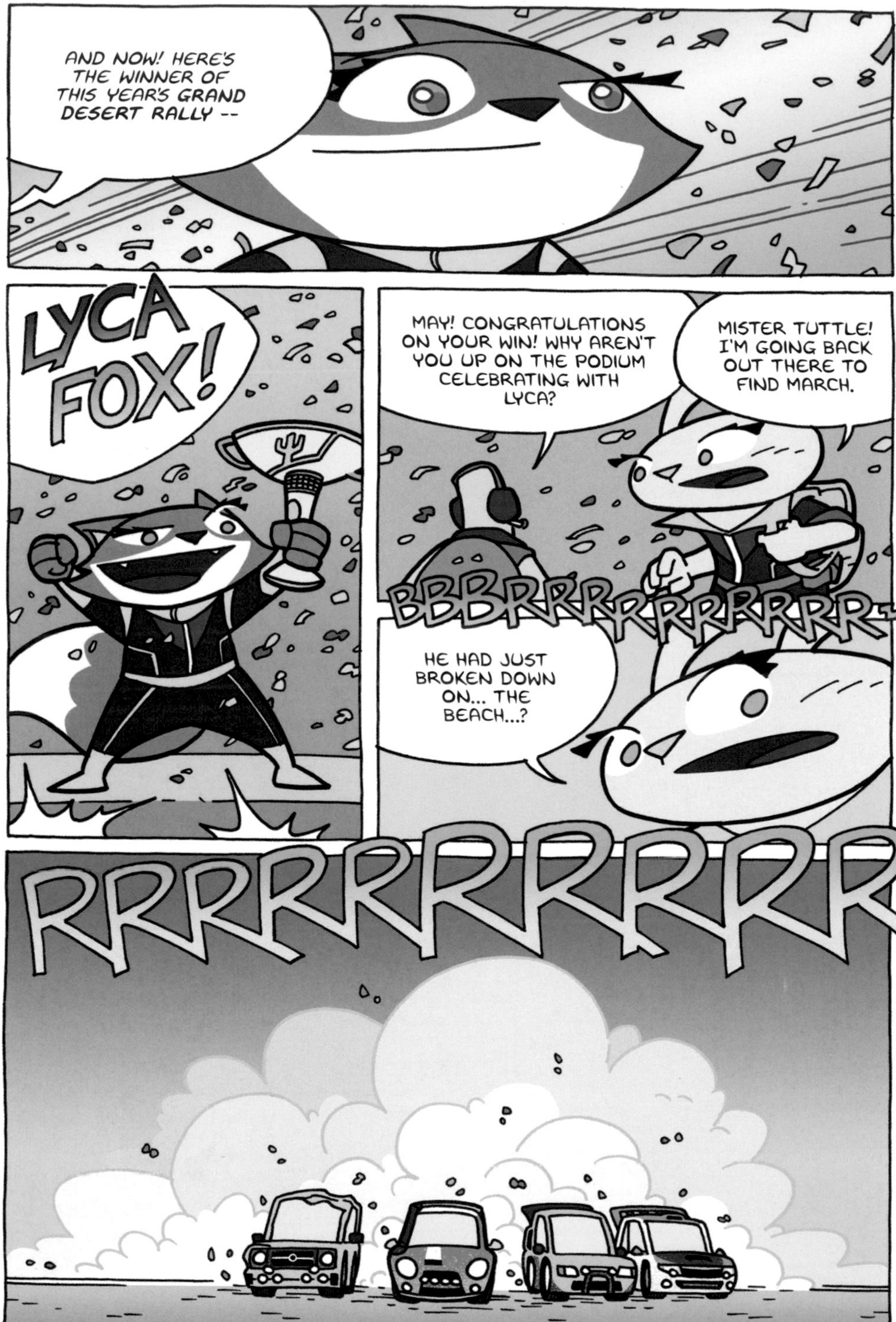
AND NOW! HERE'S THE WINNER OF THIS YEAR'S GRAND DESERT RALLY --
LYCA FOX!
MAY! CONGRATULATIONS ON YOUR WIN! WHY AREN'T YOU UP ON THE PODIUM CELEBRATING WITH LYCA?
MISTER TUTTLE! I'M GOING BACK OUT THERE TO FIND MARCH.
BBBRRRRRRRRRRRR
HE HAD JUST BROKEN DOWN ON... THE BEACH...?
RRRRRRRRRRR

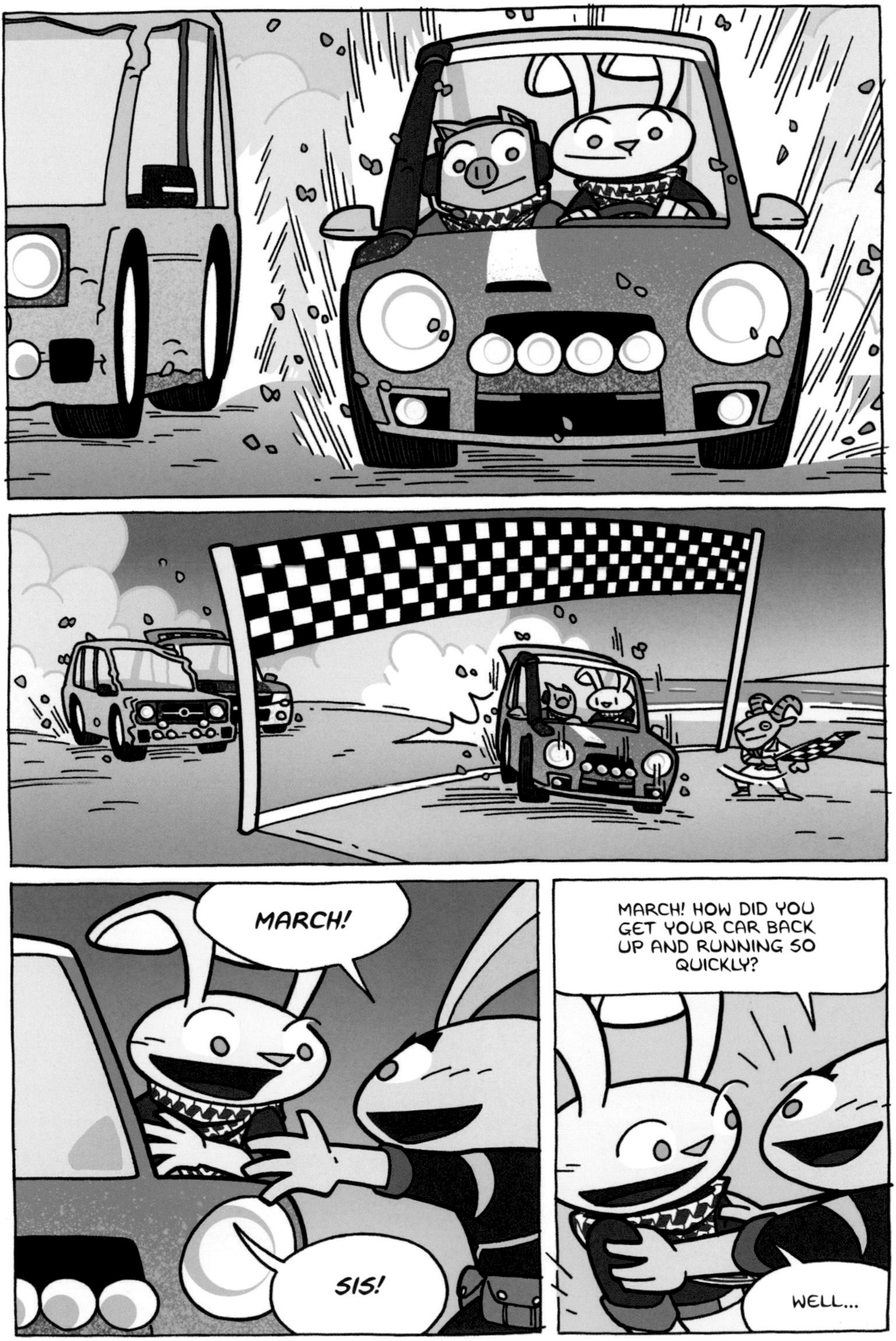
MARCH!
SIS!
MARCH! HOW DID YOU GET YOUR CAR BACK UP AND RUNNING SO QUICKLY?
WELL...

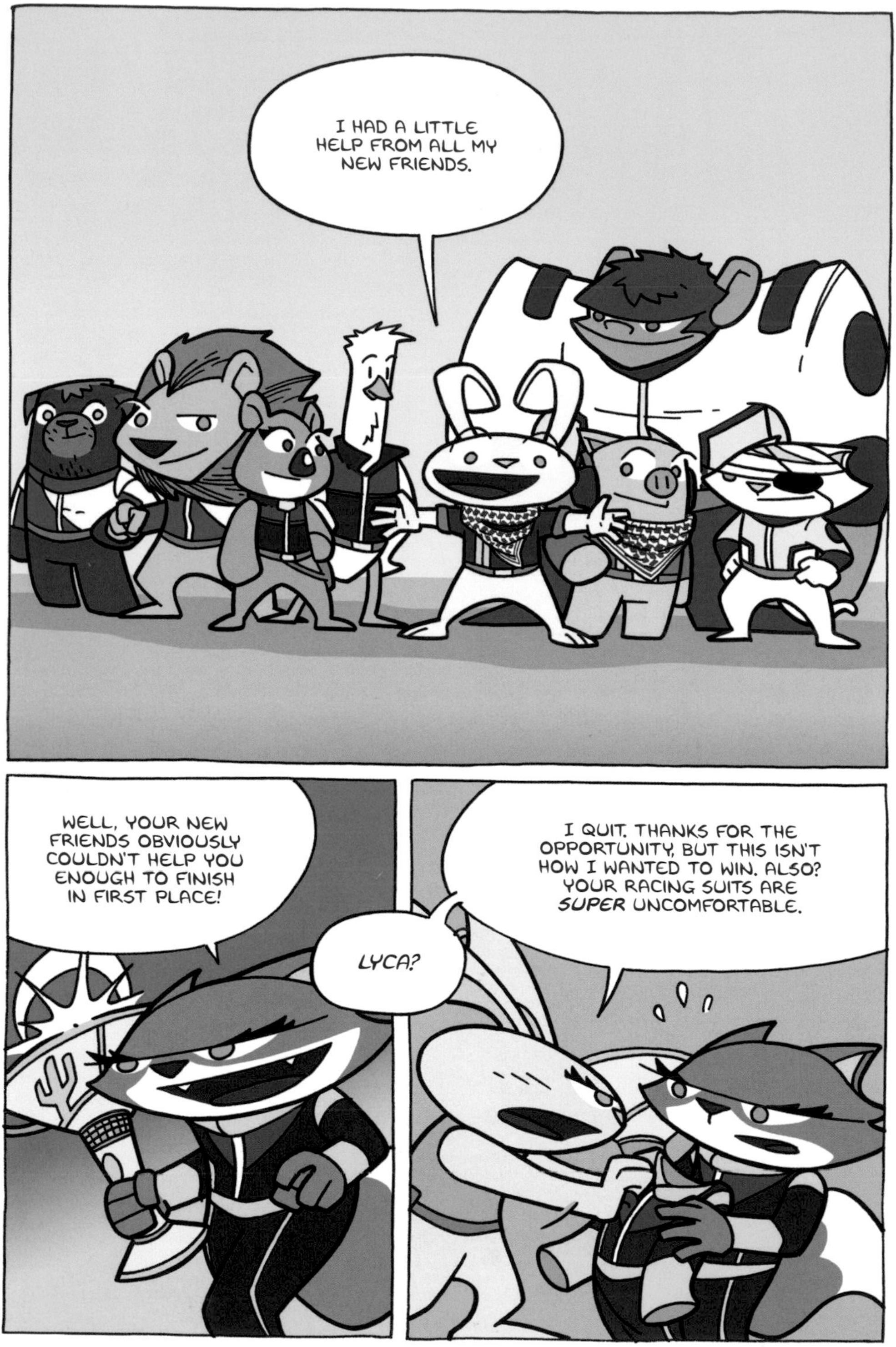
I HAD A LITTLE HELP FROM ALL MY NEW FRIENDS.
WELL, YOUR NEW FRIENDS OBVIOUSLY COULDN'T HELP YOU ENOUGH TO FINISH IN FIRST PLACE!
LYCA?
I QUIT. THANKS FOR THE OPPORTUNITY, BUT THIS ISN'T HOW I WANTED TO WIN. ALSO? YOUR RACING SUITS ARE *SUPER* UNCOMFORTABLE.

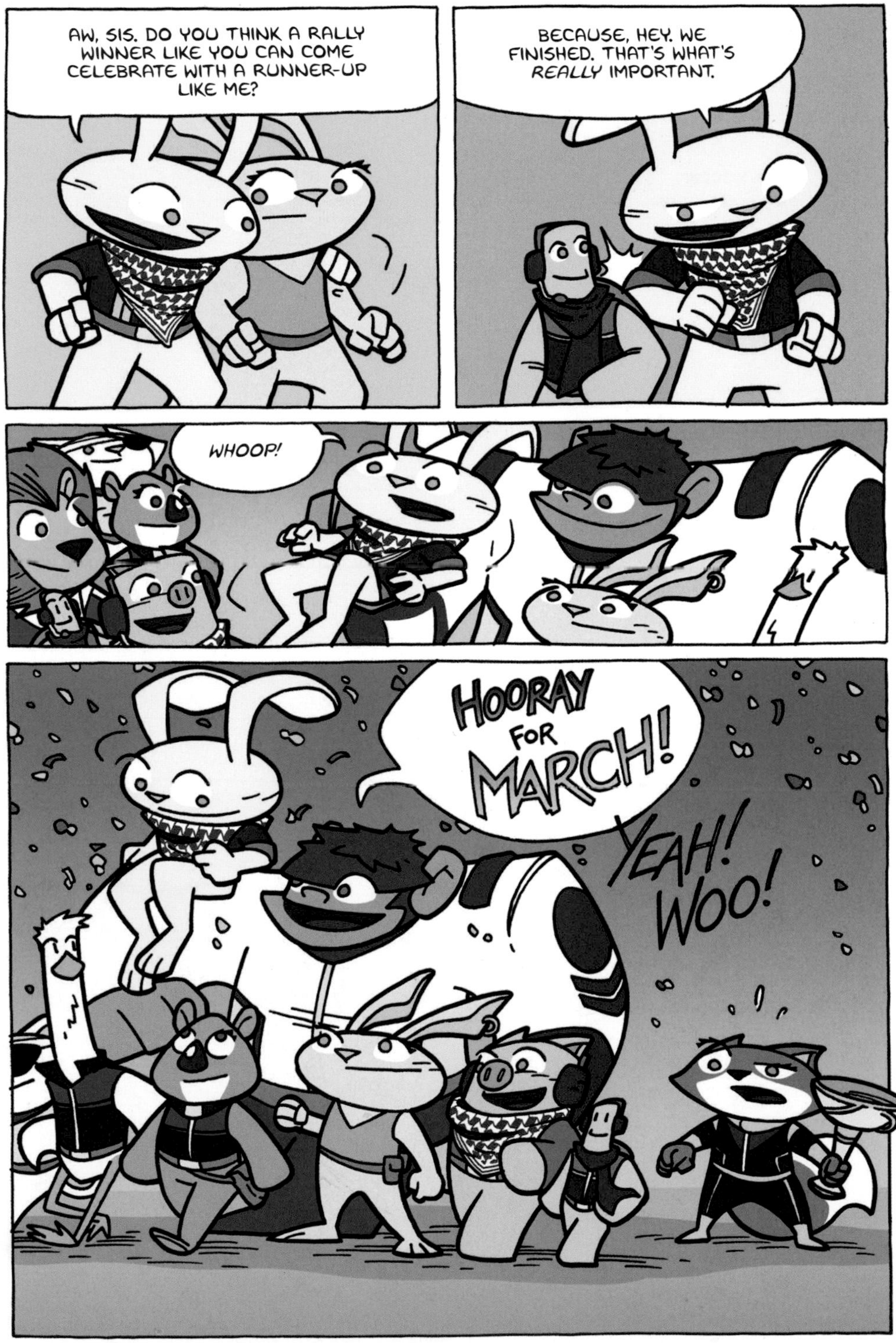
AW, SIS. DO YOU THINK A RALLY WINNER LIKE YOU CAN COME CELEBRATE WITH A RUNNER-UP LIKE ME?
BECAUSE, HEY. WE FINISHED. THAT'S WHAT'S *REALLY* IMPORTANT.
WHOOP!
HOORAY FOR MARCH!
YEAH! WOO!

SKETCHES

Character design sketches

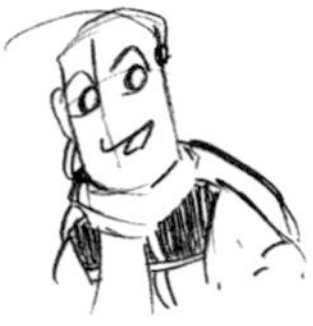

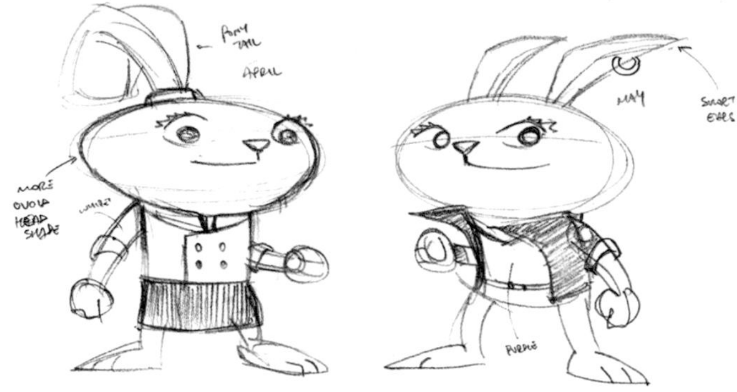
PONY TAIL
APRIL
MORE OVOID HEAD SHAPE
WHITE
MAY
SHORT EARS
PURPLE

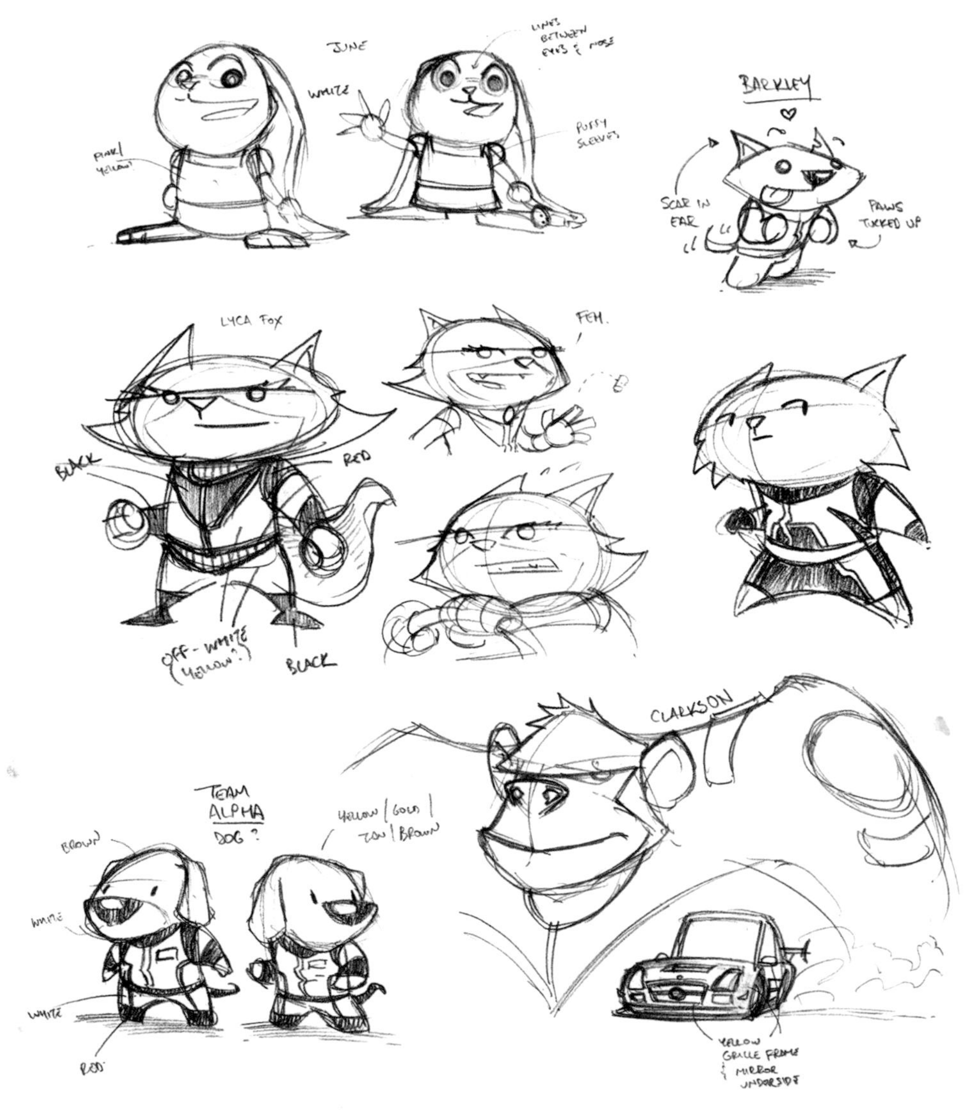
JUNE
LINES BETWEEN EYES & NOSE
WHITE
PINK/ YELLOW
PUFFY SLEEVES
BARKLEY
SCAR IN EAR
PAWS TUCKED UP
LYCA FOX
FEH.
BLACK
RED
OFF-WHITE (YELLOW?)
BLACK
CLARKSON
TEAM ALPHA DOG?
YELLOW / GOLD / TAN / BROWN
BROWN
WHITE
WHITE
RED
YELLOW GRILLE FRAME & MIRROR UNDERSIDE

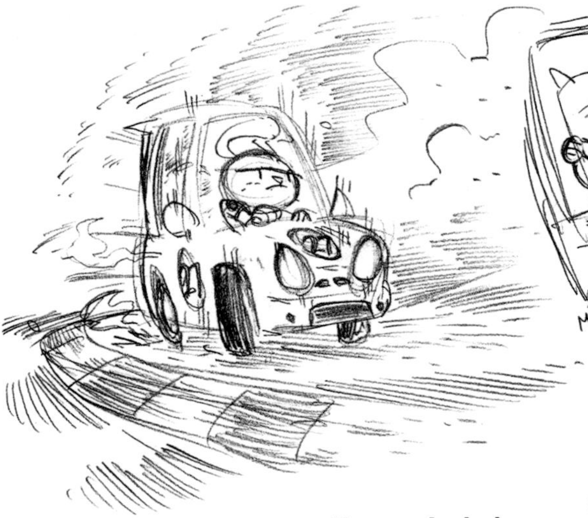

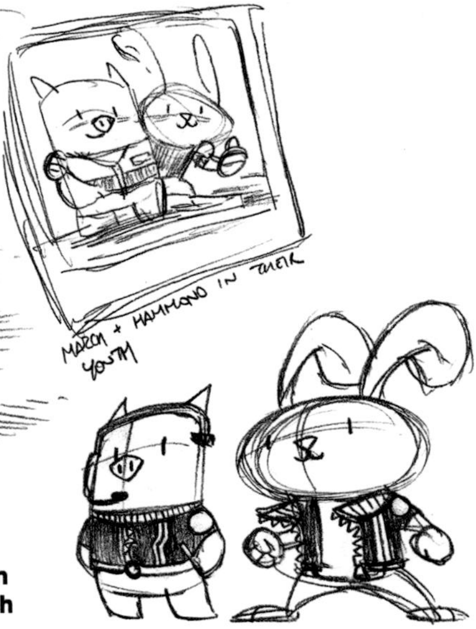
MARCH + HAMMOND IN THEIR YOUTH

Very early design sketches of March and Hammond

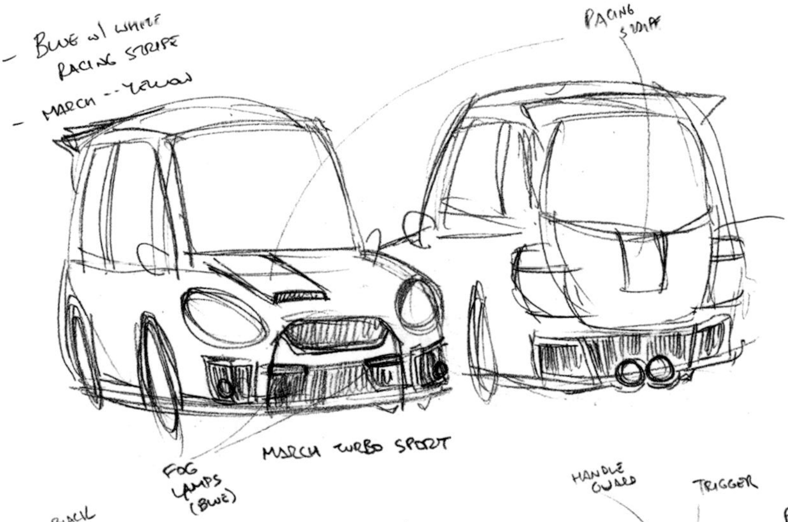
- BLUE w/ WHITE RACING STRIPE
- MARCH -- YELLOW
RACING STRIPE
MARCH TURBO SPORT
FOG LAMPS (BLUE)

Early design sketches of March and Lyca's cars

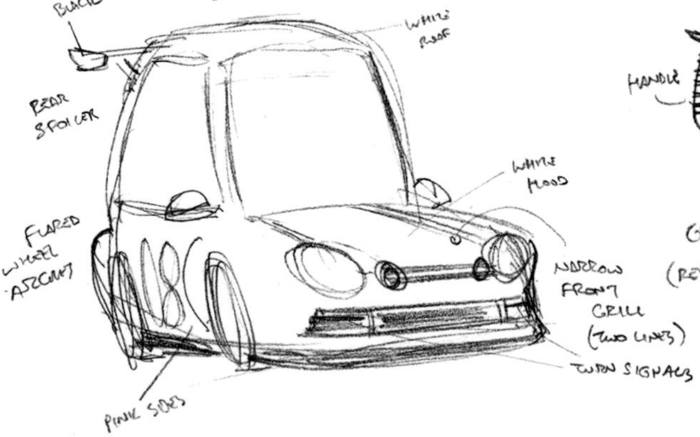
BLACK
WHITE ROOF
REAR SPOILER
WHITE HOOD
FLARED WHEEL ARCHES
NARROW FRONT GRILL (TWO LINES)
TURN SIGNALS
PINK SIDES

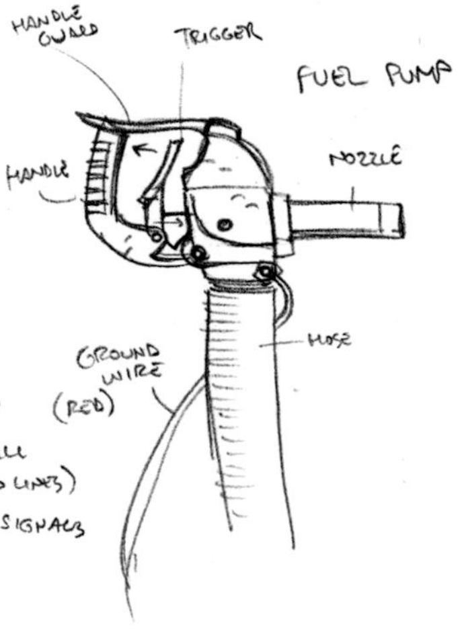
HANDLE GUARD
TRIGGER
FUEL PUMP
HANDLE
NOZZLE
HOSE
GROUND WIRE (RED)

New design sketches for The Baker's Run

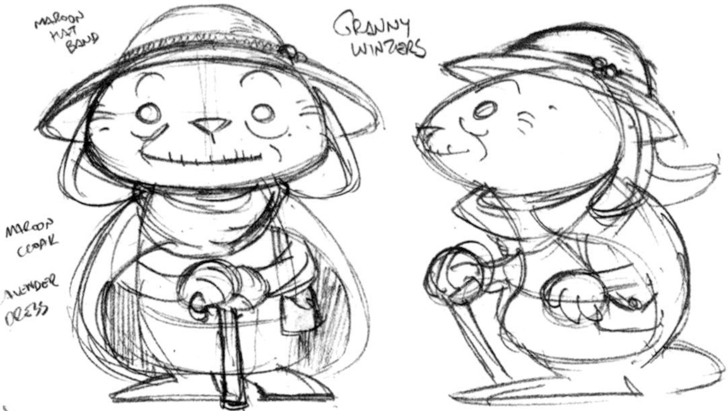
MAROON HAT BAND
GRANNY WINZERS
MAROON CLOAK
LAVENDER DRESS

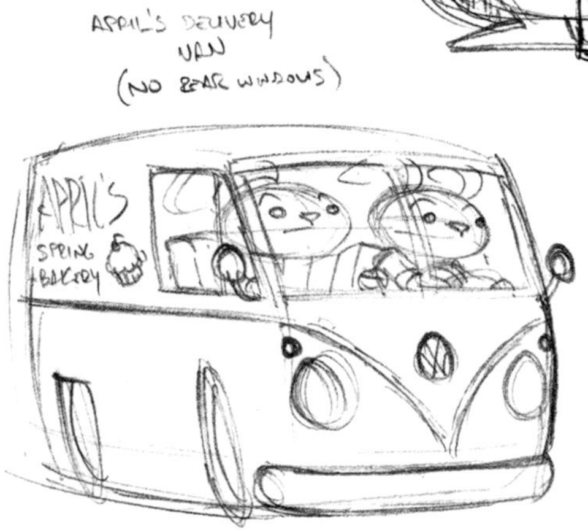
APRIL'S DELIVERY VAN
(NO REAR WINDOWS)
APRIL'S
SPRING BAKERY

I will often draw a panel several times to find the most interesting staging for a scene. The series of studies below are all different variations of panel 3 on page 80.

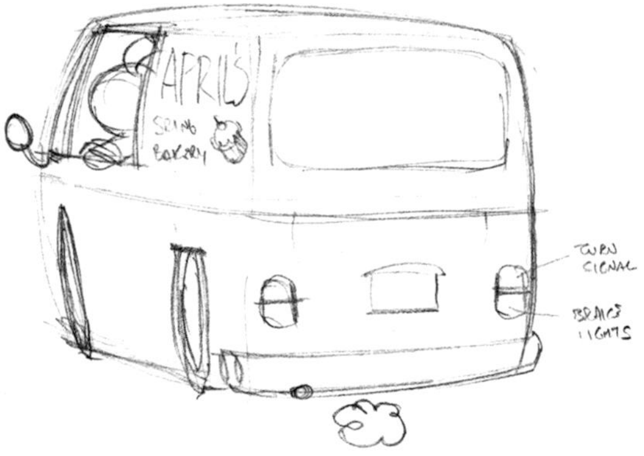
APRIL'S
SPRING BAKERY
TURN SIGNAL
BRAKE LIGHTS

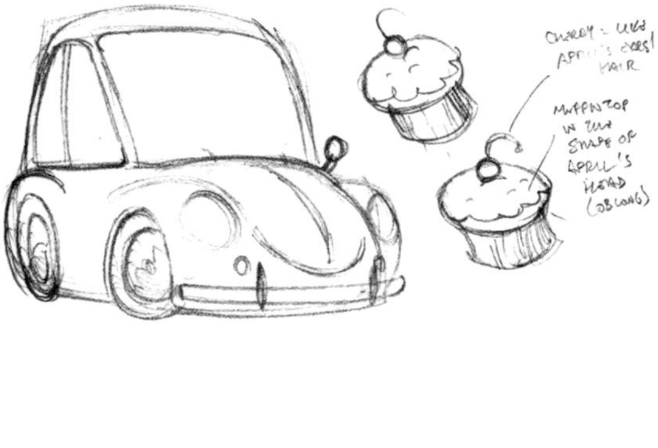
CHERRY = LIKE APRIL'S EARS/HAIR
MUFFIN TOP IN THE SHAPE OF APRIL'S HEAD (OBLONG)

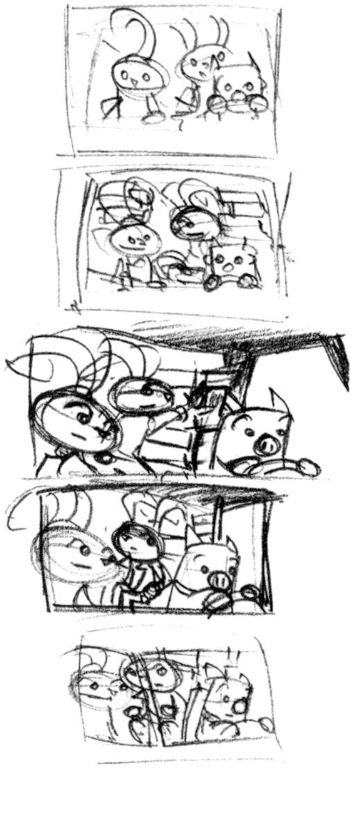

New vehicle concepts

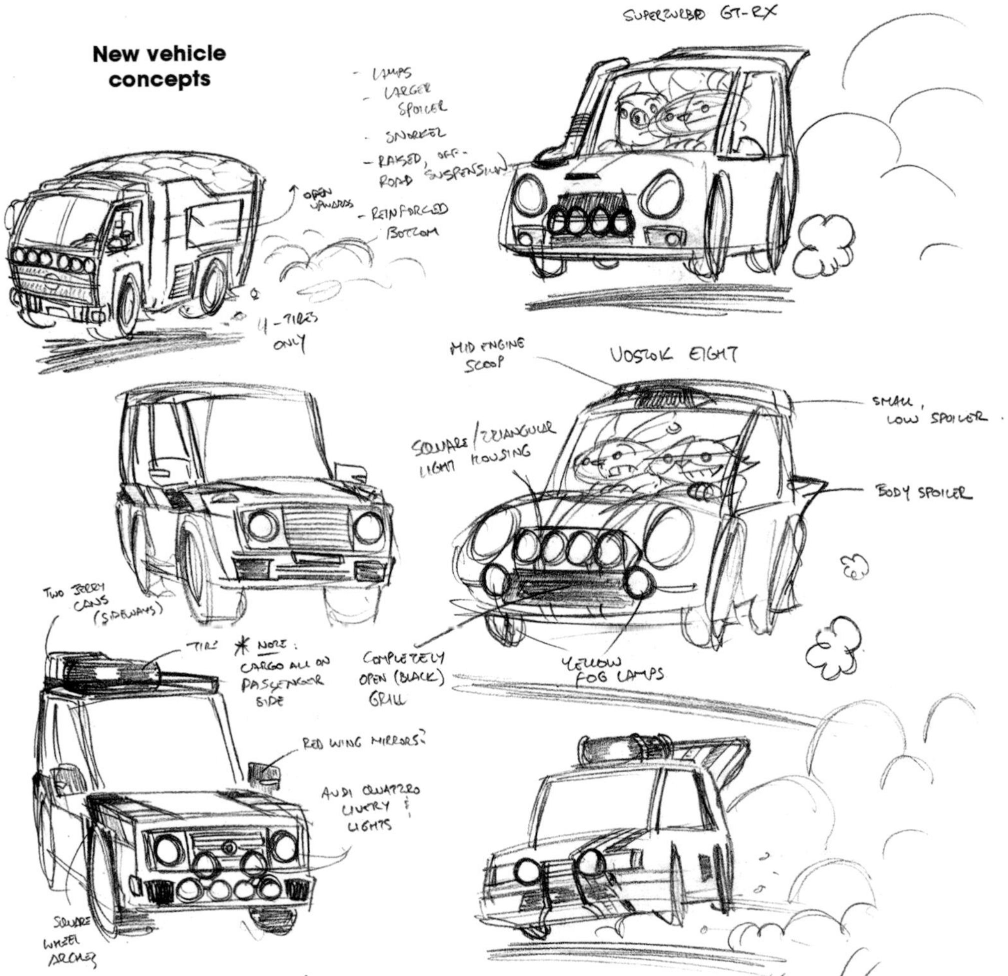
SUPERTURBO GT-RX
- LAMPS
- LARGER SPOILER
- SNORKEL
- RAISED, OFF-ROAD SUSPENSION
OPEN UPWARDS
- REINFORCED BOTTOM
4-TIRES ONLY
MID ENGINE SCOOP
VOSTOK EIGHT
SMALL, LOW SPOILER
SQUARE/TRIANGULAR LIGHT HOUSING
BODY SPOILER
TWO JERRY CANS (SIDEWAYS)
TIRE
* NOTE: CARGO ALL ON PASSENGER SIDE
COMPLETELY OPEN (BLACK) GRILL
YELLOW FOG LAMPS
RED WING MIRRORS?
AUDI QUATTRO LIVERY & LIGHTS
SQUARE WHEEL ARCHES

New character design sketches

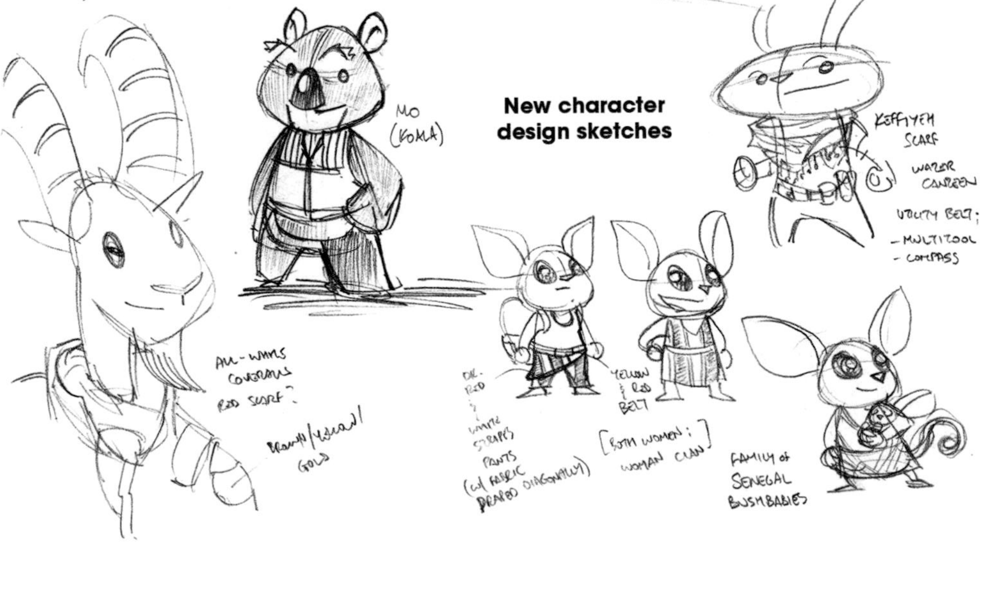
MO (KOALA)
KEFFIYEH SCARF
WATER CANTEEN
UTILITY BELT:
- MULTITOOL
- COMPASS
ALL-WHITE COVERALLS
RED SCARF?
BROWN/YELLOW/GOLD
DK. RED & WHITE STRIPES PANTS (w/ FABRIC DRAPED DIAGONALLY)
YELLOW & RED BELT
[BOTH WOMEN; WOMAN CLAN]
FAMILY of SENEGAL BUSHBABIES

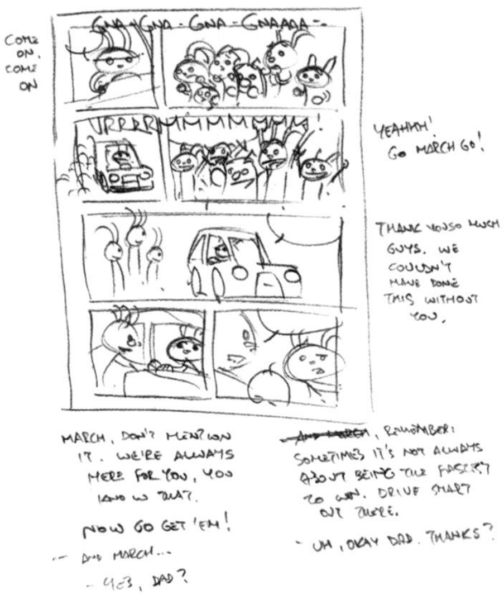
COME ON, COME ON
GNA-GNA-GNA-GNAAAA-
VRRRRMMMMMM!
YEAHHH! GO MARCH GO!
THANK YOU SO MUCH GUYS. WE COULDN'T HAVE DONE THIS WITHOUT YOU.
MARCH, DON'T MENTION IT. WE'RE ALWAYS HERE FOR YOU, YOU KNOW THAT?
NOW GO GET 'EM!
AND MARCH...
YES, DAD?
REMEMBER: SOMETIMES IT'S NOT ALWAYS ABOUT BEING THE FASTEST TO WIN. DRIVE SMART OUT THERE.
UH, OKAY DAD. THANKS?

1. Thumbnail roughs

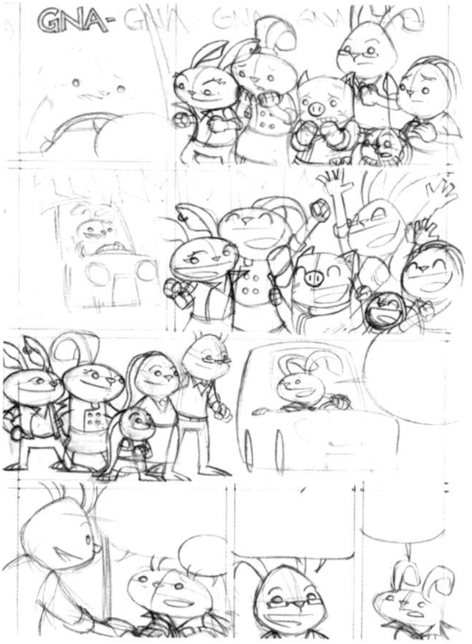
GNA-

2. Pencils

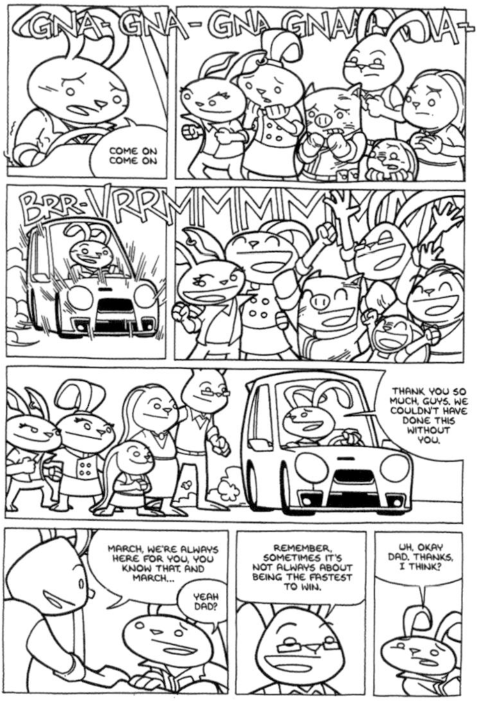
GNA-GNA-GNA-GNAA
COME ON COME ON
BRR-VRRMMMMM
THANK YOU SO MUCH, GUYS. WE COULDN'T HAVE DONE THIS WITHOUT YOU.
MARCH, WE'RE ALWAYS HERE FOR YOU, YOU KNOW THAT. AND MARCH...
YEAH DAD?
REMEMBER, SOMETIMES IT'S NOT ALWAYS ABOUT BEING THE FASTEST TO WIN.
UH, OKAY DAD. THANKS, I THINK?

3. Inks & digital lettering

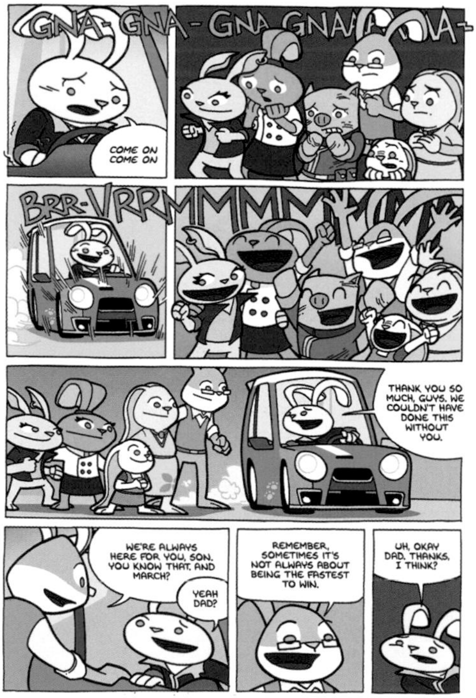
GNA-GNA-GNA GNAA
COME ON COME ON
BRR-VRRMMMMM
THANK YOU SO MUCH, GUYS. WE COULDN'T HAVE DONE THIS WITHOUT YOU.
WE'RE ALWAYS HERE FOR YOU, SON. YOU KNOW THAT. AND MARCH?
YEAH DAD?
REMEMBER, SOMETIMES IT'S NOT ALWAYS ABOUT BEING THE FASTEST TO WIN.
UH, OKAY DAD. THANKS, I THINK?

4. Final colors

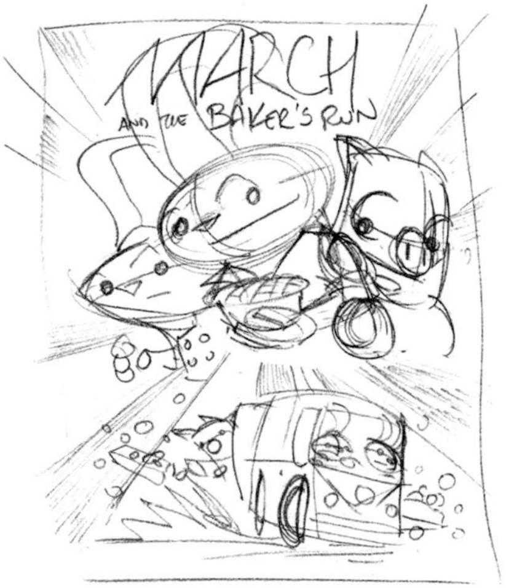
MARCH
AND THE BAKER'S RUN

1. Cover thumbnail rough

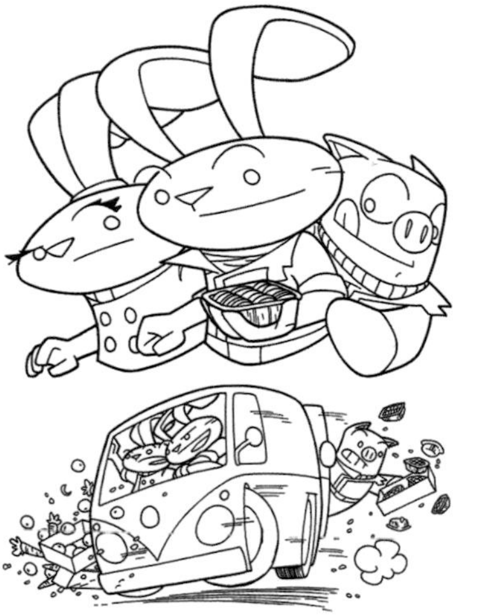

2. Inks

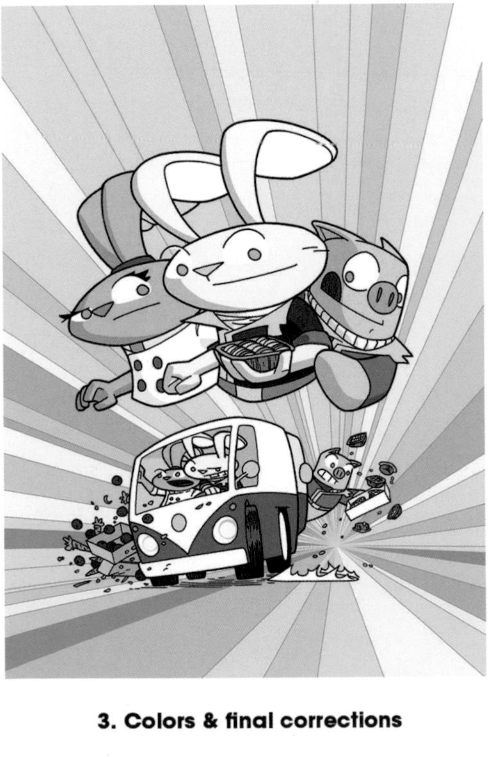

3. Colors & final corrections

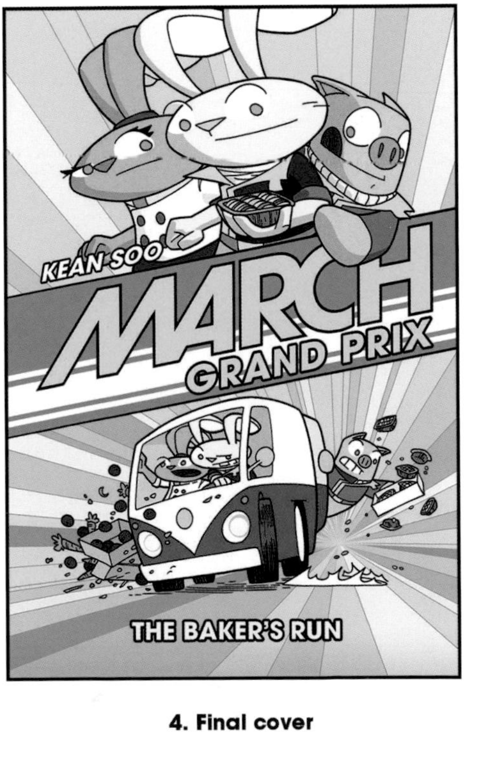
KEAN SOO
MARCH
GRAND PRIX
THE BAKER'S RUN

4. Final cover

KEAN SOO

Kean Soo was born in the United Kingdom, grew up in various parts of Canada and Hong Kong, trained as an electrical engineer, and now draws comics for a living. A former assistant editor and contributor for the FLIGHT comics anthology, Kean also created the award-winning Jellaby series of graphic novels.

Kean's first car was a 1991 Volkswagen GTI 16V, which he drove and (very occasionally) raced for over 10 years. Kean currently lives in Toronto with his wife, their dog, Reginald Barkley, and their 1992 Volvo 940 Turbo.

Kean would also like to thank Judy Hansen, Donnie Lemke, Brann Garvey, Tony Cliff, Kazu Kibuishi, everyone in the FLIGHT crew, and Tory Woollcott for making March Grand Prix such a joy to work on.